ALL THAT REMAINS

OTHER BOOKS BY THE AUTHOR

All That Remains is the first in a series of novels exploring the journeys of modern pilgrims struggling for survival and integrity amidst the confusion and disintegration of the modern secular world. The next novel, *Fast Falls the Tide*, returns to Paul Kendall. Disaster and betrayal befall him shortly after David Richards returns from Israel.

ALL THAT REMAINS

Robert L. Wise

THOMAS NELSON PUBLISHERS
Nashville • Atlanta • London • Vancouver

Published in Nashville, Tennessee, by Thomas Nelson, Inc., Publishers, and distributed in Canada by Word Communications, Ltd., Richmond, British Columbia.

All characters are fictitious, and resemblance to persons living or dead is purely coincidental.

Library of Congress Cataloging-in-Publication Data

Wise, Robert L.
   All that remains: Robert L. Wise.
      p.   cm.
   ISBN 0-8407-6783-8
      1. Americans—Travel—Israel—Fiction. 2. Christians—United States—
   Fiction. 3. Adoptees—United States—Fiction. 4. Jews—United States—
   Fiction. I. Title.
   PS3573.I79A79   1995
   813'.54—dc20
                                                              94-34519
                                                              CIP

Printed in the United States of America
1 2 3 4 5 6—00 99 98 97 96 95

Dedicated to
Rabbi Charles Shalman
fellow sojourner and *mensch;*
Lou Moses, *emah;*
and
Hela Eidinger Harris, *bubbele*

ACKNOWLEDGMENTS

I am indebted to my friends who walked with me through the journey reflected in the life of David Richards. Among those also helping with this manuscript are Arnold Fagan, Helena Rubenstein Sorenson, and Rabbi David Packman. Cliff Warren and Kathryn Fanning gave expert insight into reshaping the manuscript. In addition, Bernice McShane graciously gave editorial assistance and Dale Hammond has been a faithful secretary. As always Janet Thoma remains the ultimate editor. I am grateful for such extraordinary friends!

PART ONE

*We are pilgrims
on a journey,
we are brothers
on the road.*

—The book of Hebrews

PART ONE

ONE

Oklahoma City, January 1987

Snow gently settled across the backyard, covering the pallid lawn stubble. Freezing temperatures turned the frosty crust into a thousand diamonds. Large flakes hung in the windless sky like winter butterflies. The bright moonlight added a final touch of luminous magic to the night

David likes the snow, Susan thought. *Everything ugly disappears and is whitewashed away. Something deep within him is pacified, soothed. But someday the thaw must come. He cannot stay snow-blind forever.*

The winds suddenly picked up, dashing the calm. Flurries swirled into little waves imitating the ripples across a summer pond. Breakers frozen in a painting, the snow tide stood suspended yet poised to become a sudden blizzard.

"Oh, David!" Susan spoke to herself. "You are a tempestuous soul."

From the kitchen window over her sink, Susan Richards could see her husband bent over the potter's wheel in his makeshift studio behind their large ranch-style home. Bright January moonlight gleamed on the snow-covered backyard and reflected from the shed's tin roof. Although it was nearly ten o'clock David was still completely absorbed in his work.

Susan didn't look down as she rinsed out a dish. *Nothing clears David's mind, puts him in touch with his feelings like creating something. I just wish he didn't take everything so seriously. He is a troubled man.*

Susan could see only his head and shoulders framed by the studio window, but she envisioned his long slender fingers carefully and masterfully working the wet clay. She had always been fascinated by the graceful taper and artistic contours of his hands. David's touch was gentle and sensitive. The first time she felt the meandering veins rippling across the top of his hands, Susan was convinced an artist's soul was hidden in the body of the tempestuous young man reported to be a heart-breaker. That was twenty-five years ago! The thoroughly ro-mantic boy proved to be a remarkably innocent and naive man. David had neither been untrue nor disappointed her. To the contrary Susan could not imagine a life with another person. After all these years she still loved and yearned for his touch.

Eccentric? Susan smiled. *David is certainly unique, never one of the herd. Burning creativity sets him apart. Yet he is a driven person. Needs solitude to reconstitute himself.*

Two hours earlier David finished supper and announced he had to work outside. Susan knew the breathing spaces were the only way David kept his equilibrium when business pres-sure bore in. David worked hard, very hard.

"Looks like I could really sell my company," David had said, staring at his baked potato. "I feel very confused and frightened." He swore and stabbed the steak with his fork.

Explosive? Susan shook her head. *Sometimes. Jack Meachem gets the blast most often. Being David's business partner isn't easy, but most of the time Jack deserves it!*

Susan wrung out the dishrag and put the final plate into the dishwasher. She looked at an icicle hanging from the eave of the roof. *Getting awfully cold. I don't care! He should come in. We don't have much time left.* Susan flipped the special wall switch off and on several times. Flashing the lights in the shed meant David was needed in the house. He looked up and she beck-oned. David glanced at his wall clock and waved back. He'd be in shortly.

"Let's warm him up," Susan told the stove. "A little hot cider for our Rodin."

The coils slowly turned red as the apple juice filled the saucepan. Everywhere Susan looked around the kitchen and the adjacent morning room she saw the hallmarks of David's creativity. His large ceramic vase in the corner was filled with last fall's long-stemmed weeds. David sprayed colored paint on the tips of the seed pods, turning the pests into prizes. A large watercolor he had painted on their last trip to the ocean hung on the far wall. He had found their antique kitchen table in an old barn and refinished it. David's forte was reclaiming.

Only the two of them lived in their spacious, elegant house. Twenty-four years of marriage had not produced any children. Susan's empty womb never troubled David. She was enough for him. Although that realization always comforted Susan, she still hoped for a child.

Susan looked back at the window to see if the studio light was out. Instead she saw her reflection. She still had her svelte figure and looked more like thirty-five than forty-four. Her auburn hair touched her neck at exactly the length David liked best. Susan's high cheekbones and heart-shaped face had not yet felt the grinding wheel of time. At the same time she would have gladly exchanged the marvelous preservation for the earmarks a child might have left.

Susan poured a packet of cider mix into the steaming pan. *David isn't really a difficult person. Not demanding as much as . . . as . . . unsettled. Yes, unsettled is the right word. David is a little boat adrift on a great sea.* Susan took the pan off the stove.

Something is boiling deep down inside this marvelously complex man, something troubling and seething.

The back door opened and shut. "Sorry," David called in from the hallway. Stomping noises echoed from the breezeway. "Completely lost track of the time." David strolled into the room and threw his arms around Susan. His cheeks felt invigoratingly cold. The nippy air made his black eyes sparkle even more; his jet black hair was thoroughly disheveled, but she thought him unusually handsome in his checkered flannel shirt. David was six feet tall, on the thin side, with a lean muscular build. In the beginning, Susan was bothered when women stole a second look. David's face had strong masculine lines that made him look naturally romantic. Occasionally someone said he had bedroom eyes. With time her suspicions turned into amusement. Part of his attractiveness was that David looked exotic, maybe Spanish, at least Mediterranean. He still could smile and make her skin tingle.

"Made something for you." He kissed her forcefully. "Guess what?"

"Another teapot?" Susan poured the cider into a mug. "We've only got two dozen."

"No!" David scoffed. "Bad guess. Cynical." He sat down at the antique table. "Now you'll have to wait until it's done as punishment."

"Been thinking?" Susan put the steaming cup in front of him. "About the company?"

"Yes." David slowly stirred the cider.

"Any conclusions about tomorrow? Big, big day coming up."

"No." He sounded distant, evasive.

"When this business deal is completed let's get away from it all! Regardless of what you decide." Susan knew he'd think her impulsive. "Why don't we throw in the towel for a while? Go to Europe? Run around England. Just let life happen for a change."

David looked surprised. "Is that what you want?"

"No." Susan touched his lips. "Is it what *you* want? What does David want? Hang what everyone else is telling you *they* want."

He smiled, looked down into the cup, and stirred. "What I want?" He sighed. "I guess that's the $64,000 question, and I don't have that answer." He took a slow sip.

"Whatever you do in the morning must be what is right for you for a change." Susan squeezed his hand. "Tomorrow is going to be one of the most important days of your life."

"Thanks, baby." David finished the cider. "Let's go to bed."

• • •

When the alarm rang, David Richards fumbled for the small clock to stop the incessant electronic beeping. In the gray dawn his recurrent dream lingered. A suffocating blanket of apprehension covered him.

David's nightmares appeared with unsettling frequency. Sometimes he was chased by wild animals; on other nights policemen relentlessly pursued. Occasionally the attackers were soldiers. This morning the culprits were his parents carrying pitchforks. No matter where David hid, Mary and George Richards ferreted him out and sent David running. The alarm was a relief.

Doesn't the chase ever end? David threw the covers back. When Susan stirred, he quickly shuffled into the bathroom and shut the door. *Got to get moving.* He stepped into the shower. *Don't want to get moving.* He reached for the faucet. *Why today? Why not today?* The cold-slowly-turning-hot water finally jarred his conscious mind into gear. *Why am I taking a shower? I'll have to take another one at the gym.* He looked disgustedly at the soap. *Come on, David. Wake up.*

Combing his hair, brushing his teeth, shaving and a splash of Old Spice—the rituals of the morning were completed with the brake on. David lingered, not wanting to leave the bathroom. Only the relentless hands of his wristwatch pushed him onward. *No rest for the restless,* he thought and finished dressing.

David flipped the light switch off, opened the bathroom door, and tiptoed to the closet. Warm air poured down from the vents, but ice had frozen on the inside of the windows. He could feel the January chill waiting outside. He picked up his overcoat and scarf.

"You'll call me later today, won't you?" Susan's muffled voice arose from beneath the covers. "This afternoon?"

"Sure." David pulled the coat from the hanger.

"I've got to drive to Tulsa, but I'll be back around the middle of the afternoon. You know I'll worry about you all day." Susan sat up against the headboard. "I want everything to go well."

David looked intensely at the woman who had been his

wife for over two decades. And yet with all the familiarity that continuous days and countless nights in bed bring, David suddenly realized how much more there was to learn about her. Susan knew him far better.

"I care," she said gently. "You know that, don't you?" Susan let the cover drop.

David looked again at the lovely face framed by the jumbled reddish hair. Her warmth drew him closer. Her eyes and mouth looked especially inviting. The silk gown barely concealed her ample figure. "I need you." His words suddenly slipped out.

"What?" Susan smiled in surprise.

"Oh, I—I—I'm just a little rattled." He straightened up and put his coat on.

"I want this business deal to go well for you, David. I want you to be happy, and I know you haven't been for a long time."

David smiled weakly. "There's never been a day I've been unhappy with you. Thanks." He bent down to kiss her on the cheek.

Immediately Susan pulled him down to her and kissed him passionately on the mouth. "I *do* love you."

David smiled. "Me too." He quickly headed for the door with a good-bye wave. "I'll call this afternoon." Pausing in the hall to pick up his car keys, he could not avoid the large oblong mirror reaching close to the ceiling.

His thick cashmere overcoat gave David an athletic square look he liked. David did not see himself as a big man. People often commented on his striking wavy black hair. Yet this morning all he saw was gray creeping in on all sides. His olive skin was so much darker than the rest of his family; he always felt peculiar about his appearance.

David looked at his reflection and the ever-present mystery haunted him again. He had no idea how others really saw him nor any real perspective on himself. He always felt like an alien forced into a place he did not fit.

The mirror blurred into a cloudy mirage, transforming the wallpaper into long tan strips of wood. The glass became a door with a handle extending toward him. Somewhere behind the door was the David Richards he longed to meet. He almost reached for the illusionary knob, but the imaginary door quickly dissolved back into a looking glass.

David wrapped his scarf around his neck and reached out to repeat his daily ritual for prosperity. On the long hall table next to the door sat his favorite statue. Uncle Edward gave him the large brass bust of Moses as a college graduation present. Somewhere along the way he started rubbing the now-shiny nose for good luck. As a last act of self-fortification, David massaged the sculpture, hoping for good fortune.

While waiting for the garage door to go up, David ran through his morning agenda. *I wonder*, he thought, *is this the way destiny is found? You get up one morning, jump in your car, and just drive off toward something undefined but vaguely rising on the horizon? I hope I'm not off on another pointless chase.*

TWO

George and Mary Richards were always early risers. As with most of their daily rituals, they followed their predictable pattern with absolute precision. Breakfast was served at seven o'clock with a touch of elegance. The orange juice was expected to be on the table and the coffee poured before they sat down. Cut fresh flowers always graced the center of the table. The Richardses hoped their son, David, emulated their example as they anticipated he surely must.

"What does the paper say, dear?" Mary spread the linen napkin across her lap.

"The oil rig count continues to go down." George took off his reading glasses. "Bad sign. This country is going to pay for the lack of attention our president has given to the oil industry." Tall and imposing, George had white hair that added to his distinguished statesmanlike appearance. At seventy-two he was still a picture of health.

"Oh, my." Mary shook her head.

"Fortunately I shifted most of our assets into foreign drilling some years ago." George smiled. "Don't worry."

The kitchen door opened, and an elderly black lady carried a tray in. "Here's your soft-boiled egg, Mr. Richards. Just the way you like it." She placed the egg in a cup before him and a piece of toast in front of Mary. "Hope the coffee is fine."

"As always, Mildred." George folded up the paper. "You never miss."

"Has David said anything to you about his business negotiations today?" Mary buttered her toast.

"No." George shook his head. "The boy's playing his cards close to the vest. He wants to handle this one all by himself."

"Certainly. But I do wish he'd consult with you more, George. A great deal is at stake."

"Everything will be just fine." He winked knowingly. "I can assure you all the pieces are in the right place."

"How can you be so sure?" Mary fretted.

"Can you keep a secret?"

"Been doing so for over fifty years, haven't I?"

"I keep my ear to the ground at the bank. David doesn't know it, but his loan officer fills me in on all the details. I've known Sam Edwards as long as I've been on the board of directors at First Bank. Sam sort of slips me the inside story under the table."

"Why didn't you tell me sooner?" Mary frowned; the loose skin under her chin quivered, and her cheeks sagged. She kept her gray hair stylishly dyed blonde, but in the early morning light Mary looked every bit of seventy years. The liver spots on her hands and neck were dark against her pale flesh. "All this time I have been worrying over whether David was doing the right thing. You should have given me a hint for my own peace of mind." Her voice had an edge, authoritative and demanding.

"Now, Mary." George cracked the egg with the side of his knife. "You know I always keep a sharp eye on the boy's comings and goings. I even talked a bit with Sam Edwards about the bank backing David if he takes the advice I'll give him about politics. Got an excellent response, by the way."

"I just don't know." Mary broke the toast apart slowly. "You're going to have to approach David very *carefully* with the idea of running for governor. He can be so impractical and wander off into those strange unproductive notions he gets."

"I've already got matters lined up with the state Democratic party chairman. When David realizes what we're offering, he can't but accept the opportunity."

"Heaven knows we've laid enough of the stepping-stones in front of him." Mary took another sip of coffee. "From the private schools to the right connections, we've paved the way."

"I'm going to wait several days until after David announces the results of today's negotiations before I approach him." George's white eyebrows dropped over his eyes as he thought intensely. "He'll be in one of his quandaries about what to do with his life about then. I can spring the governor's race on him as an answer to all his problems."

Mary's sudden smile pulled her sagging face back into place. "I'll say this, George. You've always been the master of keeping David on the right track even when he was staring misfortune in the face. If we hadn't brought an end to his disastrous high school romance, no telling where he'd be today. Just think what would have happened if David had moved to California after he graduated from college. Keeping him here next to us was the best investment we ever made."

George smiled broadly. "Don't worry. I *always* keep my finger on the boy's pulse."

Sam Edwards was pumping away on the bicycle when David arrived at the health club. As he set the timer on his machine, David chided his puffing friend. "Sweating like a pig already, Sam?" Edwards groaned, and David waved at a couple of friends working out in the gym.

"Eat too much like a pig," Edwards panted. "That's my trouble."

David began churning slowing, then increased his speed. "I'm going to get an extra five minutes' worth in today if it kills me." He pulled the towel around his neck before leaning into the handlebars. "Got to get rid of a few pounds myself."

Edwards slacked his pace. "Come on, David, you're trying to make me feel guilty. You're trim as a high school football player. Look at those arms and chest." He wiped his face. "There's got to be a better place for you to meet your banker than under these humiliating circumstances. Really! Let's go back to business over lunch."

"Too much lunch *is* your problem, Sam." David rode faster. "Tell me what you found out about my worthy opponents today."

"Jackson and Schultz are sound. If they offer a buyout, they have the resources to stand behind their contract. The decision is yours. I realize Meachem has some say in the matter, but if the price is right, their company's offering is solid."

David did not break his stride. "The issue is whether I want to sell."

"Seems so to me. Look at you, David. You're an athletic specimen with every opportunity in the world at his feet. You can't lose. Really! Talk about a golden boy. You're it! Sell out high and use the money to pick another plum from the tree."

David turned slowly toward the banker. "Which fruit would you suggest?"

"Go for something big!" Edwards stepped off the machine. "Why not try public office? The field is wide open this year."

David threw back his head and roared. "Now that's rare."

"Seriously. Your reputation is spotless. You don't run around on your wife. No hidden scandals. Good businessman. The state needs a businessman for governor." He stepped off the bike and whispered into David's ear. "Take your money from Jackson and Schultz and shoot the moon. With the connections your old man's got you could—"

"Thanks for the advice," David cut him off, his sense of humor gone. "I appreciate your scoping their firm out for me. Let's see what happens today."

"Yeah, sure." Sam Edwards started for the locker room. "Good luck. Just bring the loot to your friendly banker when you're done."

David waved, but as soon as Sam disappeared into the locker room, his face froze in place. David leaned into the handlebars and pedaled furiously. The sweat quickly soaked through his T-shirt and ran down his legs. When the timer went off, he slowly straightened up. "Yes, Sam," he said to himself, his heart pounding. "What *exactly* do I want?"

Across the city in the offices of Jackson and Schultz a businessman and his lawyer studied a stack of documents lying on the desk between them. Al Jackson looked at his wristwatch.

He was large, balding, and middle-aged. Jackson's ruddy round face looked even more spherical with the stubby remnant of his receding hair clipped to the skin. "We've got about an hour left before we meet them. Is there anything in particular we must cover, Mike?" Jackson's thin gold-rimmed glasses were survivors of the 1940s. His eyes were cold and hard.

"No." The skinny lawyer sipped from his coffee cup. "I think we've pretty well covered the key areas for negotiation." Mike Alberts picked up a doughnut from a box on the desk.

"How should I read these people?" Al asked. "What strategy would you suggest?" Jackson's collar was unbuttoned to accommodate his fat neck; his tie was loosened.

Mike chewed on the doughnut. "Your best bet for attack is Jack Meachem, the blood, sweat, and tears end of the company. He'll be the one with financial need. Work on his fears about money." His thick glasses made his eyes seem larger.

"I'm not sure I understand." Jackson rubbed his chin.

"I've done business with Meachem and Richards a number of times." The lawyer picked up another doughnut. "And I've worked with Dave Richards's old man. George Richards is the moneybags financing the operation from the back room. Jack Meachem is the grunt man, does the leg work, fights it out in the trenches. David is the creative genius behind their advertising success. They've done well because of the father's financing, Jack's tenacity, and David's very considerable talent."

Al Jackson puckered his lips and narrowed his eyes. "If we buy the company without David Richards, what do we have?"

"No real competition will be left in the city." Alberts smiled. "Pretty good buy, I'd say." Mike wiped the doughnut sugar from his face. "However, if Richards starts another advertising firm he could quickly become as significant a rival as he is today."

"I need to buy Richards," Jackson's raspy morning voice rumbled.

"Get a guarantee he'll stay out of the business for a decade."

"What does David Richards need?"

"Have no idea."

"Don't banter with me!" Jackson growled. "I pay you to know everything."

The lawyer appeared irritated. "Look. Richards was born with a silver spoon in his mouth. The old man's oil money can bankroll any operation he's interested in. David has never worried about where the next buck is coming from. He simply functions as if he owns the world. I have no idea what he could possibly want. In fact, I'd love to be in his shoes. Gorgeous wife. Big house. Good reputation. Membership in two country clubs. What could David Richards possibly need?"

The bright midmorning sunlight beamed into the conference room of the Richards and Meachem public relations firm on the tenth floor of the Makin Towers Building. The marble exterior of the new forty-story center of commerce made this office complex *the* place to be if appearance mattered. Richards and Meachem, Inc., officed in nothing but what the cutting edge of political correctness and high-profile ostentatiousness dictated. A long, walnut marble-topped table dominated the luxuriously decorated conference room.

Three men stood around the table talking and sipping coffee. A woman sat in the middle chair of the table with a steno pad. Jack Meachem kept looking nervously at the wall clock. He was tall and lanky, his face narrow and pointed with an aquiline nose; his thin lips and his jutting chin made his face seem unusually long. His porcupine flattop hadn't changed since 1957.

"Get you another cup of coffee, Mr. Jackson?" Meachem turned anxiously to the other man. "Lawyers drink lots of coffee." Meachem laughed nervously. "How about another one, Mike?"

The door burst open, and David Richards bounded into the room. "Good morning, friends!" David shook hands briskly before sitting down at the head of the table. "Good to see everyone. Great morning to do some business."

"Just a mite late." Jackson slowly sat down at the table. "We'd hoped to consummate the deal by the end of the day." He spilled over the side of the chair.

"If time were only a commodity I could sell," David

beamed, "I would make us all rich. Unfortunately the best we can do is enjoy it as we spend whatever we have left."

Jackson did not smile. Meachem chuckled nervously. The lawyer's large eyes stared straight ahead.

"So! Jackson and Schultz really want to buy us out?" David asked nonchalantly. "Obviously you gentlemen recognize quality and value when you see it."

The lawyer opened his briefcase and pulled out four contracts. "We think you will find our offer to be realistic and generous."

"Aha!" David broke in. "A euphemism for hard bargaining ahead."

Jackson bit his lip and looked sourly at Jack Meachem.

"Why don't you lay your entire proposal out before we make any comment," Jack suggested. "We'll listen first."

"Fine." The lawyer passed his proposals around the table. "I would suggest we have some sandwiches sent in for lunch so we can negotiate right through the noon hour."

"Excellent." Meachem looked hard at David. "No one leaves the room until we are done. No phone calls will be taken. We'll send Mrs. Hammond out for lunch when we are ready. Let's begin."

By the time the four men finally emerged from the conference room, evening had fallen and the winter sky had turned black. They shook hands, exchanged final pleasantries, and Jackson and his lawyer left. The secretary immediately got her heavy coat out of the closet. David and Jack settled into chairs in the empty reception area.

"Here's a stack of phone messages that came today." Mrs. Hammond pushed the pieces of paper into David's hand and hurried out the door. "Got to run. My husband will kill me for coming home at this hour without phoning."

"My gosh! Susan called three times." David thumbed through the messages. "I told her I'd call this afternoon. Better make sure I'm not in trouble at home." He hit the recall button on the switchboard, automatically dialing his home.

"Hard day." Jack kicked off his shoes. "Jackson is a tough cuss. Can't believe the pile of statistics he wanted from us."

The phone buzzed unanswered in the background. "Now he knows as much about us as we do," David observed. "Whatever the intent is, his firm certainly knows how we tick."

"His intent?" Jack unknotted his tie. "He wants to buy us, pure and simple."

The phone kept ringing.

"Susan should have been home long ago. Strange." David canceled the call. "Don't be so certain you know what Jackson's really after."

"Sure, some of the fine print could be restrictive. But they made us a decent offer."

David looked around the room at the walls filled with award plaques commemorating outstanding achievement, all the signs of success. However, his eye stayed on his large watercolor in the center. The bold Colorado landscape dominated the room. In the righthand corner was his own artistic signature. "Can't always tell what people are really after."

"Don't start *that* business on me again, David." Jack's face flushed. "The day's been hard enough as it is. I don't want another soliloquy about how you'd rather be painting than be a successful businessman. You've got the bucks to indulge your fantasies. I don't have that luxury, so let's get serious. This deal with Jackson is my chance to have a decent retirement. You'll inherit yours."

"I've observed your nerves are a bit on edge, Jack ol' boy. I'd suggest your comments are a tad below the belt and rather inappropriate."

"We've been working at this business for fifteen years." Jack clenched his fist. "I think that fact alone gives me the right to tell you the truth, David."

"Truth and opinion can be confused. I've got no apologies for how you've fared for the last decade, sitting there in a pure silk tie, a sixty-dollar monogrammed shirt, and a tailored suit. I simply want more out of life than to look like a page from *Esquire*."

"Don't get condescending with me! I'm not going to let you blow a fabulous deal to placate your misplaced sense of purpose. Money makes the world go around, and that's the way you've lived as long as I've known you!"

David's neck began to turn red. "Perhaps we ought to sleep on the proposal before we say anything more that we might be sorry for." His fingers dug into the leather chair.

"Agreed!" Jack stood up defiantly. "I'll be here at eight o'clock. I suppose we can talk *whenever* you arrive." He turned abruptly, opened the closet, and picked up his overcoat. Jack didn't look back.

A policeman knocked briskly on the glass door at the end of the hall. Jack slipped the topcoat on as he hurried down the corridor to let the officer in.

"What can I do for you, sir?"

"You're David Richards?"

"No," Meachem pointed toward David still sitting in the reception area. "I'm his partner."

The policeman looked apprehensively over Jack's shoulder. "Perhaps you might come with me. I need to have a word with Mr. Richards."

"Really?" Jack frowned. "Well, yes. Sure. What's wrong, officer?"

The policeman walked past without answering. "Mr. Richards? David Richards?"

David quickly rose to his feet. "Sure. I'm Richards."

"Please sit back down, Mr. Richards. I have some difficult news for you."

"What's going on here?" David stepped toward the officer.

"I think you'd better sit down, Mr. Richards."

"No, no." David beckoned for the policeman to speak. "Be straightforward. What's the problem?"

"I'm very sorry to inform you—" The policeman caught his breath and read from a notepad. "You're married to Susan Randolph Richards, age forty-four, of 2606 Dorset Street?"

"Susan? Of course. She's my wife."

"Mr. Richards, about an hour and a half ago your wife was killed in a car wreck."

THREE

The mourners huddled around the canvas tent did not notice the taxi pull up behind the almost endless line of cars and funeral home limousines. A tall elderly man got out and quickly walked through the snow, winding his way between gravestones. The howling north wind sweeping over the Oklahoma plains covered the sound of the cab pulling away.

An Episcopal priest standing at the head of the casket poured a vial of dirt across the top. He read again from his *Book of Common Prayer*. "In sure and certain hope of the resurrection to eternal life through our Lord Jesus Christ, we commit Susan's body to the ground; earth to earth, ashes to ashes, dust to dust." The wind caught his alb and blew the white stole around him.

Buttoning the overcoat collar up around his neck, the elderly man edged between a young couple to get closer to the family. David Richards was seated in a cold metal chair between his parents. He slumped in his chair, his arms crossed listlessly in his lap. Although the bitter wind made his cheeks bright red, the rest of David's face was gray and drawn. His body seemed barely propped up by the black chair.

The crowd recited the Lord's Prayer, but the late arrival stood tight-lipped with his eyes wide open. David tried to say the words of the Our Father but broke down in the middle of the prayer. The priest concluded, "Rest eternal grant to her, O Lord; And let light perpetual shine upon her."

George put his arm around his son, and Mary took David's hand.

The priest concluded the committal with a solemn "Amen"

and closed his black book. "Because of the inclement weather, the Richardses ask that we come back to their home for our final words of condolence. A light lunch will be served. Let us return to our cars as quickly as we can and not detain David." The clergyman gestured for the crowd to leave and stepped resolutely in front of the family.

As the large group quickly dispersed, the elderly man walked toward the family. Even though the priest stood like a pillar of ice, the tall stranger brushed past. "My boy!" he opened his unusually long arms wide. "My poor, poor boy."

"Edward!" David leaped to his feet. "Uncle Edward! You got here!" David grabbed him around the neck and clung like a lost child.

"I got the first Concord out of London," the old man whispered in his ear. "Had to change planes in New York City, but I ran every step of the way." Edward's gray, stubby mustache brushed David's neck. His great, shaggy gray eyebrows quivered.

"Thank God you came," David sobbed.

Mary Richards hugged him. "What a dear, dear man you are. We never dreamed you could make it with such short notice."

George Richards shook his hand. "Bless you, Edward. Bless you for coming."

"Ride in the car with us." David grabbed his arm. "I need you more than I ever have in my life."

"I'll have to ride with you," Edward smiled weakly. "The cabby left me."

"Got you covered, Uncle Edward." David smiled for the first time in three days.

"Let's get out of the cold," the priest urged them onward. "Coldest day we've had in Oklahoma in years."

"Please ride with us too, Reverend." George Richards insisted. "Heavens, the limo will seat half the crowd."

The five people hurried into the long black Cadillac that quickly pulled away in a cloud of white exhaust. David kept looking out the back window at the tent flopping in the wind until they were well out of the cemetery.

"Reverend Paul Kendall, please meet Edward Crownover." George Richards formally introduced the two men sitting together on the jump seat.

"I believe I heard David call you uncle? You have a distinctive English accent."

"It's a long story," the elderly man mumbled.

"Edward is closer than family," David quickly added.

"We can't remember when he wasn't part of our inner circle," Mary explained. "We've sort of adopted him."

"I give the family a touch of class." Edward imitated a cockney accent. Laughter momentarily broke the tension.

"David." Edward took the young man's hand. "What happened? What happened . . . to Susan?"

"Icy road," David muttered. "Apparently the other driver had been drinking. He slid across the median into Susan's lane." He swallowed hard. "Edward . . ." David's voice trailed, and he looked at the older man with empty eyes.

"I've had the maid prepare some wonderful spiced tea," Mary broke in. She talked rapidly in an inappropriately cheerful voice. "We've prepared a light lunch, finger sandwiches, found some marvelous Russian caviar, and some steaming, hot cider."

"You have so many friends, David." George immediately added. "We've added extra servants for the afternoon. I'm sure everything will work out quite well."

"We're proud of our boy." Mary squeezed Edward's hand. "He is holding up so very well under this trial." She smiled proudly.

Reverend Kendall quickly intervened. "What part of England are you from?"

"Grew up in Salisbury. As of late, I live in London."

"Edward's been our man in Britain for a number of years." George added, almost lightheartedly. "Helped us turn many a deal in the Middle East. I must say, quite a clever businessman."

"Marvelous bridge player too," Mary chattered. "The ladies all love him." She winked.

"I've spent some time at Canterbury," Paul Kendall said. "Actually the area around Salisbury and Glastonbury is the most intriguing I've ever visited. We'll have to compare notes."

"Quite so," Edward sounded like an English butler.

George and Mary continued to discuss their afternoon menu and extol the Englishman's virtues to the priest, but Edward studied David. Black circles ringed his listless eyes. His face was blank, empty as if all remaining emotion had been wrung out of him. Crowded between the Richardses, David looked like a child held captive by two all-consuming parents.

At the slightest pause in the conversation, Mary instantly resumed her banal monologue about food. George covered any other slack with his own reflections on irrelevant trivia about the oil business in England. The priest said nothing but kept a compassionate eye on the silent, bereaved husband.

"Well, here we are and so quickly," Mary concluded as the limousine pulled through the metal gates in front of the Richardses' estate. "My, but you gentlemen are quiet."

Edward Crownover watched with chagrin as the affair unfolded. David stood between the Richardses in a reception line that looked like a macabre mixture of an awards ceremony and a wake. Most of the visitors greeted David as if he were the guest of honor. Some were openly broken, but the more emotional quickly regained their composure as was clearly expected of them. David mechanically responded to words of consolation as if reciting lines from a script prepared by George and Mary.

The Englishman promptly slipped out of the receiving line and retreated to the hallway. He paused to study the evolution of David's childhood lining the walls like a gallery of history. Among the pictures of Davey on horseback, in a Scout uniform, a football suit, Edward found several of himself standing by the boy. Edward observed himself age as the boy grew.

"Junior League won't be the same without Susan." A woman in a tight-fitting black dress chatted with a friend. The woman edged past Edward without acknowledging his presence. "We must quickly find a new chairperson for the charity ball."

"Do you think David will come?" The other woman rolled her eyes. "Maybe the dance could be *his* coming-out party!"

"He won't last that long!" The woman in black laughed as they turned the corner.

Edward shuddered. Reaching the corner, he turned in the other direction toward the drawing room. Two young men in business suits were talking in front of David's large self-portrait. Edward always admired the remarkable oil painting completed years ago in art school.

"Hear David is selling the firm to Jackson and Schultz." The first man said in a stage whisper.

"Seriously?" The second man answered.

Edward stopped and pretended to look at the picture again.

"The sly fox should make a bundle," the first man observed.

"David gets all the breaks," the second grumbled. "With his house and money, I wonder whose wife he'll go after, now that he's single."

"Care for something?" A waiter came by with a tray of drinks. Edward picked one up and moved on.

The Englishman tried to avoid trivial conversations by moving from room to room as if on some mission in another part of the house. Finally he found a secluded corner in the dining room and watched the affluent mingle. He felt highly uncomfortable and angry. Then he saw the priest at the opposite end of the room, leaning against the wall. He too appeared alienated from the gathering.

"Quite the party." Crownover strolled up and smiled thinly. "Perhaps not quite to the taste of the clergy."

The minister looked thoughtful. "Seems a bit on the frivolous side, doesn't it?" He offered his hand. "Just call me Paul."

"Americans bloody well have a knack for creating emotional distance from death. Possibly such a festive atmosphere reassures the grim reaper will not soon call again." Crownover snorted.

"Susan was well-loved. Maybe negation is the only way her friends can deal with her death at this moment."

"Reverend, you are the theologian. I am only concerned with David's well-being."

"Quite to the point," the priest agreed. "Actually I knew Susan very well, and my acquaintance with David is far from passing."

"Of course." Edward picked up another glass from the server going by carrying a tray of goblets. "The Richardses have always been faithful Anglicans. Least, that's what we call it in England."

"You're an Anglican?"

"Everyone in England is. Baptized at birth. Touched all the bases. Stood there when little David was baptized. Shan't bore you with the details."

"Oh." Paul smiled. "The faithful godparent to David, possibly?"

Edward paused and shook his head. "To be honest, godparent, yes; faithful, no. I'm not really much of a believer. Don't mean to be offensive, Reverend. Just such things as Susan's untimely death have squeezed the possibility of faith out of me. Injustice isn't easily swallowed."

"I *do* understand." The priest looked away. "We are all crushed by such a devastating tragedy. I'm available if there is something you might like to talk with me about later."

"No, no!" Edward was momentarily jolted by the minister's directness. "No one can do anything with an old reprobate like myself. Quite beyond redemption I am. But . . ."

"No one stands beyond the pale," the priest quickly retorted. "You're obviously a man of considerable sensitivity."

"Heavens!" Edward felt his face flush. "Been some time since anyone called my cards so quickly. Governor, if you knew me you'd find sensitive isn't in the accounting. No, no. I'm simply interested in David's well-being. I love the boy more than anyone in the world, and I am troubled for him. Mary acts like he's her special masterpiece of stoic denial. How does he really fare?"

"Not well at all," the priest said laconically. "David's in bad shape."

"Just as I suspected."

"Rather difficult to go on being the family's prized trophy when his psyche is crumbling like defective cement." Paul crossed his arms over his chest.

Crownover raised his eyebrows knowingly. "I hope you may be able to help him."

"David has an appointment with me tomorrow morning. During the past year we've come to know each other very well. Of course I am available to him night and day."

"Splendid. I immediately sensed you are a good man." Crownover affectionately thumped the priest on the chest. "We've both sized the matter up exactly the same way. You do what you can; I will do what I can."

"There seems to be a—well, a—mystery that surrounds David. Hard to get hold of the necessary loose ends. The times I've talked with him or the Richardses for that matter—I'm always left with the uneasy foreboding one has in trying to solve a Rubic's cube puzzle when he doesn't have the instructions. Perhaps you can help me."

"That's why I'm here." Edward set the half-full glass down on an end table. "I am the one person who has all the pieces in this puzzle. Let's sit down and talk."

The next day David drove slowly into the parking lot of old St. Mark's Church. The large gray granite edifice had the expected traditional look of an Episcopal church. Passing decades left their mark staining the rock walls and giving the long sanctuary an aged, venerable appearance. High spires and the large rose window in the center of the narthex made the church feel medieval. Directly behind the parking lot was the new educational building, which Reverend Kendall had just brought to completion. Built from the same color of granite, the addition gave a fortress aura to St. Mark's. David entered through the side door marked "Offices."

"Hello, David," the rector's secretary greeted him. "We've

been expecting you. Reverend Kendall will be with you in just a moment. You have certainly been in all our prayers."

"Thank you, Catherine." David sat down across from the secretary's desk and took off his overcoat. Her desk was surrounded by a copier, bookshelves, dictation equipment, and a typewriter stand. On the north wall was a large walnut cross and on the other an embroidered picture of a lion with wings, the symbol of St. Mark. "I will read while I wait." David picked up a copy of *The Living Church.*

"I understand a memorial fund for Susan has been established at the church." The secretary shuffled some papers as she talked. "A very nice idea."

"Thank you." David kept his eyes fastened on the magazine.

"Perhaps a picture or something for the new educational building?"

"Yes." David didn't look up.

The door marked "Rector" opened. "David! Glad you're here." Paul Kendall extended his hand. "Come in. Come in and let's talk."

The priest's inner office was lined by shelves crammed with books, which made the room appear more like a library. A large antique desk was at one end, and at the other was a small leather couch and two chairs. A *pre dieux* kneeling bench in the opposite corner faced a large Byzantine icon of Mary and the baby Jesus. The wooden wall paneling and exposed beams gave a Tudor look to the room. The office was tidy and proper.

"Glad to meet your Uncle Edward." The priest pointed to the corner of the couch. "Most extraordinary person." A gold pectoral cross dangled in the center of his clerical shirt. Handsome, with broad shoulders, he was a small man, with probing, penetrating light blue eyes. "We talked for well over an hour."

"Edward's been both a brother and an uncle." David shuffled across the room. "Strange, he suddenly left this morning for California. Said he'd be back in several days for some extended time with me. He urged me to talk with you immediately."

"I'm sure yesterday was the worst day of your life." The minister sat down in one of the leather covered chairs. "Your pain was a staggering load to carry."

David settled into the couch. "Was I so obvious?" He laid his overcoat at the other end.

"It wasn't a time for appearances."

"Father Kendall . . ." David sighed.

"David, we're really about the same age. I'm forty-nine. Right now you just need a friend. Why don't you simply call me Paul?"

"I was taught to give your position proper respect." David looked at the priest carefully. Although his hair was streaked with gray, the minister might easily pass for thirty-nine. "My parents drilled rectitude and social correctness into me, but I'll try to say Paul."

The priest took off his coat and tossed it over the opposite chair. He looked physically fit without the usual middle-age paunch. "When our members don't like a decision on the new building, I'm called 'the Rector.' If people want to keep a safe distance, they call me 'Reverend.' " He laughed. "The high church people insist on Father Kendall. People who need a shepherd call me pastor . . . or friend. I'm here as your friend, David. Your best friend."

"Excellent." David smiled for the first time.

Paul settled back in his chair. "As you've already learned in this room, we don't worry about keeping appearances. Whatever is on your mind or heart is grist for the mill. There is absolutely nothing you can't tell me and know it's kept in strictest confidence. Every word goes under the seal of the confessional."

"Thank you." David's smile faded, and he leaned forward on the couch. "Yes. Yesterday was pure torment." He lowered his head into his hands and stared at the coffee table in front of him. "Not that the funeral service wasn't meaningful," he added quickly and apologetically. "Thank you for your very comforting words. But the day was so raw, so bitter cold. And leaving Susan out there . . ." He stopped and began to weep.

The priest silently listened and said nothing. He slowly pushed a box of Kleenex in front of David.

David rubbed his eyes with the palm of his hand. "All right." He sat up resolutely. "I have to talk to someone or I swear I'm going to come unglued and start breaking up the furniture. I might just end by smashing my parents' heads together. I can't stand it any longer! Help me, Father!"

FOUR

David got up from the couch and walked to the window. Across the snow-covered patio, last summer's flowers were brown frozen stalks covered with ice. "Susan held everything in place," he finally said. "Like staves around a barrel, she held my life together. Without her, my last vestige of stability is gone."

"Susan was devout," Reverend Kendall answered. "I could count on her at ten o'clock communion every Wednesday morning. She was a mainstay of the altar guild. The entire church grieves her loss."

David put his palms against the cold window. "I thought of her as my connection with God. I always assumed her prayers for me. Last spring she insisted we read Sheldon Vanauken's *A Severe Mercy* together. Susan made me discuss the meaning of tragedy so I couldn't ever get mad at God. Can you believe it? She was actually preparing me for this time."

"Remarkable woman." The priest sighed. "We talked about you often." David ran his hands nervously through his hair again. "I wouldn't have started counseling with you if she hadn't insisted. Thank God we established a relationship before this terrible thing happened."

The priest nodded. "Because we've counseled for the last two years about your struggles, I know how hard it is for you to live with contradictions. Susan was right. You may have the head of a businessman, but you have the soul of a poet."

David turned back and looked out the window. "I'm not going into one of my monologues about the mendacity and duplicity. You've already heard more than enough of my disdain for the world of advertising; slick magazine covers that hide the truth; television commercials twisting facts with super-quickie sound bites. At least Susan won't wake up anymore to the sound of my teeth grinding." David abruptly stopped and pressed his head against the cold windowpane.

Paul sat quietly and said nothing.

"I've kept up a good front," David anguished. "My whole life has been one gigantic training session in proper appearances! Someone should have given my parents show dogs instead of dumping me on their porch."

"You are very angry with your parents?"

David slowly turned and leaned against the window. "In the last twenty-four hours I have realized just how angry I really am." He began to pace. "Off and on through the years I've caught glimpses of something seething and boiling down deep inside, but like a dutiful son, the feelings were respectfully stuffed somewhere. Yesterday the lid finally blew off."

"What happened?" Paul listened even more intently. "Susan's death would have pushed anyone over the edge, but what made yesterday so particularly different?"

"Uncle Edward noticed. He saw through the whole charade. My wife's death had to be massaged into an event. I couldn't even grieve without maintaining the proper social posture." He stopped and breathed deeply. Slowly his forehead wrinkled, and his mouth twisted with pain. "Susan couldn't even die without their controlling the event." He choked. "There's the source of the tragedy. Them! Not God."

Paul waited until David could talk again. "Are you angry because of what they did or because of what *you* allowed them to do?"

David blinked and frowned. "What a confounding thought!" He swallowed. "I'm forty-five years old. I've let myself be a puppet for so long I don't even know how to regain control. Yes ... sure ... you are very, very perceptive ... I don't get angry ... I get depressed." He dropped onto the couch.

The priest smiled compassionately. "I've seen this moment

coming for a long time. When we talked, you danced around a core issue that can no longer be avoided. Susan's death is terrible enough, but tragedy has kicked in another door you tried to avoid. Remember? We have talked before of the hidden room you keep locked in your mind. Maybe today is the right time to enter that other chamber."

"I have to," David said resolutely. "If I serve Susan's memory well, I must go on as she would have so deeply wanted. No one understood my problem like she did. If there is any meaning to be found in her death, it will come from doing what she urged me to do. Susan knew about the forbidden place. Perhaps only her death could force me inside."

"What's in the other room?" Paul probed gently.

"I'm not sure . . . but my suspicions are clear. Inside is the real David, my true self."

The priest smiled. "Yes, the authentic David has been locked away for a very long time."

"Since I was three years old," David concluded.

"Three?"

"That's when I entered the Richardses' world and my grooming began. Childhood pictures reveal how very different I was . . . small, dark-skinned with black hair. The Richards clan was fair, blond-haired, tall, and thin. I didn't even start to grow until I was in college. Obviously I was brand X, imported from somewhere."

"What do you know of your background, David?"

"Virtually nothing. Everything's been quite hush-hush as if there were something illegal about the whole matter. I suppose the records are locked away in some bank vault my father keeps under a secret account."

"So two Davids came into being," Paul observed gently. "One resided with the Richardses and the other lived in the forbidden room, behind the mirror?"

"Susan knew. She never bought the family act. In fact, Susan often encouraged me to defy my parents and strike out in my own direction. She tried to tell me how much she loved the imprisoned David. I found it impossible to believe she could."

Paul beckoned. "Why, David? Why were you such a stranger to yourself?"

"As I grew up, I bought everything George and Mary were selling. I liked the clothes, the cars, the mansion, the perks for blending in. Obviously all the rhetoric about duplicity was a cover-up. I acquiesced."

"Come now." The priest shook his head. "You are a person of considerable integrity. Oh, yes, I've watched you jump through the family hoops, but you were never a preppie, a yuppie, a whatever. Sure you wear the Gucci shoes, but you are also notorious for showing up inappropriately dressed like a bum. You have friends the rest of your social set wouldn't touch with a ten-foot pole. Your explanation won't fly."

"I sold out," David barked. "That is the truth, and Susan knew it! I wanted to go to *art school* and become an artist. I would gladly have settled for a hand-to-mouth existence as an illustrator. Maybe I could have taught in a college. Instead, the good ol' Richards corporation promised to bankroll any business I went into with potential community influence. I switched to advertising and put up the paintbrushes. I acted like the switch didn't matter, and a little piece of me died. I've been dying by inches ever since. When my partnership had trouble, I wanted to quit and go to Canada to start over in Toronto, but Dad forgave the debt and I stayed here." David was outraged. "I never got away from this flat, windy, prairie-grass prison because I just flat sold out."

"But why did you knuckle under?" Paul ignored the explanation.

"I just told you," David shouted.

"No," the priest said firmly. "You haven't told me. At least you haven't told me what the person in the secret room would say is the ultimate truth."

"Stop it!" David barked. "You're trying to confuse me. I just didn't have enough backbone to stand up for myself. The whole matter is that simple."

Paul shook his head. "Backbone? You're one of the most tenacious people I know. I'm not buying that excuse either."

"Leave me alone," David growled. "I've had enough of this conversation."

The priest sat quietly until the silence seemed unbearable. Paul finally said, "What were you afraid of, David? Fear is the key, you know. Fear controls your life, doesn't it?"

David started to shake his fist but stopped in midair; his hand trembled and slowly dropped. David's eyes watered, and his lip quivered. "Yes." His voice was barely audible. "I can't tell you exactly why . . . but I've always been afraid . . . afraid . . . I was going to die. My dreams are filled with chases, explosions, falling into empty space." He ran both hands through his hair, squeezing his scalp. "And now Susan is gone. She was the last protection I had . . . against it . . . whatever it is."

"George and Mary held your life in the palm of their hand for nearly forty-five years. They were your guarantee of survival. In the final analysis, you could never afford to stand against them."

David mechanically nodded his head. "I couldn't let myself look in that other room in my head. The person in there wasn't and would never be acceptable to them." David closed his eyes. "The only way I could protect and keep that part of me alive was to do whatever they said."

"Yes," Paul said compassionately, "you have paid a great price for stability." The priest moved to the couch and put his arm around his friend. "You saved your *self* at the price of your soul."

David buckled forward.

David fought to regain his composure as he sat in the church's chapel. The small chapel reserved for simple weddings and private prayers was adjacent to the sanctuary. Like the nave of St. Mark's, the walls were large blocks of stone, and the ceiling was crossed with massive beams. The marble altar was covered with an elegant damask green frontal. A large Epiphany banner hung from the doors that were kept closed to save on heating costs. The room was so cold he could nearly see his breath. Finally, he got up and knelt at the railing until he felt sufficiently composed to return to the rector's office.

"Ready to talk some more?" The rector got up from behind his desk.

"I must. I have to." David sat down on the couch again. "I'm sorry I got so overwhelmed. I just couldn't go on."

"Of course. We'll stop whenever you wish."

"I've bantered the word *self* around a thousand times," he began slowly, "but you understand. Tell me what is the self?"

"As you use the word, David, most simply, the self is the part of you that relates to society. It's that outer shell you think of as your identity or character. You might say the self is the front you put up. Fear and distortions have created 'the false self.' "

David shook his head. "And the soul? What's the soul?"

"I think of it as the fingerprint of God on our lives." Paul sat down in his usual chair. "The soul is our capacity to relate to God, to what is eternal."

"And that's what I have lost?"

"Let's say you've just misplaced it for the moment. I have a hunch you let Susan function as your soul, your link to the world outside of and around your true self."

David stared at the minister. "You terrify me, Paul. I didn't think anyone could know me so well."

"Perhaps only Susan did." The priest rubbed the pectoral cross resting on his chest. "However, I think your Uncle Edward will have some very strong clues about your self and soul to offer when he returns."

"A false self? Lost my soul?" David sighed and stared at the coffee table. "I don't attend services as regularly as I should, but I haven't broken the ten big rules. Of course, I'm not a particularly religious person."

"No, David. You've always been a religious person. Religious people are concerned about what things mean, with ultimate purpose and human values. You've certainly done plenty of reflection. People can be very religious but not necessarily Christian. Religious people are often quite preoccupied with outer form or ritual as the means of trying to get in touch with their souls."

David shook his head uncomprehendingly.

"There is great goodness in you, David. You must embrace it. In the days ahead you will discover Susan's death created a new crisis. Life can't ever again be as it was. Your own goodness will not let you settle for the form of things. You won't be able to go on 'going along.' David, you must find what is at the center in your life."

"Yes." He nodded his head slowly. "I can't go on being David, son of George and Mary, the young PR executive, everyone's hail-fellow-well-met." He slid back, his head resting on the couch. "Then again, I'm not sure I want to know who lives in my forbidden room. Maybe I'm afraid to find out."

"I can't tell you who is in there, but I am here to walk with you if you open the door."

"I don't have the slightest idea how to begin, Paul. Where do I start?"

"You've not yet fully faced the meaning of Susan's death. In another day, the rest of the world will go back to life as usual. Your firm will expect you to be back at the helm. George and Mary will start their social merry-go-round again. Your tragedy will be yesterday's headlines, and you will come home alone to an empty house. The pain will be greater than now."

"That's not terribly good news."

"In the darkness of the empty night everything in your soul will start coming up. Experiencing the revelation will be difficult, but if you will not run from the encounter you will begin to recover what is authentic."

"I came today expecting you to dispense a few religious answers for why tragedies occur. Instead I leave feeling maybe the way I've lived my life has been the greater blunder."

"David, there are no ultimate satisfying answers for why violent intrusions rip through the fabric of our existence. Nothing I could say would make Susan's death acceptable. Your task is not to understand as much as to use what has happened in a way that is constructive for the rest of your life. As strange and insensitive as it may sound, you have been given a staggering opportunity to start again. Your life need not be tragic; you simply need to start living it fully."

David slowly rose to his feet and picked up his overcoat. He walked toward the door. "I will be back . . . tomorrow."

FIVE

Edward Crownover caught the earliest flight possible to get into the Ontario, California, airport by noon. He picked up a rental car and drove the San Bernardino Freeway running along the edge of the high foothills until it turned south toward Chino. Edward no longer needed a map to find his way through the maze of freeway exchanges on this northern fringe of the Los Angeles metroplex. The speeding mass of cars hurtling past and around him made the old man nervous and edgy.

Edward held the firm conviction the whole area should have been left to the lizards. He didn't like the town of Chino; no history, no roots, and ten million commuters going down a freeway meant no culture. The anonymity and banality of endless neon signs and countless tract houses irritated him. As the scene blurred past, he thought of the inhabitants as a race of nomads who nightly burrowed into their individual but identical dens of apathy.

"A bloody DP camp!" he protested to himself. "The whole lot of 'em are nothing but a conglomeration of displaced persons." He turned south and back west to go directly into Chino.

Perhaps, Ruth ended up in this place for that very reason! Edward was surprised by the thought. The possibility that a community of nameless floaters might be of some comfort to her was a new insight. *Sure. Ruth had to drift where the tides took her. Once everything was destroyed, she had to accept whatever the world was, mongrel or not.*

"No." Crownover thumped the steering wheel. "Ruth is a DP of a different order! She didn't allow herself to be sucked into the Southern California ocean of superficiality and he-donism!" Satisfied by his conclusion, Edward turned on the radio and tried to find classical music to distract him. He knew seeing her again was the most pressing reason he felt agitated.

Five minutes later, he found the small stucco bungalow on a side street in exactly the variety of tract area he deplored. The adobe-colored house was surrounded by tall palm trees. An ancient spiked century plant nearly covered the entire front flower bed. A card at the bottom of the mailbox read "Ruth Moses." He knocked on the door and waited.

"Surprise!" he exploded as soon as he saw the small, white-haired woman. Before she could answer, Edward bent down and picked up the astonished woman, giving her a big kiss.

"Eddie," Ruth sputtered. "What . . . what . . . what are you doing here?"

"Ah! You are the only person in the world I ever let get away with calling me Eddie. Just look at you! Gorgeous as ever."

"Even your first words defraud a shriveled old woman. We both know I'm a faded picture, an old, cracked canvas."

"Never!" Edward hugged her. "Never in a thousand years! Especially to me."

"Why in the world are you here?" Ruth squinted, and her eye folds nearly covered her eyes.

"I'd go a million miles for one of your smiles." Edward started a bad imitation of Eddie Cantor.

"Since you are in my neighborhood, I suppose I have no choice but to invite you in for a cup of tea." She held the door open. "I won't let you drink anything stronger at this hour of the day."

"Most certainly!" Edward laughed. " 'Twould be the civi-lized thing to do."

The furnishings were spartan by Edward's standards, but the stacks of books scattered around the living room gave a unique atmosphere of intelligence and culture. "Come on back to the kitchen, and I will put on some hot water." Ruth led him through the living room. The kitchen windows were open, letting in bright California sunlight. A sprinkler system spurted outside in the dry air. The breeze smelled of a strange mixture of irrigation, orange trees, and freeway smog.

Edward sat down at the small table and watched Ruth scurry about the kitchen. Though small, the room was warm and personal in its simplicity. Each item and piece had been selected carefully to sit in its prescribed place. Everything had meaning.

Today Ruth didn't look sixty-six. There had been times he'd seen her look eighty, but today she seemed to be fifteen years younger than the calendar measured. Her grayish-white hair was striking against her dark skin. Osteoporosis bent her forward slightly, making her seem smaller than five feet. The years had given her the sage appearance of an ancient soothsayer. Ruth had an indefinable European quality when her hair was pulled back in a small knot. Her black eyes still snapped, reminding Edward she could take charge quickly should she wish. Nothing went past Ruth unless it was by her choice.

"What a couple we would have made." Edward patted her on the arm.

Ruth placed a cup and saucer in front of him and glared. "Don't start that line on me. We're far too old for you to try this with me."

"Who else would ever have been as faithful as I?" He sounded vulnerable and chastened by her answer. "Have I not been the one constant man in your life through these decades?"

Ruth poured hot water into his cup. "Eddie, you've been under no obligation to send those checks every month. How many times have I written that you should stop? Of course, I can't possibly ever tell you how grateful I am." She kissed him on the forehead. "But we both know how things really were . . ." She turned and put the teakettle back on the stove. She added, ". . . and must be."

"Nothing ever *has to be*." He put a tea bag in the hot water. "I am a firm believer we can control destiny. No one has to take what comes."

"Easy for you to say." Ruth's voice was cold.

"Well," Edward fumbled for words, "I mean to say that a . . . a . . . a . . . we can act to make things better. Start again."

"You've said so a thousand times." Ruth sat down across from him. "Let's change the subject. How's merry old England these days?"

"I didn't come here from England. Not straightaway, at least. I came to attend a funeral in Oklahoma."

Ruth stiffened, and her eyes narrowed.

"The boy's wife died. Was killed in a car wreck. Quite tragic." He stirred the tea slowly. "The terrible sort of intrusion best faced with the loving support of one's mum." He looked straight into the cup.

Ruth said nothing for nearly half a minute. "You certainly have a knack for turning up with surprising information," Ruth said dryly. She turned away and looked out the open window toward the rugged high foothills rising beyond the neighbor's fence. "I'm hardly a mum," she said harshly. "I was deprived of the opportunity."

Edward placed the spoon on the saucer. "It's time for the boy to know about you, to meet you."

"Playing God again, are we?"

"I'm doing the best I can," he answered awkwardly. "I'm not here to open old wounds. You know I've always cared about both of you. I've come across the ocean to try once more to make it all right."

After an interminably long pause, Ruth looked at him again. "Death's found David's address, has it? And I can do something about the inevitable?" She turned sideways as if determined to spend the rest of the morning silently studying the foothills.

Edward said again, "It's time for the boy to see you."

"I heard you, Edward." She pushed her cup away. "I'm not deaf."

"I recognize that tone in your voice. I know when distance is your hiding place."

She didn't answer.

"He's forty-five, Ruth. For a long time I've watched him coming to this turning point. Things have been unsettled and amiss with David for years. Then boom! He stumbles onto a volcano instead of a burning bush." He added, "You may be the only hope he has."

"I've so often wondered what he would think of me," Ruth said, as if alone. "For all these decades I've wondered so often what he might think." She got up to pour another cup of hot water only to realize her cup was still full. "You've always been faithful, Eddie. All these years, you've been constant in your reports about David. Frankly, I didn't think you would stay with it."

Abruptly setting the cup down, Ruth reached across the table and squeezed his hand tightly. "No, I cannot possibly tell you how grateful I am. In my own way I'll always love you. I'm sorry that's not been enough. Sorry for both of us."

Edward couldn't look into her eyes. He stared at her hand over his. "I'm trying to do what is best."

"I know you are."

"I thought it best simply to show up and tell you the facts in person. I know how very difficult it is for you to hear about a death, and I wanted to be here to break the news. David needs what only you can give. The boy has become a man who has lost his way. He doesn't know what he's about or who he is."

Her wrinkled face remained emotionless, giving no hint of her thoughts.

"You must tell him about the past, his past, or I fear he shan't be able to find his path. The boy must recover his sense of destiny. David needs the truth that only you can give."

"I've never interfered with his world. What right do I have to intrude in a life I didn't shape?"

"But you are the source. Without you, there would be no David. How often have I told you of his longing to know the whole story? Without knowing it, he has yearned for you."

Ruth pursed her lips and rubbed the side of her head, massaging her temple. "I must have time to think."

"You're frightened of what might happen if he came here." He saw the truth in her eyes. "You're afraid."

"Shouldn't I be?" Ruth snapped. "Who wouldn't be apprehensive?"

Edward knew he'd found leverage. "When did you ever retreat from anything fierce or threatening? Take death for instance. How many times have you faced the grim reaper himself down?" He watched her eyes for a further hint of uncertainty. "You are more than able to chance the death of your hopes and dreams."

Reaching across the table, Ruth pulled a pack of cigarettes from his pocket. Lighting one and inhaling deeply, she blew the smoke straight above his head. "Go for a walk, Eddie. Two blocks over, there's a little park. Smell the flowers down the street, look at the trees, but give me some space. I need some time to think. Be on your way."

Edward found the neighborhood park and a bench under a tall eucalyptus tree. At first he watched mothers supervising their children on the jungle gyms and swings. The boys threw sand at the girls, and the mothers threatened. Little had changed in fifty years; everything had changed.

Edward closed his eyes and let his memories float up. Surely that precious time was an epoch long since vanished. Nineteen-forty was another age in another world. Lang was Archbishop of Canterbury. George Bell, Bishop of Chichester, was preaching the British must oppose Hitler's persecution of the Jews. The likes of Ingrid Bergman and Clark Gable, Bogart and Bacall, Churchill, Chamberlain, and Delague had not yet disappeared like the morning fog; but only legends remained now, like his childhood tales of Arthur and the Knights of the Round Table. Holiday-makers journeyed to the Lake District or quaint retreats like Allington Court. The tower at Glastonbury rose above the peaceful plains extending clear to Salisbury. On the other side of fair England, the bells of Oxford rang out.

'Twas a time of style. Propriety and modesty had meaning. Decency and eloquence counted. People could be horrified by a single death and any tragedy. The regal life had its place too. The world had not yet become numb from overstimulation and desensitized by ram-

pant terrorism. Yes, the royalty, class, and style, still had their proper place.

Ruth Moses had such ways bred into her every fiber. The best of the old order had been prayed into her soul by observant parents and a long line of rabbis. Even the dust of the sunbaked Palestinian farmland couldn't hide who Ruth truly was.

The first time he saw Ruth came to mind. She was only a broken body in a military hospital, an anonymous lump in a crude infirmary bed. Like settling back in a movie theater to watch an old classic, Edward let the past completely engulf the present. Looking down a long grimy corridor into the women's ward, he could see Ruth's bed at the farthest end next to the wall. Even from that distance, he saw the IV bottles hanging from their stands. An oxygen tent covered her bed like a shroud.

"What's your opinion, doctor?" He stopped the man carrying the charts. "When will it be over for the woman in the back?"

"Should have been dead two weeks ago, Corporal." The doctor flipped open her chart. "What can I say? We didn't think she'd live through the first night they hauled her in." The tall, thin man with the forty-five-year-old's paunch had close-cropped, dirty, yellowish hair.

"Any new prognosis? Diagnosis of her problem?"

"Best we can tell, the explosion must have hit her from behind, hurling her into something solid . . . like a wall, door, tree . . . a hard surface." The doctor's face was deeply wrinkled with a dried-up double chin, making him look like a lizard. "Her coma is a result of the concussion following the impact. The broken arm and lacerations aren't nearly as bad as they look, but the head injury is still extremely serious." His thick-rimmed glasses perched on a disproportionately large, thick nose.

"Is an operation possible?"

"Here?" The doctor snorted. "Brain surgery in this place would amount to experimenting with humans. No! We'll just have to wait her out." He started to walk away and stopped. "Tell me, Corporal. What did happen to our nameless patient?"

"Our best guess is she was out of the truck when the man drove over a land mine. We surmise they stopped on the road. Maybe the mother was taking the baby to a lavatory or something of that order. She was either going in or coming out when the explosion happened. The roadside bathroom was leveled."

"A baby?" The doctor took a quick look at the chart. "There's no record of a baby coming in."

"Child's gone too."

The doctor raised his eyebrows and rolled his eyes. "Whose bomb?" He sneered in disgust. "Ours or theirs?"

"The Arabs', of course."

"Of course." The doctor shrugged. "Nothing I can do but pump fluids in her. If she survives, she could be in the coma a long time. She might turn out to be a vegetable anyway." Turning on his heels, the doctor walked away with a sweep of the hand.

The women's ward was full. Here and there nurses discreetly went about their tasks behind the white cloth partitions enclosing the beds. Ruth's corner was isolated as if a verdict had been rendered and execution was imminent. The oxygen tent didn't conceal her matted hair and soiled gown.

"She's the Jew they brought in," a woman said from behind him. "Not much to be done." The uniformed nurse was carrying sheets and bedding.

"You take care of her?"

"She's my patient." Her voice was unenthusiastic and flat. "Nothing to do but check her occasionally." She lifted the tent flap. "We'll take off most of the bandages before long. The cuts are healing, but there's no change in her status."

Ruth's skin was pale and gray. Although her chest rose and fell, nothing beyond that moved.

"Pretty little thing for a Jew." The nurse lifted her patient's head and pulled off the bandage covering one whole side like a skullcap. "We had to shave off the complete right quarter to sew her up. See. The hair's coming back quickly. The swelling is going down, don't ya see?"

"You think she'll live?"

"Nurses don't offer such opinions. What's your interest?"

"Off the record—just a guess? An opinion?"

"Yours is as good as mine, governor. Head damage is strange business."

"Has anyone come asking about a baby?"

"A baby?" The nurse shook her head disdainfully. "We take care of their bodies, not their problems." She pulled down the cover sheet revealing just how small Ruth was. "If they're not English, we don't ask or want to know. Are you here on official or private business?"

"Purely official. I have papers and forms to complete."

"I got nothing to add and don't want my name mentioned. I have to wash her and tidy up a bit. Best you'd be going on."

"Has anyone come to visit, to see her, to make any inquiry?"

"Her chart is marked confidential. We don't breathe a word about those kind. As far as the record goes, she ain't even here."

"Thank you, nurse. That's quite good. If there are any changes, please let me know."

With a nod, she started moving tubes and cords to get down to her work. "I'll say this," the nurse called after him. "If 'twas me, I'd folded my cards long ago. Must be something powerful inside driving her to stay alive."

Slowly the scene faded, and Edward opened his eyes. A mother was calling for her child to stop being so reckless on the swings. The warmth of the Southern California afternoon settled around his thoughts once more. For all those years, he had been Ruth's link with the boy. In time, his guilt had turned to fascination with David's development. Concern became affection, and the boy became the son Edward never had. As much as anyone, Edward mourned David's losses and applauded his successes.

Would I have married Ruth? Oh, in a minute. If the privilege, the opportunity, the possibility had been mine. But the future was sealed in one night. Once she knew that I was involved in taking her child, there was no reason or excuse that would ever redeem me. The future was thereafter swallowed by the past.

A child pointed at him, and he waved. A mother quickly

took the little boy by the hand and led him back to the swings, scolding as she went.

Do I still look so guilty? he thought. *Ruth would say so, I'm sure. I'd have gladly settled to be anything but her friend. The loss of the child tied us together and forever separated us. She was always thereafter on her way to a place of her own choosing, and I was never in the running. The friend, the confidant, and the compatriot, yes, but I was never invited to go beyond the door that I would have paid any price to enter.*

Edward stood up slowly, feeling completely seventy-seven. He looked at his watch, shook his head, and started back to Ruth's house. He remembered her as she was, with magnificent thick black hair hanging dramatically over her shoulders. When the sun bounced off her, sometimes, her hair looked almost blue. Her impeccable olive skin had seemed to glow. Often he thought of her as a gypsy princess.

Petite but powerful. Somewhere along the way, Ruth Moses became the ultimate survivor. Not afraid to match wits or cross swords with any man, she was still warm and compassionate. Through the decades, as the black hair turned gray, her winsomeness turned to wisdom.

Edward thought of how she would disappear from sight for years at a time, coming back into his life wanting some news of her boy. Her German accent became more neutral, although faint traces of the several languages she spoke still lingered.

He walked, thought, remembered . . . regretted.

SIX

Edward knocked lightly and immediately walked in. Appropriate or not, he liked the feeling of familiarity. "Ruth, I'm back." He sounded like a husband returning from work. Edward hesitated, making sure his audacity wasn't a blunder. On an end table next to the couch he saw David and Susan's picture, taken on David's college graduation day. The young couple waved optimistically toward a future somewhere far out beyond any camera's range.

For the first time, Edward fully realized how furious the Richardses would be if and when they found out what he was up to. Should confidences be broken, George and Mary probably would never forgive him. Then again he had long since paid his dues to the family. For over four decades he had made oil deals around the world and represented their oil business in England. He could live with the consequences.

"I'm in here," Ruth answered from the kitchen. She hadn't moved an inch. "Sit down." The little woman took control immediately. "I am ready to talk." She leaned forward against the table, placing her chin in her hand with her first two fingers pressing against her temple. Edward knew the gesture always meant Ruth was thinking very carefully.

Edward sat down with the solemnity of a judge taking the bench. "Enjoyed the park." He tried to seem casual, knowing his British accent would still make him sound unbearably pompous.

"Notice how much Chino is like Israel?" Ruth lit another cigarette.

Edward blinked several times. The connection had never occurred to him.

"Same longitude and latitude." Ruth blew smoke toward the window. "The climate, seasons, terrain are identical." She concluded, "Why else would I settle here?"

"Well . . ." He started to venture his opinion but thought better. "Yes, the connection is striking now that you mention it."

"Never been to Oklahoma," she continued with a logic he couldn't quite grasp. "But I know there is no similarity between here and there. Cowboys, Indians, flat land, four seasons, lots of Baptists, few Jews."

"I'm not sure I follow."

"They have no place for me there," Ruth answered laconically. "Traveling to David would be a mistake. I have no business there."

"If I might be permitted an opinion—"

"David must come here," she interrupted. "The only possibility is a meeting on my turf."

"Well, my goodness!" Edward blurted out in relief. "If that's a concern, heavens, I can bloody well take care of his trip out here in a heartbeat. Why—"

"Please quit playing God." Ruth blew smoke in his face. "None of us are abandoned children any longer. The decision has to be David's. I'm not going to force myself back into his life. If David, *and David alone*, wants to meet, then I am ready."

"Excellent!" Edward snapped his fingers and waved his fist in the air. "Mission accomplished."

"Edward . . ." Ruth glowered at him. "Stop trying to manipulate fate. Simply tell me everything you know about David's situation."

Halfway across the continent, David Richards sat in front of Paul Kendall's desk. Outside the church, a late winter snow drifted leisurely to the ground, the large flakes disappearing in the afternoon shadows. The priest listened intently before speaking. "As strange as it may seem, I'd like to shift subjects and talk about something different from Susan's death."

David looked relieved. "You *are* perceptive. For the last four days I've done nothing but respond to questions about Susan's death, her effects, her will, her whatever. I am completely drained."

"I want to explore your recurring dreams." The priest opened a notepad on his desk. "I think the secret room in your mind will open more quickly if we take a look at what your soul has been trying to tell you for a long time."

"Whatever you say." David shrugged. "Susan and I attended your seminar on dream interpretation last spring. She thought I needed to hear your thoughts. Absolutely fascinating! I had no idea dreams were so significant in the Bible or that so much could be learned from them. Susan was quite taken that a clergyman should have studied psychotherapy in Switzerland." He paused, raised his eyebrows, and rolled his eyes. "Sorry, but I must confess I still have some reservations about the whole subject. I guess I didn't get very far."

Paul ignored his explanation. "Let's allow my method to speak for itself. I've used dream work in spiritual direction for many years." The priest wrote the date across the top of his pad. "You have the gift of artistic vision, David. You intuitively look at the inner qualities and meaning in a subject. You're a natural to profit from exploring your dreams. Once you find out who you are, I expect you might even be the sort of person who has visions."

"You're not serious," David scoffed.

"Quite. In fact, your dreams are very much like visions being offered to you as a gift from your soul. Even though you feel as if everything is coming unglued right now, a great push toward wholeness and integration is bubbling up inside you." The priest winked. "Don't let my expectations put you off. Let's start. Tell me about the dream that has become your ostinato, the recurring inner theme. Try to remember what came up last night."

"I'll try." David closed his eyes and breathed deeply. "I am trapped in the midst of a riot, a shootout in a large house. Men with high-powered assault rifles are firing on the windows while other attackers storm the doors . . . strange . . . the attackers are wearing red suspenders. I seem to be inside with police officers trying to protect the house . . . the house is my house . . . or it bears a resemblance to my house . . . at the same time I seem to be standing back watching the fight happen . . . objective, detached." He stopped and shook his head. "No, the attackers are the policemen, and I'm inside trying to keep them out. Nothing kills the cops. My bullets hit them, but they don't die . . . but I have another problem . . . I'm also fending off the family who lives in my house. I can't stop their invasion or the intrusion. The dream fades, and then the old familiar refrain starts up for the thousandth time." David opened his eyes.

"The usual?" The priest scribbled furiously on his pad. "What do you mean?"

"The same dream has been there forever. I can't ever remember not dreaming of the explosion. It's like watching a home movie over and over again."

"And?" The priest gestured with his pen for David to continue.

"The sequence begins each time with an atomic bomb explosion. The sky lights up, and the sounds of the stupendous explosion totally engulf me. I see nothing but fire and hear only the roar. I try to run but can only crawl. Debris flies past me. No matter how fast I try to move, I can't make my legs work. I know I am about to die . . . and then I wake up. Terrified . . . frightened . . . disoriented."

Paul studied his notes carefully. "I can't actually tell you what a dream means." The priest laid his pen down. "But I can help you discover for yourself what the symbols embody. The pieces of the dream are about you. They're parts of yourself. Your experiences. Every dream has many layers and the deeper we go, the more we discover."

"What in the world have you been writing?" David peered over the desk.

"I have a method for diagramming dreams." Paul Kendall

held up his pad. "Dreams tend to break into three segments just as every good story should. I discovered there is usually a setting, a problem, and a solution."

"What's my answer?" David grinned skeptically. "Let's get right to it."

Paul frowned at the notepad. "That's the problem, David. There's no solution here."

"I don't understand."

"You're stuck in the middle. Recurring dreams are a sign that a basic life problem isn't being solved."

"Sure fits me! I've been stuck forever . . . somewhere. What's my obstacle?"

"I know enough about your life to venture a guess about the most superficial layer of the dream. You feel attacked by the circumstances of your life. The pressure and compromises of success are a personal assault on your values and ideals."

"What's your clue?" David smirked.

"The red suspenders." The priest answered his challenge with ease.

"You're kidding!"

"Any of your yuppie friends *not* have a pair of red suspenders these days?"

David's mouth dropped. "Amazing. I hated the style when suspenders became the rage last year. I refused to wear them when my mother gave me a pair for Christmas. Astonishing!"

"How do you feel right now?"

"Why . . . I seem to be filled . . . with insight. Of course, you already knew how much I resent trendiness and conformity."

The priest chuckled. "Yes, I had a head start, but your dream tells me how seriously these contradictions affect you. You say one thing with your mouth but feel another in your heart. You are a man under assault. Susan's death will only aggravate your problem unless you turn this tragedy into an opportunity."

"Opportunity!" David snarled.

"You see yourself as trapped by circumstances." The priest's voice was soft and reassuring. "You've never known how to manage the pressure. Things just happen to David, and he takes whatever comes next. Susan's death must not be just another in a long line of events to be massaged some way or the other into the basic life script David follows. If you continue to read your prescribed lines, I can predict what will soon follow."

"What?"

"You'll marry the most eligible divorcée at the country club, take a Caribbean cruise for a honeymoon, and come back to do it all over again. Your dream will turn into a nightmare."

The color left David's face. He wrung his hands and turned sideways in his chair. "Am I so obvious?"

"Not to yourself. The dream wants you to discover your own lack of insight. You've allowed yourself to become spiritually bankrupt, and you're trying to save what's left in your improvised house, your soul."

David ran his hand nervously through his hair. "If this is your idea of superficiality, I'm not sure I want to go deeper."

"We can stop at any time."

"Paul," he stopped. "Paul, right now I've got to think about something other than Susan's death. When I let my mind wander, I see her out there in that frozen ground." He covered his face. "Go on," he mumbled. "Please continue your interpretation."

"Dreams are really about ourselves. Remember, symbols are aspects of our personalities. For example, the house in the dream is a representation of your self and what's going on inside. By the same token, the attackers are also parts of your personality, pieces of your past, memories, and events. They help us understand why your inner turmoil is so severe. Do you have any idea what the other intruders might represent?"

David looked down at his hands and the wedding ring he was still wearing. He twisted the gold band. "My parents pecked away at me like chickens obsessed with some irregularity on a barnyard stray. Yes, of course, my parents have camped in my living room forever."

"But only because you allowed them to have such power." Paul smiled. "Remember, we are dealing with what's inside your soul. You let them become part of your superego, your conscience."

"I don't understand." David shook his head. "What are you driving at?"

"The issue isn't *them*; it's *you*. What must be deciphered is your inner conflict."

"You're telling me to stop blaming George and Mary?"

"I'm suggesting you have a George and Mary living in your head, shouting messages to you in your moments of indecision. You have been forever at war with them to your own detriment."

David winced. "The idea hits me like a Mack truck!"

"Your battle isn't with them; it's with yourself, your own compromises. The recurrent dream is trying to get you to wake up and recognize the warfare for what it is."

Paul watched David's rapid eye movements as if he were reading something only he could see. For several seconds David sat transfixed, gripped by what was racing through his mind. He chewed on the side of his lip and twisted his wedding ring around and around. "If what you are saying is correct . . ." Each word slowly followed the other. ". . . I am basically attacking myself. Can that make any sense?"

The priest nodded.

"Why would I assault myself?" David frowned. "Guilt?"

"Sure. You punish yourself for compromise. But I believe something much more profound is happening. Feel, David. Let yourself *feel* the turmoil."

Once more David slipped into a trancelike stare. His body was immobile, while his eyes moved rapidly. "Perhaps . . . the reason for the battle is not destructive. Now I see there is a room in the basement of the house in my dream. Yes, the fight *is* over access to the basement. Someone is locked up down there in that dark place. The battle is to gain access to that cell . . . maybe the point of the assault is to set the prisoner in the dungeon free . . . maybe . . . the point is to break down the prison door."

"And who is the prisoner, David?"

"I am."

"Correct." Paul sat back in his chair, waiting for the insight to sink in.

"But . . . how . . . could I be in the dream, an observer of the dream, and the prisoner . . . all at the same time?"

"With the exception of the prisoner, each of the persons in the dream is a facet of your own personality. In the past you have mistaken one particular aspect of your life for the totality of who you are."

"Then who is the captive?"

"The real you, the David longing to be free, to live without restriction or suppression." The priest arose and walked to the window. "Often we spend decades living behind a facade, not recognizing the disguise for what it is. Finally the past will no longer be denied and explodes. What feels like death turns out to be the first breath of real life we've had for a long time."

"Yes." David exhaled slowly. "I have been both prisoner and my own jailor?"

"Please don't think me insensitive." The priest watched the new snow cover the remaining flower stalks protruding above the old snow. "A disaster has driven you to this crossroads, but as terrible as is Susan's death, you have actually come to a place of painful opportunity. Yesterday's gardens are dried and shriveled, but a springtime is still ahead . . . if . . . if . . . you are not afraid of a resurrection."

David continued twisting his wedding ring. "I have heard almost more than I can digest. Perhaps I'd best be alone to think things through. But I must ask you one more question before I go."

"Certainly." The priest returned to his chair.

"What about the other dream? The explosion?"

"You're right. We have had enough for one day." Paul closed his notebook. "Next time."

"I can't simply leave the matter there. Please give me some hint of what you think the dream is about."

"Does this dream always come in the same way?" Paul leaned back in his large desk chair.

"Exactly." David threw up his hands. "I feel like someone watching the same VCR tape over and over again."

Paul nodded his head knowingly. "Have you ever heard of post-traumatic stress disorder?"

"No." David shook his head.

"People have terrible experiences that etch a memory in their minds. The horror won't go away. I think your dreams reflect an experience which permanently marred your psyche. You've never come to grips with something that happened to you long ago. You are reliving the trauma which you can't face consciously."

"I don't even vaguely remember any such a thing occurring."

"That's why you have the dream. The experience is too traumatic to face now."

"My parents never mentioned an explosion." David plunged his hands into his pockets. "I really wouldn't have any idea where to look." He walked thoughtfully toward the door.

"I have a suggestion." The priest stood up. "Start with your Uncle Edward. Talk to him when he returns. He might surprise you."

SEVEN

"This is your mother as she looks today." Edward placed the picture on David's office desk. "We made this five-by-seven just before I left California yesterday. Got in late last night." On the top floor of Makin Towers the morning sunlight glistened on the portrait.

"Quite a way to start my day . . . the rest of my life." David ran his fingers slowly across the slick finish and leaned back in his chair. He rubbed his temple gently and stared. "Ruth Moses," he mumbled.

"Here are a number of old pictures taken about the time you were born." Edward dumped a brown envelope upside down on the desk and pulled out one particular snapshot. The yellowish paper was brittle, and the black tones faded to brown. "I believe this is the only surviving picture of your father. Unfortunately he's a bit far away. You obviously got your height from him, not your mother. Ruth's not quite five feet tall."

David gawked at the couple, leaving the snapshot exactly as it fell in front of him.

"Your marvelous black eyes certainly mark you as Ruth's boy. While the picture doesn't show the details, the color and texture of your hair is exactly like hers! Quite extraordinary, isn't it?"

"People forever speculated about whether I was Italian, Lebanese, Greek, or something," David muttered. "Never could put it all together, and now here's the answer in front of my eyes: Jews. All the time I've been a Jew."

"Your face has a composite Mediterranean quality. Sort of gives you an air of mystery." Edward looked at the picture of David's father again. "You are a chip off the old block, have the same aura. Your mother met him at the kibbutz after she came to Israel. Apparently his family returned to Israel from Damascus around the turn of the century."

"Didn't he have a name?"

"Forgive me." Edward cleared his throat. "You see, I knew your mother so much better. Well, actually I never met him. Ruth was the name always on my tongue. I suppose I tended always to refer to your father as him."

"Did he have a name?"

"Certainly . . . certainly. Your family name is Moses, of course. In Hebrew the name is often pronounced Moshe. His given name was Yaacov. Yaacov Moses."

"And years ago you gave me a statue of Moses . . ." David's face remained completely motionless, making it impossible for Edward to read.

"Seemed very appropriate at the time. I'm sure each revelation is quite a shock to you, old chap," the Englishman hesitantly concluded.

"Reverend Kendall said you had some information for me." David picked up his father's picture. "What an understatement!" He looked at the picture and kept shaking his head. "Jews! We're all Jews!"

"I've included a number of pictures taken shortly after your adoption. Your mother was in terrible condition for quite a long while. Doesn't look well in this picture."

David slowly sorted through the additional pictures. "This is a British soldier." He stopped and held the picture to the light. "Who is the man?"

"As if you don't know! Not a bad likeness of me at the time. Probably eighty pounds lighter."

"You've known the whole story from the very beginning?" David was distant and strained. "You've always known everything there was to know about me?"

Edward nodded.

"I'm sure you will understand if I study the pictures privately." David gathered the collection together and slipped them back into the brown envelope. "Thank you." His indifferent inflection revealed nothing.

"I have prepared complete directions and a map to find your mother. I'm also giving you a file with information accumulated over the years. I anticipated you would need these facts some day." He opened his black briefcase. "Basic background material you will find helpful in filling in many blank spaces." Edward shoved the bulging manila folder across the table. "Read it all. The material will help you prepare for your meeting with Ruth."

"Meeting?" David rocked forward against the desk.

"I took the liberty of making your airplane reservations for the day after tomorrow." Edward reached inside his coat pocket for the travel packet. "The extra day will help you digest my files."

"Wait . . . just . . . a . . . minute." David's emotional front cracked. "What are you suggesting?"

"I think you will find the Reverend Kendall is in complete agreement with my decisions . . . at least about meeting your mother. I'm the one who feels the urgency about timing."

"Do you have any idea what you're saying?" David stood up.

"Quite." Edward sounded like a soldier executing a command to charge up an unassaultable hill. "The hour has come!"

"I couldn't possibly consider such a trip right now." David gestured frantically. "The whole idea is out of the question."

"Anticipating such a response, I have one more item to give you." Edward reached into the back pocket of his briefcase. "Ruth sent you this letter. Asked me to hand-deliver it to you, she did." He placed a small blue envelope on top of the tickets. "You'll notice the correspondence is in her own hand."

Across the top in an artistic flourish was written, "To David." He read his name again and again before picking up the letter. David turned the small envelope over several times but didn't open it. "I must read her letter privately. It's been some time since we corresponded," he answered sardonically. "Somewhere over forty years as a matter of fact."

"Some things don't ever change, my boy."

David probed Edward's eyes until the intensity forced the Englishman to look down. "I know everything you have done has been with the best motive. Always has been, Uncle Edward. I trust you. Beyond that point, I have no idea even how I feel right now except I'm completely blown away. Just about as numb as when I went to the funeral home."

"This isn't an end, but the beginning." Edward took David's arm. "You need a new dawning in your life. Believe me, the sun is still coming up." He pointed to the window.

David squeezed the old man's hand. "I . . . I . . . don't know. Just don't know what to think." He stepped back. "Edward, you're coming on like a steamroller. I can't accept these tickets you bought."

"You most certainly can! They're paid for. Just get on with it."

David turned away and looked out the tenth-story window of his office, peering down on the Oklahoma City financial and business district. Edward could see snow was still piled up along the curbs. People hurried down the windswept streets. "I can't simply fly out to California and knock on some woman's door and say, 'Surprise! I'm back from the bulrushes. You've won a delayed visit from the stork. I was misplaced in shipping some forty years ago.' "

"Let's simply start with a phone call. Ruth is expecting you to ring her up. I jotted her number on the inside of the file. Read her letter first; then a little chat over the phone will be the right way to break the ice I should think."

"A *little* chat?" David sounded exasperated.

"Certainly! You're an artist with words. You'll know what to say. Things of this sort simply unfold; word after word, sentence after sentence, and before you know it, you'll have leapfrogged over any barriers. The result will be quite lovely."

David wrung his hands and shook his head. "I . . . I . . . don't know."

"Oh, of course you do. Surely you've got something to drink around here. How about something for your old uncle?"

David pointed toward a credenza against the wall. "Help yourself. Nothing for me." He looked out the window again while Edward rummaged through the cabinet until he found a glass.

"What can I say to you?" David sounded peeved but resigned.

"Thank you will be quite sufficient." Edward raised his glass in a toast. "Oh, yes. One more thing. I trust this matter is strictly between us. I prefer to keep my dealings with your parents in the business of petrol and not personalities. I hope such will be possible."

"The last thing I'm interested in is having Mom and Pop Richards walking through my private world, much less this corner of my past. No problem there."

Edward gulped his drink and set the glass on David's desk. "Davey, I'll leave you with your thoughts." He picked up his overcoat and started for the door only to look back. "I'm proud of you, lad. Very proud. Look at you! Savoir faire, you are. The best-dressed gentleman in merry old England would have nothing on you. You're a handsome man, indeed; but even more, you're a fine human being. Don't worry now. Everything is going to work out fine, just fine. Read the letter and give your old mum a call. You'll never be sorry."

David waved weakly, and Edward walked out.

An hour later David went straight home from the office. He changed clothes and immediately went out to the flat shed behind his rambling ranch-style home. The large open room was cold, but the smell of paint and clay invigorated him.

He spun the potter's wheel and walked toward the large kiln on the other side of the room. The last piece he'd done, the vase for Susan, sat on the vat covered with plastic. He didn't touch it. Along the row of shelves, he felt the chalky dryness of the curing pots and paused to turn the gas heater up.

Lifting the lid from a large plastic bucket filled with wet

clay, David pulled out a wad of sticky Oklahoma red clay and began working the mass. He sank down on a stool in front of the small table, closed his eyes, and let his fingers shape something, anything.

A gnarled, twisted shape arose between his fingers. The little form appeared to be filled with despair, bent by an unseen wind. Pulling another hunk out of the large lump, David worked the clay into an abstraction of a bird's wing.

The wing seemed to be broken, but with his index finger David smoothed the side of the sculpture straight and finished. He flattened the bottom to give the piece stability to stand alone. For a long time he stared at his creations. Smiling for the first time in days, he set the shapes in the center of his workbench and put the rest of the clay back into the pail.

David washed the clay from his fingers in a small basin beneath the studio window. He could see the garden plot running from the edge of the shed completely across his backyard. The glory of last summer was brown, withered, and frozen. Parched, shriveled cornstalks hung in sad disarray. Banks of snow hid the last of the beanstalks and tomato vines. And yet David saw the scene had its own strange design. Chaos had given way to nature's unique hidden order where everything had its place.

David closed the shed door behind him and walked resolutely to the house. He sat down at the kitchen table and placed the phone in front of him. Inhaling as much air as he could hold, David dialed the number he had scribbled on his desk notepaper.

"Hello." The woman's voice didn't sound half a continent away.

He breathed deeply again. "May I please speak with Ruth Moses?"

There was a long pause. Finally the woman said, "This is Ruth Moses."

"I'm David," he said with wavering uncertainty. "I'm David Richards. Once . . . a long time ago . . . my name was Moses."

EIGHT

The flight to California seemed interminable. David read and reread Edward's personal archives on the Moses family, drew sketches on scraps of paper, drank Coke after Coke, paced the aisles, but time only increased the tension.

Eventually David simply watched the billowy cloud cover rolling to the horizon like a peaceful ocean. The undulating mass of a thousand shapes looked solid as ocean swells appeared from the shore. The airplane abruptly descended with the ease of a diver plunging into the sea. As brine blurs the swimmer's vision, the mist turned into vaporous, obtuse cotton obscuring everything. The reality of the previous moment disappeared, transformed into an illusion. Beneath the overcast, David knew another world awaited him, as mysterious as the inside of a cloud, as unknown as the depths of the sea.

When the airplane landed at Ontario, David seriously considered boarding a return flight without even leaving the airport.

Edward's map and instructions were clear enough, but nothing relieved David's growing apprehension. He hoped getting out of the rental car parking lot would settle him down, but even the distractions of freeway traffic couldn't placate his mounting anxiety. After he'd made the loop south and back west toward Chino, David knew destiny was only minutes away. The thought clutched at his throat; waves of apprehension swept over him like a riptide.

David pulled to the side of the road, trying to clear his head. For the first time he realized how warm the weather was. He had lost any sense of stepping out of winter into springtime.

David took off his coat and watched the thousands of automobiles whiz past. The constant pulsating bursts of air slapped him in the face. Only after gaining some composure did he pull back into traffic.

The exit sign into Chino wasn't far ahead. He followed Edward's map and quickly located the neighborhood. Creeping slowly around the last corner and down the street, he saw a small gray-haired lady waiting in front of her house. Just as Ruth had promised, she was sitting in a blue lawn chair reading a book. He was too far away to make a final judgment, but there was little question he had found his mother.

David drove slowly up the street, watching the house numbers but knowing his destination was just ahead. The woman seemed to be completely absorbed in her reading. He pulled up to the curb and watched for some reassuring response.

The little woman dropped her book and pulled off her reading glasses. She stared for a moment and then called out with hesitancy. "David? David? Is that really you?"

Her voice was the same—just as on the telephone—but everything was different now. The voice was attached to a face, a form, and nothing was the same, or would ever be again. A human being was coming across the lawn toward him. Her arms were open, extended, reaching.

David tried to get his coat. Thoughts of appropriateness raced through his mind. Worrying about the right thing to do momentarily detached him. His heart was pounding like a flat tire slapping the pavement. David forgot the coat and hurried around the car.

"Oh, David!" She was not ten feet away. "You look just like your pictures."

He swallowed hard and tried to smile but felt completely embarrassed. She was small as Edward described, and yet there was none of the reservation he predicted. Nothing could stop this indomitable force sweeping toward him. His arms came up mechanically, reaching out for her embrace.

"Aaahh," she sighed in his ear, hugging him tightly. "You are here." A momentary fragrance of perfume felt heavenly and very feminine. She stepped back with her hands on his chest. "Let me look at you." Her smile nearly consumed her face. "Just let me look at you!"

"Ruth?" barely slipped from his lips. "Hello."

"*Oi vey.*" Ruth looked up at him. "You are just as handsome as I always knew you would be."

David laughed nervously, fighting his erupting emotions. He bit his lip but couldn't keep the tears back. "I . . . I . . . don't know what to say." Impulsively he hugged her again. Ruth felt small, fragile, breakable, and yet her grip was fiercely powerful.

"I understand." Ruth clung to him almost with desperation. "Everything is all right now."

"I . . . I . . . just can't find the words," David stammered. "Yesterday I thought I knew what I would say, but I can't remember any of those things."

"Not important." Ruth waved her hand as if banishing the thought into oblivion. She wiped her eyes. "None of that's important now." She reached up and felt his hair. "Don't you have beautiful hair! All of our people do, you know."

"Our people? Yes!" David hugged her again and laughed. "Yes, *our* people!" They both laughed and cried at the same time.

Ruth took his arm. "Well, we can't stand out here letting the neighbors watch." A hint of an accent slipped into her voice. "Let me show you my house." She whisked him across the lawn toward the front door.

Once inside, David quickly glanced in every direction, mentally photographing the exact details of the living room. He drank in the atmosphere, absorbing himself in the ambiance of her space. By the Richardses' standards the place was spartan; yet there was an economic simplicity of traveling light and keeping only what had meaning and value. He saw intelligence and thoughtfulness in her belongings.

"My home is simple." Ruth pointed to a chair.

A large painting on the far wall caught David's eye. "That's an original?" He stared in amazement. "I would swear that's Courbet's *The Stone Breakers*." He walked closer to the picture of a boy carrying rocks to a man with a hammer. "Can't be," he murmured. "It was lost from Dresden during the war."

"Edward told me about your love for art. Yes, that is a Courbet."

"This work is genuine!" He gently touched the canvas. "This painting is worth—" David turned and stared at his mother.

"I'm glad you approve of my taste."

"Where did you get this picture?" he asked, awestruck.

"I'm filled with surprises." She sounded guarded, clearly conveying she would say no more on the subject. "Sit down right here where the light is good." Ruth pointed to a chair next to the couch. "I want to look at you and soak up every detail."

David backed toward the chair, gawking at the picture.

"I have a few Goya etchings left you'll appreciate. All in due time."

"Museums are still looking for *that* picture." David stumbled into the chair.

"You are just as I knew you would be." Ruth sighed. "I had lost hope this day would ever come." She kept talking, ignoring his questions.

David finally turned back and looked deeply into her face, trying to read between the wrinkles. She was like, but different from, her pictures. No question their hair was the same texture and the contour of their faces remarkably alike. Her nose was different; time had narrowed her face and drooped her eyelids, but nothing had dimmed the intensity of her black eyes.

"I must feel your ears." Ruth ran her fingers along the outer edge with the strange notches. "*Mazel tov!*" she exclaimed with glee. "You have the marked ears, our family trademark."

"I always thought something went wrong when I was born. Maybe forceps marks."

"Heavens no!" Ruth giggled. "The Holy One marked us. No question you are my boy."

David kept staring at her face.

"Do you mind what you see?" Ruth puzzled.

"I . . . I have this obsession with faces." David tried to sound nonchalant. "In art school I painted portraits. I study people in restaurants, on the street. I sketch endlessly. See . . ." David pulled some scratch paper from his pocket. "I drew the flight attendant on the airplane, trying to pass the time."

Ruth flattened out the paper and smoothed the rough edges. "You catch the essence of the face with such a few lines. I'm very impressed."

"Here's another one I dashed off in the airport." David pulled an envelope from his pocket. "I have this thing about eyes. I was trying to capture the unusual quality I saw in this woman sitting in the waiting room."

"Indeed!" Ruth laid the envelope on top of the other drawing. "Her eyes could almost leap off the paper into your soul. I am reminded of the work of George Grosz. Have you heard of his painting?"

"Of course. He came to this country from Germany before World War II. I believe his school was called 'new objectivism.' "

Ruth smiled. "Excellent. We called his work *die neue sachlichkeit*. He and Max Beckmann did extraordinary work until the Nazis ran them off. They were both good friends of my father. We lived in Leipzig, you know."

"Your father?" David's mouth dropped in astonishment. "You knew these people?"

"Art was in your blood before you were born, my boy. Our family has always been patrons of the arts. How it would have pleased my father to see such talent in a grandson."

"He is buried in Germany?"

Ruth stiffened, tilting her head back in a proud but defensive posture. "David Eidinger died at Auschwitz."

The word shot through him like a bullet. David tried to find some word, some expression but nothing seemed appropriate. Auschwitz ricocheted off the walls of his mind like a piece of jagged shrapnel. He thought of Susan's death and the terrible pain returned in his throat; he felt empty.

"We will speak of the matter at another, more appropriate time." Her voice was distant again, aloof and almost hard.

"Let's talk about you now. What questions do you have about your past?"

"I have so many questions." David tried to focus once more. "There is so much I have wanted to know for so long."

"Ask anything. I have nothing else to do for the rest of my life but answer your questions." A smile returned.

"My birth certificate was obviously altered. What was my real name?"

"Yaacov and I called you Dov, the pet name your father gave you. You were our little Dov. But your real name was David. David Moses, named for your grandfather."

David sat back in the chair, pondering her answer. "How did I keep my first name?"

"We can thank Edward for that turn of fate." Ruth's smile twisted cynically. "He persuaded them you'd have an easier time if your name wasn't changed. At least he did that right!"

"How did Edward accomplish *that*?"

"Edward was always the link. He brought you from a hospital to the family who stole you away. Once he made contact with them, Edward somehow signed on for the long haul. Apparently everyone became fast friends."

"Dov," David rolled the name around in his mouth. "Dov? Sounds very nice." David smiled. "You mentioned my father. Tell me about him."

"Yaacov loved to talk, to talk of the future. I couldn't believe that any of us had a future, but Yaacov believed in the destiny of our people. He would hold you over his head and tell you tomorrow was going to be better. You were such an important part of his dreams." Her smile tightened. "He talked so often about the potential of our little Dov." Tears filled her eyes. "He would be so happy . . . with you."

"Do I look like him?"

"Perhaps now is the time for his picture." Ruth reached beneath the book table and pulled out a yellowed cardboard folder. "I let Edward think he carried off the last photograph I had." She laughed. "We have to humor poor old Eddie." Ruth peeled off old, dried rubber bands. "This picture was taken for a passport the year you were born." Ruth carefully opened the folder and took out a brown-toned picture.

David turned the aging print from the light to prevent glare. For a long time, he simply stared. Finally he said, "I don't think we look alike."

"Of course not." Ruth puckered her lips and shook her head. "You look like my family. You are most like my uncle, Zac. They are all gone now, but you do look so much like him."

"Gone?"

The forebidding look returned to Ruth's eyes. David let the question drop and looked at the picture again. He began to see a familiar shape of the head, a slant to the jaw, a curve around the chin. Each discovery was exhilarating. His questions began as a trickle but quickly became a river of inquiry. Names of Ruth's brothers, places, events spilled out as Ruth became an encyclopedia of the past, each detail capturing David's imagination.

Both Ruth and David jumped when a distant hall clock chimed. "Look how long we've been at this!" Ruth stood up. "Three hours. I must start fixing supper for us. Perhaps a little wiener goulash?" She watched his face for some response. "Some red cabbage? Maybe a little schnitzel, no?"

"Anything is fine." David followed her into the kitchen. "I'm afraid I may not be too hungry. So much is still swirling around inside me."

"Nonsense." Ruth began pulling covered dishes out of the refrigerator. "I've been planning this repast since you called. Won't take me long to put it all together."

David looked over his shoulder at the large Courbet painting in the living room. Ruth Moses was a woman of stunning contrasts; a simple house with priceless art treasures, a gentle woman with an ironclad will. He watched his mother scurry about the kitchen looking like any grandmother in Chino. Yet, lying up on the corner of the kitchen cabinet, stacked on top of an international edition of the *Jerusalem Post* was a copy of Berman's *All That Is Solid Melts into Air*. Next to both was a worn paperback edition of Dostoyevsky's *Notes from the Underground*. Ruth Moses was not a simple person.

NINE

Ruth slowly poured cherry topping over the blintzes. "Can your mother cook or not?" She handed him the heaping dessert plate.

"Oh," David groaned in mock pain. "I can't eat any more or I'll pop. What a supper. You've done Christmas and Easter in one fell swoop."

Ruth looked askance. "Actually I've *never* done either of those days in my whole life." She refilled his glass. "Eat some more. You're way too skinny."

David took a big breath and picked up the fork. "What a challenge."

"My, but your father loved to eat! When I made him cheese blintzes he'd eat until he was nearly sick." Ruth sat back down and rested her head on her hands. She watched him eat in total delight. "Now I can cook for you once more."

Halfway through clearing the plate David stopped. "Strange." He left the fork on the plate. "I feel I've always been here . . . like I've come back after a brief absence." He looked around the room at the cabinets, the ceiling, the floor. "Yes, I seem to have just come home from college or returned from a vacation. Strange, everything feels so familiar."

"It should," Ruth said. "It's yours. Anything I have is yours. You have come home. Of course, the interval since your little vacation was considerably longer than expected." Ruth laughed at the irony of her own joke.

"What do I call you?" David hesitated. "Shall I call you Mother?"

Ruth started to drink from her glass, then stopped. "No," she said after a long pause. "No, too much water has gone under the bridge for you to call me Mother. Someone else paid for the right to that title. Just call me Ruth."

"Then Ruth it shall be." David reached awkwardly for his glass. "I'll drink to that." He clicked his glass against hers. "Ruth and Dov against the world forever!"

"Forever!" Ruth held her glass above her head. "Absolutely." She exclaimed and suddenly stood up. "Let's dance! Yes, this is the moment to dance. We have named each other." Ruth grabbed his hand.

"Wait!" David pulled back. "I . . . a . . . well . . . I wouldn't know how to do something like that. We never did things . . . er . . . a . . . in the family where I grew up. . . . I guess we were too proper."

"What a pity!" Ruth let go. "We always danced." Ruth held her hands toward the ceiling, looked upward, and swayed back and forth. "The hora, folk dances, ballroom dancing! Your father and I laughed and sang all the time. When good things happened, we jumped up from the table and danced about it."

"I'm afraid we were much too reserved. We didn't touch much. Things were kept decent and in order . . . distant."

"Such coldness violated your spirit." Ruth stared intensely as if plumbing the depths of his soul. She shook her finger at him. "It wasn't in your nature to do well with people who were so dead. Was it?"

David tried to answer but could only shake his head.

"I understand you. We're family, you know. You're bone of my bone, flesh of my flesh. I know what's hidden in your heart. Am I wrong?"

David bit his lip and fidgeted with his fork. "Where were you all those years?" He bore down on the tablecloth with the tines of the fork. His eyes filled with tears. "Where were you when there wasn't anyone who understood?"

The joy washed from Ruth's face; she instantly looked old and worn. "I'm sorry. I'm sorry for more than I can tell you. We were both sold down the river without a choice." Silence fell between them, and she didn't respond when David reached for her hand.

"I didn't mean to sound as if I blamed you." He tugged at her hand. "There were just so many empty spaces. I wish we could . . ." He stopped, unable to complete the sentence. "I'm so very glad to be here." He squeezed her hand.

A taut smile crossed Ruth's face. "My, my, but we do have a lot to say to each other." She got up from the table and began shuffling dishes to the sink. "You're sure you don't want something more to eat?"

"No, no, thank you. Couldn't eat a bite more. Please sit down. I didn't mean to ruin the moment."

Ruth froze in place by the cabinet. "Nothing could spoil tonight. No, my son. I expect joy and pain to be served on the same plate. It has always been so for Jews."

"I see," David hesitated. "Could I probe further?" Before she could answer he continued, "You spoke of Auschwitz. Can we talk about what happened to your father, your family?"

"To *our* family," Ruth corrected him.

"Of course."

"I was smuggled out of Germany and into Palestine in 1935." Ruth sat back down and lit up a cigarette. "Jewish boys and girls were selected for their capacity to adjust to the difficulties of life in Palestine. We were trained to live in the primitive conditions of the kibbutz." She inhaled deeply, closed her eyes for a moment, and blew the smoke toward the ceiling. "That's where I learned to smoke these worthless cigarettes. I had to do something to live with the isolation, the tension. Yes, the terror."

"And the family stayed in Germany?"

Ruth nodded her head. "We knew things were going to get bad, but no one . . . no one . . . dreamed of the death camps even in their worst nightmares. My father had connections, important friends. But in the end, nothing proved to be of much value." She began to smoke in quick rapid puffs. "Our family didn't live in a ghetto or isolated from the rest of society. Of course we were observant Jews. My mother's father was a rabbi, as was his father. My father was well-known and highly respected at the synagogue in Leipzig. He often made aliya and read the Torah on the Sabbath. Mother always kept a kosher house. Yet our family were intellectuals, artists, avant garde in their ideas, cultured people. Unfortunately the family also believed in the inevitable advance of society. The ideals of humanism nourished us. Our expectations were shaped by democracy and socialism." She bit her lip. "We believed reason would triumph over ignorance and prejudice."

"And they waited too long to leave?" His voice was nearly a whisper.

Ruth picked up the empty glass. She inhaled deeply, then filled the glass with smoke and quickly set it on the table. The cloudy wisp slowly drifted and curled upward. "They disappeared into thin air. Their entire generation evaporated. I still can't quite grasp how such a thing could be." Ruth stared at the glass. "The joy, the laughter, the dreams, the memories of a whole family vanished like the morning fog. Very real, tangible, flesh-and-blood human beings simply disappeared like this little cloud . . . of smoke." She watched until the glass was completely clear.

"How have you lived with these losses? All these years so alone. First the family, then a husband . . . and finally . . . a son lost. How have you endured?"

"Your losses are less, David? They were your family, too. And now your wife is gone." Ruth shook her head. "No children will return to you someday, from somewhere. No son can reappear to fill the emptiness of your old age."

David bit his lip. "How did you sustain your pain?"

Ruth slowly got up and walked hesitantly to the window. The contour of the high foothills was still barely visible in the vanishing sunlight. The winter rains had turned the dead brown grasses green once again. The sage and underbrush were in full flower. "Life does go on," she concluded. "The tides creep in and slowly ebb out, but their flow never ceases. Regardless of how black the night, morning comes again."

"But sometimes the night is too long?" David pressed on. "Exactly what happened?"

"I was still in the hospital when I learned that both my husband and child were gone forever. A few months later I received word my mother and father perished at Auschwitz. For the next ten years I felt nothing. I ate, drank, breathed, made sounds, went to bed, got up again, day after day, year after year I went through the motions of living. I mechanically executed the functions of life like an automaton." Ruth began pacing back and forth. "When the terrible suppressed pain finally erupted, I was even more immobilized. My festering wounds had contaminated my every dream and hope. Gangrene poisoned the wellsprings of my vitality. I still cannot remember many of those days." Her eyes looked frenzied, darting back and forth in rapid movement like a caged animal. "The period is only a blur, a painful detachment from life. I was swallowed in the whale's belly of despair." She closed her eyes and leaned against the cabinet. "Understand?"

Tears filled David's eyes. "I understand, not fully of course, but enough . . . enough."

"One spring afternoon a friend drove me down to the Gennesaret, the Sea of Galilee. I sat on the bank and watched the sea gulls swoop down over the waters. Light danced on the gentle waves like a thousand diamonds. As was done for thousands of years, men hauled in nets filled with fish. The meadows were a blanket of color, the flowers swaying in the gentle breeze, rolling down from the Golan Heights. I could no longer resist the beauty and began to listen to the sounds of life. Sitting alone, I commenced to feel the rhythm of life once more. I started to touch again the indomitable ethereal goodness which links the seasons together. The smell of it filled me, and I felt the breath of God on my face. When I returned to the kibbutz, I was ready to live again."

David tried to envision what she must have looked like, such a small woman trying to hold back the crushing weight of the world, one little light fighting against the constantly returning darkness of night. "The breath of God?" He asked in wonder.

"I hadn't gone inside a synagogue for years. I wanted none of it. *It*—the only word I could find for a faceless unfeeling deity. *It* was the only definition left in me. I knew of nothing but a cold, impersonal, unyielding, unmerciful force kicking the universe along its way. And then up from those meadows came the sweep of fresh life, new promise, and the undefinable was no longer sterile, indifferent, distant."

"I'm not sure I comprehend." David shook his head.

"Nor can I. But like a dance, the movement began to animate my legs and my arms. Suddenly the sound was no longer hidden; it became an ostinato surfacing like the driving force in a sonata or a symphony, I knew what I hadn't been able to hear had not been lost. The Holy One had always been there. The music began anew."

David choked. "My problem is I've never really lived at all. I've been a pale reflection of everyone else's dream. I can't find the key to unlock the door holding everything in. At least you danced on the edge of the sword; I've acquiesced so long my emotions are atrophied. My hopes are stale beyond resuscitation."

"No, David." Ruth shook her head fiercely. "You still have eyes. Marvelous eyes that see inside people and put the truth on paper. We must start there and work until your ears are open. Then the heart will be set free, and finally the forbidden door will open."

He shook his head despairingly and wiped his cheek.

"David, you can't know what's behind that inner door because you've never met that part of yourself which is Jewish. You need a human mirror to reflect what you can't see. Your people will reveal the rest of you. In our music, our dance, our talk, our laughter, you will find the reflection. The joy of the Jew is a wondrous thing indeed! You ask me how I stood the pain. I will tell you our secret. We believe laughter is stronger than pain. We know joy is more enduring than suffering. Our way is to surround catastrophe with stories and jokes which swallow the pain and digest the hurt through laughter. Every Jew is a storyteller and comedian of sorts because that's how we face tragedy."

David ran his hands through his hair, scratched his head, and rubbed the back of his neck. "I can't quite get my hands around what you are saying. The words touch my mind but I . . . I . . . the idea . . . slips through my fingers."

"I will tell you why." Ruth pointed her finger at his face. "You are a product of the affluent American way of life. Oh, yes! I am glad wealthy parents spared you the deprivations of poverty, but luxury has exacted a great price by creating a terrible gulf between you and life." She shook her finger like an angry teacher lecturing a dilatory student. "Ease is the enemy of vitality. In your world, clothing labels are mistaken for culture; expensive cars are confused with personal worth. Turn on any radio and listen to your horrifying music debase every value Western culture has taken centuries to recover." She shook her fist at the ceiling. "You have to turn up the decibels to the pain threshold even to endure the words! Your never-ending pursuit of security is far more deadly than any threat of political annihilation I faced."

"Yes!" David nearly shouted. "Yes! You are absolutely right. I know, I know," he sobbed. "Susan, my wife, knew. Yes, I want out, but I don't know what to do, where to turn."

Ruth lit another cigarette, and her countenance changed again. Her eyes narrowed like a lawyer sizing up a jury. "Sometimes the answer is found inside, and someone must bring it forth. Such is the way of the psychiatrist. There is a proper place for this work." She exhaled slowly and the smoke lazily curled toward the window. "But this is not your problem. You must discover what you have not known, what lies on the outside. You must become a wandering Jew walking around the edges of society as our people have always done. The Richardses gave you the resources to be an insider. Now is the time to become an outsider. Find out who *you* are by finding out who *we* are."

He blinked several times before smiling. "What an incredible suggestion." David laughed softly. "How in the world would I do such a thing?"

Ruth put the cigarette out in a ceramic ashtray. "Yaacov loved the land. Certainly the work was terribly hard back in those early days. The Arabs wouldn't sell us anything but mosquito-infested swamps. The Moses family drained the fields and learned how to irrigate. In time those swamp bottoms grew wonderful vegetables. Yaacov loved to plunge his hands into the soil and feel the dirt slip between his fingers. The land made him alive."

"What are you saying?"

"When I was so deeply depressed, the *terra firma* became the place where I found both myself . . . and God. Galilee was healing balm for my soul. Israel *is* holy land. Our people have returned to life there. In such a small place there's everything from barren wilderness to fertile fields. Yes, both the wretchedness and enchantment of life is mixed into the dirt itself. The journey of our people through history is etched into the terrain."

"Then why did you leave?"

"You would never have found me if I hadn't."

Her candid answer jolted David. For a moment he tried to digest the implications. "I see," he said slowly under his breath. "But I'm not sure what you are suggesting."

"You want to open the door to your soul?" She leaned toward him. "Then why don't you move to Israel for a while? Go there. Walk where your father walked. Sit by the sea. Breathe the air. Meet the people."

"You're not serious." David sounded bewildered.

"Do you know a better way to find yourself?"

TEN

Edward Crownover eased the borrowed car into the driveway. David's rambling house reflected both Oklahoma and Susan's taste. George and Mary Richards surely liked the prosperous appearance. They inevitably confused square footage with class. But Ruth would take exception to the pretentiousness. After all, such a prairie estate was designed for a large family. Two people rattled around in all those rooms like rocks in a tin can.

Although Edward never liked the house, he always stayed in his own permanently reserved room when the inevitable business trips brought him to town. A robe and slippers awaited him in his closet. Susan even hung a quaint picture of an English pub on the bedroom wall. This time he stayed in a hotel.

The house was Susan's. Edward turned off the car. *The studio out back is David's. The arrangement was his compromise. Everything's been a compromise for David until now.* He rested his head on the steering wheel. *Sounds like things are bloody well about to change. I hope he's not terribly angry. I wonder how long David will continue to stay here.*

Edward felt apprehension again. David's phone call the night before he left California sounded too much like a summons from the Lord High Commissioner. He promised to call again immediately upon his return.

Good sign he wants to talk to me first. He groaned. *Then again, David gave no hint about what was really on his mind. Not like him at all.* He got out of the car slowly, slammed the door, and looked across the yard. The snow was slowly melting, leaving bare brown spots where the dead grass poked through. *Too flat and barren for my taste. Unbearably hot in the summer, brown and stripped in the winter.* He inhaled the sharp crisp air. The clean freshness invigorated and stirred the old man. *Springtime is wonderful. Have to give the place that much credit.* He walked to the front door.

Edward gave a brisk, proper knock before inserting his own key in the lock, opening the door, and calling out hesitantly into the dark house, "Davey, are you here?"

"In the den," David's voice echoed through the empty house. "Come on back."

David was sitting in an overstuffed chair in front of the large picture window overlooking the spacious backyard. The lights were out, and the room was filled with shadows. Only the morning sunlight illuminated the den. Uncharacteristically, David didn't get up.

"Welcome home!" Edward dropped on the leather sofa. "Good trip last night?"

"Sure," David's voice showed no emotion.

"I imagine the last week has been the most extraordinary of your life." Edward's smile was forced and artificial.

"Susan's been gone two weeks and five days," David sounded factual and detached. "Seems like a few seconds . . . more like an eternity."

"I shan't possibly try to imagine the pain you've faced, Davey." Edward folded his hands in front of his face and stroked his mustache. "But I hope your time with Ruth helped."

"Why didn't you ever tell me any of this?" David hunkered down in his chair "All these years you knew every crying detail."

Edward nervously ran his hands through his hair; his mouth went dry. "I never worried much about where life was going or the meaning of what went past. Taking matters seriously sets a man up for a nasty fall. Well now, that's not quite so. I must confess some terrible pangs of conscience over what might have been. Yet, overall, I didn't allow myself to think too far ahead of the day at hand. I knew someday the right moment would come." He shook his head and finally lowered his head into his hands. "I did the best I could . . . at the time." He felt the same terrible, gnawing ache as when Ruth confronted him. A bubble of pain rose up from his stomach and lodged in his throat. "I'm so sorry." He choked. "I tried to do what was right."

"Couldn't you have told me something, anything?" David's mask of indifference broke, and he grimaced. "If I had only known about Ruth."

"One word and your parents would have made sure you never saw me again." He sniffed and choked. "I waited until you needed her the most."

David finally stood up and walked over to the couch. "I'm sure you did what you thought was right." He patted Edward on the shoulder. "Yes, her help was very important. She's going to be my bridge from the past to the future."

Edward felt more at ease. "Good, good. 'Tis a relief to hear it."

"I don't sleep well." David sat down on the edge of his small desk. "Without Susan I . . . stay up too late . . . then can't sleep. I read, constantly, incessantly." He picked up a book. "Ever read this one, Edward?" He held up a gold-edged collector's edition. *The Diary of Anne Frank*. Rummaging quickly through a pile of booklets, he found another book of pictures. "This little volume came from a museum in Israel, the Yad Vashem." He flipped the pages to a black-and-white photograph of a pile of human bodies. "Sure, I knew about the Holocaust, but I also read about Christian martyrs. Didn't really pay a lot of attention to the facts. Oh yes, I heard about the slaughter of the Jews, but I also read about Armenians being killed by the Turks. My generation grew up with disaster. I became numb to it, I suppose, until this week." He opened another booklet titled *Auschwitz: Voices from the Ground*. "My grandparents could be in one of these pictures." He quickly shut the book.

"I know, I know," Edward mumbled.

"Ruth tells me her displacement and our separation would never have occurred if we hadn't been Jews. The British army wouldn't have allowed a child of any other race to be kidnapped."

"You've never known anti-Semitism, Davey." He cleared his throat. "I never knew anything else. Have to hand it to your parents. George and Mary wouldn't tolerate such trash. They kept you from being exposed to the scourge."

"Here's another gem Ruth gave me." David picked up a thick paperback. *"Sophie's Choice,"* he read the title. "Quite a story about another woman who had her child taken away. Know how it ends? Remember what happened to Sophie's sanity?"

"Please, please!" Edward balked at the thought. "No more! I can't stand any more animosity. Is that what's happening to you? You're going to get the infection and start hating the people who hate Jews. God help us."

"No," David answered calmly. "I'm just trying to find out what it means to be a Jew."

Edward's hopes dwindled again. He felt a void hovering around him like a dark cloud. The house seemed so peculiarly empty without Susan. He got up to find something to drink.

"Little early, isn't it?" David picked up another book and pointed at the nearest chair. Edward sat back down. "Ruth gave me this volume the second day I was there. Chaim Potok's *History of the Jews.* Extraordinary. Never knew any of the story of the Jewish people through the centuries. I found out persecution's not new. Been going on for centuries."

"David," Edward pleaded.

"Come now! You're the jolly Englishman, the final finished product of Christian civilization. Tell me, why were people put to death because of their racial and religious origins? I don't understand how families were torn apart because of ethnic differences."

"Must we go on?" Edward cleared his throat again.

"Oh, yes. We *must* go on. I have to know why all those bodies were piled up like so much firewood. Obviously the world's not the same place I thought it was just a week ago. I have to understand."

Edward pulled at his collar. "Perhaps civilization ran out in this century. Maybe we became so scientific we simply researched personal worth right out of existence. I don't know the answer, but there is no such thing as Christian culture anymore. The days of Christian kings and knights-errant are gone. Thomas à Becket died eight hundred years ago, and Sir Thomas More's integrity has vanished like heraldry. No one looks for the Holy Grail anymore."

"Let me read a bit." David opened the book, ignoring his answer. "Potok's introduction describes Jewish history as being the task of helping the Almighty bring creation to perfection while preparing for a Messiah to bring redemption. He writes, 'It was the sacred duty of the Jew to lead man along that path; it was the demonic intent of unrighteous gentiles to try to kill us along the way.' " David closed the book. "Tell me. What do those words mean?"

"I don't know," Edward held up his hands in a plea. "I'm not a religious man. Never made any pretense of running into the Divine on any of the world's street corners. Maybe I grew up in the shade of one too many cathedral. I watched the tourists come and go, never intending to enter myself. Just had a perpetual disinterest in the subject of religion." Edward unbuttoned his collar. "Perhaps my problem was not indifference as much as an abiding premonition that if I got too close my style might be cramped. I suppose I could never bring myself to renounce the devil in all his works and ways."

"My question isn't academic." David crossed his arms over his chest. "I have a baptismal certificate which says David Richards is a Christian. I have a Jewish mother who tells me I am a Jew. Who am I? Dachau, Auschwitz, and the Yad Vashem remind me the answer is a life-and-death question."

Edward looked at the ceiling and shook his head.

"Look." David pointed at him. "I feel like I've been catapulted out of this cozy midwestern ghetto into an ancient desert. Right now, I am caught between something called Christendom and a conundrum called Judaism. Two great grinding wheels are bearing down on me. You started this. You tell me what to do."

Edward tried to clear his throat one more time. "I can't," he said dryly. "Oh, that I could! Tragically I've bloody well spent my life running from such questions." He stopped and inhaled deeply. "But I can tell you this much." His voice cracked. "Don't stop the quest. Don't flinch. Because if you do, someday you'll be an old man looking back over your shoulder at a pile of meaningless check stubs, a trail of broken hearts, and pointless receipts from a past that evaporated into nowhere. Yes, David, I sent you to California, and I have no apologies. No, no! Don't stop looking—ever! The Grail may yet be out there somewhere."

David watched Edward drive off and then walked back through the dark house to the den. He spent the rest of the afternoon reading and not once answered the telephone. For supper he ate a precooked frozen dinner from the microwave before returning to his books. Even though it was midnight when David turned the light out, he was awake at five o'clock.

His dreams had changed somewhat. A new cast of characters emerged. Rather than being chased, David was discovering hidden stairways and road maps. Doors were opening in front of him, and paths appeared out of nowhere. Still, the forms were illusive, and he hadn't slept well. David felt exhausted.

He left for the office around 7:00 A.M. for lack of anything else to do. This time when he passed the statue of Moses in the hallway he thought about the significance of the graduation gift. "Edward did leave a few hints around," he spoke to himself. "Maybe I was too severe." David didn't rub the nose.

On the top of his desk David found a monumental pile of mail. Cards of condolence were sifted in with circulars and junk mail. Catalogs and bills were lumped together. He thought about calling Ruth but realized California time would be around 5:30. Shortly after eight o'clock he heard Jack Meachem come in.

"Davey? You're back?" his partner called down the hall.

"Yes."

"Welcome back." Jack walked briskly through the door. "Haven't seen you for what seems like forever." He offered his hand and sat down in one of the brown leather chairs across from the desk. "How are you?" Jack's voice was sincere and sober.

"Better." David smiled. "It's not easy, but I'm getting there."

"I think the little vacation trip to California was a great idea. You needed the space. Get in some sun by the ocean?"

"Yes." David glanced at Susan's picture still placed on the credenza behind his desk. He immediately looked away.

"What'd you do?" Jack removed his brown cashmere coat and brushed his stubby crew cut.

"Just bummed around." David kept trying to smile. "Thanks for the flowers." He pointed to a potted plant of primroses. "Great selection. You know I love the colors."

"I'm so sorry, David." Jack's eyes filled with tears. "I know we've had our differences through the years, but honestly, I'd do anything if I could make this time easier."

"Thank you, Jack." David bit the side of his mouth. "I'm sure you would. I hope my absence hasn't made work too difficult."

"Don't give it a thought." Jack shook his head and then inhaled deeply. "There is one item we must look at today. Unavoidable . . . I wish we could put it off another week."

"Jackson and Schultz are calling?" David leaned back in his chair.

"They've been very understanding. Haven't pushed any, but they want to have some idea what we are going to do."

"Certainly." David pulled a Mont Blac pen from his inside coat pocket and began tapping on his palm. "They have every right to a response."

"I still strongly favor selling." Jack's voice took on a nervous urgency. "Of course, you have to work for them or not at all. I suppose it's all become even more complex for you now."

David turned his chair sideways and looked out the tenth-floor window. "Ever do business with Jews?"

"Jews?" Meachem snorted. "Are you serious? Don't tell me you've struck a deal with some California Jews."

"I'm interested in your opinion."

"Of Jews?" Jack raised his eyebrows. "I don't know much of anything about them, except they're all rich and have big noses. I'd expect them to be mean, hard-driven money-grubbers."

David slowly turned back and looked hard at his friend. "Is that really your view of Jews?"

Jack blinked and frowned. "Well, I guess. Sure. I don't know why, but I don't think I'd trust them. What's the scoop? You got something going with a Jew?"

"Yes." David crossed his arms over his chest. "As a matter of fact, you might say I have something rather important going with a Jew."

Jack shook his head. "My old man always said to watch 'em in a business deal because they will skin you alive if they get the chance. You know that old expression? 'Don't let them Jew you down.' Must be something to it."

"Did anyone ever suggest to you that you might have more than a touch of anti-Semitism?" David's eyes narrowed. "Do you really know any Jews?"

"Anti-Semitism?" Years of trading verbal punches brought Jack to instant rancor. "What are you talking about?" He didn't conceal his irritation. "You ask for an opinion, and I gave you an honest answer without prejudice."

"Do you know any Jews locally?"

"What is this with you? I don't like the third degree. No, I'm sure there's some around here." He frowned. "Well, yes. I know of a couple of attorneys who are Jews. Everybody knows about the Silvermans and the ton of real estate they have amassed."

"Did you know there are two synagogues in town?"

"You planning to buy one of them?" Jack returned the jab. "Is that your next business project? Look. I don't have the slightest interest in what the Jews are doing. If you have a business deal going, put it on the table. Otherwise, let's get on with Jackson and Schultz. At least they're not Jews."

"You go to church most every Sunday, Jack. Do you ever learn anything about the history of the Jew? After all, the Christian faith came out of a Jewish world."

"What is going on with you?" Jack's face turned red. "Is this another one of those bizarre philosophical rabbit trails you love to run down? Half the time you spin off into antisocial tirades about compromise. Is this the new kick? Be nice to the kikes week?"

"Kikes is clearly pejorative, racist."

"I don't care what it is!" Jack suddenly slammed his fist on David's desk. "I don't want to mess up this contract with Jackson and Schultz. No!" He was nearly shouting. "I don't know any Jews. Moreover I don't want to know any Jews. Even more, I don't want to learn anything about Jews." He swore. "I want to sell this company and get into business with somebody who's not a nut. You were bad enough before Susan . . ." Meachem stopped and cringed. "I'm sorry." The words rolled out in a sigh of exasperation. "Just sorry." He stomped out of the room.

David stared at the pile of mail. "Where was I?" He fumbled with the unopened letters. "Yes," he continued his soliloquy to himself, "where am I?"

David looked around the room and out over the city. "How in the world did I ever get to this place?"

Edward sat alone on the veranda of the Oklahoma City Country Club enjoying the privileges of being a friend of the Richards family. The skylight transformed the cold winter sky into warm, soothing sunlight. The aroma of his second cup of coffee tickled his nose. He poked at the cherry sweet roll with his fork.

David's question kept coming back to him. "Why didn't you ever tell me any of this?" Edward tried to dismiss the accusatory query, but David's voice would not be denied. "All these years you knew every crying detail."

"Why?" Edward said to himself. "Why indeed!"

He closed his eyes and tried to remember how it was

Robert L. Wise

forty-three years ago. *Over four decades ago!* Images of Palestine floated up from his memory. Everything was so different . . . then. He began to see himself as a young man. The scene rolled forth once again . . . like a replay of an all-too-familiar television rerun.

The first light of dawn was breaking through the dirty window of the makeshift military headquarters overlooking Tel Aviv. Periodically an explosion scattered the dusk and lit up the sky. The smell of smoke hung in the air, but nothing interrupted the annoying staccato clicking of the typewriter. He paced nervously, his khaki pants wrinkled and the military jacket stained. Edward Crownover was tired and worn.

He stopped and ran his hand through his dark brown hair. He puckered his lips, and his mustache stuck out like a bedraggled brush. "What are we going to do with this baby?" Edward pointed a long, bony finger at the little boy holding onto the desk. His voice became strained. "We've bloody well got enough trouble fighting the Nazis and keeping the Arabs from killing the Jews without baby-sitting some nameless orphan." He swore and began pacing again. His combat boots clomped against the wooden floor.

"Corporal, you worry too much," the adjutant shot back without looking up from his typewriter. The nails were chewed away on his fat fingers. "Mate, let nature take its course. The only thing I know is one of our patrols found him crawling near the remains of the truck. Matter of fact, the hull was still burning when our boys arrived. Well, someone's got to take responsibility. Don't they, deary?"

"I tell you, Williams, I don't like any of it." Edward stiffened to rigid attention, looking like the embodiment of Victorian propriety. His long dangling arms and large hands made him appear even taller. Pouting caused his stubby brown mustache to look more prickly. "We're heading for trouble straightaway." Edward's unusual bushy eyebrows lowered to half-mask his brown eyes.

The toddler pulled the handle on the front of the gray shabby desk, opening and closing the bottom drawer. His soft

— 84 —

olive skin was smudged with grease, and his dirty, worn T-shirt was torn. Long black curls hung over his ears. His shoes were gone. He smelled of smoke. Suddenly the little boy started throwing papers out of the open drawer.

"Cute little devil," the adjutant chuckled. "Better stop him from tearing up something important." Williams had a bulbous shape like a pear. Only his belt appeared to keep his belly from spilling over like a broken sack of flour. The fat around his neck absorbed his chin and jaw line. His soiled brown uniform was too tight. He shut the drawer and set the child on the floor several feet from the desk. "I'd say he must be about two years old. Might be four and small for his age."

"Seems so to me." Crownover dangled a ring of keys in the air, and the child immediately grabbed them. "Can't be more than three years, anyway."

A flash of light shot through the window. A few moments later the sound of a far-off bomb explosion rattled the windows. The child instantly began to scream.

Edward immediately picked up the crying boy and hugged him. He swirled the child around in his arms, trying to distract him, but the terror ran deep. A number of turns were required to stop the outburst. Only by holding him close to his chest could Edward stop the sobbing.

"Look at those huge black eyes!" Williams chuckled.

Edward sat him down. The orphan shook his mop of black curls and toddled off across the rough wooden floor of the crude officers' headquarters. The British corporal yawned as the adjutant locked the desk drawer.

"Things work out, Corporal Crownover. Your trouble is not keeping your nose out of what doesn't directly concern you. Nasty habit, isn't it?"

Edward defiantly picked up a clipboard and read from the top of a form. "Says he was found not far from the kibbutz called Afikim close to the Sea of Galilee. Truck blown to pieces. Must have run over a land mine. Not much left of the driver. The woman was lying about fifty feet from the point of the blast.

Found the boy crawling on the ground under a large tree. All quite lovely."

The adjutant pulled at the ends of his long tapered mustache. "Just another Arab bombing." Williams's ruddy complexion was a product of cold English winters, not sultry Middle Eastern summers. "Well, Corporal, my boy, we have a baby to dispose of." He began typing again.

"Come now, Williams! I have no taste for kidnapping," Crownover barked. "If this matter isn't handled right, we could deeply regret—"

"Come now, *yourself*, Corporal. Don't get self-righteous on me. And let's jolly well not forget rank here." Williams picked up the child from the floor and set him on top of the worn desk. Immediately, the small hand reached for the brass buttons on the solider's uniform. "Out here in this desolate Arab dump, the British army is the only thing that stands between anarchy and any semblance of order. We have to do the intelligent thing and let the chips fall where they may."

Edward looked down at his scuffed boots and shook his head. "I'm not convinced."

"Look around you, man!" The adjutant clenched his fist. "Even this new so-called city of Tel Aviv is nothing but an experiment in futility. We're England! We have to do as *we* see fit."

"Sir." Edward's jaw tightened. "Relatives must be out there somewhere. Someone's bound to show up sooner or later. Babies don't just disappear and no one comes looking."

"Read the report again," the adjutant snapped. Williams's sharp outburst startled the child, and the boy looked up apprehensively. "Sorry, matey." The adjutant patted the child's head roughly. "No alarm intended."

Edward scanned the report form again. "What's left out is as significant as what's here. Whoever wrote up the explosion was avoiding every possible critical detail concerning identity."

Williams jerked the clipboard away. With the contempt of a schoolteacher lecturing a failing pupil, he underlined the sentences with his index finger. "The father was killed in the blast. As I read it, the father isn't coming back to claim the lad."

"Doesn't say father, but the woman's not dead yet—"

"Any minute, soldier! Any minute now they'll be haulin' her worthless Jewish carcass down to the morgue." Williams's voice became more shrill. "Probably dump her in an unmarked grave. After all, these things happen every day!"

"How can we dispose of a child until we get a death certificate for both parents? If they are the parents? I mean . . . what if—"

"Good heavens!" The senior officer exploded. "We're dealing with Jews! Remember? Miserable Jews. These unwanted refugees somehow or the other keep crawling into this land and drivin' us crazy. Who cares what they want . . . or think for that matter? We oughta throw the whole lot of these Christ-killers into the sea anyway! Britain runs Palestine. Jews have the rights *we* say they have! Anyway after the war's over, the Arabs will annihilate what's left of 'em anyway."

The child crawled across the desk toward Crownover's more gentle voice. Slowly reaching up, he abruptly clutched Crownover's hand. Peering up with arresting eyes, the little boy pulled himself up by grabbing the corporal's uniform and rubbed his cheek against the officer's hand.

Crownover clutched the baby to his side and looked over at the clipboard again. "Wait a minute. Look here. We know a considerable amount about the child. The report says the family name is Moses." He whispered to the child, "Moses, little boy. You're a real biblical Moses set adrift in a cruel world."

"Don't mention that name ever again!" Williams snatched the clipboard away. He talked faster in rushed tones. "We need to get this baby out of here immediately." The adjutant pulled wrinkled identification papers from the back of the clipboard and tossed them into the trash basket.

"At the risk of insubordination, I must protest again, Williams. If something goes wrong, I'll bloody well be the one on trial. Really now! Why are we breaking every rule of protocol in dealing with an abandoned child with a dead father and a mother who may not even be—"

"Who *will* be dead by morning! Right?" The adjutant sat down and spread the papers out on the desk. He stared angrily at the corporal. "You know how protective those Jews are about their children. If the word gets out, every Yid from the kibbutz will be down here claiming to be the uncle, brother, aunt, whatever. Come on, Crownover. Don't you have enough military problems without playing nursemaid?"

The child placed his head against the soldier's shoulder. The corporal looked away from the senior officer.

"Corporal, Corporal," Williams pleaded. "If the word gets out, *you* will be the one trying to make these squatters happy. Think about it. Don't these Jews give you enough grief without throwing in the problem of disposing of an orphan?"

"Okay, mate, level with me. What *else* is afoot with this child? There's more you're not saying."

The adjutant pursed his lips, squinted his eyes, and began drumming on the desk with his fat fingers. "Crownover," the adjutant drawled out every letter in the name as far as possible. *"I have already promised the baby for adoption."*

"Well now, governor! We have come to the bottom of it, haven't we? Perhaps we have a nice Bedouin couple to raise the boy out in the fresh air of the desert? We're doing Isaac and Ishmael in reverse these days? Do I know this lucky family who won the local raffle on Jewish children?"

"Don't push me, Corporal. I've promised the baby to an American couple." He unwrapped a piece of gum and began chewing furiously.

"They know the baby is Jewish?"

"They don't care if the child is half-Martian! In fact, they don't want to know anything except that the baby is healthy. What more could we ask for? Since the Arabs will eventually do these Jews in anyway, we are saving the child's life . . . actually." Williams immediately went back to the papers, making quick pencil checks.

Crownover cleared his throat. "Quite lovely. Only Americans around here would have to be some of those oil-rich business people negotiating lucrative war contracts. I meet them in the club all the time. I bet they have plenty of resources to cover all the costs."

The adjutant nodded but didn't look up.

"Who knows? Maybe there is even a hefty finder's fee for some lucky solider who should turn up such a baby?"

Williams froze in place. His neck turned red. Without looking up, the adjutant whirled around in the swivel desk chair and walked to a file cabinet next to the wall with his back to the corporal.

"All right, governor." Edward fought to sound casual. "You are his majesty's officer in charge, and I am your humble servant. Let's just leave it with the understanding that at some future date you owe me one. A big one."

"Make sure the boy's healthy," the adjutant snapped. Williams did not turn around.

Edward glanced at the crumpled identification papers in the trash can. Carefully balancing the child in one arm, he pulled the forms out of the trash in one swoop and quickly crammed the information in his side pocket before hurrying toward the dispensary.

The scene faded, and Edward realized he was staring at his white napkin. David's question returned and brought Edward's mind back to the present moment. "Why didn't you ever tell me any of this?" Edward crumpled the linen into a ball.

"How could I ever have explained?" he asked himself.

ELEVEN

David missed Susan.

She had been his stabilizer, a monitor, a beacon on dark nights. Without her presence, the wrangling over the sale of the company was quickly becoming intolerable. Slowly passing days dragged into weeks as the tension mounted. David uncharacteristically vacillated over final terms for settlement.

Confrontation with Meachem stayed at explosive levels. David was willing to sell but wanted no strings attached to his future. Jackson and Schultz waffled and groaned. Each delay made Jack more agitated. Jackson implied their firm was on the verge of dropping the negotiations.

A terribly cold February made matters feel worse. Winds howled constantly, and the windchill factor plummeted. The terrain was dead, frozen. But time and events did not stand still. David's life had become a white-water ride. The journey into the rapids began with talk of selling the company; then Susan's death capsized the boat. The reunion with Ruth Moses was another wild plunge into roiling foam; the sale of the company became a boulder in the river.

David missed Susan a lot.

She was the quiet backwaters, the warm place of retreat. Her influence was like a regulator, an on and off switch. Without their evening rituals, David found it nearly impossible to go to sleep. He read into the small hours, dreading the relentless alarm awaiting him a few hours later. He studied *Everyman's Talmud* and pondered Elie Wiesel's stories of the Ashkenazi Hasidic masters of central Europe. He read Chaim Potok's intriguing novels about contemporary Jews. A new world filled with strange customs, diverse beliefs, and a strange vocabulary of Yiddish phrases opened before him.

After finishing a book, he called Ruth for answers and insights. This new Jewish mother always left him with too much to digest. Like a sumptuous lobster dinner drenched in butter, her responses were too rich and too heavy. She sent him down other unexplored roaring rapids, washing away cherished preconceptions about himself, his past, his future. Each ride left him soaked in new ideas and foreign concepts. Often David could only stare at the walls. Large gulps of time were required to digest Ruth's unorthodox and alien responses.

The hidden inner room where the unknown phantom David hid opened slightly. Frequently the shape and dimensions of this other person slipped out of the shadows, but insights were brief and fleeting. Paul Kendall helped clarify these moments, but there was no one else with whom the discoveries could be shared.

David missed Susan.

He increasingly realized Paul was right. David had related to the world through her. Susan had been his connection to God, to the church, to his soul. Without her steady hand, his little boat felt wobbly, vulnerable, and perilously unnavigable. Only after one of his weekly sessions with the priest was David finally able to quit wearing his wedding band.

"I put both our rings in the bank safe-deposit box." David looked at the back of his hand where the slight indentation and lighter skin color on his ring finger remained.

"What did you feel?" Paul Kendall leaned back in his chair.

David looked around the pastor's office, studying the books and pictures. "Well," he drawled slowly, "hard to say. Felt very final."

"Did it hurt?"

"I ... I ... don't ... think I know for sure." David frowned.

"You stuff your pain, David. Staying in touch with your true feelings is hard for you. During childhood you learned to conform to other people's expectations and to discount your deepest emotion." The minister nodded his head slowly. "Try it again. What did you really feel?"

David closed his eyes and sighed deeply. "I don't want to talk about it."

"Just let what's there come up. Live in the experience."

"Why are you doing this to me?" David slowly opened his watering eyes.

"Your grief won't heal unless you go through it." Paul's voice was soft and kind.

"Maybe I don't want to—as you say—'heal' my grief," David snapped.

"Correct." The minister abruptly sounded clinical. "But you will wallow in depression and self-pity until you deal with denial."

David crossed his arms over his chest and glowered. "What denial?"

"That Susan is dead and not coming back."

"Who do you think you are?" David's voice was shrill, strident. "How do you know?"

"Have you taken Susan's clothes out of the closet? Cleaned out her drawers?"

"That's absolutely none of your prying business!" David stood up and pushed his chair back. "Nobody is going to remove one stitch of Susan's things until I'm good and ready. Do you understand?" He screamed at the priest. *"Do you understand?"*

In barely a whisper, Paul answered, "Yes, David. I really do understand."

David started to pound on the desk but stopped. His face and neck turned crimson, and his lips began to quiver. "I can't just give her clothes away," his voice broke. "Susan's parents died long ago . . . and . . . she was . . . an . . . only child." His voice trailed away. "Everything would go to strangers." Slowly he sunk into the chair. "I couldn't stand for someone else to wear her dresses." His words slurred together. "I need her things . . . to be there . . . please . . . I couldn't stand . . . empty drawers." He slid back into his chair and buried his face in his hands.

"We have to let Susan go," Paul answered quietly. "Grief is a bridge we must cross, but we can't park on it." Walking around the desk, he put his hand on David's shoulder and waited for several minutes.

"You're praying for me?" David finally sniffed.

"Yes."

"Strange." David stared at the floor. "I can feel it. I can actually tell the pain is lifting."

"Good." Paul fingered the cross hanging around his neck. "And how do you feel right now?"

"Sad. Yes, very sad."

"The more of everything you feel, the quicker you will heal."

"What's wrong with me, Paul?"

"You don't want life to go on. Everything around you is in flux, every piece of your world changing. You need Susan to help sort it all out, and she's gone. You're trying to live with the brakes on again."

David blinked rapidly several times, clearing his eyes, "Yes," he said slowly. "I don't want any more surprises." He settled back into the chair. "But I can't stop the alterations." He reached up and squeezed the hand on his shoulder. "Thank you. Thank you for being here."

The minister sat down on the corner of his desk. "You're trying to survive a suffocating avalanche of personal discoveries. Anyone would be terrified."

David ran his hand through his hair and rubbed the back of his neck. "This Jewish thing is eating my lunch. My wife goes out the back door of my life, and my biological mother comes in the front one. Before one world dissolves another comes careening in like a Mack truck. I don't think I can absorb the impact."

"What's your next step?"

"I know I have to get rid of Susan's things. You're right, painfully right." He exhaled slowly. "But I don't know what to do with what Ruth is teaching me. I'm becoming a veritable encyclopedia on Judaism, and yet I feel disjointed."

"Perhaps, the insights are too abstract, too cerebral. Maybe you ought to visit the local synagogue. Get to know some of the Jewish community. Get more visceral."

"You're serious?"

"Take your quest out of the abstract. Get out of the books. Find out what the Jewish world is really like."

"I couldn't do that!"

"Why not? Rabbi Sol Berkowitz over at the synagogue is a friend of mine. I can tell him you're coming. Explain something of your situation. He's confidential."

"Heavens no!" David shook his head tenaciously.

"And why is this suggestion so threatening?"

After a long pause David answered, "Another change." Picking up his overcoat, he slowly turned toward the door. After a couple of steps he stopped. "Of course!" He pivoted. "That's why I've made the business negotiations so difficult! Trying to keep my foot on the old brakes." He snapped his fingers and darted toward the door.

But David still missed Susan.

Eating alone at a nearby Mexican restaurant, David thought of what he wanted to tell Susan about his afternoon discoveries. He could see her eyes sparkle with approval as he described his new insight into the hide-and-seek game he played with pain. But no one was there.

During the next week, David wrestled with the idea of attending the synagogue. The suggestion made him apprehensive and uneasy, but he tried to remember he was resisting every new experience. A curious thought occurred to him. His entire adult life was spent in Oklahoma City, but he had not even driven past the synagogue. The place seemed hidden away in one of the older parts of the city. Isolation of the Jewish community had never occurred to him before. Christian and Jewish worlds simply didn't mesh.

Two more weeks slipped past before David showed up for the Saturday morning Torah service. The exterior of Beth Israel didn't look particularly different from a church. The flat-roofed, red-brick exterior was old but ecclesiastical. An iron fence ran around the sparsely filled parking lot. People were getting out of their cars and filing into what was obviously the entrance. He circled the block several times before finally stopping.

Ruth had sent him a yarmulke to wear. He reluctantly slipped the small black cap on the back of his head and worried that the little prayer cover would slide off, causing him to look like a fool or a spy. Hurrying up the stairs beneath bronze plaques memorializing deceased members of the synagogue, he held the yarmulke in place. At the top were double doors obviously leading to the place of worship. Next to the heavy wooden doors was a rack of long white cloths trimmed in a black design with long dangling fringes on the ends. From his reading David knew talliths were worn over the shoulders by observant Jews. It just didn't feel appropriate for him to put on one of the white and black prayer shawls, so he went on through the doors into the sanctuary.

The large assembly room wasn't entirely unlike a church but was still different. Obviously there were no crosses or Christian signs but neither was there the rich symbolism he expected in his own church. The room was more spartan, like unadorned Evangelical churches often looked. In the front was a raised platform with a large cabinet containing ornate scrolls standing upright behind a thin veil. David recognized the ark and knew it contained a handwritten copy of the Old Testament. Two plain podiums stood on each end of the platform. An old stained-glass window attached to an adjacent wall was obviously preserved from a former time or another place. People were scattered across the sanctuary in theater-style seats, making the small congregation appear like a collection of individuals. The sparse attendance made David feel conspicuous.

The service was already under way, so David quickly slipped into a row near the back. No one seemed to notice. He grabbed a book from the rack in front of him, attempting to look like he knew what he was doing. For a moment he wondered if he should kneel, but, seeing no kneelers, he plunged into the book. To his amazement, most of the pages were in Hebrew. Bewildered, he looked around again and for the first time really listened.

A low, quiet, rumbling babble arose from the people reading from the service books. He immediately thought of a Pentecostal tongues gathering. A small man with a tallith pulled over his head walked to one of the podiums and prayed in Hebrew. The man looked Semitic or at least eastern European. Certainly the leader would never be mistaken for an Oklahoma country boy. He was small, had a short black beard, and wore wire-rimmed glasses, much as Paul Kendall had described Rabbi Berkowitz.

Losing some of his self-consciousness, David listened in rapt fascination as the Sabbath service continued. People didn't seem to be meditative as much as rotely reading from the service books. Children wandered in and out, adults came and went as if disconnected from any spiritual flow in the service. Other men helped the rabbi take the scrolls out of the ark, remove the velvet cover, and unroll the large Torah. Several members of the congregation came forward to read the sacred writings. Some read the Hebrew words slowly, but one tall man in particular read rapidly with strange nasal inflections as if chanting an ancient Middle Eastern rhyme. He stayed by the Torah when the rabbi began his explanation of the lesson for the day.

The rabbi had barely begun his dissertation when the thin man interrupted, questioning the rabbi's interpretation. The rabbi joked, responded, and went on. After a couple of minutes, the man intruded again, and a lively debate over the rabbi's explanation followed, making David feel extremely uncomfortable. Breaking into one of Paul Kendall's sermons would be the gravest insult and was unthinkable. The two men railed back and forth like lawyers locked in a courtroom dispute. Slowly David began to realize the debate was the way the teaching was done.

Once David assimilated the peculiarity of arguing, he was able to hear what the rabbi was really saying. In extremely erudite form, Berkowitz explained the story of Abraham's offering up Isaac to be a potential human sacrifice. A strange, unique perspective emerged. Berkowitz suggested Abraham had been wrong, gone too far. In his zeal to follow the will of God, Abraham had misunderstood the directions, consequently traumatizing his son for the rest of his life. The rabbi argued that sons must understand the best intentions of fathers often go awry when offered up on the altars of zeal and fanatic best intention. The only recourse is to forgive as hopefully one's children will someday forgive.

Suddenly the rabbi's mood darkened. "Of course we could speak of the *akeda* theme, the binding of Isaac, as the final test of faith. Is not the *akeda* used by many writers to describe the Holocaust when there was no divine intervention?" The synagogue became deathly quiet. "Many of us have struggled to understand how the Holy One of Israel could turn his back . . . even as Abraham seems to have been able to do . . . before the utter abandonment of the sacrificed. So we, like Yitzchak . . . like Isaac . . . have lived traumatized lives attempting to probe the meaning of such a possibility . . . as utter abandonment."

David felt undone. He came as a tourist, not a participant, but was leaving confronted. The rabbi's viewpoint seemed slightly heretical to his Christian ears and yet was obviously profoundly true. The service ended with David knowing he was back in the cold roiling rapids heading for a new bend in the river.

David watched the congregation file past him toward the door. For the first time, he realized many of the people bore a striking resemblance to his mother and himself, like distant cousins or certainly people of common origin. He watched with fascination, following the crowd into a fellowship hall. Wineglasses, decanters, pickled fish, bagels, and lox were set out on a large table. People snacked, talked, and nodded to him in a distantly friendly way.

"You must be David Richards."

David turned around to find the rabbi walking toward him with his hand extended. "Ah . . . yes . . . I am."

"Welcome to Beth Israel. Paul Kendall told me you would

be coming." The man seemed to be about David's age, somewhere between thirty-five and forty-five, but the rabbi was smaller, maybe around five foot five.

"Good of him." David felt stiff and awkward. "Great guy . . . Paul Kendall."

"Indeed." The rabbi shook David's hand enthusiastically. "A true friend of our community. Fine man. He tells me you've found a Jewish mother in your past." The rabbi's intense eyes were black and twinkled, hinting at a keen sense of humor.

David felt naked and looked quickly to see if anyone was in earshot. "Apparently so."

"Happens to the best of us." The rabbi laughed at his own joke. "Ashkenazic or Sephardic?" His accent was strongly eastern, a New York Brooklyn sound.

"A few weeks ago I wouldn't even have understood the question." David sensed genuine interest. The rabbi's casualness was reassuring. "Sephardic. As best I can tell, the family descended from Jews driven out of Spain."

"I hope you'll feel at home." The rabbi pointed toward the table. "Let me pour you something to drink, David. We're certainly glad you're here." He handed David a plain, small goblet.

"All rather new." David raised the glass as if to toast.

"Of course." The rabbi clicked his glass against David's. "*L' Chaim*! To life." His hands seemed unusually large in proportion to the rest of his body. "We're a strange little group. Lots of immigrants. A few Israelis. A number of descendants from Jewish families who settled the area. And I'm a New York City Jew . . . went to Hebrew Union Seminary. Get to know us, and I think you'll like our people."

"Thank you." David suddenly felt very uncomfortable as if he'd come too close too quickly and needed to retreat. The large hands might suddenly grab hold of him. "I have a noon appointment and have to rush off . . . but another day. Look forward to the meeting." He quickly set the empty glass back on the table.

"Give me a ring, and we'll set a time." The rabbi waved as

David backed toward the door. The phrase "our people" lingered in his mind.

Although going nowhere, David hurried toward his car. Urgency gave the appearance of purpose and appropriateness. "What do I feel?" he said to himself, putting the key in the ignition. "Inappropriate . . . in a no-man's-land . . . displaced. At the same time exhilarated . . . excited . . . intrigued." Pulling into the street, he thought, *Paul Kendall ought to be impressed. I'm in touch with myself for a change.*

Images kept rolling around in his mind. He could see the large Torah scrolls with their velvet covering and the silver knobs at the top. The lyrical phonetic sound of the Hebrew stayed like the sound of a new song. He heard again the clanking of the silver chains and emblem over the velvet when the rabbi and the men carried the scrolls around the synagogue. People had reached out in the aisle to touch the bundle with the tip of their service books. Berkowitz's face loomed before him once more. The rabbi was the embodiment of what David expected a Jew to look like. The beard, the wire-rimmed glasses, the profile were the vintage midwestern prototype of a Jew. The slight Brooklyn accent was frosting on the cake. The longer he drove, the better the whole experience felt.

Best of all, people looked like him. Every childhood memory was tainted with the painful awareness of looking different, being from somewhere else. Like an Angus in a corral of Herefords, David never fit in the Oklahoma human landscape . . . until now.

But, then again, he pondered as he drove, *what would people really think if they thought I was Jewish? Obviously many people don't look kindly on . . . on . . . us. People wouldn't understand.*

David wanted to tell someone. He could call Ruth, but long distance wasn't what he needed. He wanted to touch someone who could appreciate what the morning meant to him. He needed a flesh-and-blood someone whose eyes he could see. Someone.

David missed Susan. And it hurt.

TWELVE

One set of stairs led up to the sanctuary and the other down underneath the synagogue to the rabbi's office. At the bottom was a hallway lined with pictures of previous rabbis. Sol Berkowitz was clearly one of the younger leaders. He stood in the door waiting for David and their three o'clock appointment. In contrast to David's stylish suit, the rabbi was dressed casually in a blue shirt unbuttoned at the neck. His brown work pants were held up by plain suspenders; he wore white jogging shoes. A blue yarmulke trimmed in gold was pinned on the back of his head.

"Shalom. I'm delighted to see you've come back."

David shook the rabbi's hand. "Thanks for making time. Passover is not far away, I thought you might give me some insights since this year might be the first time I have kept the observance. At least that I can remember."

"Come into my office, David. Come in and I'll tell you all the hidden secrets of the Pesach." Rabbi Berkowitz laughed.

Once inside, David looked around in amazement at the disordered office. His compulsively neat disposition recoiled at the piles of books and papers jumbled together everywhere. Bookshelves were crammed full with books wedged on top of the stacks. Children's crayon drawings were taped at odd angles to the walls, adding color to the confusion. A pencil sketch of a man blowing a shofar looked like the only object that was not askew.

The rabbi caught David's rapid assessment of his study. "In the beginning the Word was 'let there be light,' not 'let there be neatness.' " The rabbi laughed at his own joke. "Sit down, David." He pointed at a desk chair. "Believe it or not, there is order to all this disorder. Somewhere in here I'll find you a Haggadah, the service book to use on Passover. Maybe I can get you started saying kiddush on Sabbath eve or even learn the Sh'ma in Hebrew. Who knows where all of this will lead?"

"Actually I don't know what to do with all the material I have now." David sat down on a faded brown couch. Nothing about the office was like Paul Kendall's except for the multitudinous books. "I basically just wanted to talk to you."

"Certainly!" The rabbi took off his small round glasses and began cleaning them on his shirt. "I am an open book. Whatever I have to offer, I am delighted to give." His large hands wrapped around the glasses. "As you can see, my style is rather laid-back."

"Perhaps, you know something of my story?"

"Paul Kendall gave me an overview of your voyage down the river of life. Says you're a regular latterday Moses come back from among the bulrushes." He laughed again.

"Lately it's been a little more like a ride down the Colorado River through the Grand Canyon."

The rabbi's disposition changed instantly. "I am very sorry also to hear of the tragedy of your wife's death." He pulled at his black beard. "Such pain." He clicked his tongue against the roof of his mouth. "Such pain, indeed."

"Lot of changes." David cleared his throat. "So, here I am. Most of all I want to know what it means to be a Jew. Even though we have always been a very small percent of the population, a lot of attention comes our way. And a lot of it has been simply awful. Why?"

"Get right down to it, don't you?" Berkowitz raised his eyebrows. "I must say, public acceptance has certainly improved in my lifetime. Jewishness hasn't changed, but gentile perception has. When I was a boy I often found 'dirty Jew' scribbled on my desk. My family couldn't join any country club. Often college fraternities ruled us out. Believe me, there was no honor in being called a kike."

"This is all new to me. I didn't experience such prejudice growing up here in Oklahoma."

"Oh, but I think you were exposed to more of it than you recognized. Probably Jews were invisible to you. Since World War II much of the obscurity as well as the old stigma has changed." He put his glasses on, letting them slide down his nose. "Paradoxically, the Holocaust shocked people into an awareness of the ultimate end of their intolerance. Of course, we were influenced dramatically too. Jews are never going to let it happen again. You can bet on that!"

"I am not ignorant of history." David chose his words carefully. "Even had a minor in it during college. Somehow I never picked up the stories about Christian persecution of the Jews through the centuries."

"History reads different when the professor is Jewish," the rabbi said dryly. "And 1492 is a different date when you discover our people were being run out of Roman Catholic Spain at that time. Those glorious stories of the Crusades look a little less glamorous when you discover that killing Jews was a major preoccupation of the Holy War." He looked over the rims of his glasses and sighed, like a professor admonishing a pupil.

David turned uncomfortably on the couch.

"Of course, we also have our dear friend Martin Luther who advocated burning the synagogues and Jews who didn't convert. Caught up with *that* story yet?"

David nodded his head.

"Good! Good. Your education in Judaism must include a healthy dose of historic reality."

"You hate Christians?"

"Heavens no!" The rabbi sounded annoyed. "I try not to hate anyone. The challenge is to keep Christians in perspective. As a matter of fact, they have become the best friends Israel has today. Right-wing Fundamentalists have gone to the other extreme now and romanticize us. We are astonished at how they believe everything Israel does is politically correct. I wouldn't even intimate such a thing! They think we're God's time clock ticking away to bring the Messiah back." Berkowitz roared. "My boy," the rabbi slapped David on the knee, "you've come at the right time. Jews are back in style."

"I don't understand."

"Go to one of your Christian bookstores! You'll see shelves of books on our customs, our festivals, our history. Jews convert to Christianity, write their stories, and make big bucks." He laughed again. "You know the Hebrew word for the Holocaust is *shoah*. Here's one for you: There's no a-business like a-shoah-business."

"Sounds rather dark to me." David's forehead furrowed, and he frowned. "Black comedy, no?"

"Of course it is!" the rabbi snapped. "Don't be deceived by the adulation. When those same Fundamentalists find out their Second Coming theories are wrong, they might turn on us with the same enthusiasm the medieval Inquisition had in chasing us across Europe. Persecution could start up again as easily as it did when Hitler made us the scapegoat in Germany." He looked hard at David. "Make no mistake about it, boy. Many, many people will not find it good news to hear you've got Jewish blood in your veins. Study carefully the road before you."

"That's why I want to know what it means to you, a rabbi, to be a Jew." David persisted.

The rabbi looked at the ceiling for a few moments. "Actually you are asking me two questions." He looked thoughtfully out of the corner of his eye. "First, you ask, what is it to be Jewish? But there is also the matter of being Jewish in this part of the world."

"I don't understand." David shook his head.

"I grew up in New York City. Went to a yeshiva and on to seminary at Union. I was virtually reared in a ghetto. Didn't have to see colored lights and Christmas trees on our block during Hanukkah. Very nice. Very easy. See what I mean?"

"Yes." The word slipped slowly out of David's mouth. "I think."

"Quite easy being Jewish in a world where you can even

order kosher Chinese food. Slightly different when you get hit below the Bible Belt." He grinned.

"So why'd you come to Oklahoma in the first place?"

"Growing up in Brooklyn I thought civilization ended with the Mississippi River. Kennedy's assassination in Dallas proved to me there was nothing out here but maniacs and cowboys." He looked over the rim of his glasses again. "Know what I mean? Then I came out here with my father on one of his business trips. Couldn't believe it! I loved the openness, the uncrowded way of life. People were warm, open, and caring. Life wasn't jaded like it is in so much of NYC. To my consternation, I found life in the great southwest still had a touch of the untamed and unexplored. I loved the independent spirits. I came back the first chance I got."

"But there weren't many Jews here. Were there?"

"The Jewish population in Oklahoma City is smaller than the statistical error in the census." Berkowitz laughed again. "Here you fish or cut bait. Back east, Jews can be quite marginal and float. No one pushes. But not here! You're either Jewish or not. Religion is unavoidable in the Bible Belt. People feel the pressure to decide. Our people have to take the synagogue seriously if it is to survive. Makes a great context for ministry."

"So you pull the troops together and keep the fort running out here on the frontier?"

The rabbi grinned slyly. "Not exactly. I must also care for the converts, you know."

"Converts?" David puzzled.

"Surprises you, doesn't it? Yes, one out of six of our members have chosen Judaism. One out of three couples are converts."

"I thought only Evangelical churches produced converts. These new members are the product of mixed marriages?"

"No. About three fourths of the inquirers just walk in off the street. Generally they are either former Roman Catholics angry over one of the church's social positions or Fundamentalists who've had too much fire and brimstone poured on them. Smoke got in their eyes." The rabbi burst into loud laughter.

"I'm astonished." David shook his head.

"Generally the converts had questions their churches wouldn't answer. They were squelched for asking too many questions." The rabbi pulled at his beard. "They were taught faith is acquiescence and told they should shut up. We're different here. We welcome any and all questions."

"I have never heard of anyone in this city ever converting to Judaism!" David frowned. "I didn't know it was possible."

"You're not likely to hear, either," the rabbi squinted and looked out of the corner of his eye. "Methodists can become Presbyterians and Roman Catholics change to Southern Baptists, but a Christian becoming a Jew is anathema. People who admit conversion to our community have lost their jobs, their friends! No sir! Christians get very upset by such a thing."

"Yes, I can see why." David ran his fingers through his hair. "There is an issue here of eternal destiny. In Oklahoma, churches generally preach about salvation." David gestured nervously. "I don't mean to be offensive, but what can you possibly offer these people?"

"A great deal of relief!" Berkowitz raised his eyebrows and leaned forward. "You must remember that for us salvation is in the deed not the creed. What someone believes isn't as important as what he does. We don't think Jews have a corner on the salvation market. Any person who does sufficient good has a place in eternity."

"And what is heaven?" David shot back. "I'd be very interested in what you think the place looks like."

"Jews have many images." The rabbi shrugged. "Who knows? The rabbis of the Talmud expected an academy on high where you studied for twenty-four hours a day and always came out with the right answer. On the other hand, the prophets wrote of a messianic age where we will be resurrected to a better world. The lion will lie down with the lamb and we can all plant gardens. To make any one exact description final is illusionary."

David rocked back in his chair. "I've never heard of such an idea before."

Berkowitz shook his finger in the air like an ancient rabbi. "No one is trying to convert you, David. The issue is whether you belong here or not."

David nodded. "I understand. Tell me more about what a good Jew does. What constitutes your daily habits?"

"We call it *kavanah*, sincere intention to be authentic. Of course, public worship is important in developing Jewish spirituality. Praying, seeking the Holy One, studying the Torah are all essential disciplines."

"Much like Christianity?"

"Certainly." The rabbi kept pulling at his beard. "And we believe charity is of great consequence. One should seek to do noble causes for the sake of God."

"Then what divides us?" David beckoned for an answer. "I don't understand where the line is between these two religions? Is believing Jesus was the Messiah the problem?"

"No." Berkowitz shook his head. "You may believe Jesus was the Messiah and still be a Jew. The problem comes when you believe that Jesus was God. God in the flesh. The doctrine of the incarnation creates the uncrossable chasm between Christians and Jews!"

"My goodness! What can I say? You've certainly opened my eyes. I must carefully digest our conversation," David slowly rose to his feet. "It will take some time."

"Of course," the rabbi smiled. "Weighty matters. Each one is truly worth a lifetime of discussion. You ask very good questions, David."

"Thank you. Actually we didn't ever get to the Passover. Perhaps next week I could return and start there."

"Excellent. I'll have a Haggadah in Hebrew and English waiting for you. I'm sure in a week I can find something in here." He laughed. "How about the same hour and day?"

"I'll be here!"

David slowly drove away, trying to remember each word of the conversation. He felt frighteningly stretched, not knowing where to put the explanations. He stopped for a red light and wished everything would halt. If the old days would just come back again. Even when things got boring, life was predictable. Instantly he was aware Susan would never return. One thing was crystal clear: if Susan wasn't in heaven, he wasn't going.

The unusually cold winter weather began to break up near the end of February. The nights hovered around freezing, but the temperatures during the day climbed back into the fifties. David could feel his own thaw within. Life had not returned, but the promise of spring was foreseeable.

Driving down the expressway to work, David thought about his reading, Ruth, the rabbi at the synagogue, and what was happening inside him. His wild river ride past the narrows and through the whirlpools seemed to have settled into a more peaceful, gentle pace—for the moment. Maybe he could now face closing the deal on the company and getting out. David was so absorbed, he missed the Sixth Street turnoff to his office and had to double back.

Nothing had changed on the tenth floor of the Makin Towers. Except for replacing Susan's picture with Ruth's, David's office was the same. He stopped and looked at his Colorado watercolor before hanging his overcoat in the small side closet and putting his briefcase under his mahogany credenza. Sunlight poured across the mail waiting on his desk. On the top of the pile was an interoffice memo sealed in an envelope marked confidential. David recognized the handwriting. He opened the letter.

TO: David Richards
FROM: Jack Meachem

I have tried very hard to understand why you can't come to a decision in the negotiations with Jackson and Schultz. All other parties have long since arrived at a conclusion. Unless a figure is reached quickly, the sale will be lost.

I must reluctantly conclude you want a larger share of the profits. The only way I know to break the ice is to give you a larger cut of my return. I can ill afford to do so, but neither can I stand to lose the retirement benefits coming from the deal.

OK. You win. How much more do you want?

David winced. He folded the note and reached for the intercom.

"Jack?" David called into the phone box. "Jack? Are you there?"

"Yes." The voice sounded far away, from another city.

"Got a minute? I'd like to discuss your memo."

"I'll be right down." The intercom was silent.

Meachem shut the door behind him and quickly dropped into the office chair on the other side of the desk. He slumped, not concealing his despair. His eyes were ringed with dark circles and looked hollow.

"Jack . . ." David sounded exasperated. "I never intended matters to come to this."

"You don't need to explain," Jack spoke rapidly in a professionally aloof voice. "Just tell me how much you want. An extra 5 percent? 10 percent?"

"Please." David held up his hand and gestured for silence. "Let me clarify. The problem isn't money or the terms." He shook his head and widened his eyes. "It's been me . . . facing the changes . . . resisting decisions. Jack," he pleaded, "you've been my best friend for years. I wouldn't undercut you. I don't want a dime more than I have coming."

Meachem stared, expressionless.

"I know so much of what I'm doing right now doesn't make a lot of sense to you, but it doesn't to me either." David turned around and looked out the office window toward the west. The bright morning sun felt warm and pleasant. "We both know what George and Mary Richards are saying. They want me to get out and make a fresh start in politics." David turned around and laughed. "Can you imagine me as a politician?"

Jack smiled thinly and looked away.

"No, I suppose right now you wouldn't nominate me for county jerk. Last night I talked to Ruth . . . How shall I say it? My mother in California will do. I know this new relationship sounded unbelievably bizarre to you when I explained it last week. Anyway, she is urging me to do something you'll probably find to be the most absurd of all. Ruth wants me to make a big break and go to Israel for a while."

Jack's mouth dropped. He blinked rapidly and exhaled deeply. "Israel?" His voice raised into a high squeak and his face twisted into a look of disbelief.

"Yeah, I know. Sounds pretty wild. Keep it between us."

"Israel?" The repetition sounded more like a plea than a question.

"Well, now you can see something of what has been keeping me so preoccupied, or as Uncle Edward would say, 'in such a muddle.' "

Jack covered his eyes and looked at the floor.

"I'm saying all this to reassure you that my indecision has nothing to do with money." David sat down in his chair. "But I know no explanation will help until we get these negotiations off high center; so here are my final terms."

Jack leaned forward apprehensively. "Please go on." He bit his lip.

"You finish the deal, sell the company, and I'll take whatever is acceptable to you. That simple."

Jack's mouth opened again. "You're kidding."

"Nope. It's a done deal. What makes you happy is completely acceptable to me. I want out immediately."

Jack stood up. "Do you really mean it?"

David smiled. "Absolutely."

"Thank you, thank you." Jack, on the verge of being speechless, extended his hand.

"I wouldn't want this partnership to end without us being the best of friends." Jack squeezed his hand firmly. "And I want you well taken care of. Forgive me for my vacillations during these past weeks."

"Forget it." Jack spit out the words. "I totally understand. No problem." He began backing toward the door.

"And let's keep the idea of a trip to Israel between us."

"Of course! Certainly! Mum's the word!" Jack waved over his shoulder and hurried out of the room.

David laughed hard for the first time in a long time and felt good, deep-down genuinely good.

After finishing the mail, David reviewed several pending projects. He checked plastic color overlays and penciled in suggestions. Eventually he drank a can of Coke and later sent the secretary after a cup of coffee. Nothing seemed exciting or challenging, and by 10:30 David knew for sure he belonged somewhere else. The spark was gone, and work was dry. His conversation with Jack had sealed his fate, allowing him to confront the obvious. Truthfully, his heart had never been fully in the business. At least he felt very good about how matters were being settled. Jack would do the right thing and forever feel grateful. When Mrs. Hammond returned, David smelled the cup of coffee in front of him and savored the rich flavor. He had made Jack happy and liked the feeling.

"Mr. Richards," the secretary's voice boomed over the intercom. "You have a call from your father on line one."

He picked up the phone. "Dad?"

"David! Are you all right?" George Richards sounded irritated. "Haven't heard from you in a long time."

"Hello, Dad." He tried to sound warm. "Everything's fine. Just sitting here working away on several projects."

"Good," George Richards boomed over the receiver. David held the phone away from his ear. "Haven't seen much of you lately. Your mother and I were concerned to know how things are going."

"Well, you know how business is," David waffled. "Early bird gets the worm. Can't slow down."

"Excellent! That's what I like to hear. Certainly can't ever let much slack slip in. Overkill never hurt anyone but the victim." He laughed coarsely. "What do you hear from Edward Crownover these days?"

"Not much." David bit his lip. "I see him about once a week. He seems ready to settle into life in Oklahoma."

"Humph! He needs to go back to England before he croaks, the old frog." George cleared his throat. "Had a bad cold last week, but it's about to go. Son, your mother has something she wants to tell you."

The phone was silent for a moment. David thumped impatiently on the desk with a pencil. "David?" Mary Richards spoke in an elderly high pitch. "How are you, Son?"

"Doing quite well, Mother. And you?"

"Fine. Fine." She chirped. "Been busy as usual. So much to do . . . at the country club I have the spring Beaux Arts Ball to plan . . . you know how demanding life can be."

"Of course."

"Which is exactly what I want to ask you about. I'm sure you will want to be part of the season this spring. And . . . well, I have somebody quite lovely we want you to meet. I was thinking of a little supper this Friday night at our place and . . ."

"Mother," David broke in, "I'm far from ready for that sort of thing. At this time—"

"David, you must get out. Camille Everest ran into me at the club, and I know she would be a delightful diversion for you. She is available Friday and . . ."

"Please," David was firm, "I'm quite capable of handling these matters myself. I am not available Friday."

"David," Mary's voice quivered, "you don't sound like yourself."

"I have a previous social engagement Friday," David lied. "I'll get back to you about any openings on the calendar."

"Oh." His mother's voice trailed away. "Well, here's your father."

"Blast it, Son!" Once again David held the phone away from his ear. "All these women think about is getting you married off again. Hear about it all day long." He cursed. "Listen, Son, how's the sale of the business going? People at the bank haven't heard a thing from you in a while."

"What do you mean 'people at the bank'?" David set the pencil down on his desk.

"You know how talk is around the business community," George fumbled. "Everyone meddles in everyone else's affairs."

"Who is doing the talking?" David asked with the same sternness with which he rejected the Friday night date.

"No one in particular," George prevaricated. "Aren't you about to get the matter settled?"

"Just can't say." David stared at his desk. "Issues have become so complicated it may take another several months. Who knows? The whole thing may yet fall apart."

"Oh, no! I hope not." George's voice lowered in his confidential insider baritone. "Son, we've got to use this springtime to get positioned politically. Why, just last week, the Democratic state chairman buttonholed me. He thinks you're a shoo-in, boy. Just say the word and we're off!"

"We're off?" David mused. "Sounds about right to me."

"What?" George's voice returned to the normal shout. "I don't think I understood you right."

"Dad, thanks for the encouragement. I'm thinking about the matter seriously, but Jack has just come into the room with some urgent business. I'll be back to you."

"Sure, Son. Of course. We're here waiting."

"Naturally. Good-bye, Dad." He hung up before any other response was possible.

David turned uncomfortably in his chair and looked out the window. Time lost significance as he stared into space.

"Another cup of coffee, Mr. Richards?" His secretary's voice startled him.

"Thank you, Mrs. Hammond. But I'll pass." He turned back and looked around his office. His watercolor of a Colorado mountain stream threw the rich colors of sky and water into his face. The cascading creek sprinkled with life and invited him to come right out of his chair and step through the frame. He looked at the picture of Ruth in Susan's place. "I've got to get out of here," he said aloud. "I've come to the end of it."

THIRTEEN

During the weeks following David's agreement with Jack to conclude the sale of the company, their relationship recovered the old warmth. Cordiality returned, and the tense atmosphere faded.

David's weekly sessions with Paul Kendall made his grief more bearable. Edward kept showing up unexpectedly at odd hours with a wide assortment of ideas and suggestions. His conversations with the two men made life and change manageable.

After a long lunch with Uncle Edward, David called California. The two-hour difference guaranteed Ruth should be home during mealtime.

"Hello." Ruth's familiar husky voice sounded blunt and uninviting.

"Mother?" The name slipped out of David's mouth unexpectedly. He hadn't said *that* word before and wasn't sure where the *faux pas* came from. "I mean . . . Ruth. It's me. David."

"Ah, my boy. I wish you were here. Just making a sandwich. I'd share it with you."

"Sorry, I just finished lunch with Uncle Edward. He sends his love."

"He always did," Ruth quipped. "How is the old limey?"

"Quite well. He's been trying to turn several oil deals while he's still in the area."

"Just what that old man needs," Ruth scoffed. "More oil to peddle. Tell him to do volunteer work in a hospital so he can do something useful for a change."

"Don't be cynical," David chided. "Edward and I have a proposal for you."

"Proposal? I don't pay any attention to him, but from you? Ah, that's another matter. Tell me, *mon cher*! What do you have in mind?"

"I want you to come to Oklahoma City to observe the Passover with me."

Silence. Complete silence.

Finally she answered. "You're serious, aren't you?"

"I want you to visit my world. See my house, my studio. My office. You need to know what my lair looks like. You can meet my friends."

"David," she begged, "I have my own closed doors too. The past can't be opened without great personal cost."

"Come now, surely I haven't pushed *you* out of your comfort zone?" David teased. "Sounds like a retreat in California to me."

"Some things are best left alone."

"Is this the advice of the woman who has relentlessly blown the doors off every bastion of privacy I ever had?" David chided humorously. "Surely not." He waited for a response, but when none came he turned more serious. "Perhaps I can't face some of my secrets until you face yours. Could I possibly offer you some encouragement in return for all the support you have given me?"

"Oh, my boy." She sounded very far away. "My dear boy. Of course you are right. But . . . I just don't know."

"I will not push you across any lines you don't wish to cross. You really wouldn't have to do anything you didn't wish. It's just that Passover is coming up," he paused, trying to frame the request more poignantly. "I thought it would be most special for us to celebrate my first Passover, at least in a long time, *together*."

"I have not been to a Seder with a member of my family in decades," Ruth sighed.

"I've studied with the local rabbi." Sensing he was winning the tug of war, David became enthusiastic. "I have a Haggadah and have been learning to pronounce the Hebrew words. We could have the meal in my home. You could cook. What do you think?"

"What can I say?" Ruth groaned.

"Edward can come and . . ."

"Yes, of course!" She sounded exasperated. "We couldn't keep Edward away."

"Pesach is for the family, is it not? Edward would have to be here. I could bring Paul Kendall and possibly my business partner Jack Meachem. Passover is the feast of freedom. What better time for you to come?"

"*Mon chou*! I never planned on any such a thing."

"Then it's decided," David nearly shouted. "You are coming, and the time of Pesach is at hand."

"David—"

"For once I have *you* speechless. Undoubtedly the major accomplishment of my week!" He laughed. "I'll check on airline schedules and call you with some options. See you then."

"David—"

"Bye."

During the weeks that followed, David was completely preoccupied with preparations for the Passover. Jack Meachem was overwhelmed with the prospect of meeting Ruth, and Father Kendall was intrigued. Edward was ecstatic. Ruth's reluctance slowly turned into acquiescence. By the time the night of April 13 arrived, the table was set, the candlesticks in the center, and David wondered if Elijah might even appear. Even a menorah was placed on the serving table.

The doorbell rang once, and David was instantly there. "Ah, Paul! Shalom." Their voices carried down the hall.

"Shalom." The priest followed David into the entryway between the living room and the dining room. His black suit and clerical collar were tailored and stylish. "Shalom aleichem."

"Very good pronunciation!"

"Actually I studied a year of Hebrew in seminary." The

minister looked into the living room where the guests had gathered. "Tonight will be good practice."

"I think you know everyone." David pointed toward the living room. The lights were turned down, and candles were burning around the room. "Jack and Kay Meachem are here. Of course, you know Edward Crownover."

"And where's this mysterious mother of yours?"

"In the kitchen completing the final preparations for the meal."

"Quite a night." The priest winked. "I'll just make myself at home."

Edward Crownover had been listening since the door opened. He had crossed the room and had his hand extended.

"Jolly good!" Edward Crownover slapped the minister on the back. "Been too long since we last talked. Wonderful to see you this evening. Just arrived myself. Actually haven't even seen Ruth yet." He grinned like a naughty schoolboy and wiggled his eyebrows.

"No, no." Paul Kendall waved at the couple at the other end of the long living room. "The Meachems are old acquaintances."

"Quite so." Crownover lowered his voice to a confidential whisper. "Never liked Jack much. Saw him as an opportunist, a leech on David's good graces. While I'm at it, I want to congratulate you on the extraordinary job you've done with Davey. Really pulled him together, you have. Hats off to you, Reverend."

David returned in the entrance with Ruth on his arm. "Look who's here," he called to Edward.

"*Bouleverse?*" Ruth swept into the room with her arms open. "No?" She gave Edward an affectionate hug.

"*Tout à fait!*" He beamed. "But more pleased than I can possibly say."

"And you are the minister David speaks of so fondly?" Ruth offered her hand to Paul Kendall.

"I am deeply honored." Paul kissed her hand.

"What an elegant man." Ruth curtsied slightly.

"And I want you to meet Jack and Kay Meachem." David introduced his friends.

"My pleasure." Ruth shook hands with the couple. "You are David's partner?"

"Yup!" Jack answered. "Sure can't believe I'm meeting you all."

"I think everything is ready." Ruth's "th" sounds betrayed an accent. *Is* sounded more like *ist*. "Shall we go to the dining room and begin?"

Ruth and David led the way, and the guests fell in behind them. Edward sauntered through the hall into the dining room, giving Moses' nose a quick rub.

The strange little group gathered about the Passover supper table like true exiles: a dissipated, remorseful Englishman next to an Episcopal priest at a Jewish festival, a former business partner and sometimes adversary staring at a reluctant Jewess and her long and still lost son. Each nervously looked at the others before the expatriates sat down to the ancient celebration of freedom.

David handed out little books edged in scrolls and flourishes of color. "I have a Haggadah for each of you. The rabbi found a version with both Hebrew and English which will help us follow and read together more easily."

Reverend Kendall quickly thumbed through the pages, pausing here and there to read a Hebrew phrase. Ruth had to show Jack the book was read from the back forward. Kay kept nodding pleasantly while obviously not having the foggiest idea what was happening.

"The men will want to wear a yarmulke." David handed out black skullcaps. "This is normal Jewish custom."

"Looks like a beanie," Jack smirked.

"I will read the part of the father and ask the men to read the children's question," David explained. "I guess we're all a bit out of character." He smiled nervously, and the supporting cast laughed in response.

Everything in the room had David's artistic touch. From the picture on the wall to the large arrangement of spring flowers gracing the center of the table, taste and elegance prevailed. The finest silver and china were carefully placed on the best linen. In the center were two elegant candlesticks. Exquisite handcut Scandinavian crystal was set at every place.

"Ruth is going to light candles," David continued. "She made sure the food is kosher even if we're not."

Once again polite laughter.

David stood up and put his Haggadah on the table. "Tonight is very important for me. Each of you is here because you know something of Ruth's and my story." He became more steady and serious. "I've tried to learn the pronunciation of the Hebrew. I suppose the occasion is both a Passover and bar mitzvah of sorts for me." His voice rose from another place within him. Uncharacteristic display of emotion spilled over. "I seek to touch something I can't quite see. Please forgive my mistakes."

Instant reassurances resounded around the table.

"I am going to wear my grandfather's tal—tal—it? Correct?" He turned to Ruth.

"Tallith." Ruth nodded encouragement.

"My prayer shawl, my tallith, is one of the few items that survived when everything else was destroyed, so I wear it tonight to honor the family I never met."

Picking up the large white cloth with black edging, David reverently draped the shawl over his shoulders. "This mantle is the only connection I have left between me, this Passover, and our past generations. You see, Ruth and I are all that remain."

Ruth's stoic face looked impervious, but her eyes instantly filled. She looked very small, vulnerable, and alone.

Edward bit his lip and looked out the window. He remembered the first time he heard Ruth speak.

"Corporal?" The woman on the telephone sounded urgent but distant. The connection was bad.

"Yes? This is Corporal Crownover. What can I do for you?"

"You said to call. Well, she's awake. Has started to talk, she has."

"Who?" Crownover frowned. "Who in blazes are you talking about?"

"The Jewish woman. I'm the nurse at the hospital. Remember? A month ago you left instructions with the chart to call if she survived. You know—the woman who has been in a coma for nearly five months."

"Yes, of course." The soldier sat up rigidly in his chair. "Most certainly." He pressed the receiver more tightly to his ear.

"You'd best come and see, sir. Yesterday she opened her eyes and looked around the room. Today she's asked for water, she has. I think 'er mind's a-coming back."

"Thank you, nurse. I'll be there at once."

Thirty minutes later, the corporal found Ruth propped up in bed with her eyes closed. The white dividers still isolated her from the rest of the world. He watched for five minutes before stepping behind the partition and sitting down. She stirred.

"Actually, I'm sorry to bother," he spoke cautiously.

Slowly the small woman opened her eyes. Black hair had grown over the side of her head but she still looked disheveled and unkempt. Her naturally dark skin had faded in the dim room. Her eyes were blank and empty.

"How are you?" The Englishman probed.

She said nothing.

"Guten morgen. Sprechen sie Englisch?"

"Ja," her speech was slurred.

"Lassen sie uns dann Englisch sprechen."

The woman nodded.

"Can you say your name? In English?"

"Ruth." She barely exhaled the word. "Moses. Ruth Moses."

"Do you know where you are?"

She shook her head. "In . . . a hospital."

"Have any idea what happened to you?"

"They said—" She stopped and blinked her eyes several times. "There was an explosion—they said—I—I don't remember." Months of immobility had left her frighteningly frail. "My husband? Do you know . . . about my husband?"

"Ah . . . yes! Well you see, unfortunately I suppose I must be the one to tell you. The facts are terribly unfortunate. Your husband was killed in the explosion."

There was no expression, as if she already knew. She looked away in silent resignation.

"I have a child, a baby boy. Where is my baby?"

The corporal stared in sheer terror, shaking his head from side to side.

"My son is dead?" Her voice was faint, as if about to fade forever.

"He is gone."

"He's gone?" she whispered. "Gone?" Her eyes widened in puzzlement and then closed tightly. One thin line of tears ran down her sunken cheek. "Then I, too, shall die."

"Oh, no!" The corporal leaped to his feet. "No, you can't! Heaven help us! We've had enough death. No, I won't let you die!" He grabbed her hand. "I will help you live!" He grasped her hand, hovering over the bed. "Please don't talk like that!"

She turned away, but her hand limply lay in his.

"You shall not die!" He repeated again and again.

Edward looked back at Ruth sitting so vulnerably at the end of the dining room table. He wanted to go around and stand next to her but knew he couldn't. He thought again of that decision he made so firmly in the hospital room. He simply could not leave her alone. Ever.

FOURTEEN

As the evening progressed David moved nervously from person to person, playing the host, like a novice conductor trying to direct an amateur symphony. Sour notes and more than an occasional faux pas punctuated their performance. At one point, Jack Meachem told Ruth he thought she didn't really look like a Jew. Uncle Edward kept trying to impress Paul Kendall with his meager knowledge of the Anglican Communion. The Richardses called in the middle of the meal, wanting to know what David was doing home by himself and letting him know they were more than willing to drop by. David tried valiantly, but his Hebrew pronunciations were painfully halting. Nevertheless the displaced persons society kept playing their parts and marching onward through the Seder.

"*Baruch ata Adonai elohenu.*" David set the Elijah cup down and put the matzo crackers back on the plate, covering them with the white linen napkin. He gave a quick sideward glance at Ruth, seeking reassurance. She kept nodding. "*Baruch atah Adonai elohenu melech ha-olam shehecheyanu v'kiy'manu v'highianu lazman.*" David read laboriously. "Ruth will now recite the prayer over the candles." Paul Kendall smiled broadly, signaling his approval of the reading.

Ruth covered her head and hovered over the candlesticks. In hauntingly lyrical tones, she began to chant the ancient prayer. "*Melech ha-olam asher kidd'shanu b' mitzvotav v'tzivanu l'hadlik ner shel yom tov hazzeh.*" She paused, looked across the table at David and repeated the prayer in English. "Blessed are

— 121 —

You, O Lord our God, King of the universe, who has kept us alive and sustained us and brought us to this season."

As each candle caught fire, shadows highlighted different portions of Ruth's face. Edward watched the mystical mosaic unfold and her wrinkles fade. Ruth's gray hair was once more blue-black, sparkling, and she was the loveliest creature in the world. The candles became singular in a wine bottle flickering against a restaurant wall in the quaint little port of Haifa.

The night smelled of the Mediterranean with a hint of spring flowers exploding everywhere. The nice little waterfront cafe was a million miles from her dirty little kibbutz. The corporal's romantic ploys were with clear design and intent. Good food, intimate talk, and the ocean would hopefully spin the magic web. But Edward knew he was in trouble as soon as he picked Ruth up at the kibbutz. She said virtually nothing during the long ride into Haifa. Romance was not in Ruth's eyes. Something awful was rolling loose in her soul.

"I must say, Eddie, you've been very good to me." She picked at the appetizer. Her natural olive color had returned to her face, giving her a gentle glow. "These past three months have been a daze, but at least I can walk now." She dipped the artichoke into the butter sauce. "I never would have expected a British soldier to have interest in my rehabilitation."

"Mustn't believe the party line. We Brits aren't as bad a lot as you've been told by your taskmasters back at the farm."

"We have good reason for apprehension." She looked at the butter covering the artichoke.

"Come now. A little faith in your fellow man."

Ruth's head snapped as if hit with an invisible hand. Her eyes were hard and cold. "Faith? You must be out of your mind. Faith is the last thing I have. I don't believe in you, England, America, God, much less tomorrow. Give me one reason to trust anybody. To believe in anything!" She tore the appetizer with her teeth.

"Come now!" Edward puckered his lips, bristling his mustache. "You're a Jew. Jews believe in God. Don't they?" He tried to chuckle and sound lighthearted.

"Believing in God never got me anywhere!" She took a big drink from her glass. "Sure, my family was religious enough to keep a kosher kitchen. Once my father even told me he would declare me dead if I married a gentile. Now he's dead and here I am. Want a hunk of dead meat, Eddie? You've certainly pursued me hard enough." She eyed him mockingly.

"Ruth, you know my intentions have been nothing but honorable," he lied. "Have I not been the gentleman?"

"And I don't care if I am dead," she continued as if he had said nothing. "Death is not so hard. Living is the torment."

"Ruth... please... I have no desire but to make you happy."

"Believe? The only thing I have left is my grandfather's tallith. My father gave me the rag just before I left Germany for reassurance. Can you believe it? Absolutely the only thing that remains of my family is a prayer shawl."

Edward nervously reached for a cigarette.

"And we don't even use such things as talliths at the kibbutz. No one at Afikim prays. Never. We know we are our own salvation or there is none." Ruth sneered. "So you think all Jews believe in God? Hah!"

The corporal lit the cigarette and inhaled deeply. "What... I mean... well... I'm trying to say..."

"You want to know what Jews believe today?" Her eyes narrowed as if ready for a fight. "Take that worthless Russian womanizer, for instance. You know, the one who married my friend Shula. He is the new true Jew. He can't even say kiddush. Guts and a few souvenirs from the old people are all that is left."

"Something else?" The waiter slipped up with pencil in hand. He looked tense. Obviously Ruth's voice had carried across the room.

"Look again, my love. We can't be pessimistic before such cuisine. What will it be?"

"Anything is an improvement on the ninety different ways we eat eggplant and tomatoes everyday," she snapped. "You order."

"The fish will be excellent," Edward said in the waiter's direction.

The waiter smiled formally. "Excellent choice." He scribbled on the pad and was gone.

Silence fell between them. Edward watched obliquely, trying not to stare. Earlier he guessed she was pushed to her limits well before the explosion. Life on the kibbutz was exhausting. Up at 5:00 A.M. in the summer, it could be so hot by nine that work would have to stop until the late afternoon. In the worst summers, the sun could become so hot that the fields spontaneously burst into flames. Nutrition was bad, and existence was marginal. The only reprieve was their night life. Living hard produced playing hard. The kibbutz had an unconfirmed reputation for wild parties.

Ruth picked up his pack of cigarettes and lit one from the candle. She held the smoke for an interminable amount of time before blowing a cloud toward the ceiling. "They are all dead, you know. Some new refugees came in last week with new information." Her voice was frank and flat. Ruth seemed to be talking to someone in another place. "My father had been hiding on the Polish frontier when he became homesick for my mother. He tried to return to Leipzig, but they caught him on the train. The SS held him until they arrested the rest of my family. They loaded him, my mother, the others on a train and sent them to a death camp in Poland." Her eyes were empty, her face completely expressionless. "The Nazis obliterated my whole family, *et voila*."

"Heavens! I had no idea. My dear." He reached for her hand. It was lifeless as in the hospital. "I—I—I'm sorry. Let me help." He squeezed her fingers. "I will take care of you. You can move in with me."

Ruth pulled away. "I don't need *that* sort of help." She stiffened. "I can take care of myself."

"I didn't mean anything improper. I didn't." He nervously ran his hand through his hair. "I say, I've never heard anything so bloody horrible."

"You will hear much, much more." Ruth sat back in her

chair and crossed her arms over her chest. Her fingers dug into her arms. "Oh, yes! You and the rest of the world that denied us asylum will hear a great deal more. This time Pharaoh came at us with tanks and machine guns, but there was no pillar of fire to turn the devil back. There was no government to offer shelter . . . in America . . . in Britain." She pointed as if he were personally responsible. "Death is in the air, and you still can't even smell the stench."

"I don't know what you are talking about." Edward gestured nervously. "I've been nothing but your friend."

The waiter slipped alongside the table. "Our best." He smiled artificially, trying to appear unaware of the obvious confrontation unfolding in front of him. "Enjoy." He placed their food on the table and quickly disappeared.

Ruth looked at the plate. The fish was steaming, and the vegetables were colorful and bountiful. Even though she could not have seen such abundance for a long time, Ruth didn't pick up the fork. "My father was a man of considerable learning and intelligence. He found it inconceivable a crazy racist paperhanger could control Germany. He didn't think Hitler would stay in power six months. After the Nazis stole the family fortune, he started to see. Takes a great deal to make some people understand."

"I know nothing of these death camps, you see." Edward stopped and coughed. "Well, there have been rumors of Nazi excesses, but after all, war is always a bloody terrible thing."

"No, I don't see. I don't see at all. Know how my mother survived after the SS stole our bank account? This refined cultured daughter of a well-known rabbi donned a wig and sold corsets door-to-door to survive! She stuffed away a few hidden deutsche marks to buy the British visa that got me out. But even she didn't dream of cattle cars, gas chambers, and crematoriums. Mother didn't see so well either."

"Please eat." The corporal pointed to her plate. "Your food will get cold."

"Let me tell you how I got here." Ruth lit another cigarette. "You probably never heard of Henrietta Szold. Through the women's Hadassah groups in America, she raised the money for us. Even Schoenberg and Einstein were part of Carnegie Hall concerts to raise funds to resettle children like myself. We were sent to Berlin for secret training in survival on the frontier. They taught us how to live on nothing." She puffed rapidly on the cigarette, blowing quick puffs of smoke toward Edward. "One night the Nazis rounded up our people and declared all Polish Jews *nein statten*! I was put on the next train out of Germany. A dirty, leaky Yugoslavian cargo boat brought us to a wharf not far from here. You know about our coming ashore?"

Edward tried to eat without looking at her. "Yes, I know something about the illegal boats trying to land around here."

"Of course you do, Corporal! British Intelligence puts in overtime trying to stop us. Ever see our ragtag band of Hebrews descend on the docks when one of the forbidden ships sails in? We hop around like a hoard of crickets passing out clothes so the wayfarers can be absorbed in the crowd before you catch them."

"Someone has to maintain some law and order." Edward viciously speared the fish. "I'm not responsible for every injustice in this world. Didn't I come to the hospital every day? I've tried to make things right. Haven't I?"

Ruth looked straight into his eyes without flinching, and he tried not to look away but did. Starting at the top of his head, her eyes traced a line down his face to the bottom of his chin. "There must be *some* reason you have been good to me. You are British after all." She pushed the untouched plate away. "I must see things more clearly. I am all that is left. Me. Ruth Eidinger Moses. No husband. No son. No family. I am the only survivor. Alone. All that remains."

Edward jumped.

David offered him the Elijah cup. "Edward, would you place the cup outside in the hallway? We must recite our hope that the Messiah will come soon."

"Yes, of course." Edward reached for the cup. "I'll put it there." He left the silver goblet next to the Moses statue.

David struggled on, reciting Hebrew again.

Edward returned and kept watching Ruth. He found it difficult not to think about the night so long ago in Haifa. He had offered compassion and hoped for romance; she had resisted his advances and offered destiny. For the first time in all his wandering ways, the soldier from Salisbury trudging through a dreary military assignment, he had been caught up in something larger than pleasure and mundane routine. And now here he was decades later, watching the Americanized Jewish baby standing there with his grandfather's tallith hovering over his shoulders.

David continued his explanation. "I will read the modern litany of remembrance in English. No generation has known a catastrophe so vast and tragic."

The group answered from their books. "The blood of the innocent, who perished in the gas chambers of Auschwitz, Buchenwald, Dachau, Majdanek, Treblinka, and Theresienstadt, cries out to God and to man."

"How can we ever forget the burning of synagogues and houses of study?" David continued to read. "The destruction of the holy books and scrolls of the Torah, the sadistic torment and murder of our scholars, sages, and teachers?"

The Meachems were clearly overwhelmed. The minister and Edward looked pained but continued. "In the Warsaw Ghetto, Jews valiantly defied the overwhelming forces of the inhuman tyrant. These martyrs lifted up their voices in a hymn reaffirming their faith in the coming of the Messiah, when justice and peace shall finally be established for all men."

David almost shouted his response, "I believe with a perfect faith in the coming of the Messiah, and though He tarry, nonetheless, do I believe He will come!"

David abruptly stopped, and silence fell across the room. His uncharacteristic display of some other emotion than anger or grief was confounding. Jack looked nervously at his wife, and Edward blinked at the minister. Ruth's eyes fastened on her plate.

"David?" Paul Kendall broke the silence. "Perhaps I might interject a thought or two at this point?"

Clearly relieved, David nodded and sat down.

"David, the *meaning* of this night and these words is the most profound for you and your mother. Yet, as one who believes that the Messiah has come and prays for His coming again, the meaning is no less significant. In a different way, Christians too look forward to a coming day of justice and equity for the whole world. In the meantime, I, for one, want to pledge tonight to do everything possible to maintain dignity and oppose every form and manifestation of prejudice."

"Here, here!" Jack soberly raised his goblet.

"Never again." The priest lifted his glass.

Without a word the rest slowly held their glasses up.

Kay answered. "Our young people sing a song that goes something like . . ." She tried to hum a line. "We will guard each man's dignity, and save each man's pride."

"Everyone has a right to be who they are," David answered.

Edward looked at the bust of Moses in the hallway. The ancient bronze statue seemed to scrutinize everything happening in the dining room. Edward felt under observation.

The Haggadahs were put aside, and the eating began. Ruth brought in a first course of chicken soup with matzo balls. Plates of gefilte fish followed. Jack stared at the stuffed carp placed beside bowls of vegetables. Matzahs were piled high again. She continued until the guests begged for mercy.

"Can anyone cook like my little Ruth?" Edward boasted. "To the best cook in Europe, Israel, and America." He applauded loudly. The group laughed and agreed.

"Time to conclude with the ancient response," David said, "next year in Jerusalem!"

Paul Kendall responded. "Next year in Jerusalem."

"Indeed!" David looked at his mother. "It shall be so. I have a little announcement to make." David smiled and looked at each person thoughtfully. "Please keep my secret for the time being, but I did want you to know on this night. I will be leaving for Israel shortly. I don't know how long I will be gone." He turned to his mother. "I'm hoping Ruth will join me. Maybe you too, Edward?"

"Smashing!" The Englishman cheered. "Of course, a family reunion in Haifa."

"For how long?" Jack asked.

"I don't know." David shook his head. "I just don't know. I guess . . . for as long as it takes."

FIFTEEN

David stirred and tried to cover his eyes. Spring sunlight burst through his bedroom window, leaving him no place to hide. He rubbed his eyes and sat up in bed. Last night's Passover felt like a fantasy, an episode from some other lifetime. And yet he knew he had crossed a bridge. The light felt good.

The evening celebration had filled David's dreams with strange images. He covered his eyes and tried to recall each shape. Something in his psyche had slipped into place even though his recollection made him feel remotely disconnected. David slowly replayed the Seder in his mind and once more an awareness of something deep and of great significance was evoked.

He tried to see the "other David," the one walking behind the hidden inner door. No one appeared, but he was aware of how rich and immediate his feelings were. He felt a freedom beyond anything he could remember, even though the terrain felt uncertain and amorphous, like trying to walk on a cloud. Yet he was keenly aware of what he needed. At least the lock had been broken off the door, and nothing but time kept him from entering.

A sudden urge to create pushed through his reflections. Energy spilled over, and his hands tingled. David knew he had to get his fingers into the clay. Something within was trying to emerge, insisting on the moment at hand like a woman whose term is full in a pregnancy that will no longer wait.

Putting on a dirty sweatshirt and pants, David didn't shower or even comb his hair. He slipped down the hall to avoid waking his mother. He paused only to scribble a note, explaining he was out in the studio. Edward was coming by midmorning to take Ruth for brunch, leaving plenty of time to work before they returned. He grabbed a bagel from the refrigerator and swigged down orange juice straight from the carton, remembering how much Susan disliked his drinking from the container. On this morning the memory didn't make him sad anymore.

Once the wad of clay was centered on the vat, David lost himself in the whirl of the wheel as his hands blended with spinning earth, water, and the moment. A wall of mud rose magically between his fingers and a cylindrical form spun upward. He relaxed, allowing the form to take its own life and shape.

Centering is everything, he thought as the wet kaolin oozed between his fingers. *In life, in art, you have to find the center, live at the center, exist out of the center. If not, the tension is too great and everything falls in.* He sat up to relieve the muscle cramp in his back. *Unless the center holds, nothing maintains the circumference. The center must be exact and secure or everything slides into disaster.*

The hours dissolved like a morning mist burning away while David floated with whatever came from within. Restoration and reconstruction worked within him as well as on the potter's wheel.

"Davey?" Edward's disembodied voice drifted in from the backyard. "Still out there?"

David looked up at the old clock on the wall. Magically the hands had raced forward to two o'clock. "Sure. Come in."

The door opened, and Edward stepped in. He was wearing one of his English tweed sports jackets over a gray sweater. His paunch pushed the sweater well in front of the coat. "Ah, my boy! I told Ruth you'd be out here. Saw your note. She's in her room tidying up a bit."

"Enjoy your brunch? Where'd you go?" David let the wheel slow down and began wringing the clay from his fingers.

"Smashing time!" Edward dusted off the top of a stool and plopped down. "We went to the country club." He puckered his mustache and grinned. "Of course, I had to use your father's membership to get in. Fortunately I still remember the number." The Englishman winked.

"Quite an experience last night." David started washing his hands under the faucet. "I hope everything met your expectations."

"Enchanted time, it was. Certainly took me down memory lane."

David smiled. "Last night, I noticed you watching her. You've got quite a thing about my dear old mother, Edward."

He tilted his head and arched his bushy eyebrows. "Frightfully so. No denying it. I suppose just being with Ruth occasionally makes the rest of my drabness bearable."

David washed his hands and looked out the window as if more interested in the plant stalks and residue of winter than in what he was about to say. "You know," he tried to sound casual, "you've never said much about why it didn't work out between the two of you. Give me some clues."

"I tried to make it happen!" He shook his finger in the air. "Heaven knows I tried." His voice dropped. "Even came close. Very close. Guess it just wasn't to be." He folded his arms over his protruding stomach. "I suppose the details have become dim in my feeble mind. I'm am old man, you know."

"You're old like a fox gets hard of hearing." David started drying his hands on an old dirty piece of a towel. "Don't kid an old kidder. For years I've watched your eyes every time a sweet young thing goes through the room. You're an incorrigible but lovable old conglomeration of lechery, larceny, and sentimentality. Now fess up and tell the real story." David smiled wryly.

Edward stood, walked to the door, and looked toward the house. "Never in me life ever met anyone quite like 'er." He seemed to be talking more to himself than David. "What a woman." The old man turned slowly back. "Yes, you want just the facts. After Ruth fully recovered she joined the British Army to help kill Nazis. Shocked the pants off her comrades at the kibbutz. They blamed it all on me, you see."

"Oh, I *do* see, Uncle Edward."

"No, nothing like you're thinking. She joined purely because of the possibility of getting at the Krauts. Truth was, I knew all along about Ruth's goings-on back at the farm. Had access to intelligence reports, I did. Facts were all there in her file. She'd been in the Hagganah and was quite good with a pistol. Ruth even knew Morse code. When our soldiers raided the kibbutz for weapons, she'd sit on the hills and alert the surrounding communes. Absolutely fearless."

"With such a record, how'd they ever let her in your army?"

Edward waved his hand in the air aimlessly. "Tough times. Scarcity of people. We needed women like her." He lowered his hand as if he were writing invisibly in the air. "I also altered her file and retyped some of the findings." He winked. "Never told anyone that story before. I finally got her shipped over to Ben Gaza to do hospital work."

"You made sure Ruth was just close enough to continue your pursuit. Very clever, Uncle."

"Not clever enough. Ben Gaza was where the big trouble began. Now that Ruth was military personnel she had access to records. One morning she was sent to Haifa to pick up some patients. On a hunch she looked up her own files. Of course everything had been destroyed except for the admission form. An unfortunate notation indicated a baby had been admitted without injury." He breathed in deeply and exhaled fully. "The signature at the bottom was mine."

David covered his face with both hands. "Oh no!"

"I pleaded. I promised. I talked. I tried to put matters into perspective, but the possibility of any future romance was dead. With my signature I signed my own death warrant."

"What kept the relationship from ending right there?"

"You, David." Edward chuckled. "Quite ironic. Hadn't been for you, my boy, Ruth would have disappeared into the desert that afternoon she found the forms with my name. But we made a pact . . . struck a bargain. I promised to be a liaison to the baby. If she'd keep in touch with me, I'd keep her up on your progress. With great hopes in mind, I launched out to do business with Richards Petrol and made sure Ruth had my permanent address in Salisbury. And from there the decades unfolded."

David ran his hand down the side of the wet clay pot sitting on the wheel. "Never in my life have I heard anything quite like it."

"The war ended, and I kept making oil deals. The Richards family thought I was wonderful, and Ruth barely tolerated me. David grew up, and we grew old."

David scanned his tutelary friend. Edward looked old and tired. His face sagged as if weighted down with disappointment. "Ruth obviously has a great deal of affection for you. She banters and jabs, but I can tell she cares deeply."

"Time has mellowed and worked its way." Edward's eyes looked unusually large and watery. "I've always loved her, and I know, in her own way, she's come to care for me. Care? Indeed, that's the right word. Yes, cares a great deal, I do think. But her trip into the hospital file room ended any journey we might have made together through life."

"What's ahead now?" David wrapped cellophane around the clay vase. "What's your next move?"

"I am going to leave about the same time Ruth goes back to California. I'd rather be on my way out of the area when you let the Richardses in on your big family secret and tell them about your trip to Israel."

"What a hero." David laughed. "Getting out of town before the big shootout at the corral. Don't worry, I don't think we're going to have any wars to speak of, and I'll make sure your back is covered."

"Have no doubt of your intentions, but I've been here long enough." He paused and smiled. "You're doing much better, Davey. Perhaps, you don't see it, but I can tell the difference. You've come a great distance since that frozen day when I arrived here from England."

"Thank you, Uncle Edward." David glanced up at the clock again. "You've saved my life . . . again." He set the vat and the wet pot to one side. "I've got to talk with Reverend Kendall shortly. Guess I better hurry in and get cleaned up. I'll see you and Ruth for supper tonight."

" 'Tis done. I'll be in the house later."

David walked out but paused halfway across the yard and looked back. The old Englishman sat in the shadows by himself, staring out into the field behind the studio. For the first time David realized how alone Edward truly was. Born in the shelter of the great Salisbury Cathedral, Edward's life had full measure of adventure, drama, history. And yet in these twilight years, the glory was fading fast and he was all that remained.

David's session in Paul Kendall's office moved quickly to the ongoing issues they discussed each week. Little time was wasted in small talk.

"And why were you able to *feel* the meaning of what you read from the Haggadah last night?" The priest's voice took on his quiet, psychiatric sound.

"For the first time in my life I felt like I truly had a history," David answered. "I wasn't a displaced person dropped into the great Southwest. I was in continuity with the fathers of my fathers. I felt very whole."

"What does 'whole' feel like?" Paul Kendall rubbed the gold crucifix around his neck.

David looked away, unable to answer. "I . . . I . . . I don't know what to say. I suppose my identity has always been more like a great black hole. Every attempt at meaning tends to get sucked into that vast emptiness and disappears." He rubbed his temples. "I think the discovery of Jewishness has plugged the gap. I feel like a wall has been constructed. I have a place against which I can bounce my thoughts and measure my person-hood."

"You identified with the Jewish race last night," the minister observed.

"I think so," David mused. "It certainly felt natural enough."

"I can still see your face as you read of the burning of synagogues and the murder of sages and teachers," Paul continued. "You changed. You were no longer reciting a ritual. You looked like a haunted person. When we said back 'Buchenwald, Dachau, Auschwitz,' you flinched slightly with each place. Did you know?"

David shook his head.

"It's true. Last night you claimed a part of you that was displaced a very long time ago. You didn't notice because you weren't acting or putting on a costume. You had stepped into your own skin."

"That's progress." David hedged. "Isn't it?"

"Significant accomplishment," the priest beamed. "Excellent."

David waved both arms toward heaven like he'd seen Tevya do in *Fiddler on the Roof*. "Now I have another problem."

"Shoot."

"People of Christian faith were among the German persecutors of Jews, were they not?"

"It's a mixed bag." The minister reached for a book on his library shelf. "Unquestionably people who held Christian faith not only acquiesced but participated in the Holocaust. On the other hand, here's a book about some of our heroes." He handed him a copy of *The Pastor's Barracks*. "Ten percent of all prisoners in Dachau were Christian clergy. One third of all Roman Catholic priests in Poland died there."

"No one's told me their story!"

"Read the book. You will be surprised. *The Hiding Place* is a similar story."

David looked at the cover. "But why have Christians and Jews had this running battle for centuries? I'm appalled."

"Most of us are," the minister agreed. "We grieved over the struggle. But I don't think the problem has much to do with being Christian or Jewish. It's a human problem born of arrogance and intolerance; the sin is one of self-righteousness and spiritual pride."

"How so?" David put the book on the coffee table.

"We all forget we have a blind place, a shadow side. In religious disagreement our ignorance can become quite lethal.

In the name of love, people start killing each other. Nothing's more vicious than a church fight, especially when both sides claim to have a corner on God's will."

"But the story of Christian and Jewish antagonism is particularly appalling."

"Certainly. Yet is it any different from what happened in the Civil War? Northerners killed to liberate black slaves while practicing child labor, which was every bit as inhumane. Was one side more right than the other? Here's a real tough one to ponder. Homeless Jews invaded Israel after 1945 and took away the residences of many Palestinians, herding them into refugee settlement camps near the Dead Sea. You might have thought the dispossessed would have been more sensitive. Most of those natives were Christian Palestinians."

"I see." David muttered. "No, I really don't see. The whole issue is becoming very complicated."

Paul nodded. "Life is complicated. Most things aren't as simple as they first appear."

David held up one finger. "I have a final question. Since I talked with Rabbi Berkowitz I've been haunted by the question of eternal destiny. I didn't think much about heaven until Susan died. After that I haven't let myself explore the subject. The idea of separation has been too painful to touch. But I look at my mother, think about my observant Jewish grandparents, and consider how good a man Berkowitz obviously is. Well, I don't know any other way to say it. Do Christians believe they are all going to hell?"

"Depends on who you talk to, David. Yes, some Christian groups think no one's going to heaven but them. And John's Gospel does record Jesus saying, 'No one comes to the Father but by me.' "

David moved to the edge of his chair. "So? What's your answer?"

"My answer isn't important. What counts is your conclusion." The minister settled back. "I don't want to give you my answer or an easy solution. The question is too important for the sake of your own identity; you must not accept uncritically what I or anyone else tells you. Sorry, I think this issue may be your next major life problem to solve."

David rolled his eyes in exasperation. "At least give me some clues, some alternatives."

"Sure," Paul Kendall's voice changed and became professional. "You must realize this has been a problem since the beginning of the Christian era. In fact, it separated Jewish believers in Jesus from the other traditionalists. Generally the answers have fallen into about three broad categories." The minister held up one finger. "Some groups condemn all Jews to perdition. Just that simple."

David crossed his arms over his chest and nodded.

"Other groups believe in a dual covenant theology. They believe an agreement was made for all Jews through Abraham, and this contract is in effect for all eternity. A new covenant was made for the gentile world through Jesus Christ. Gentile and Jew are covered under different terms. After all, both groups believe in the same God. Got it?"

"I think so." David answered thoughtfully.

"Other theologians teach the issue is not so much what is believed but what is practiced. Jew and gentile alike will be judged by how well they followed their consciences. Each can only follow the light they have received. Jews are not condemned for what they don't understand or cannot accept because of historical circumstances. The real judgment will come according to how faithfully they have practiced with integrity what they believe in their hearts to be true." Paul shifted back into a more conversational voice. "How's that for further complication?"

"You certainly put it all out there on the table." David frowned. "And now you want me to single-handedly answer the question that you theologians haven't settled for two thousand years? Some assignment!"

Paul grinned. "Never said it would be easy, David. But I can guarantee the quest will be very profitable."

"At least help me with this one." David beckoned with his hands. "The rabbi said the issue isn't whether one sees Jesus as the Jewish Messiah as much as believing Him to be God. Berkowitz's distinction left me speechless. What do we believe?"

The minister laughed. "No, no, my friend. The issue isn't what *we* believe. The question is what *you* believe. The rabbi has framed for you the pivotal issue. Was Jesus the fulfillment of Jewish hopes or is He as the book of Acts states, *Xristos o' Kurios,* Christ the Lord? Again you must decide. You and you alone."

"Paul . . ." David begged. "Don't play a game with me."

"No game!" The minister ignored David's consternation. "You are forty-five years old seeking to understand the truth about yourself. You've been around the church most of your life. You must find your way through the question just as you have worked to discover the truth about your past. Perhaps your trip to Israel becomes even more significant in this light."

"You're the priest!" David charged angrily. "You're supposed to tell me what the truth is."

"Ordinarily I would jump at the opportunity to proclaim to someone what I believe is true." Paul's voice was soft and gentle. "Your situation is different. You've heard the preaching many times. Today you became a pilgrim. The best I can do is walk with you, point out sights along the way. I'll always be here as your friend, a guide, but I must not rob you of a verdict you alone must render and a discovery you have to make for yourself."

David groaned and looked away. After several minutes he slowly stood. "I feel very agitated, and I'm sure you'd tell me that's good. That makes me ever more angry!"

"What else do you feel?" Paul insisted. "Think about it. What do you want to do right now?"

David puzzled. "I don't know." He shook his head and almost started toward the door. "I guess . . . I wish . . . I could talk to Susan."

"And that is why you must decide for yourself."

SIXTEEN

Ruth carefully folded and tucked her light blue dress into her suitcase. David watched her pack. The guest room was taking on its usual unused look. Ruth placed her airplane ticket in her purse and strapped the bag shut. A teapot and a half-filled cup sat on the bedside table.

"The room's ready for Edward to move back in next time he comes." Ruth glanced at his dressing gown and slippers in the closet. "I'm sure he gets quite sentimental about sleeping here. He gets sentimental about *everything* else."

"I doubt if he ever stays in the room again." David poured tea into the two teacups. "I plan to put the house up for sale when I leave for Israel. If it doesn't sell I'll decide later." He took a slow sip from his cup. "The Earl Grey tea Edward brought from England is particularly good this year."

Ruth looked around the room and at the picture of the English pub. "You have many memories attached to these walls." She smiled. "But, you are right. Inevitably there comes a time to move on. Some places have to be left behind."

"Did you ever go back?" David asked. "Back to Leipzig after the war was over?"

"Yes." Ruth sounded pensive. "Ten years after the war, I returned. Of course, Leipzig was in East Germany, and the Communists controlled everything." She sat down on the bed and drank from her teacup again. "I was concerned the Communists might try to detain me, but fortunately I had no trouble. Apparently they had lost all record that I was ever a citizen of Germany. I sneaked in. I slipped out. That simple."

"Hmmm." David tried to sound casual but didn't. "What did you see? Tell me what you learned."

Ruth looked at the fragile Wedgwood teacup. Obviously a woman had purchased the lovely little piece of china. "I learned if one keeps looking back she eventually turns into a pillar of salt. Just as all rivers run down to the sea, life goes on. We must go with the flow."

David nodded his head. "Yes. But what did you see? What was left?"

"Everything and nothing." She smelled the aroma of the tea. "Most of the bricks were still in the same place they had been for centuries, but the city was in bad shape. Citizens paid their taxes, and the Russians simply put the money in their pockets. The Communists did absolutely nothing to restore or refurbish the city after the war. Streets looked like time had stopped the day the Soviets took over. Tragically little remained of our way of life."

David drank again and looked as if he were trying to frame a question.

Ruth watched him. "You want to ask me how it all felt? Did it make me sad?" She patted his hand. "You don't want to hurt my feelings, but you want to know what this place of your grandfathers was like."

"Well," David muttered. "Anything you can tell me . . ."

"Of course." Ruth smiled. "I understand. I came prepared to share this memory . . . as painful as it is." She put the cup back on the table. "I was able to contact a childhood friend, Hilda Bebel, to meet me. Even though Hilda's father was in the army and a member of the Nazi party, she was still my friend and very sympathetic with our plight. She tried to help. Hilda watched when everyone was deported."

"How did you get to the city?"

"By train." For a moment Ruth saw the train she left on as a teenager. An older woman was standing by the side of the car beckoning her to join quickly the twenty-eight youths bound for Berlin. The group sat in their seats like statues. The heavyset woman hurried her onto the train, barking in her ear that delay was dangerous. Ruth had quickly complied, tossing her single bag on the overhead rack. When she turned to go back and say her final good-byes, the woman blocked the door insisting no one could get off the train. She had desperately tried to open a window to touch her sister and parents but couldn't. The family didn't realize Ruth couldn't come back for final good-byes. They watched helplessly as the train pulled away from the station. She never saw them again.

"You say you came by train?" David broke the silence.

"Oh, yes!" Ruth blinked several times. "I came in from Frankfurt about five hours away. The *Hauptbahnhof*, the train station, was the one building which had been completely rebuilt. I suppose it was bombed in the war. I walked up and down the tracks trying to remember exactly how it was, but everything had changed. My visit got off to a painful start. Hilda arrived shortly, and we walked into the town."

"Leipzig's big, lots of people?"

"Probably 750,000 people," Ruth explained. "Leipzig was always a great center of culture and world trade. People were everywhere, scurrying off to their jobs." She laughed. "Work? Hah! The Communists made work a joke. No one made much money, and no one did much work! There was hardly a telephone in the whole city. What a mess the Russians made of everything."

"You and your friend walked back to the old familiar haunts?"

"Haunts? A very good word." Ruth smiled weakly. She once more felt people brushing past as she walked from the Hauptbahnhof down the Platz der Republik. For nearly a decade she hadn't heard German, and the words hurt her ears. She thought Germans bit off their words like animals tearing at meat. "Of course, the language came back to me, and we spoke in German."

"Did that bother you?"

"No, of course not." Ruth snapped. "We must not let ourselves succumb to the base emotions of our persecutors." She took another sip of tea. "At least one must struggle to keep the negative in proper perspective. Let's see, where was I?"

"Hilda was taking you through the city."

"Yes. We walked down the platz toward the Jewish cemetery. Our path took us by the place where they herded all Jews before deportation. Hilda pointed out a ditch down in the valley near the river. She told me the local citizens threw rocks at our people while they waited for transportation. The last time she saw my father and mother, they were standing down there by the river. I looked and simply walked on."

"To the cemetery?" David asked.

"Of course all of the Eidingers died in the camps. But my other grandparents and ancestors were buried in Leipzig." She said factually. "I put flowers on my grandparents' graves, and we went on. I wanted to find my old house."

"Was it difficult?"

"No. Just as I did as a child I looked for our family synagogue and knew the right street was very close."

"The synagogue was still there?" David pushed his cup and saucer aside.

"Oh, no. The building was burned during the *Kristal Nacht*, the night of broken glass when the Nazis attacked Jewish businesses all over Germany. There was only a stone monument left to mark the site. We stopped, but I didn't want to stay long. I wanted to find my house."

Ruth stopped. Memory pushed her words aside. She could see two little girls walking down the Katharinenstrasse. Multicolored, tall, baroque-style buildings loomed above her eight-year-old eyes. The huge gray stone image of the Thomaskirche seemed again to be the biggest church in the world. In the back was the cemetery with Johann Sebastian Bach's grave. His statue was so austere and massive Ruth covered her eyes when she passed.

"We lived on Gustof-Adolph-Strahse in number 34." She began again. "I was surprised when we found the steps up to the great wooden door. The entry was the same, but the house seemed so much smaller to me. But it was still a three-story structure."

"It's always that way." David smiled. "Strange isn't it, the tricks our minds play."

"Many people lived there now," Ruth sighed. "All the rooms had been let out for tenant apartments. Hilda wanted to go in and see if someone would let us look in the place where my bedroom had been, but I couldn't stand to go any farther. I became so overwhelmed I had to walk away. I couldn't stand to see people living in my house stolen by the Third Reich. Some doors can't be opened."

"Didn't you ever go in?"

"You think I'm very strong, David." Ruth's face dropped. "I'm not strong at all. I want to run and hide all the time, but life gives me no choice but to go on. I must make my confession. Inside I've always felt soft and so terribly vulnerable. Whatever I am, I became in spite of myself. That afternoon I *had* to walk away. I could not stand to go back into rooms where only the family ghosts lived. My life was too empty to walk alone into such an abyss. That afternoon would have swallowed me if I had not known that you still existed somewhere in the world. I simply couldn't stand to look in like some tourist and observe that nothing remained of my past."

David reached out and took her hand.

Ruth cleared her throat. "I had been told that family records were still kept in the synagogue on Keilstrasse. Fortunately, that building fared better than our synagogue. Still a beautiful place."

"Was anyone there?"

She nodded her head. "Yes. The *shamash*, the caretaker, was cleaning up, and he knew about special files hidden in the basement. We went down to a dark room in a remote corner of the cellar. The place was damp and smelled bad, but he found an old wooden cabinet maintained by the Jewish Federation. The *shamash* knew exactly where to look. Everything was alphabetical and in good order. The federation had kept careful records of what happened up to the moment the last official was taken away."

Ruth opened her purse and found a little black notebook and took out several yellowing pieces of paper. She unfolded the heavily creased forms and handed them to David. "I thought my visit might come up, so I brought a copy of the forms with me. Here is what the *shamash* gave me." David looked, trying to decipher the German.

Ruth explained, "The bold letters across the top read, 'Israelitische Religionsgemeinde zu Leipzig,' the Jewish Federation of Leipzig." She pointed to the small print. "There is my mother's name, Rebbeka Rive Eidinger, born November 16, 1884. Rive is a Yiddish name." Ruth put two other papers on top. "This form is for my sister, Margit, and the other is my father's certificate. David Israel Eidinger." She read, "Born July 7, 1885."

David ran his fingers slowly over the smudged forms, looking at each one from several different angles.

"Notice what is written on the bottom?" Ruth underlined with her finger. "The dates are all the same. 21-1-42; the day of deportation. Only at that moment did I fully understand. My family had disappeared over two years before I even knew they were gone. The report had come to me more as a rumor than a fact. Somewhere in the back of my mind, I thought maybe it would all prove to be a mistake, but that afternoon the charade was over. I fully closed the door and all hope for them died." She took a deep breath. "I sat down on the floor and wept for a long time. Finally Hilda and the *shamash* helped me climb back up the stairs. I slumped down on one of the synagogue desks and lay my head on the wooden top."

After a small but awkward pause, Ruth continued. "At the front was a very large golden Star of David and beautiful red velvet drapes above the ark. On each side were two great golden menorahs. I stared for a long time before I realized that the people of Israel did remain, even in Leipzig. The Holy One had preserved our people in the face of such a great loss. He had not abandoned us. Like Moses in the wilderness, I had to go on, but I was not really alone. I was part of a people. We still traveled together. Your father Yaacov believed in our people, and now I must do the same." She took the registration forms back and looked at them with great tenderness. "So strange. These little pieces of paper are all that remains to prove David and Rebbeka Eidinger and their daughter Margit lived. But they did. After that afternoon I put my hopes in the destiny of our people. Our family lives on in us." She put the papers back in the black book and dropped it into her purse.

David rubbed his temples but didn't speak.

"Have you guessed the other secret I found on this trip?"

David looked puzzled. "No," he said slowly. "I don't understand."

"You wanted to know about my special picture." She smiled slyly. "You know the Courbet, *The Stone Breakers* picture that disappeared from Dresden?"

"Of course!" David exclaimed. "That picture might well be priceless."

Ruth stood up and put her purse on the table. "Who'd ever believe a poor old woman would have such a treasure? It's quite safe with me. No burglar would trouble with what must surely be a cheap fake." She laughed. "Really, I never worry about the picture. You want to know where I got it?"

"Certainly."

"Hilda was as devastated as I was by our trip through Leipzig. She was quite grief-stricken by what they had done to me and rightly guessed I had nothing left to my name. She kept wringing her hands and lamenting. She said over and over, 'I must do something for you.' When I got on the train, she pressed a long, round bundle into my arms. She said simply, 'My father stole it from the state. Now it can serve a good purpose.' With that Hilda disappeared back into the crowd, and I never saw her again. When I unrolled the bundle I discovered it was a canvas taken off the frame and rolled up to protect the canvas. In time I realized she had in effect bequeathed me a fortune."

"I'm speechless." David settled down in his chair. "Just speechless!"

"Then, perhaps it is time for me to let you talk." Ruth's eyes twinkled for the first time, and the sadness slipped away. "Now I have a question for you, my boy. What have you learned from my story? What have you learned about yourself during these last few days?"

"I thought about this amazing odyssey last night," David answered. "Instead of reading, I wrote in a journal Paul Kendall gave me some time ago. I made a time line of my experiences since I met you and what I have discovered from each of these junctures. I was surprised." He shifted in the chair and scratched his head. He looked at the mirror above the dresser. "I'm not sure I can state it simply. Possibly I don't even understand, but a door has opened, a part of me has come forth. You told me if I opened my eyes, then my ears would hear and finally my heart would be free. The hidden David has stepped out. Being with you has been like standing in front of a mirror, showing me what I can't see. Your voice made me hear." He struggled to find the right words. "Really quite different though." He paused and chewed at his lip. "You see . . . in the past I've been sort of a reflection of those around me, a pale reflection. I was their mirror imitating life. Being with you created something of a different order. Rather than being a copy, I am becoming an original."

"*Oi vey!*" Ruth applauded. "My son, you have done very well. I think you are finding your way home even as I did in Leipzig. And what does this original masterpiece that is you really look like?"

"Perhaps I am still unrolling this bundled-up canvas you brought to me," David answered. "I don't think the picture is yet ready for display, but some of the sketch is clear. Like Moses striking out into the desert with one foot still in Egypt, I am a man astride two worlds. What seemed hollow, void, formless, and with little value has turned out to be filled with profound possibilities. My empty little world has turned into a treasure chest, but the journey is far from done. The work of integration remains. Many pieces must still come together."

Ruth hugged him tightly and kissed him on the cheek. "You will get there. I have no doubt that you will."

SEVENTEEN

The phone in David's den rang twice. David looked at his watch and knew he had only two hours left before he took his mother and Edward for their final supper together.

"Hello," David answered.

"David! This is your father. Your mother and I want to talk to you at once!"

David held the receiver away from his ear. "What . . . what's wrong?"

"We are extremely upset. Your mother and I are on our way over to your house."

David glanced at Ruth walking down the hall with a dress in her hand. "No, no. That won't be necessary . . . a . . . actually . . . I was just going out the door. I'll drop by your house on my way . . . to . . . the . . . store."

"Then we'll be expecting you immediately!" George Richards slammed the phone down so abruptly David jumped.

"What in the world?" David slowly put the receiver down. *I wonder if telling them I'm not running for any public office whatsoever has just now sunk in.* He reached for a sweater and hurried toward the door. *Sure don't want them over here.* He grabbed his car keys and called over his shoulder. "Be back in a minute, Ruth. Shouldn't take long."

In fifteen minutes David pulled through the gate in front of the Richards estate. He left his car parked before the large front door and walked in without knocking.

"Yoo-hoo!" David called out. "Anyone here?"

"In the drawing room." George's voice echoed down the hall. "Come back here."

David walked in hesitantly. "Came over immediately. What's going on?"

Mary Richards sat on the edge of the couch, her hands folded tightly over her lap, clutching a handkerchief, her lips set in grim resolution. She was wearing a black suit with a high-necked ruffled blouse. George stood at the french doors looking out over the backyard gardens. The silk cravat beneath his tailored white shirt and checkered sport coat added to his naturally elegant appearance. No one moved.

"What's happened?" David stopped. "Has someone died?"

"You tell us?" George turned slowly from the window. His eyes were cold. "We need a *full* explanation."

"Of what?" David slipped down in a plaid wingback chair.

"Don't toy with us," Mary's voice cracked. "We know what's going on at your house."

"And who is staying there!" George added. "I know Edward Crownover is behind it all!"

"Wait!" David held up his hand. "Just wait a minute. What are you talking about? Let's get specific."

"Took some doing to put the pieces together." George pointed his finger at his son. "Of course, we couldn't get anything out of Father Kendall, but I put the screws on Jack Meachem and he told me enough."

"We even talked to the housecleaner and she told us an older woman was staying with you." Mary sniffed and looked away. "Didn't take much to figure out it had to be *that* woman."

"What woman?" David's face began turning red. "What do you mean 'you've put the pieces together'?"

"Blue blazes!" George nearly shouted. "I knew something bizarre was afoot when you turned down the crack at the governor's office! Just couldn't put my finger on what was wrong. Now the whole thing makes sense!"

"And the woman is a *Jew!*" Mary dabbed at the corners of her eyes.

"Stop it!" David pounded on the chair. "Do you have any

idea what you're implying about me? I'm not about to stand here and put up with any anti-Semitic remarks, regardless of the reason. Now cut out this nonsense and shoot straight."

"You have no idea how much money I pumped into local candidates and the state party to make sure you got the nomination," George Richards began talking rapidly. "You are throwing away the opportunity of a lifetime!"

"Your father and I spent our entire lives planting stepping-stones for you to get to the top." Mary wrung her hands. "Everything we've done has been for your best interests. Now you're turning your back on us for some ... some ... stray alley cat out of the past."

"What did you say?" David slid to the edge of his chair. He gritted his teeth.

"The instant I heard of this crazy trip to Israel I had a strong notion of what was afoot." George began pacing between David and his mother. "Several months ago I ran into Saul Silverstein at the country club. He told me he'd seen you at the synagogue and wondered what you were doing there."

"Silverstein?" David puzzled.

"You don't know him," George shot back, "but we've done a few oil deals together. Silverstein said the rumor was you were telling people you had a Jewish mother."

"Oh, the humility of it all." Mary closed her eyes tightly and threw her head back. "To think you were telling people you had *another* mother."

"I've always known I came from somewhere else," David growled. "No secret there. You just never were honest enough to tell me all of the facts."

"Honest!" George exploded. "After all of these years you've lived off of my money, my bailing you out, my bankrolling your projects, my—"

"Stop it!" David shouted. "If you're worried about money, I'll pay you back every dime you threw at the politicians. Moreover, I've paid back every debt I ever owed to you. Don't you dare wiggle money under my nose." He abruptly stood up and shook his fist in his father's face.

"Please." Mary pulled at George's coat. "Money isn't the issue. David's betrayal is what is killing us."

"*Betrayal?*" David shrieked.

"You've set us aside for some woman you don't even know." Mary began to cry.

George crammed both hands in his pockets and turned his back.

David slowly sank back down in the wingback chair. "This is just really *too* much," he answered in disgust. "Too much to believe."

"We took you in," Mary stopped and sniffed, "when there was no one else to—"

"I know the whole story," David cut her off. "I know the details from top to bottom. You bought me like one picks up a prize dog at the kennels. Furthermore you probably took me illegally out of the country of Israel. So don't give me any sob stories about taking in the destitute waif that . . . that . . . ."

George Richards started to shake. He put his hands over his eyes and dropped down beside his wife. Mary reached over and took her husband's other hand. The Richardses leaned together and wept.

David stared at his father and mother, waiting for another response.

George finally pulled out a handkerchief and wiped his eyes. "Edward Crownover's told you this story, hasn't he?"

"Uncle Edward doesn't have anything to do with it," David lied. "I'm the one who went to California and made the contact. I have a right to know about my past."

"You're not a Jew!" Mary lashed out. "You're our son. We've raised you as a good Christian American. I'm not about to stand by and let someone confuse you with nonsense about a past that is long since dead and gone."

"The past is never dead," David answered resolutely. "Whether we are fully aware or not, we are shaped by what happened. Everyone has a right to know what formed them."

George shook his head. "We always feared this day might come. Just didn't really think it would."

Mary began to cry again.

"All we've ever wanted is what was best for you," George added.

"And those intentions were always wound together like rope strands with what was best for *you*," David added.

"I can't believe you would say such a thing to us." Mary wrung her hands. "After all we have done."

"I think this conversation has already gone too far." David stood up. "I don't intend to let you talk to me in such a demeaning manner ever again. Through the years I've put up with this humiliation too many times."

George looked up abruptly. "What on earth are you talking about? I don't understand what you're accusing *us* of doing to you."

David studied the old man's face. He obviously didn't comprehend.

"We've invested our whole lives in raising you," George continued. "You were our dream, our hope, our hobby . . . everything."

"We don't have anyone left but you." His mother's voice crackled. The whining accusative sound David detested faded. "Without you we're just lonely old people." Mary sounded desperate and afraid. "We need you." Her voice trailed away.

George stared at the floor. "You're the only family we have." His anger had turned to hurt. "Mary and I are getting old," he said slowly. "What would we do without you?"

David thought of the decades Ruth endured alone. Her desperation to survive when there was no money, no opportunity, with all hope having gone up the chimney of a death camp. He looked around the room. Oil paintings hung on the walls. The cherry wood table was trimmed with handcarved inlaid mahogany. A large silver candelabra graced the table. The curtains were imported. The contrast between the Richardses' world and Ruth's was painfully obvious. Her treasure was stored in the real stuff of life.

"I've never bucked you." David felt pulled between two irresistible forces. "But the time has come for me to be my own person." He was surprised at how unsteady he felt. The words were harder to say than he had thought. "I'm not going to be bought off anymore. What I do, I do because I choose to do so. I have a right to my own life." He felt confused. Anger was being pushed aside by a faceless fear, making him feel wobbly. David realized he needed to leave quickly, lest he crumble.

"Son." George reached out to him. "We need you."

"Right now I have to think about myself." David looked nervously back and forth between the two parents. "I'm going to Israel," he said resolutely. "I have nothing more to explain or say." He stood up and marched toward the door.

"David," Mary faintly called after him, "don't leave us for someone else."

He didn't look back.

Edward and David waved good-bye one last time before Ruth disappeared down the ramp, into the airplane. "Don't have much time left before I catch my plane." Edward pointed toward a ticket desk at the other end of the long corridor. "I make the changeover in Chicago to British Airways."

David put his arm around the old man's shoulders as they walked, and he carried Edward's flight bag in the other hand. "Can you believe this has all happened? Been like a dream."

"Was more like a nightmare when your father called to say good-bye." Edward puckered his lips, and his mustache bristled. "He's bloody well steamed. Fairly well guessed I was behind your turning up a Jew and deciding to go to Israel. Actually I didn't say anything. Right smartly he gave me an earful and then hung up on me, he did."

"I'm afraid Father and Mother are dealing with a severe change of plans right now," David answered. "Father dropped a bundle in the Democratic party coffers because he thought he'd badger me into running for office. He like to have had a stroke when he discovered I meant what I'd been telling him for two months."

"You haven't said 'no' often, David."

"Unfortunately. But I'm not about to be seen in public with

that Camille whatever-her-name-is that Mother has picked out for me to take to the spring prom."

"Your mother's not happy with me either, I'm sure."

"The rabbi taught me that sons have to forgive fathers when their best wasn't good enough." David stopped at the ticket counter. "The same goes for mothers. We both have to try and keep them in perspective."

"Remarkable insight, Davey." Edward glanced up at the flashing red boarding sign over the ticket counter. " 'Tis a shame, but the airlines are ringing me up."

David put his hands on the slumping shoulders. "Uncle Edward, you saved my life again. I will always owe you everything I have."

Edward's eyes filled with tears, and his nose turned red. "I love you, David. I love you more than if you were my own flesh and blood. I want this to turn out to be a good time in your life."

"You will bring Ruth to Israel, won't you?" David handed him the flight bag. "Paul Kendall has given me names of people to contact, but I'll need both of you to talk with. Can you get her to come?"

"Ruth?" Edward laughed heartily. "No one makes up Ruth's mind but Ruth. If there is any way in God's creation it can be done, I'll bring her." He started backing toward the door. "Do be careful over there. Don't get into any of the scrapes I did."

"God bless you, Uncle Edward." David kept waving. "Stay off the sauce and watch your health."

Edward handed his boarding pass to the agent at the entryway and waved one last time.

"This year!" David called after him. "This year in Jerusalem."

PART TWO

. . . but now they desire a better country.

The book of Hebrews 11:14

EIGHTEEN

Because the 747 flight from New York City changed carriers in Rome, David arrived in Tel Aviv in the late afternoon. The urge to explore the city immediately drowned in irresistible drowsiness, sending him to bed shortly after supper. To his consternation he was wide awake at two o'clock, and the rest of the night was a loss. At the crack of dawn he stored his excess gear in his hotel and caught the first bus to Jerusalem.

Following Ruth's advice, David's fashionable suits didn't make it into his luggage. Israeli style was casual and basic. Over a short-sleeved blue cotton shirt, he wore a correspondence vest with multiple pockets for notebooks, pencils, a camera, candy bars, and junk. In one zipped pouch was a small map and the address Paul Kendall had given him for Dr. Shlomo Cohen. Docker pants and crepe walking shoes made him look a mite touristy next to the locals, whose faded, patched blue jeans and worn, plain shirts had never been fashionable. Sprinkled throughout the bus, Arabs in long white and black checkered headdresses sat next to wives in long white robes. Some women had on brightly colored, floor-length Palestinian mantles. No one seemed to notice David until he began frantically sketching his fellow passengers.

When the Egged bus pulled into the Jerusalem station, he leaned over to a particularly dark-skinned woman staring at him and said, "We're sure not in Kansas anymore, Dorothy." She obviously didn't comprehend.

The hotel clerk had told David the stop was within walking distance of the Old City. He simply followed the crowd streaming down to the ancient marketplace. At the first view of the Damascus Gate David stopped. The sight was straight out of a Cecil B. DeMille biblical movie. The huge stone walls ran at irregular angles as far as he could see. People were walking across the medieval wooden bridge over the moat in front of the massive gate with ancient wooden doors. Across the top of the turret-capped ramparts were openings where ancient warriors shot arrows down on attackers charging the towers with swords in hand. Surely nothing had changed for two millennia.

David joined the throng surging under the ponderous wrought iron portal and tromped into the Holy City. He walked down the broad Street of the Gate until he came to an intersection. At the end of the unmarked thoroughfare, he found a teeming bazaar bustling with bargaining and haggling customers. He looked in every direction in rapt fascination until he noticed a young soldier guarding the area.

David carefully studied the Israeli soldier casually leaning against a stone wall. The boy in the loose-fitting khaki uniform couldn't be over twenty. His unusually large leather military boots looked out of proportion to the rest of his slender body. The blue yarmulke bobby-pinned in his thick black hair seemed strangely incongruous with the heavy machine gun slung over his shoulder. The boy's hand rested lightly over the trigger. The Israeli kept looking up and down a narrow passageway submerged in shadows cast by the high stone walls lining the cobblestone streets. Boy or not, the solider was ready and cocked; he made David apprehensive.

David slipped past the guard and ambled on down the ancient thoroughfare. Two days in Israel had not cured jet lag, and he knew fatigue and chronic sleepiness might overtake him any minute. When it hit, a fog of drowsiness made everything turn into a blur. Since walking helped clear his mind, the continuing tour of the old marketplace was more than a tourist inspection.

Strange smells enticed him. Spice and vegetable odors blended with the aroma of slabs of meat hanging outside. A strong whiff left David feeling slightly nauseated. Around the next corner he found another outdoor food market. The stalls of the vendors were quaint and primitive. Most of the food was set out in the open air. Buyers and sellers haggled over the price of a cabbage as if it were gold. Some of the men's worn suits must have been World War II discards. The small and crowded area bristled with life; David was invigorated once more by the sights and sounds. Everywhere he saw faces to sketch. Arab and Jew, Palestinian and tourist blended into a rich mosaic. He felt like a time warp had swept him out of the twentieth century, hurling him two thousand years backward.

For a moment David felt released and set free from whatever and whomever he had been. He seemed to be floating outside of time, independent of the restraints of a former life. He couldn't remember ever feeling so alive.

The irregular meandering pattern in the stone paving of El Wad Street beckoned him on to other inviting mysteries. He tried a few more blocks to see what turned up. The street descended and became granite slab steps, worn dangerously slick. Children and women brushed past, hurrying on their way. At the bottom David turned to his left and discovered he was standing in front of a door opening into one of the Stations of the Cross on the Via Dolorosa. Awestruck, David simply gawked.

A group of tourists quickly crowded in from behind him, and a guide began an explanation in English. Their trendy T-shirts and souvenir hats marked them as Americans. David wondered if he was as obvious. He made a mental note to dress down further and never wear anything but jeans.

David listened until the lecture on the Fourth Station was finished. The group moved on, and he remembered his purpose was not sightseeing. Paul Kendall had written the address of Dr. Shlomo Cohen at the top on the small Jerusalem map he pulled from his pocket. He traced his route from the Damascus Gate to the Fourth Station. Fortunately, he wasn't far off course. The Jewish sector was not far away, and the apartment building shouldn't be too hard to find. He held the map in his hand and continued on down the winding way toward the Street of the Chain.

Faces leaped out at him, begging to be captured on paper. Vendors selling everything from postcards to fur hats accosted him at every turn, but he kept moving. David loved every minute of the unending distractions. Jet lag had to wait. Too much vitality was exploding around him.

The buildings in the Jewish sector didn't look particularly different from those in the Arab Moslem Quarter, but the environment was distinctly Jewish. Men were wearing yarmulkes, and every doorjam had a mezuzah, an oblong plaque containing a biblical blessing. Occasionally, a Hasidic Jew walked past with long curls dangling down the side of his face, the fringes of his tallith hanging out beneath his black vest.

David carefully studied his map again. The apartment building was straight ahead. Only then did he realize some of the residences were new, their architecture almost identical with the ancient city so as not to interrupt the timeless quality of Jerusalem. He quickly found the right door.

A simple sign read, "Dr. S. Cohen." David touched the long narrow mezuzah and rang the doorbell. In a few moments the door cracked. He could see a woman's eye peering out at him. "I am David Richards, an American." The woman opened the door slightly and stared intensely. "I believe Professor Cohen is expecting me this afternoon."

The door swung open. A little, fat, swarthy woman grunted but said nothing. She only beckoned David to follow her up the two flights of stairs that led to another door, opening into a small living room.

The terrazzo floors were plain and the house spartan like Ruth's place; no superfluous decorations here. The room had white walls and simple angular furniture. Once inside the living room, David could see down a hall to an office crammed full of books, pamphlets, and papers of every size and shape. A short, rotund man stood up after the woman whispered in his ear.

"*Boker-tov.*" The bowling-ball-proportioned man bounded

down the hall with his hand extended. "Shalom and welcome to Jerusalem." Shlomo Cohen had the same black eyes and dark olive skin as most of the people on the street. Over sixty-five, his balding head and round, sagging face looked like an ancient sage from the Old Testament. His silver-white fringe of hair made his skin seem even darker. "So you are the protégé of Paul Kendall! No?" He pumped David's hand. "Yes, Paul not only wrote me of your coming but rang me up across the ocean to discuss this quest of yours." He pointed to a small plain brown chair. "Sit down, my boy."

David felt himself completely swept away by the natural forcefulness and intensity of his new acquaintance. "You teach history and the humanities at Mount Scopus University? Correct?" David began timidly.

"Of course!" Shlomo sparkled. "Such knowledge is the way to truth. But tell me of your trip. How have you found our land so far?"

"I've just been here a few hours, but I've never seen anything like Jerusalem. Frankly, I'm overwhelmed by the wonder."

"Of course!" The professor rolled his eyes. "There is magic in the air. A most sacred place, indeed. And where are you staying?"

"I haven't scoped out the hotels thoroughly, but the clerk at the Tel Aviv hotel told me of an inexpensive Arab place, the Hotel Ritz, near the Old City."

Cohen scoffed. "Inexpensive? Cheap! Deplorable." He beckoned to the housekeeper. "We must find much better accommodations for our friend. Bring us some coffee!" He waved the old woman toward the kitchen.

"Any help you can give is deeply appreciated. I'm afraid this whole experience is rather overwhelming."

"Of course, of course." The scholar wrinkled his brow and patted David on the hand. "You have come to a very disturbed world in the midst of an impossible time under complex circumstances. This Holy Land is in a great upheaval and could explode at any moment. Our country is still not sure of what it's about. Our identity is still emerging."

"Sounds frighteningly like myself."

"Yes." The professor shook a pudgy finger in the air. "Paul told me you are trying to discover the meaning of Jewishness." He smiled knowingly. "What it means for *you* to be a Jew."

"Paul told me you could help with my questions."

"Oh, a curse indeed!" The old man bellowed with deep rumbling laughter. "All Jews seem to be possessed and obsessed with this unfathomable problem that began with our father Abraham. The Holy One told Avram to go, but we've never been sure where he was supposed to go." Shlomo laughed again. "You've taken up with most difficult traveling companions."

"If there's anywhere in the world where people should know the meaning of Jewishness," David answered, "I'm sure it's here."

"Not so!" the professor frowned. "You see, we don't even know ourselves what a Jew is anymore. On one hand, we have the ultraorthodox and the Hasidim trying to pass laws to ensure only their religious definitions are accepted. On the other hand, most of the pioneers who founded this confused state didn't even believe in God! In between these two poles we have a hundred different opinions."

"And you?" David pursued. "How do you define yourself?"

"Perhaps our word *mesarti* says it best," Shlomo said thoughtfully. "The Orthodox have stolen the meaning of religious. I would not call myself a religious person. *Mesarti* simply means traditional."

The housekeeper brought in two cups. The coffee looked extremely black and very thick.

"My mother didn't explain any of this to me." David reached for a cup. "You make the task sound more formidable than I thought."

Shlomo laughed again. "A true professor can't let you settle for easy answers. Jew or Christian, we are speaking of a much more complex matter than merely taking off or putting on some religious coat of many colors. I promised Paul I would be a dog nipping at your heels. If I smell any form of dishonesty, you will find me to be a friendly but persistent nemesis."

"You also understand what it is to be a Christian?" David smelled the strong aroma from the cup.

The old man nodded. "I know about being a Jew." He puckered his lips. "I know about being a Christian. Maybe equally important, I know about being a human being."

David took a sip of the coffee and choked. He tried to catch his breath, but the bitter taste gagged him.

"Our Turkish coffee is strong medicine." Shlomo grinned. "Nothing like your American watered-down version. One must learn how to appreciate the bitter in order to get the full taste." The old man raised his eyebrows and nodded his head knowingly. "A good metaphor! You are now in a world where everything is done with gusto . . . and a lot of bitterness."

David sputtered. "Strong stuff indeed! I know my journey's under way for sure." He began to take another sip but didn't. "Where do I go from here?"

"What was your original name? Your parents' name?"

"Moses. I was David Moses."

"Ah, Moshe!" Shlomo settled back in his chair. "Let me suggest you begin by being David Moshe for a while. Just be a Jew, be a Moses from America."

"How would I start?" David set the full cup back on the table. "I'm not sure what to do. I've got to be more than a casual observer."

"Of course, of course," the large man agreed. "I have two ideas in mind. You will begin by meeting a friend of mine. Yosef Blum is a guide and can easily include you in one of his lecture groups. He is a typical agnostic Jew making his living by telling the tourists stories about places he doesn't believe in. He'll help you take a quick look around and show you one side of Israeli life."

"Excellent idea." David edged forward in his chair.

"Next you will move in here in the guest bedroom." Shlomo pointed down the hall.

"I couldn't do *that*," David protested.

"The space is small but adequate." Shlomo ignored his objection. "I thought of the idea when I received Paul's letter, but I wanted to meet you first. You need to stay in a good kosher house where I can keep an eye on your progress."

"I would be an inconvenience."

"Shulamit, my housekeeper, comes only on the off days anyway." He disregarded David's reluctance. "Now, we must start your education at once." He stood up and beckoned David to follow. "Look out!" He pointed to the large arched picture window in the center of the room.

To David's surprise a vast panorama opened beneath him. He was looking down on the Western Wall.

"Know the place?" Shlomo chuckled. "I want you to go down to this holy remnant of the past and pray like a good Jew should. Write your prayer on a piece of paper and stick it in a crack in the wall. Stand before this lone reminder of the glory of the past and look into your heart. Then you will know the most important thing to ask of the Holy One."

David stared at the crowds of people coming and going from the Wall. "Couldn't be a more appropriate place to begin."

"Wear this." Shlomo opened a drawer in a long chest and picked out a brightly colored yarmulke. "Yemenites make these. They're no tourist souvenir." He tossed him the prayer cap.

"Go now?" David looked again.

"Of course, of course." Shlomo shrugged. "Why not? I will call the tour agency and they will relay word to Yosef. He will come shortly and be expecting you. Listen to his instruction. At the end of the tour, he'll take you to supper and get better acquainted. You will quickly learn a great deal about our world."

David looked down at the ornate cap bordered in bright red and gold thread. "Why?" David puzzled. "Why are you doing all of this for me? I'm very grateful, but I don't understand."

"For the time being, let us simply say that I owe Paul Kendall a great debt. You must remember that I too must struggle at being a human being. Perhaps, as I help you on your journey, you will help me with mine."

"I . . . I . . . I'm not sure I understand." David looked baffled.

"Let me tell you a tale of the Hasidim." The professor looked out over the ancient ruins. "Once in Poland an old rabbi went up and down the streets of all the villages crying out, 'Be a human being!' When the rabbi met travelers on the road he admonished them, 'Be a human being.' One day a peasant stopped the sojourner. 'Good rabbi,' the farmer said, 'why do you continue with this plea? No one listens to you.'" Shlomo turned back to David. "The rabbi answered, 'I persist so I will not forget.'"

The old man took the yarmulke and placed it on David's head. "You are trying to find something that was lost in your past. All of us must struggle to recover the truth about who we are and what a human being is. None of us has an easy task remembering."

NINETEEN

Warm spring sunlight covered the crowd gathering on the rock-floored plaza in front of the lone surviving remnant of the days of Solomon. The air was dry, and David again felt invigorated. Women walked to one side of a metal dividing rail and men to the other. David blended with the men walking toward the stupendous stone blocks of the Western Wall.

The observant were a strange assortment of shapes and sizes, coloring and dress, alike only in that no head was uncovered. Many men wore simple black business hats; others had peculiar, large, circular fur hats. The long curls of the Hasidic Jews rolled down the sides of their heads and dangled at their temples. Their long, black frock coats and black beards were identical; some pulled their black and white talliths over their heads. A few old men with great shaggy white beards sat dozing on wooden folding chairs with their large, black hats tipped to shade their eyes. Fair-skinned blue-eyed Jews stood at the wall next to dark-skinned Middle Eastern types. A few men looked like David.

A constant babble of prayers filled the air. One cluster of men kept swaying up and down reading from their prayer books. As they davened, bobbing up and down, their prayers arose more like groans and moans. David inched his way forward until he stood before the cracked, pitted blocks of ancient stone.

David felt self-conscious and silly, but no one seemed to notice him. He reached out and touched the rough stone surface. As he ran down a crack between the stones, he inadvertently knocked a rolled piece of paper out of the rock. Immediately he picked up the wad and opened it. The handwriting was in English. David felt as if he were eavesdropping on some eternal secret conversation, but he continued reading:

> O Great God of the universe, please hear my prayer. Save me from the darkness that has settled in my mind. Keep me from death that lurks at every corner and fill the emptiness within my heart. Ariel

The handwriting was sprawling and urgent. The personal words seemed sent by some forever unknown soul mate. David read and reread the message, then took out a pencil and wrote on the bottom, "Me too. David Moses."

He rolled up the paper and stuck it back in the wall. A million fingers must have touched these rocks. He put both his hands against the wall and closed his eyes. Immediately he thought of Susan. George and Mary Richards's anger came to mind. He could see Ruth's face and then Edward's next to her. His imagination returned to Susan again. David no longer felt clumsy and the act contrived. His prayer slipped out in a barely audible whisper. "Help me find my way."

Calm fell over him. David felt as if he had stepped into a wondrous place in space, suspended above time and circumstance. Almost as if he had stumbled into the ancient Holy of Holies, David knew he had crossed into the realm of the sacred. He remembered Ruth describing life coming back to her by the Sea of Galilee and the experience of Father Kendall praying for him in his office. He tried to absorb the ambiance of the encounter so completely that the moment would never leave him.

Long after the gentle mantle lifted, David stepped back. He patted the rock and turned away. Without looking at anyone, he found his way back to the partition rail at the back. Leaning back against the metal bars, he tried to assimilate the experience. Finally he simply watched the never-ending procession of tourists marching past the Western Wall. Varying only in style, the guides repeated over and over the same story of how the wall was the last remnant of the glory of the Temple.

The sun felt warm and good. David was surprised when he glanced at his watch and realized it was three o'clock. He looked up at the banks of apartments at the back of the plaza and identified the arched windows and Shlomo's apartment.

"You must help me look for my friend," a guide shouted to his group. "He will be in this area somewhere." The heavy accent sounded Polish.

A short, thick muscular man led his group toward the barricade. He looked to be about fifty with a ruddy complexion. There was no yarmulke on his thinning hair. The man had on a brown sweater as Shlomo had said he would. The twenty-five American tourists, chattering like sparrows, wore funny navy-style orange and white caps with "Fellowship Tours" stenciled across the brim.

"Yosef?" David waved. "Yosef Blum?"

The guide smiled and waved. He hurried toward the partition. David jumped over the side and met him halfway. "Exactly as Shlomo described." The guide extended his hand. "Welcome to our little group."

"Thanks for taking me on." David shook his hand.

Yosef introduced David as if he were an old friend and explained David would be with them the rest of the day. The guide told a joke about Americans and launched into his lecture on the Western Wall with a rhythm that hypnotized the little birds, leaving them baffled and silent. Most of the pilgrims were tired, travel-saturated widows who had already seen one too many holy sights.

Blum didn't seem to notice the fading attention. With sweeping flourishes of his arms, he lectured about the Romans, Turks, and Arabs denying Jews entry and visitation. His voice rose as he described the Six Day War that finally restored right of access. He slid into his close, noting the Israeli government was more equitable in a few decades than all the combined centuries of gentile power. Then he sent his flock of sparrows down to investigate on their own. The two men walked to the back of the plaza.

"Care for a cigarette?" Yosef offered the box to David.

"Thank you, no." David smiled. "Great lecture."

"Shlomo says I am to make an Israeli Jew out of you." Yosef blew smoke into the air and grinned.

"Think it's possible?"

"Sure." Yosef pulled a handkerchief from his pocket and wiped his forehead. "Look at me. When we were chased out of Poland only eighteen years ago I couldn't even read Hebrew. Now I even speak English." He puffed on the cigarette. "You going to make aliya? To immigrate?"

"I'm just looking." David shrugged. The question surprised him. He had never considered taking such a drastic step. "Getting a feel of the land." He tried to sound casual.

"I'll do my best to convince you," Yosef chided. "Sorry all I have to offer you this trip is an assorted collection of old bags from Cincinnati." The guide pointed to the orange and white caps bobbing up and down before the Wall. "Time to reel them back in." He started waving an orange flag on a stick over his head.

"Thanks for letting me tag along."

"Sure." Blum put his cigarette out on the pavement. "I was a student of Dr. Cohen at Mount Scopus. I owe him a great deal. Glad to help. In Israel we have to help each other." He continued waving, and the group came trudging back.

Yosef cajoled and encouraged the stragglers up the steps and through the security gate into the Temple Mount. His unending lecture about the Temples of Solomon and Herod was timed with precision to coincide with the exact sites they passed. Even his jokes and puns must have been told a thousand times at these precise places. Nevertheless, David was hypnotized. He followed obediently as the Israeli pied piper led the flock into the Al-Aks Mosque. The guide pointed out the spot where Anwar Sadat prayed as well as a myriad of other obscure facts about the mosque.

"Now we go on to the Dome of the Rock." Yosef helped a

large lady put her shoes back on. "The site is holy for Jews, Christians, and Moslems. The rock is Mount Moriah where Abraham offered Isaac up."

As the group walked across the top of the Temple area, David remembered his first visit to the synagogue and Rabbi Berkowitz's sermon on the binding of Isaac. Never would he have expected to be standing on the exact spot where the event that had touched him so deeply occurred. *What a haunting story, he thought, so unsettling. A knife poised above the heart . . . and God looks away. Thereafter, sons forever traumatized by fathers. Parents forever haunted by unfulfilled obligations of parenthood, the ways of God obscure and contradictory.*

"Take off your shoes again." Yosef assembled the group before the entry of the magnificent tiled mosque exploding with blue and gold color. "Inside you will see the imprint of the hoof of Mohammed's horse left when the prophet leaped into heaven." Yosef winked at David. "Go see the great relic for yourself." The flock of tourist birds scurried inside to walk on the lavish red oriental carpets and see the great rock.

David found the building to be an architectural achievement of striking beauty. He walked by himself, quickly making the circle around the massive outcropping called Moriah. The dome-shaped building was singular and obviously contrasted with everything else in the Old City. The size of the great rock was equally impressive. The surface was flat, bare, ugly as David imagined the site of sacrifice must have looked to Isaac. He didn't like the feel of the mosque and was the first to leave.

"The Moslems created quite a masterpiece." David pulled his shoes back on. Yosef had stayed outside to watch the shoes.

"Sure." Blum shrugged. "Every thousand years or so the worthless Arabs do something right. What we ought to do is bulldoze this mosque down and let the Hasidim rebuild their temple."

David stopped tying his shoelaces. "You're serious?"

"Why not? The quicker we get rid of these dogs of the desert, the better."

"You'd have World War III in your backyard." David rolled

his eyes. "Every Arab in the world would be down here with a gun."

Yosef began waving his orange flag once more to assemble the covey of quail. "Of course. The Ayatollah, the U.N., and all the bleeding hearts of the world would descend on us in screaming rage." Yosef started walking away from the mosque toward steps at the rear. "Still the thought of tearing their playground apart amuses me."

David fell in step alongside the guide. "Are you saying you believe in the reconstruction of the Temple in this place?"

"Me?" Yosef mocked a look of consternation and laughed. "I couldn't care less about a temple. I would just enjoy watching the Arabs dance in fury." Yosef led them down a stone stairway and out onto a parking area where the group boarded a sightseeing bus. Windows rolled up the side and across the top for a complete view. The driver quickly steered the vehicle into an alleyway and out toward the Lion's Gate.

David sat in the back and made notes on what he had heard. He scribbled his impression of Yosef as the bus wound its way down the curved road descending the Kidron Valley and then up the Mount of Olives. On the other side he could see a panoramic view of the Old City.

He stared in astonishment. Nothing he had seen before was quite like seeing the whole city. The Golden Dome of the Rock looked like the sun rising over the granite wall circling the past. He could see the sealed Golden Gate, and at the far corner of the ramparts the Pinnacle of the Temple towered above the Kidron Valley. Recently excavated steps to the Temple looked like jagged building blocks rising out of the Valley of Tyropoenon, the old Jebusite city of David. Minaret prayer towers and church steeples punctuated the skyline. Sunlight bounced off round tops, square shapes glistened from the gilded Dome. Two millennia of history exploded before every blink of the eye. The sheer magnitude of the scene swept over David's imagination like a tide rolling in from a distant mystical sea.

The bus wound through back streets until it reached the top of the Mount of Olives. The neighborhood changed and took on a more contemporary Arab look. Some people waved; others scowled with hostility as they rocked past. The bus finally stopped in front of a high, dirty, stucco wall. Yosef assembled the group inside the gate and explained the site.

"On this spot," Blum pointed to a small tower as he spoke, "Jesus ascended to heaven. The story is told in the book of Acts, and we call this place the Mount of the Ascension. The footprint of Jesus was left on the rock inside the building. There you will see the last memento of Jesus," he paused and said dryly, "just like you saw Mohammed's horse's hoofprint in the Dome of the Rock. Please take your pictures now."

"Do you believe the story is true?" one of the elderly women asked.

"About Mohammed?" the guide feigned sincerity. Everyone laughed.

"As I said in the beginning, some sites are authentic and others legendary. You take your pick." The group hurried away.

"What's the scoop on this place?" David remained outside with Yosef.

"Roman Catholics devour this site," Yosef said under his breath. "With these Baptists, it's usually different. They're not as apt to buy the pious propaganda. I have to be careful." He tossed his head cynically. "Jesus' footprint and Mohammed's horse. Hump! The old lady's got to be kidding."

"How do you tell the difference between fraud and the real thing?"

"Oh, most of the sites have some genuine historical background." Yosef started back to the bus. "I just don't go for the legends, the Jesus junk. But I have to make a living, you know." He put his arm around David's shoulder. "We'll dump these people at the hotel and head for a nice spot. Maybe we can even find some women and make the evening count." He chuckled and slapped David on the back.

By the time the Fellowship Tour group emptied out and were tucked away in their hotel, it was after six o'clock. The bus pulled away for the security barn, and Yosef chauffeured David in his small old Volvo.

"The place is called 'The Cave' because that's exactly what it was," Yosef explained as he drove through the downtown streets. "Some enterprising soul turned the old hole into a nightclub of sorts. There's not much nightlife here." He held up a finger instructively as he spoke. "We say, 'In Jerusalem we pray; in Tel Aviv we play.' "

The night spot was plain and subterranean. In the center of the oilcloth-covered wooden tables, Chianti wine bottles held half-burned candles. The top of the cave made a dark ceiling over the spacious cavern that held twenty tables and a dance floor.

"They have singers?" David pulled out a chair.

"Indeed! Yardena's very popular. Maybe she'll sing early and come over and talk to us. A few women always show up."

"You're not married?" David looked around for a menu. Several couples drifted in.

"No, never could afford the luxury." Yosef lit another cigarette. "Inflation's rampant. Too much uncertainty. I just grab at what comes by. And you?"

The question had a cutting edge, and David didn't want to give explanations. "I'm single." He cleared his throat.

"Mel-tzar!" Yosef hollered at a waiter. "A liter for us." A young man in jeans and an apron signaled from behind a bar.

David leaned back in the chair and took full measure of his guide. "You don't seem to be particularly religious. Does that affect your work as a guide?"

Yosef puckered his lip and swore. "I don't know anything about God. I went to guide's school and learned the history of the Bible and this land better than any of the preachers who contract for my services. I don't buy or sell anything that's not history."

The waiter placed a liter and two glasses on the table. "How about a steak this evening, *schmoszal*?" he chided Yosef, obviously knowing him well.

"Still serving horse meat?" Yosef shot back and grinned.

"Give us time to get limbered up. Bring two more glasses in case we hit it lucky." The waiter sauntered off.

"You want to know why I don't believe?" Yosef narrowed his eyes. "I am the only one of my family to survive. We lived in Krakow, Poland, when I was a boy. I escaped; the rest died up the road at Auschwitz." He inhaled long and hard. "If there is a God, he let the Nazis burn my family. Understand?" He leaned on his elbow and pointed rapidly with his finger as he talked. "I don't think there is a deity, but if there was one I would spit in his face!" He sat back and took a drink.

"I understand." David took a sip from his glass.

"At least there's more of us here than there are of those religious crazies with the long curls." He looked around their dark surroundings. "Can you believe those fundamentalist nuts have gotten a hold on the government? Ridiculous! No! Most of us Israelis are secular, nonobservant."

"So, Yosef. What makes you a Jew?"

The waiter set two more glasses next to David.

"I believe in the people." He reached over and took hold of David's shoulder. "Our nation is the last hope we get. No God from somewhere is going to take care of us. We must stand together." He squeezed David's shoulder. "I am prepared to kill anyone who threatens me or my future."

David searched for something to say. The guide's forcefulness made a casual answer impossible. He bit his lip and looked at the table.

"I live by one creed." Yosef sounded like a preacher making his final point. "Never again! We will die before we give up one inch to anyone . . . particularly the worthless Arabs."

"You fear them?"

"No," Yosef sneered, "I despise them. And you better too, lest they slit your throat some dark night. The PLO, the terrorists, even their rotten children would annihilate us with the wink of an eye. Don't you *ever* forget it."

David felt uncomfortable. Yosef's words dripped with hate, and his eyes became hard as he talked. There was no middle ground with him. David again cleared his throat. "A . . . a . . .

what about the recent invasion in Lebanon? Was that a mistake?"

Yosef pursed his lips and became more reflective. "We had to do something about the terrorists sneaking down from the North. Sure, Sharon and his generals went too far and got us bogged down in a swamp up there. They weren't smart about what they did."

Two young women walked past the table, and Yosef was on his feet at once. Attractive and in their late twenties, the pair were dressed casually with a sensual flair. "We have two very special little sabras among us." Yosef called after them. "Ruth! Hannah! *Mah-shalomech*. Sit with us."

"Sabras?" David turned and looked.

"Native-born. Not immigrants." Yosef pulled two chairs over from the other table. He beckoned. "Come, my delights of the night, and grace our ugly table with your beautiful faces."

"Look," one woman said to the other, "it's Yosef, king of the male chauvinists." She walked back and dropped her purse on the table. "Still up to your old tricks, tour guide?"

"Now, Ruth." Yosef reached for her hand, but she pulled back. "Let bygones be bygones. I want you to meet a handsome American come here to consider making aliya."

The other woman sat down on the opposite side. "I trust he has better intentions than you always do, Yosef."

"See how forthright and brazen they are?" Yosef smiled as if imitating Charles Boyer or Paul Newman. "True sabras. No finesse. All brashness, yet fresh and eager for life."

"Overlook Yosef." Ruth tossed her head away from the guide and smiled at David. "He has a one-track mind." The small brown-eyed woman's sparkling black hair was pulled back and tied behind her head. She was deeply tanned and wore little makeup. Her natural beauty needed no assistance. "You obviously have a great deal more class."

"What can I say?" Yosef groaned and joked. "They know me well. Meet my friend David Moses from America."

"Hi, hunk." Ruth laughed. "This is Hannah Sarid and I'm Ruth Bilayeva."

The lights lowered, and a woman walked out on the small stage. "And now the voice that all Israel wants to hear," an announcer boomed over the PA system. "Yardena!" The music started.

The stunning, raven-haired entertainer's voice was low, rich, and sultry, like an Israeli Marlene Dietrich. A single spotlight centered on her while she swayed back and forth, singing with passion and conviction. Her accompanist in a plain black T-shirt played a small grand piano tucked away next to the wall of the cave.

She had barely finished the song when Yosef was on his feet applauding wildly. "Yardena!" he called. "My true love!"

Before the applause faded, the piano broke in with a more upbeat tune and Yardena's style changed. She bounced around the floor, swaying and dancing to a samba beat. Halfway through the third song, the audience started to sing with her. Yardena followed with another folk song, and the crowd sang lustily. She carefully orchestrated the audience until even David was part of her act, trying to mumble along. Yardena ended with a plea for faithful Jews to return to their homeland and help rebuild the country. The piano hit it again, and Yardena was back singing and dancing.

David had never seen anything quite like the rapport the entertainer had with her audience. He felt like he wanted to dance. Someone from the audience called, "The hora! Let's do the hora!"

The audience piled out onto the dance floor. Hannah grabbed David's hand, pulling him behind her. With no idea of what he was doing, he swirled away with her like a native. David hopped and kicked, imitating the person next to him. The girls clapped and moved with graceful ease. The hora was instantly followed by another, more complicated folk dance. David stayed and stumbled along. His new friends laughed good-naturedly at his mistakes. Then the song ended, and he uncharacteristically twirled with his arms in the air as if he were the solo dancer of the evening. People applauded.

Hannah abruptly kissed him and put her arms around his

neck. "What a man!" She squeezed lightly. "We must get much better acquainted, David Moses from America." She kissed him again, waved good-bye, and walked toward the door with Ruth.

Her kiss was the first touch of passion David had felt since Susan's death. The unexpected, spontaneous ardor shocked him. He stood on the dance floor with his arms dangling at his sides, watching Hannah disappear through the door.

"Now you are learning to be an Israeli!" Yosef slapped him on the back. "Good work. Hannah's a real fireball!"

David followed Yosef off the floor. He was sweating and felt the need for fresh air. After a few steps, his head started to spin. The heat and jet lag had turned into an inebriating concoction.

Yosef directed David toward his car. "You will do well here." Yosef walked with his arm around David's shoulder. "We work hard. We play hard," Yosef confided. "We must live for the hour. It's all we have, but the sheer joy of the moment is enough."

David smiled sluggishly. "*L' Chaim*," he answered.

"Exactly!" Yosef laughed and raised his hand as if in a toast. "*L' Chaim!*"

TWENTY

The second day David toured from the Dead Sea to Jericho. He sat on the edge of Masada's sheer cliffs, letting the breezes from the ancient Roman encampments far down below sweep over him. In order to shake free of the Fellowship Tour's collection of hens, he ran all the way down the steep winding trails, beating the group back to the bus. Yosef's periodic iconoclastic asides and caustic caveats didn't impede David's captivation with this strange new world etched with deep valleys and sheer cliffs. Even the stark wilderness was hauntingly beautiful in an inimitable ascetic way.

The next day the bus went in the opposite direction toward the West Bank. In Bethlehem, as people had done since the third century, David walked through the Church of the Nativity and down to the Grotto that was the ancient stable when there was no room in the inn. He saw the shepherd's field and the unavoidable tourist traps, offering everything from plastic Jesus dolls to ceramic plaques proclaiming, "Shalom Y'All." Finally the group loaded up and left the little town of Bethlehem behind. Jet lag immediately put him to sleep in the back of the bus. When he awoke, the Cincinnati tourists were collecting their belongings from the overhead rack and filing into the hotel.

"You missed World War III," Yosef said in his face while shaking David's shoulders. "Wake up, and I'll buy you a drink in a classy place." He pointed to the side of the hotel. "My car's in back. I'll meet you there, and we'll take off."

David yawned and nodded. "Coffee sounds better to me." He followed Yosef out of the bus.

After disposing of the last of his covey of American quail, Yosef drove back toward the Kidron Valley and up the other side. The exquisite Seven Arches Hotel dominated the top of the Mount of Olives looking down on the Old City. The two men found the hotel's bar and listened to the piano as they discussed the day.

"Really, this is not a good place for us," Yosef complained. "The only single women are tourists, and I sure don't want to hustle them."

"What was her name?" David meant Hannah but didn't want to seem interested. "You know. The one I danced with last night?"

"I knew she caught your eye."

"Come on." David squirmed. "I just didn't get her name."

"Hannah." Yosef grinned. "Hannah Sarid. She lives somewhere out there on a kibbutz and comes in when the crew hits town. I can probably put you in contact with her."

"No, no," David retreated. "Actually I ought to turn in early. I need to talk with Dr. Cohen for a while before I leave, and I must catch him at breakfast. Tomorrow I'm going up toward Ashqelon. I'm still fighting the jet lag. It seems the earlier I go to bed, the better I tick."

"Sure. We can take you close to the town." Yosef picked up a Hebrew newspaper from the next table. "You might be interested in the big debate going on in the Knesset right now. The politicians are fighting over the legal definition of what a Jew is." He laid the paper out.

David stared at the bold Hebrew headlines and the long illegible columns. "What's the uproar about?"

"The religious sects and the Orthodox are fighting to narrow the definition of Jewish identity to fit their convictions." Yosef traced down the column with his finger. "They're pushing a 'Who is a Jew' amendment that would affect the Law of Return. As it stands now, any Jew is welcome here."

"What's your opinion?"

Yosef sniffed indignantly. "Since millions of Jews were put to death for even a hint of Jewish ancestry, I don't think it's right for anyone to narrow the definition of who we are. Anyone who could have perished as a Jew is certainly entitled to call himself one and claim this land as his home."

"Be precise, Yosef. What is a Jew?"

"Anyone who sincerely identifies himself as a Jew is a Jew!" He pounded the table. "Being kosher has nothing to do with it. Only soul-searching can tell anyone whether he is a Jew or not. Politics is politics. Religion is religion. Mixing the two is disaster. Hang the religious busybodies and their nonsense!" Yosef stood up and folded the paper. "Let's go before I get angry and ruin my evening."

David paid their bill, and they walked out together. "I think I'll walk back," he suddenly decided. "I can take the path down the side of the cemetery and cut back up the other side through the Lion Gate. It's a short distance to the apartment."

"Come on," Yosef protested. "That's a long walk at this time of night. There's a lot of Palestinians between here and there."

"The exercise would help me sleep better." David shook his hand. "Don't worry. I've watched lots of John Wayne movies and kung fu on TV."

Yosef laughed. "Well, watch out for the wild women. Hannah Sarid may still be in town."

David waved and started the steep descent down the back alley known as the Palm Sunday route of Jesus. The hillside was covered with headstones and stone sarcophagis over Jewish graves. Halfway down the slope a sign identified the place where Jesus paused to weep over Jerusalem. The marker described the site as a traditional burial place for infants and children.

Lights began to appear in windows on the other side of the valley. The sun was disappearing, and shadows fell across the alley. Oklahoma seemed a lifetime away. He was walking down the roads his fathers had traveled and was among his own people. And yet . . . and yet . . . he was not a product of the land. He was not a sabra nor did he even understand the burning political issues of the day. Yosef was amusing, intriguing, bewildering but certainly not a soul mate of any variety. No matter what he might wish, David knew he was still a tourist at best.

Paul Kendall's voice came back to him. *"What do you feel, David?"* And indeed he felt many things. The other David no longer hid behind a sealed door. No restraints here. He felt the complete freedom to escape from behind the forbidden side. Being David Moses was exhilarating, fun, a great adventure. And yet . . . and yet . . . was he truly David Moses or only parading in a temporary masquerade to be put aside when the costume ball ended? Two Davids walked beside each other down the increasingly dark path. Neither identity was entirely clear.

He glanced over at the cemetery and could still see small rocks placed on the headstones by mourners. He wondered if anyone still visited Susan's grave. The thought hurt, and he didn't want to linger long on that distant burial ground.

The fact that he could push on was a sign of progress. Susan would have been thrilled with all the sights he had seen, and he wished they had made more trips together.

David heard footsteps and looked up. A young girl, avoiding eye contact, hurried past.

What would Susan have thought of the exotic Jewish girl at the Cave? The kiss Hannah planted on his mouth? David knew the answer to *that* question. For the first time he let himself realize how attractive the raven-haired beauty was. He tried to feel Hannah's lips again.

Well, he thought, *I'm sure I won't ever see her again. What a story to tell Jack Meachem. I'll have to add a few details to tantalize him.* David laughed at the thought. *Would old Jack ever be impressed!*

Only then did David realize he could no longer remember what Susan felt like. Her face was there, but her features lacked sharp definition. The touch of her hands was gone.

Somewhere off in the distance, a bullhorn on a minaret sounded the Moslem call to prayer. David's concentration was broken. The sound was forlorn and strange, as peculiar as his situation was, walking down a back street carrying in his hands pieces of himself that didn't yet fit together. The two Davids walked side by side, but they did not touch.

David was asleep almost before the light was out. Exhaustion and jet lag could no longer wall out his old recurrent dream. The ball of atomic fire roared up from his soul with a deafening explosion; a mushroom cloud of boiling smoke filled the black sky, quickly turning red. The scene slid into slow motion as if being played frame by frame. Pieces of debris drifted overhead; a lifeless form flew past. David's arms and legs turned into putty. He frantically willed motion, but nothing responded. A shriek of pain echoed from somewhere. The sounds of horror wrapped around him like a suffocating blanket of dread. Panic was total and annihilating. He thrashed under the covers, trying to escape the ever-descending horror.

David finally awoke; the wild, frantic images of his dreams faded. Sweat beaded his forehead. He lay in bed to let the turmoil settle. When he finally looked at the clock, he leapt up, afraid that Shlomo would already be gone. He threw on his clothes, but the anxiety lingered. David left the room without combing his hair.

"Come in, come in," Shlomo waved from the kitchen table. "Take a little breakfast."

David slid into his chair. "I was afraid I overslept and might miss you."

"Try a bagel." Shlomo pushed a plate toward David. "The pickled herring are nice, and the vegetables excellent."

David stared at the typical Israeli breakfast of plain yogurt, raw fish, cucumbers, and tomatoes. "Perhaps I will start with a little coffee."

"Of course, of course." Shlomo poured from the large stained pot. "Tell me, what have you been learning from Blum?"

"Yosef is an excellent guide." David sipped the thick black coffee very slowly. "I have learned volumes."

"Excellent!" Shlomo beamed and scooped up a spoonful of prunes. "And what have you learned about being a Jew?"

David pushed the fish aside but put the bagel on his plate. "Seems like Jews are having as hard a time as I am figuring out what Jewishness really is." He broke the bagel apart. "However, lack of definition doesn't stop people from singing and dancing. Everyone wants me to make aliya and return, even if they're not sure what I would be coming back to."

Shlomo roared. "What a perceptive young man you are, David."

"And I also have discovered that I should hate Palestinians and Arabs."

"Oh, my!" The professor took a big bite of his fish. "Apparently Yosef has exposed you to both his vices and virtues. Did you like the dancing?"

"Yosef and his friends shook me free." David put a fig on his plate. "I could learn to get into those wild stomps going on down at the Cave."

Shlomo applauded. "I will take you in Mea Shearim where the Haredi nest. You haven't danced until you've been with the Hasidim. Perhaps we can find a wedding to attend." The professor wiped his mouth and settled back in his chair. "What do you think makes Yosef Blum tick?"

David washed the bagel down with a slow sip of coffee. He grimaced and poured some water into the black syrup. "I think my cynical guide is a survivor who has lost his past. He doesn't look far beyond next month." David thought for a minute. "Perhaps he is not so different from my former business partner who also sells what he doesn't believe in. Yosef Blum may not be much of an idealist, but he certainly is a patriot."

"I underestimated you, David. You are a man of considerable promise. You have analyzed my old student quite well. Very penetrating." Shlomo stroked his small black beard. "To see the error is to begin to find the truth. Unfortunately, I was not able to raise Yosef's sight much above hope in political security."

"You don't approve?"

"Of course not," the professor snapped. "Yosef is a type but only one example. I am, perhaps, another type. Israelis come in many sizes and shapes."

"You are less afraid of the Arabs?"

"I tend to be an idealist." The professor smiled sadly. "Arabs are no less human than we are. They are not animals but people having a bad political experience. You must remember some Arabs are Moslems, some are Christians. There is a great difference. During my Marxist days, I had more passionate optimism about what politics could accomplish than I do now."

David's eyes widened. "You were a Communist? I've never met a live one before."

"A Marxist," Shlomo corrected him. "As an American, you would tend to not understand the difference." He pointed his finger at David. "As a matter of fact, you are closer to the Marxist view of things than you realize."

David grimaced. "Come on. You can't be serious."

Shlomo looked at the ceiling as if starting to read from an invisible book. "A line in the *Manifesto* runs something like this: All that is solid melts into the air, all that is holy is profaned, and at last man is forced to face his real condition and his relations with his fellow men. Sounds like David Moses' problem."

"I'm not a Communist," David recoiled.

"No, no." Shlomo chuckled. "But Marx saw what the modern world has done to you, David. He foresaw nihilism causing people like you to lose their reason for why they create. He saw personal worth becoming a commodity for exchange."

"Didn't hear much of that perspective in the public school in Oklahoma." David thought of his former company and why advertising had become a painful occupation. Conversations with Jack Meachem and his father flashed through his memory. Ideas he couldn't quite grasp raced across his mind.

"You cannot understand Yosef unless you understand where our tired world has gone." The professor stood up and took a book down from the shelf behind him. "I have been preparing a lecture on what Friedrich Nietzsche wrote nearly a hundred years ago." He thumbed through the pages and began reading. "'When people have lost their purpose and everything that they depended on is vanishing like smoke up a chimney, then there is one very predictable place where they will run for security.'" Shlomo looked up at David. "Yosef's love for Israel is what Nietzsche called 'the new idol,' the state." He read again, " 'State is the name of the coldest of all monsters. Coldly it tells lies; and this lie crawls out of its mouth: I, the state, am the people.' "

"But isn't Israel the Holy Land?" David argued.

"Yosef ran from the fascists and the Nazis, and yet he is frighteningly close to believing the identical party line of salvation through blind loyalty to a political order. The most dangerous state is one claiming to be ordained by Providence." He shut the book and put it back on the shelf. "The grand deception is completed once a people is found to despise. The Nazis hunted Jews and now Jews hunt Arabs. For all his patriotism, Yosef makes a poor Jew."

David ran his hands through his hair. He tried to frame a question and a response but felt confused. "Isn't Israel supposed to be a nation created by God? How can anyone explain the fact that after two thousand years the nation came back into existence?"

"After the Babylonian exile, the great prophets taught us that we must never confuse the people of God with any political system, even right here in this chosen place. For that reason alone my idealism in any political order has vanished. We must believe in more than the state."

"Therefore," David answered slowly like a pupil struggling to find the right answer, "a Jew must be much more than a citizen of this country, even a fiercely loyal patriot."

Shlomo nodded his head. "I told you, David; the issue isn't being a Jew or a Christian... or even an Arab. The basic question is being a human being. Human beings don't hate other human beings, regardless of their differences of opinion. When we quit being human, we join forces with the Monster."

David thought of his anger during the Civil Rights era and

the Vietnam War. How often had he longed for a passionate allegiance to some cause he could never quite define? In the end he succumbed to the comfortable status quo that sucked the life out of him.

"I happen to passionately believe in Eretz Israel," Shlomo continued. "But being part of a people, of *Am Yisrael*, is not the same as a particular political allegiance, whether Communist or capitalist, Jew or Christian, socialist or Zionist. The answer is in finding values that transcend the divisions that tear people apart."

David stirred uneasily in his chair. "Only you and my mother talk in such penetrating terms. No easy answers here." He rested his head on his hands and frowned at the table. "And how do Christian and Moslem Arabs differ?"

"Very significantly!" The professor lectured with his finger in the air. "The radical Moslems believe killing Jews fulfills a divine obligation. Very frightening! Christian Arabs are much like Christians anywhere in the world."

"I see," David said slowly. "Where do I look next?"

"There is no hope for the satisfied," the professor said politely without smiling. "But for one such as you, great possibility lies ahead. Remember our father Abraham was simply told to go. Moses went into the wilderness without a map. Maybe the answer is not to have an answer but to make a journey. The holy place is never real estate, whether it be Moscow, Washington, or Jerusalem. *Medinat Yisrael must be more*."

"Or Oklahoma," David added. "So, where is it?"

The professor lifted his coffee cup in a toast. "*L'Chaim,* David! To life!"

TWENTY-ONE

David closed the apartment door behind him and dropped his vest on a chair. The afternoon sunlight streaming through the large bay window was fading. Shlomo's apartment was refreshingly cooler than the streets. David kicked off his shoes, letting them fall with a clunk on the floor.

The professor called him from the kitchen. "Good day of touring? Come in here and tell me of the many discoveries Yosef Blum led you to see."

David walked slowly down the hall.

"Get a cold soda from the refrigerator, David." The professor laid his *Jerusalem Post* on the table and took off his half-glasses. "You look a little sunburned."

"Great day. I took a ton of pictures. Made some great sketches." David sat down across from his mentor. "I didn't know so many important things happened so close together. Every ten feet you discover you're standing where some mind-boggling story unfolded." He popped the cap off the cold drink. "What's the paper say?"

Shlomo shook his head. "Serious business. Confrontation is increasing in the West Bank area. Too many hit-and-run incidents. The Arab villages are turning into warring camps."

"So? What's new?"

"The problem is more than business as usual. Matters are deteriorating," Shlomo explained. He twirled his reading glasses. "But tonight I have something much more delightful for you to consider. I hope you are not too tired to add another chapter to your story of what a Jew is."

"Sure!" David tried to sound interested in spite of the recurring jet lag. "What's up?"

"We are going to Mea Shearim tonight so you can see the Hasidim up close. In America you were acquainted with moderate Jews. Over here you can experience the whole spectrum. Yosef Blum and his friends are the nonobservant atheistic types. Tonight I am going to show you the opposite end of the scale, the most extreme of the extreme, the Haredi. I think you will find the followers of Reb Arele Roth to be quite fascinating. I can guarantee some colorful sights." The professor slipped on a jacket and picked up his keys. "Gets cool quickly after the sun goes down. We'll catch a taxi and be there in ten minutes at most." The professor handed him a brown paper sack. "I've made you a sandwich and put in some fruit. You can eat on the way. Get your jacket."

"Thanks." David took the sack and started for the living room. "Why do you want me to see these people?"

"They have become very powerful, politically," the professor answered. "A true force to be reckoned with. If we have time, I also want you to meet some Messianic Jews. In contrast, this group is completely powerless."

David followed obediently, and Shlomo Cohen led the way downstairs and through the familiar back streets until they found a taxi stand at the corner of Shivtei Yisrael and Haneviim Street.

"Wear your yarmulke," the professor instructed while the taxi sped through the new city. "The Haredi take everything very seriously. You wouldn't last five minutes in there if you looked like a tourist or a nonobservant."

"Who are these people?" David watched the crowded streets and ate the chicken sandwich from the paper sack.

"The Haredi are the ultraorthodox, the Praetorian guard fighting off all subversions of the true faith." Shlomo settled back with his hands over his protruding stomach. "Their name comes from the Hebrew root word for agitation, fear. They are literally a denomination within the larger framework of Jewish faith."

"Fear?" David peeled a banana.

"Haredi fear the secular world. Jerusalemites changed their name from an adjective to a noun. For most of us they are the epitome of everything we loathe." The professor stuck out his lip. "Superstition, rigidity, fanaticism, judgmental. Understand?"

David nodded. "Sure. Americans aren't keen on Fundamentalists either."

"No one noticed the Haredi always had large families." Shlomo leaned over as if to confide. "In the Diaspora the population growth is below zero. Jews are drying up." Suddenly he shook his finger in the air like an orator. "But not the Hasidim! Not only do they multiply like rabbits, they have become extremely successful businessmen! And now this minority has gone into politics and is exerting tremendous influence in the government." He rolled his eyes and stroked his beard. "The bogeymen in black coats are scaring the wits out of the liberal who expected Israeli religionists to disappear before the end of this century."

David noticed increasing numbers of men walking down the streets in the distinctive frock coats. A few had knicker-style pants with long socks. Even small children with locks of hair curled around their ears always wore the skull cap. The taxi stopped in front of a food vendor's stall, and Shlomo jumped out. David dropped the brown sack in a large trash bin.

"These are possibly the most separated people in the world." The professor nodded toward an old man leaning over a table filled with onions and corn. His flowing silk dressing gown and extraordinarily long shaggy white beard made the shopper look like a hybrid between an ancient prophet and a refugee from eastern Europe. "Their faith permeates and defines every aspect of their lives," the professor explained. "Totally devout!"

The two men walked casually toward an alley entryway. Children dashed in and out of the Quarter. The professor pointed at a large tin sign nailed to a brick wall. The top half was in Hebrew and the bottom in English. David quickly skimmed the long list of prohibitions defining how men and women could be dressed inside the ghetto.

Once past the entrance, they strolled down a narrow sidewalk before turning to the left. "Reb Arele and his disciples are a fairly new movement. Arele inherited his position from his father-in-law, who was their original spiritual guide. They have recently constructed a new synagogue. Tonight we are going to watch their service."

The buildings were venerable but not ancient like the Old City. Most storefronts seemed to have been built a hundred to a hundred and fifty years earlier. Small shops selling a strange assortment of hardware, dry goods, and sundry items lined the narrow streets.

Hareidions stood in groups talking, watching David as much as he looked at them. The atmosphere felt unique, not quite definable but very foreign. David couldn't connect with these people. Obviously a considerable chasm separated their worlds.

"A modern scholar of Marx and Nietzsche must be quite contemptuous of these people," David finally commented.

"Quite the contrary!" Shlomo protested. "These strange people passionately love God. Their bizarre customs are an attempt to keep the modern world from consuming them. Surely Marx would have been impressed with their attempts to prevent the holy from being profaned."

"I'm surprised at you," David answered.

"Why?" the professor challenged. "I can believe their political and social ideas are crazy without losing respect for their willingness to pay any price to preserve what is ultimate." He took David's arm and directed him toward a rough two-story concrete structure straight ahead. "Sure, they are fanatics, but we can learn from everyone. Even their radicalism is a lesson in myopia."

Children ran in and out of the unfinished synagogue. Several Hasidim entered ahead of them. A young man stepped out, pointed at David, and began shouting in Yiddish.

"He says you're a disgrace," Shlomo translated and pulled David along.

"No beard!" The protestor pointed at David's face. "You disgust us. You look like the goyim!" He spit on the ground and stomped up the street.

"Beards are *that* big here?" David rolled his eyes.

"Reb Arele's followers take everything very seriously." Shlomo chuckled and opened the door. "Very seriously."

Children were running under the tables and over chairs scattered around the large assembly room. Bearded men milled around talking to each other. The stark concrete walls and floor gave the room a barren, austere feel. Shlomo and David sat down in the back. A few men looked critically at them, but others didn't seem to notice. The gathering appeared to be a meeting waiting to be called to order.

An old man in a rumpled shirt and a worn black vest came in from a side door. He walked to the front and yelled, "*Shabbos!*" and banged his fist on the table. "*Muktzah!*"

Shlomo explained, "The *shamash* is calling everyone to prepare. The service is about to begin."

Men stopped talking and the *shamash* herded the children to the back. The side door opened again, and a tall, thin man dressed in white stepped in. His face was thin and elongated as if much fasting had taken the rabbi too close to emaciation. He had unusual haunting blue eyes and pale skin. Blondish brown curls at his temples made him look more like an American picture of Jesus than a Jerusalem rabbi. The men surged forward and the *shamash* immediately leaped to the rabbi's side, pushing the singing followers out of the way.

"His hair is wet," the professor whispered. "He has just been to the *mikveh* for a ritual cleansing. He is preparing to welcome Queen Sabbath."

David stared incomprehensibly straight ahead. "Queen what?" He finally asked.

Shlomo leaned closer speaking even lower. "Every Sabbath an extra soul is offered to those who are ready to acquire. They are trying to make sure they are ready to receive what God may give."

The congregation began to chant and pray. An elderly gray-bearded man humbly crept to the podium near the curtain-covered ark. He began to pray loudly.

Shlomo translated, "May His great name be magnified and sanctified in the world which He has created."

"Amen!" a young man directly in front of David screamed at the top of his lungs.

David jumped and bolted forward in his seat. Shlomo reached for his hand.

"Amen!" The back of the man's neck turned red. He continued yelling in Hebrew. Other men joined in with terrifying intensity.

"They've gone crazy!" David started to stand up.

"No, no." The professor restrained him. "Reb Arele teaches the 'amen' should be said with total abandonment of the soul. Unfortunately his followers equate loudness with sincerity."

The yelling faded, and the rabbi sat down at the central table. Someone put a wine cup and a loaf of bread before him. The congregation circled the table. David stood on the chair to see what was happening.

The rabbi appeared to be giving some sort of a blessing before breaking the bread. He called out names and broke off pieces of the bread. Men leaped forward, stuck out their hands and snatched the morsel of bread from their leader. Reb Arele kept handing out pieces of the bread until the loaf was gone.

Plates of food were carried in from another room and set before the rabbi. He would eat a forkful of food and pass the plate to a follower, who gobbled the food down. Once the plates were empty, the men squeezed even more tightly around Reb Arele. David could only faintly make out the teacher's words.

"He is giving Torah," Shlomo explained. "The rabbi is giving them a short teaching."

When the instruction was finished, the *shamash* jumped on the table and began singing. Immediately, other men broke into boisterous raucous song. As the tempo and crescendo increased, the entire group began dancing, swaying, and moving around the room in hypnotic rhythm.

Suddenly, two men jumped up on the table with the *shamash* and danced like Russian Cossacks. The circle of dancers widened, and other men locked arms with the swaying, gyrating Hasidim. Stomping shook everything in the room. The air became hot and stifling, but the followers were undaunted. Dust created a cloudy atmosphere. The singing and dancing alternated between the sounds of a frightening roar and a party going out of control. The candles cast shadows of gyrating bodies with hands held high bouncing across the walls.

"Enough!" David pulled Shlomo toward the door. "I've got to get out of this chaos." Once outside he gulped fresh air and coughed. "I've never seen anything like *that* in my life! Sheer madness."

"Quite the contrary." The professor looked up at the stars filling the sky. "You must understand what they are trying to change."

"Do explain." David sounded caustic.

"The Baal Shem Tov, the founder of the Hasidic movement," Shlomo shifted into his lecture mode, "didn't believe in accidents." He sauntered back down the street leading out of the ghetto. "He believed everything is linked to what happens above. Worship down here can change what's planned up there." He pointed to the stars. "Reb Arele's disciples were affecting both eternity and time tonight."

"You don't believe that nonsense," David scoffed.

The professor plunged his hands into his pockets. "David, let's take another look into the soul of these Haredi. Remember what I told you is the prime motivation for their behavior?"

"Yes," David answered thoughtfully. He looked in a window as they passed a residence. Around candlelight, a family was gathered at a dining table with the father at the head of the table instructing the children. The streets were strangely empty. No one loitered in the alleys or on the curbs. Everything in Mea Shearim was under control. "You said fear created their extreme lifestyle. They are afraid for survival."

"Do you have any idea what such anxiety feels like?"

David stopped.

"Fear does strange things to people," the professor continued. "Some people become nonconformist—"

"And some people become conformist," David interrupted.

"Exactly. Reb Arele in his own peculiar way understands well how his followers could be quickly swallowed up in the modern age and turned into nothing but a commodity. He is fighting to preserve their uniqueness lest nothing remain of the past. Perhaps they are doing a better job than their liberal, sophisticated counterparts in our society. On the other hand, these nonconformists are also the most conformist people you will ever meet. Are they not clones of each other?"

The two men walked along silently for the rest of the block. Finally David spoke. "And where did they develop their uniqueness?"

"They stayed faithful to the ways of their fathers." Shlomo no longer sounded like a teacher. His voice became mellow, reflective, and wistful. "No one in this place is cynical about the past. Tradition is a holy thing because it is the path to God."

"And which God is this?"

The professor answered with enthusiasm. "The God of Avraham, Yitzchak, and Ya'akov. I have no question they worship the one true God. Christians would call Him God the Father."

"The Father," David mused. "Finding one's father seems to be a common denominator in Israel. For Yosef Blum the discovery is called patriotism; for the observant like Reb Arele the solution is religion."

"You ask me if I believe their worship behavior affects anything." The professor started David down a different street. "There was a time in my life when I despised the synagogue and believed Judaism to be nothing but nonsense. I lived through my own great losses," he cleared his throat and said with hard finality, "of which I never speak. I escaped to the United States to study. I was a broken man with no hope. The only possibility for change that I could see was in politics." He walked out on to a broader boulevard, leaving Mea Shearim behind. "I lived in perpetual despair."

The professor stopped talking. David wanted to say some comforting word, but nothing seemed to fit.

"Bitterness infected my soul," Shlomo finally continued. "Fortunately I became well acquainted with an unusual American. Contrary to most of the people I knew, this man had a fierce experience with the Holy One. More than believing in God, he *knew* the Divine on a first-name basis. Although a Christian, he spoke constantly of the God of Abraham, Isaac, and Jacob as being Father to both of us. His suggestion was that I must embrace what my past had already given me." The professor stopped and looked up at a street light. Night had completely settled over the city, but the bright halogen light cut into the blackness, even on the other side of the street. "Shortly thereafter an agnostic Marxist found his way back to the synagogue."

"What did this man do?" David asked cautiously, not to trespass on tender ground.

"He sent me home to the remains of yesterday." Shlomo began walking again. "Perhaps, most important of all, Paul prayed for me almost without ceasing."

"Paul?" David's mouth dropped. "You're talking about Father Kendall!"

The old man's eyes filled with tears. "I cannot tell you how it happened. But Paul's prayers lifted the terrible darkness that had settled over me. He reached into heaven and changed what had happened to Shlomo Cohen on earth." He pulled out a handkerchief and blew his nose. "Far be it from me to despise whatever Reb Arele's followers are about in their shouting and dancing."

"This is why Paul Kendall sent me to stay with you!" David was nearly speechless. "You've known each other for a long time."

"Paul Kendall saved my life." Shlomo concluded but said nothing more. He looked ahead with the fierce intensity that signaled no more questions allowed.

"Oh, my." David shook his head. "Does this mystery ever end? Amazing."

Shlomo said nothing. At the next corner, the professor took a small address book from his pocket and quickly thumbed through the pages. He squinted at the street corner sign and pointed toward a narrow lane. "This way," he grunted. "We have time for a quick visit. I want you to meet one more person who happens to live in this area. You will find Ilan Sharon to be as interesting as Reb Arele. Ilan too is a fanatic of sorts . . . at least in Jewish eyes. He's a Messianic."

TWENTY-TWO

Shlomo Cohen turned down Ben Yehuda Street. The world of the Haredi was totally displaced by the hustle and bustle of modern Jerusalem traffic. Young people in jeans and slogan T-shirts hurried past. Some wore yarmulkes, many did not.

"Ilan's private studies led him to the conviction that Jesus, or as is the Hebrew name, Yeshua, was the true Messiah," the professor talked as they walked. "Particularly remarkable since Sharon was born on a kibbutz before his family moved into Jerusalem. But remember he and his followers are as kosher as anyone in this land."

"Run your definition by me again," David said. "What are Messianic Jews?"

"Most simply put, they are Jews who have no desire to be thought of as Christians but still believe Jesus of Nazareth was the promised Messiah."

"Are there many of these people?"

"They are still a small minority," the professor explained. "Perhaps there are thirty congregations. Most encompass no more than a hundred people, but they create consternation far out of proportion to their actual number of members."

"They meet in churches?" David watched a bus go by packed with Jews and Arabs.

"Usually they gather in apartments or homes on Saturday." Shlomo stopped and pointed at a storefront. "The group which meets here is more successful than most. Ilan Sharon has done quite well with his followers. I called him earlier in the day. So he should be expecting us." The professor knocked on a side door.

A young man with a black beard and blue yarmulke rushed out of the shadows. Whatever the young Israeli said sounded angry. He thrust a piece of paper in David's hands and hurried away. David looked at the picture of a man and his wife holding a child on their lap.

"I see Ilan now has a publicist." Shlomo laughed and began translating the Hebrew sentence. " 'Watch out for these people. They are always smiling and helpful. They love you because they want you to love Jesus.' "

"What's this flier all about?" David watched the young man return to a secluded place between two parked cars where he could observe anyone who stopped at the side door.

"Probably one of the Yad L'Achim," Shlomo explained. "The group exists to counter the Messianics. These activists even disrupt the worship gatherings of the believers. Bug their phones, open mail, and break into homes!"

"You've got to be kidding!" David stared again at the flier.

The door opened a crack. A small man with glasses and a short beard peered out. "Shalom," he ventured.

"It's Professor Cohen. Can we come in?"

"Of course. Watch out, Shmuel Golding's people are out tonight." The man swung the door open. He was dressed casually in a plain shirt and looked like a typical observant Jew. "They'll be on you like a snake devouring a mouse."

"They already have." Shlomo held up the flier and stood back to allow David to go first. "A different group of antagonists," he explained. "They run the Jerusalem Institute of Biblical Polemics which exists to unconvert Ilan's converts." Cohen laughed.

"Thank you for the phone call." The man led them into a small assembly hall. Thirty to fifty folding chairs were scattered around the plain room that might have been only a social hall. "I'm glad you could stop by tonight. Professor Cohen has told me about your quest." He held out his hand. "I'm Ilan Sharon."

"My pleasure." David shook his hand. "The name is David

Richards. I've had quite a wild evening. The professor spares no expense in entertaining his guests."

Ilan laughed. "Sit down please. The Hasidics consider us to be their archenemies and the epitome of evil. The extent of their harassment is considerable. One of our congregations in Tiberias was stoned several times by the Hasidic during a period of six months."

"Something doesn't quite add up." David scratched his head. "Most of what I've heard portrays Israel as a land of religious freedom with all faiths having access to all holy places. Jews allow atheists to call themselves Jews. Why would you be attacked for offering another option?"

"Evangelism of Jews is chutzpah," Ilan spoke with urgency. "Something completely unacceptable." He was slight and at first glance looked about thirty. A second look added at least fifteen years. "Newspapers will not even accept our advertisements because they fear the pressure and backlash from the Hasidics. Ultraorthodox put great pressure on zoning officials trying to keep us from using this building." The longer he talked the more he sounded like a man living under considerable stress.

David puzzled a moment before chuckling. "After all Jesus *was* a Jew."

Ilan shook his head. "Jews can't think of Jesus without remembering centuries of Christian history when we were the victims. Jesus isn't the issue as much as *what* faith in Jesus has cost Jews for nearly two millennia."

"In the minds of many Jews," Professor Cohen added, "Nazism was another aspect of Christianity. If they get too close to Jesus, they will end up with his friends who put their relatives in the ovens at Auschwitz."

"That's not fair!" David protested. "The Nazis were not only pagan but blatantly anti-Christian."

"True," Ilan agreed, "but many of our people believe the Third Reich used traditional church hostility toward us to achieve their anti-Semitic goals. I have people in my congregation who believe everything regular Christians believe but would never allow themselves to be called Christian. They feel the word has been too contaminated."

"Listen," David felt his temperature rising, "hate can be annexed to any religion. All week I've been with a Jew who hates Arabs. Your papers are full of stories of Moslems who hate Jews. Christianity is not inherently anti-Semitic!"

"Of course, of course," the professor agreed. "But there are too many victims of persecution in Israel for an objective view of Messianic Jews to exist. Maybe in a hundred years the climate will change, but for the time being the Holocaust has left too many wounds."

"What can you do then?" David asked Ilan.

"More than one might think." Ilan picked up a manuscript from a desk next to him. "We are currently completing a Hebrew-language New Testament with special explanatory footnotes. I am personally writing a multivolume New Testament commentary in Hebrew. Professor Cohen has helped me several times in translating Greek accurately. We have musicians developing unique songbooks with Jewish melodies. Each effort is like laying down a stepping-stone on the path to understanding."

"You *help* these people?" David turned to the professor.

"I told you being a human being, a man of truth, is the most important thing." Shlomo shook his finger at him. "Perhaps I didn't elaborate my meaning with enough clarity. Ilan and his people truly care about what happens to our people. That's enough for me."

"For the first time in nearly nineteen centuries," Ilan continued, "there is a new attempt being made by Jews to take the gospel to Jews. Yeshua's followers are doing everything in our power to truly offer love to His people."

"And Ilan's people live with great Jewish integrity," Shlomo added. "No one can question their adherence to halakah, to Jewish law."

"David," Ilan squeezed his shoulder, "you are a rare find for us. A Jew with Christian training! We could use you at once. What a tremendous addition you would make to our congregation. You already know more about the faith than almost any of our people."

"Wait . . . just a minute." David felt himself backing away. "I am an advertising man." He paused. "Well, I used to be. Now, I . . . I . . . at best I'm in transition. My background is quite limited, you see. I suppose I'm more a Christian who is trying to figure out what it means to be a Jew."

"Don't you believe in Yeshua?" Ilan pressed.

"Of course . . . certainly." His profession felt strangely different from any David had made in his life. Such an admission in Oklahoma City was no more than a social statement of religious affiliation. "I was baptized as a child and confirmed as a youth." David realized he sounded more as if he were trying to convince himself. "I've never thought of myself outside of this context."

"Then you have a faith to share," the minister urged. "Here we have the great privilege of being misunderstood, even persecuted for our convictions. We are very fortunate."

David looked carefully at the man who must be about his age. Other than being born in the same country there was little similarity between them. *Was their faith truly the same?* He asked, "How did you come to believe?"

"I will give you the short version of a long story." Ilan settled back in his chair. "As a child I saw many Christian missionaries come through our land. Of course, my parents taught me to despise them." He laughed. "However, I came to disdain these goyim for my own reasons. We began to find boxes of Bibles left in the alley behind the houses on my street. We learned the missionaries had quotas to fill, and our people wouldn't take their free Bibles. The proselytizers simply dumped the Bibles to make it appear they had distributed them." He smiled sheepishly. "You must understand the times were difficult, and everyone was short of basic supplies. We ended up using the Bibles as toilet paper."

Shlomo winked at David. "We are a resourceful people."

"I was learning English in school and practiced reading anything," Ilan continued. "One afternoon I decided to see if I could understand this strange book we kept stacked in the bathroom. To my delight, I could understand it rather well. The more I read, the more surprised I was. Nothing was as I expected." Ilan thumped his manuscript. "Here was the story of a Jewish man who was truly one of us. I was attracted to his Jewishness and his interpretation of Torah."

"You must have encountered painful resistance," David concluded.

"I had to fight for every inch of what I profess. Trust me! I have been stomped into the ground many times by far more capable debaters than the likes of Yad L'Achim or Golding's institute students hiding out in front. Everything I hold to has been chiseled out of granite. In the end my family forsook me."

"I'm not like you," David apologized. "In my world, we saw the church as sort of a . . . a . . . an object of convenience. You see," he fumbled, "everyone was a Christian of sorts. Or at least, we assumed we all believed the same things."

Ilan's eyes became hard and unrelenting. "Then the time has come for you to leave such a shallow and banal world behind. Americans worry over parking places and diets. Such luxuries are inaccessible to us and our Messianic believers. Our constant concern is with living and dying. We need you." Ilan's tone was demanding, unyielding, and unapologetic.

"Ah . . . thank you," David mumbled. "It is an honor—"

"No honor," Ilan cut him off. "Rather a responsibility if you actually believe what you say you do. You are by definition a Jew who believes in Jesus. Are you or aren't you?"

"Certainly," David answered defensively.

"Then do something about it," Ilan insisted.

David stared at Ilan. No excuses were left. The moment felt long and awful. The Messianic Jew looked back with stoic resolve.

"Thank you very much for seeing us tonight," the professor broke in. "I think you have certainly helped David discover another dimension of what it is to be a Jew." Shlomo stood up. "Unfortunately, the hour is late."

"I hope I've helped him see the basic truth about who he is." Ilan's tone offered no social compromise.

"We must talk another day." David offered his hand. "I will carefully consider what you have said."

"The time is short." Ilan did not smile. "We must seize the moment."

"Yes," David answered awkwardly. "I will do my best."

"The issue is not necessarily your best," the Messianic replied, "but your integrity."

David once again couldn't find an answer. He had offered a polite social response, but the minister returned confrontation. Jews often seemed to follow this pattern, and it befuddled David. Ilan Sharon's intensity was particularly intimidating. In the end David could only nod his head.

"I will shortly have some new information for you on your manuscript," the professor chatted as they walked to the door. "I have consulted with Dr. Flusser about the first-century setting of the group called the Pious Ones. Call me this week. The insight will help make your commentary more comprehensive."

"Yes, yes," Ilan answered, opening the door for them. "I hope to see you again very soon, David."

David waved and looked for the young man who had been hiding between the cars, but he was gone. "Sure thing." He hurried away.

"I believe Sharon upset you more than Reb Arele did," Shlomo chided as they walked up the street. "Got in your face, didn't he?"

"No, certainly not," David perjured himself. "Just not used to his style."

The professor laughed and slapped David on the back. "Permit me to make an observation. Regardless of who the person or the group is, we must not mistake sincerity for truth. Fervor isn't the same as veracity. At the same time we must not let a strange behavior or a lack of social finesse keep us from penetrating the camouflage covering reality. Tonight you have been through a considerable exercise in attempting to remove veils."

"It's a whole new world," David answered politely.

"And what have you learned?" Shlomo persisted.

"A hymn is often sung in American churches. The words run something like, 'Faith of our fathers, living still, in spite of dungeon, fire, and sword; faith of our fathers, holy faith.' Both the Haredi and the Messianic Jews seem to be singing the same song to a very different melody. Possibly I sing to yet another tune."

"Profound," the professor said thoughtfully.

David walked for an entire block before he spoke. "Perhaps I'm seeking what only my father can give me. I found my mother, but can I find a man who died long ago?" David asked.

Shlomo walked a long way before he answered, "Ilan Sharon and Reb Arele believe you can."

TWENTY-THREE

By May 16, the sweltering promise of summer was clearly ahead. Even in the early morning hours, the glow of the sun quickly covered the cobblestone streets of Jerusalem and radiated back from the asphalt pavement. The air was dry and no rain would fall for a long time. David could feel things heating up.

"Something big is brewing in the West Bank towns," Shlomo Cohen told David as they walked through the narrow street leading from his apartment into the plaza before the Western Wall. "I am concerned. You must be very careful. Many Palestinians are on the verge of revolt."

"Why?" His walking shoes clicked against the stone streets.

"Palestinian refugees are a festering sore on the body of Israel." The professor shook his head. "At least a half million Palestinians live in the Gaza Strip. Maybe 400,000 displaced people exist on the West Bank. If we add the number living in Jordan, Syria, and Lebanon, we are talking about two and a quarter million Arabs in exile. Most of these people live in appalling conditions. Time is running out on their discontent."

David looked at an Arab sitting at a small cafe table smoking a cigarette. His long, brown robe could have been preserved since biblical times; the black igal headband of his kaffiyeh was tipped at a casual angle of suggestive indifference. But when David and the professor passed, the Arab's stare was hard and cold.

"We have not always treated these people well," the professor added. "Occupation has pushed them into hatred."

David glanced back at the Arab. The dark-skinned man was still staring at him. "You think matters are coming to a head?"

"A new book about this problem has just been published." Shlomo put his hands behind his back and looked at the street as he walked. *"The Yellow Wind* is a good title. *Rih asfar*, as the Arabs call the hot, terrible east wind that comes once in a generation. The heat is so intense the grass bursts into flames spontaneously. Rocks turn white from the heat. The Yellow Wind blows from the gates of hell."

"I still hope to get down to Hebron after I've spent some time at the kibbutz." David ate the last of a bagel as he walked with his thick duffel bag slung over his arm. "Maybe I could take a weekend trip by bus. I really want to see the burial place of Abraham." Even though he wore a light T-shirt, he still had his many-pocketed correspondence vest on. His faded blue jeans and plain walking shoes made him look like the natives they passed.

The professor shook his head. "Hebron has always been hostile to Jews, but now the situation is quite volatile. A group of Jewish settlers moved into the town, and immediately a yeshiva student was murdered. The settlement countered by attacking the marketplace stalls of the Palestinians. Fighting erupted and now everyone carries weapons. You would be quite vulnerable in Hebron."

David walked under the stone arch and out into the vast expanse in front of the Wall. "Maybe David Richards, not David Moses, will have to go." He shielded his eyes from the bright sunlight.

"You have enough to learn at the kibbutz," Cohen said, ignoring David's suggestion. "Don't be afraid to stay as long as you wish, but don't discuss Shulam's Messianic Jews. Yosef and the bus will be here any moment." The professor pointed beyond the military checkpoint where tour groups were already starting to assemble. "Yosef must go by Ashqelon to take his group to the airport. You won't have any trouble finding the Afikim kibbutz from there."

David nodded to an Israeli sentry as they passed. The young

man wore the familiar khaki green fatigues and army beret with his machine gun close to his side. The soldier waved back as if greeting a countryman. "My mother sent me a map and ample instructions on how to find Afikim. I can't tell you how excited I am to visit the place."

The familiar orange Fellowship Tours bus pulled up to the curb. "Spend plenty of time," Shlomo advised. "Work on the farm a while." Yosef was sitting in the front guide's seat. "A little hard work is always good for the soul, or so Marx thought." The professor winked. "Settle in. The people will accept you as one of their own."

The heavy metal door swung open, and Yosef beckoned for David to hurry. Other buses were pulling up behind. "Thank you, Shlomo." David tossed his bag to Yosef. He turned back to hug the rotund little man. "You've given me much to think about. I spent most of yesterday digesting our one breakfast conversation. Thanks so much."

"Keep in touch." The professor patted him on the back as David stepped into the bus. "Watch out for the Yellow Wind. If you need something, simply call or drop me a letter. Your room will be ready when you return." Shlomo pressed a piece of paper in Blum's hand. "Yosef, get him as close as you can," he instructed and then stepped back to the curb.

David waved, and the bus quickly pulled away.

From his customary seat in the rear, David watched the strange conglomeration of ancient and new buildings blur past as the bus sped from the confines of the ancient city into modern Jerusalem. In a few minutes they passed the Knesset, the parliament building, and on by the Shrine of the Book, housing the Dead Sea scrolls. Even before they reached the city limits, Yosef began his predictable morning recitation of Hebrew idioms, which the ladies from Cincinnati were supposed to have acquired in their week in Israel.

"*Boker-tov*," Yosef roared into the microphone.

"Good morning," the women's chorus giggled.

In quick order, the guide ran through the repertoire of *shalom, toda-rabah, bevakasha,* and each time the answers were clumsily parroted back. The city soon disappeared, and the road plunged into thick pine forests. "We will go down to the ocean," Yosef explained, "and we will find the airport out on the coastal plain."

David opened the vest pocket where he kept his small collection of maps, instructions, and addresses. He again found Ruth's instructions.

"Before we part," Yosef's voice boomed over the microphone, "we have one last opportunity to speak of the history of our many difficulties in this land that God has given only to us." Even though the group had already heard the story two days earlier, Blum continued a tedious discussion of the Arab attack when Israel became a state in 1948. He rambled on about his part in the Yom Kippur War and described again how he was wounded. Gray heads with tightly curled perms began nodding and dropping forward. The road descended out of the pine forest and cut across open fields where workers were tending young shoots bursting from knurled grapevine stocks. The vines were stuck between the rocks, which appeared to be the more significant crop on the steep slopes. David found himself drifting away as the steady droning of the redundant lecture lulled him into drowsiness.

"David Moses!" the PA system boomed.

David jumped. He had been dreaming of walking through his old house in Oklahoma City. For a moment he had no idea where he was and felt bewildered.

"A little surprise for you," the voice was telling him. "We took a slightly different road and are close to the kibbutz. The entrance is just ahead."

David rubbed his eyes and peered out the window. The bus slowed and pulled to the side of the road. A large arrow pointed to the left. Painted beneath Hebrew letters was the word *Afikim*.

"Our friend is leaving us here," Yosef explained to the group. "Let us tell him shalom and wish him well."

The ladies waved and blew kisses. David jumped down, and Yosef tossed him his duffel bag. The guide leaned from the step and grinned. "Now I know where you are going." He shook his finger and laughed. "Happy hunting! See you at the Cave." Yosef winked, closed the door, and waved.

David watched as the bus disappeared, with no clue to Blum's innuendos. He shrugged, put the bag over his shoulder, and started up the driveway. The fields were carefully cultivated; the buildings were in excellent condition, with flowers blooming in the beds surrounding the quarters. Every inch of the property was well kept, and the kibbutz looked prosperous.

At the end of the lane was a flat-roofed one-story building. Posted over the entry in English was the word *Administration*. David walked faster. From his vest pocket he fished out Ruth's letter with instructions about the kibbutz. He scanned the details about his birth and read again the strange name of the woman he should contact.

David quietly slipped into the administration building. Two women and a man were busily working behind a large counter. Their clothing was basic and austere. No one looked up until David shut the door firmly behind him. The trio did not stop what they were doing. David stood before the counter for what seemed like an eternity before the unkempt, rumpled man got up and came forward.

"*Boker-tov,*" the old man sounded brusque and impersonal. His drooping face was gnarled and worn.

"I'm sorry," David apologized. "I don't speak Hebrew. Does anyone speak English? *Ha'im atah m'daber Anglit?*"

"Simma," he grunted to the younger woman and walked away indifferently. A squat, fat old woman was comparing bills with the young one called Simma. The man mumbled something, but neither looked up.

Around thirty, Simma had a natural, country look. Her black hair was pulled back in a bun. The simple dress didn't conceal how attractive she was. After about a minute Simma pushed back from her desk and finally came to the counter. "*Mah-shalom-cha.* Need help?" Her accent was thick.

"If it's not *too* much trouble." Irritation crept into David's voice. "I am seeking some information about Afikim."

"You want to buy plywood or produce?" The young

woman pulled out a notepad without looking at him. "What do you wish to order?"

"No, no." David couldn't get her to look at him. "My business is personal. I am looking for one of the older residents' My parents once lived here."

Her head snapped up. She turned to the old man and woman who immediately stopped their work. "I'm not sure I understand you." She put her pencil down.

"Many, many years ago," David thought he must sound foolish, "my parents lived in Afikim. I was born here."

The other two Israelis immediately walked to the counter and stared at him.

"Probably no one would remember them, but I had hoped." He stopped and reached in his pocket. "I have the name of an old friend . . ."

"Lived here?" the old man suddenly understood English. "I have been here almost from beginning." His broken English had a French accent. He squinted at David skeptically. "Just *who* are you?"

"My name is David," he stammered. "David Moses. My parents sometimes called me Dov." He pulled at his vest and ran his hand through his hair. "My father's name was Yaacov, and my mother is Ruth—"

"*Kwais!*" the man exploded. "Friend! I can't believe my ears." He rushed around the counter. "I knew them well. Yaacov! Ruth!" he exclaimed. Rounding the corner he held his arms out. "My boy, you are Dov?" The two women were right behind him. Each in turn hugged David.

The old man stood back and covered his mouth. "We thought you were dead." His eyes filled with tears. "I can remember the tragedy as if yesterday. *Une catastrophe totale.*" Tears ran down his cheeks. "Oh, your father! My friend Yaacov. What a man!" He hugged David again. The old man's tears dampened David's neck. "Ma belle! We thought you were dead."

David didn't know where the rush of emotion came from, but he began to weep. He trembled and tried to find a handkerchief. The older woman kept hugging him and began crying also. "I can't believe I have found someone who remembers," he sputtered.

"So many come and gone over these decades," the old man's lip quivered. "But never, never we forget their faces, their lives. They are our family." He patted David on the chest. "And Ruth. What a little gem! No one could forget your mother."

"She said one of her old friends might still be here." David kept trying to find the paper. "I think her name is Shula."

"Shula!" the older woman exclaimed. "Of course, Shula Schransky. Even now she is in the infirmary. Sick, you know." The woman clapped her hands. "What joy you will bring her!"

"I hoped she might give me some details about my past, something I might remember . . ."

"*Tout à fait!*" the old man puffed out his chest. "We all can! Yes, everything. We can tell everything." He struck his own chest. "But I have given no name." He laughed. "I am Yisrael Dinitz. Meet Simma, our daughter, and my wife Rosalie. Consider us *your* family now."

"Oh, thank you." David tried to regain his composure but felt extremely self-conscious. "This isn't like me." He struggled to swallow. "I'm just rather undone."

Off in the distance a shrill whistle blew one long blast.

"Lunchtime." Yisrael took David's arm. "You are our honored guest. Come. At the cafeteria we celebrate."

Simma led them through the back door. The three Israelis chattered and continuously interrupted each other, pointing in every direction, explaining the kibbutz to David. They pointed out a large swimming pool and long low manufacturing buildings.

Yisrael enthusiastically described their growth into one of the country's most affluent settlements. When they reached the commissary David was pushed past the long line waiting to enter the large dining hall. Yisrael led him to a raised area in the center of the cafeteria.

Yisrael held his hands over his head and clapped for attention. Before people quieted he broke forth in Hebrew. Silence fell over the room. He pulled David toward him. "Something wonderful!" Yisrael shouted in English. "One of our own has returned." People burst into loud applause. "David Moses!" He held up David's hand. "This son of Israel was born here." Cheers broke out. "We thought he was dead." Yisrael's announcement became emotional. "His father Yaacov was killed helping our settlement live. Bless his memory! We receive his son back with joy and remember Yaacov's gift to Eretz Israel."

Suddenly all the people in the cafeteria were on their feet applauding. The boisterous tone subsided, and solemnity and honor emerged. Once again, profound emotion gripped David, and the knot in his throat made it difficult to speak. He tried not to weep. Yisrael hugged him again.

The people sat down, and David was taken to the head of the line. People reached out to touch him, shake his hand, wish him *mazel tov*. Servers smiled, nodded, and heaped food on his plate as he filed past. Finally he dropped in a chair, fearing his knees would buckle.

"You have come home," Yisrael smiled kindly. "Every person is truly touched you are here."

David tried to eat, but he felt disconnected, almost dizzy. Insight and confusion pulled him in opposite directions. Once more, pieces were coming together. He stared at the steaming food.

"I must leave soon," Yisrael explained. "We are a very large operation. You know, we send our own ships to Africa for materials." He shrugged. "No, no, you don't know. But I must go to the warehouse as soon as I finish. Simma will take you to see Shula in the infirmary."

David could see people pointing toward him. With no idea of what the Hebrew words buzzing around his ears meant, David knew he was at the center of every conversation.

Like a computer producing an endless printout, Yisrael deluged David with facts on their plywood production, the amount of vegetables grown in the fields, clothing manufacturing, the security system, on and on the description rolled out. Yisrael finished eating at the same time he came to the end of his stockholder's report. "Simma knows Shula well." He hugged David again. "She's an excellent guide."

Simma smiled politely but said little, as if embarrassed.

David was grateful for the silence. He yearned for solitude to absorb the avalanche of sensations rolling over him. He looked out the window at the flowers, shrubs, trees; each flower bed magnificently manicured. The new multistory apartment complex was freshly painted. The displaced had carved out a secure place in a hostile world.

"May I get you something more to drink?" Simma asked.

"No, thank you." David said simply.

He was aware people continued to stare at him. Not sure how to respond, he kept looking out the window. He knew the crowd was thinning out but could not shake the nagging sensation of eyes burning holes in the back of his head. Slowly he turned to look across the cafeteria. At the other end of the room a small deeply tanned woman leaned against the door smiling knowingly. The raven-haired beauty waved.

David's mouth dropped. Hannah Sarid.

"You know Hannah?" Simma asked.

David stuttered. "I met her several days ago in Jerusalem. I'm surprised to see her."

"She lives here." Simma didn't look up.

"A friend of yours?"

"We are all friends."

"I mean . . . a . . . do you know her well?"

Simma looked at David quizzically. "Very well, why?" There was a touch of misgiving in her voice.

"I'm amazed to see anyone I've . . . a . . . met here. That's all."

"Of course," Simma answered politely. "Hannah does get around." She gathered up her dishes on the tray. "We can go when you're ready."

David looked again, and Hannah Sarid was gone. "Sure, let's go."

Simma explained the kibbutz on the way to the hospital. David listened and said little even after they went inside. The long halls of the infirmary were immaculately clean. The furniture was simple but well kept. Brightly colored curtains gave the clinic a cheerful appearance. The building had a freshly washed white, sanitary smell.

"Shula Schransky is in the next room," Simma explained. "She is not sick as much as worn out. Her condition is poor. We called ahead and explained your coming so she would not become too excited."

"I won't stay too long," David assured her.

Simma knocked and then opened the door. The room was small but adequate to hold a hospital bed, nightstand, and two chairs. A large picture of Masada hung on the wall.

"You are here." The frail little patient held out her thin arms. "Come to me." Her gray hair was flat against her head; she looked worn and drawn. "Ruth's little Dov! Let me hug you."

David bent down, and her bony arms encircled his neck. Shula had the stale smell of the infirm. The brown pupils of her eyes were encircled with yellowish deterioration. Her skin hung from her arms. Her lips against his cheek felt paper thin.

"I don't see so well now." Shula put her hands on his neck and drew him close. "I never dreamed I would see you again." Her eyes moved rapidly across the terrain of his face. "And your mother? Is Ruth well?"

"Hardy as ever." David smiled. "She sends you her love."

Shula wept. "I would so love to see her before I die. We lived through so much together."

"I will leave you to talk." Simma went to the door. "Perhaps your conversation is best alone." She waved. "Come to the administration office when you are ready."

"Afikim is quite impressive." David pulled up a chair.

"My dear young boy," Shula's voice cracked, "if you could have seen what little was here when your mother came. Only huts and mosquitoes. Our diet was so meager we often broke out in boils and sores."

David tried to envision Shula with the wrinkles ironed out. Ruth's fading brown picture of daring pioneers with their hair blowing in the wind came to mind. He imagined her hair as black again.

"There was almost no pastureland, and the summer heat nearly consumed us." Her yellowing, faded eyes stared at the ceiling. "But we were part of a great adventure. The whole world was against us, but nothing stopped our progress."

David remembered Shula was at least ten years older than Ruth. He thought the woman looked much older. Her arms and hands were dry and leathery from too many years in the unforgiving sun.

"I was there when your father and mother stood under the *chuppah*, the wedding canopy. What a striking couple!" Shula beamed.

David pulled the chair closer to the bed. "You *really* saw them get married?"

"I was there when you were born." Shula reached for David's hand. "The building is gone, but the place is close to the new barns. Yes, I was there."

David held her hand tightly. "Can you remember anything about that night?"

"No English doctor would come out to this strange settlement of Jews. And the night was very dark." Shula whispered an aside. "We had to be careful because snipers often shot at our windows at night. You picked a dangerous time to come." She laughed gently. "Your father was very nervous, so we kept him boiling water. One of our own midwives and I brought you into the world. The delivery was not hard." The old woman sighed. "And now you have come back to us."

"Do you remember when my father disappeared?"

"Of course!" Shula's voice turned raspy and forceful. "Terrible! Just horrible! Your family left for a ride and didn't come back. By nightfall we were sure they had been ambushed." Shula pushed herself up on her elbows. "Danger was everywhere." Her voice cracked. "Snipers shot at us as we worked in the fields. The Arabs rushed in and raped our women or cut our throats. A person could just disappear and never be heard from again. Such atrocities were common. The British wouldn't lift a finger to help."

"Did anyone know where they had gone?"

Shula shook her head. "Privacy was a luxury in those days. To steal a few hours away together was precious. Possibly they hoped no one would even miss them, but one of the men saw your father drive off the kibbutz in a pickup. We had no other clues."

"What happened?" David bit his lip. "How did you find out what occurred?"

"Days turned into weeks. Yaacov and Ruth had vanished from the face of the earth." Shula's eye widened. "Then one of our men heard about the wreckage of a truck on one of the backroads going up to Nablus. We took our rifles and five of us went up early in the morning." She searched David's face as if telling the story for the first time. "We found the truck...upside down . . . completely incinerated. A bomb crater was about twenty feet behind the wreck. There was a little house, a sort of rest room, that was flattened. We had to assume that animals dragged away . . ." Her voice trailed off. "Of course, your father had driven over a booby-trapped Arab road."

"Thank you." David let go of her hand and settled back in his chair. "You have helped."

"Months later a British solider brought your mother back. We were elated as we were sure she was dead. Her mind was blank. She couldn't tell us anything. For a long time she wouldn't talk to anyone. She would not mention your name, David." Shula shook her head and slipped back onto her pillow. "She was never quite the same again."

"Shula, is the backroad still there? Could I find the place?"

"The road is a paved thoroughfare now. Sure. The 'Y' in the road where they stopped is quite obvious. I could even have someone make a map."

"Please do." David smiled. "Yes, I would very much like to find the place where my father was last seen."

"Stay with us," Shula reached for his hand again. "Your coming back is a confirmation we have not been wrong. Perhaps you truly belong among us. Yisrael will find a place for you to stay . . . a night . . . a week . . . a month." She squeezed his hand hard. "A lifetime."

"You are tired." David stood. "I will come back later. Yes, I will definitely stay here for a while." He bent down and kissed her on the forehead. "After you've made the map, I will find the place." He stopped at the door. "Thank you, Shula. Thank you."

TWENTY-FOUR

David finished his letter to Ruth and scanned it quickly. The small apartment in the new complex was detailed and Yisrael Dinitz's greetings were included. He urged Ruth to visit Shula before time ran out. He described the hard work in the fields but didn't say anything about the encounters with Hannah Sarid. David sealed the envelope and set it on top of a letter to Edward. On the bottom of the stack was a card to George and Mary Richards and in between were a few lines to the Meachems.

The first week at Afikim flew past in spite of the aches and pains of physical labor. Residents needed to know he pulled his own weight, and David recognized the work assignment with the day laborers was a test of sorts. The sunburn still stung, and he knew his letters had to be completed quickly before he fell asleep at the desk. Fatigue was not an enemy, and his stamina was increasing. David felt alive and vigorous.

Sheer exhaustion limited his conversations with Hannah in the evening. She had certainly been available enough, but the capacities of the flesh were spent by six o'clock. She had a way of showing up just as he was eating with the other workers. When Hannah came, Simma left. Table conversation was difficult because many of the residents didn't speak English. Hannah translated and kept the conversation alive. She also lingered after the others left.

After polite exchanges, the workers were often distant and disinterested in David's world. Many were critical of life in the United States. They didn't seem to connect emotionally with

David. By the week's end David knew he was not one of these settlers.

Putting the pile of letters aside, David made final preparations for bed. He could hear the beat of rock music in the distance. Hannah was probably down in the recreation room . . . dancing with anyone available. David's legs wouldn't stand the test tonight. She had certainly telegraphed an invitation, but he had slipped away.

This little sabra was cut from a different pattern. The first time he saw Hannah, she was certainly attractive enough, but during the last week, the magnetism increased. Simma was responsible, thoughtful, but Hannah conveyed an earthy sensuality.

David picked up a pencil and started to sketch. The contour of Hannah's face beneath the sweep of her hair came quickly and with accuracy. He made light lines to place her eyes and mouth in proper proportion. The shape of the lips was easy, but to David's surprise, he couldn't draw her eyes. For the first time, he realized he really hadn't been able to look within this inviting woman.

He crawled into bed wondering. The thought crossed his mind he should write Paul Kendall. The resolve to do so was quickly engulfed in sleep.

During the next week, he had three conversations with Shula. She rallied but couldn't leave her room. Seeing his mother through the eyes of this old friend filled in missing details. Clearly, Edward had never fully grasped the depth of Ruth's losses or how her personality was changed by pain. Shula's vivid description of the metamorphosis of a carefree wife with boundless optimism into a creature of dark foreboding thoughts and reclusive tendencies deeply touched David.

Shula often wandered off into folk tales and stories of the wisdom of rabbis. But Shula's version of the past hardly connected with the present moment. Her European world of the shtetl and the ghetto was from another time long since consumed by fire. Only fragments lingered in the memory of an aging woman. David left their conversations with a profound sadness for her, for Ruth, for grandparents, uncles, and aunts he would never know.

The exhilaration of David's personal discoveries evaporated before the onslaught of constant demand, production, and routine. Yet, for many of the other residents endless toil seemed to be a wall that covered what was best left unexamined.

Many survivors' children were raised to trust no one. "Parents and children often cannot cry over pain," Shula explained. "Pain is always measured against the possibility of death, so difficult moments are simply discounted." She explained the endless guilt of being alive when so many weren't. "Little ones often unconsciously think they must justify their parents' survival." Shula took his hand. "You were a very fortunate boy, David. The Holy One saved you from terrible pain." He remembered staring at her, not sure whether to be grateful or remorseful.

"Food takes on a strange meaning for the survivor," Shula explained rather clinically one afternoon. "I have friends who still take a snack with them wherever they go for fear of being detained. Strange," she mused, "some even eat rotten food rather than throw it away. Makes you a little crazy sometimes," she concluded.

Each time David left the hospital keenly aware he could not lay claim to being a sabra of any sort. He was the child of a world across the ocean, and mercifully spared the worst horrors of the twentieth century. Paradoxically, as kibbutz life became more familiar, he was aware of how different life in Israel really was.

Loneliness returned. The old sense of displacement emerged. David often preferred distance between himself and the others. The second week came to an end, and he decided to go it alone that evening.

After the tractor was parked in the barn, David quickly showered, grabbed his vest, and went to the cafeteria. He chose an isolated table in the back to eat alone. Trying to be the "good ol' boy" with a table of immigrants had been a self-imposed sentence. Solitude felt familiar and comforting.

"Hard day?" A feminine voice broke the silence.

"Hannah!" David sounded surprised but wasn't. "I didn't see you come in."

She set her tray across from him and sat down. "You look very lonely tonight." Her inflection meant more than the words said. "Perhaps things have not gone so well."

David tried to organize his thoughts. "Nothing in particular," was the best he could say.

"Such a strange man," Hannah teased. "Very different." The sabra frowned. "Not one of us." Suddenly she smiled. "But definitely not one of *them*. Perhaps you need a little pleasure in your life."

David tried to avoid the temptation to dance verbally with her. He didn't like the tease. "Happiness? Sure, I'd like a touch of joy." He tried to look into her eyes. "I need to get connected to life again."

Hannah buttered her bread and looked around the table for the salt. She studied a piece of fish as though trying to decide whether to eat. "To be so serious is a mistake." She speared the fish with her fork. "We must find a way to lighten your life."

David pushed his plate away. "I would like to draw your eyes, to sketch your face." He became more definite. "Yes, I *want* to find out what is in your eyes."

"Draw *me*?" Hannah scoffed. "Of course! Why not? I always wanted to be a model."

"I was trained as an artist. Faces are my thing." He took several last bites. "Yes, drawing would be very good for me."

Hannah listened with an air of indifference and quickly finished eating. She picked up her tray and beckoned for him to follow. He slipped on his correspondence vest with pad and pencils in the pockets.

"So you want to look into my eyes?" She slipped her hand into his. "Okay. We need a good place, Mr. Van Gogh." Once outside, Hannah turned in the opposite direction of David's apartment. "My place, of course." She squeezed his hand.

Her apartment building looked older, dated, but in good

repair. Hannah's flat was at the end of the first floor. She unlocked the door, let David in, and locked the door again.

David immediately felt a lack of taste. The few pictures were tourist-variety photo reproductions of Israel. Like most of the apartments, the furniture was simple and basic. The room was cold, flat, stark. The only personal touch was an old family picture on a small table. At the end of the living room was a single barrack bed and an adjacent kitchenette. Green military fatigues hung from a wall hook. Black boots were stacked underneath. David slipped his vest off and took out his sketchbook.

"My eyes?" Hannah sat on the end of the bed. "You like my eyes." She giggled.

"The eyes are the windows of the soul." David picked up a pencil without looking away. "They tell me who you are." He tried to see behind her facade.

Hannah undid the shirt button at her neck and tossed her head from side to side, letting her hair bounce free, but she didn't look at him.

With several quick flourishes David established the place of the face on the page. "I want to feel . . . the essence . . . the center." He looked at her intensely.

Hannah smiled cynically. "We don't have to do this routine. It's not necessary to tickle my ears with sentimental nonsense." She kicked off her shoes.

David's surging inner drive stopped. At one time he thought maybe Susan's death had ended that other sense of life, but the urge was still there. Yet Hannah's purely physical indifference severed the sensual tie that was pulling him onward. Her words lacked warmth. She moved with instinctive intent, not romance, love, or even caring. David saw nothing in her eyes.

"I am a beautiful woman." She shrugged. "You are a lonely man. It is a lovely evening. Just that simple. Nothing more."

David thought of Susan. "No. There has to be something more." He put the pencil down. "If there were not, the pain and regret would be even greater tomorrow."

Hannah looked amused. "Love has nothing to do with anything."

David persisted. "I want a friend, a confidante, someone to share my heart with."

"What's the matter with you?" she taunted. "I didn't invite you to get your hands on my soul. Who do you think you are? We may both be gone tomorrow."

David watched her eyes. Brown turned to black. She couldn't see beyond his skin; she never would. Salaciousness was turning into anger.

"Forgive me." David snapped the notebook shut. "My loneliness has betrayed both of us." He slung the vest over his shoulder. "I'm sorry. I had best be going."

"You're crazy!" Hannah reached for a shoe.

"Maybe so." David shrugged. "Maybe not."

As he unlocked the door, her shoe sailed past his head and bounced off the wall. He closed the door behind him without looking back. David guessed she was swearing in Hebrew.

The evening breeze felt cool, and David quickly put his vest on. He walked hard and fast toward nowhere, feeling bewildered and confused. He was angry with Hannah, himself, and life as it was. He had come a long way from Susan's death but not from her influence. He didn't want any changes there.

When David reached the far fence line, he realized he was too close to the security perimeters to keep going. Someone might mistake him for an intruder. He turned back, walking more slowly. Only then did he begin to sense clarity. Certainly he was an ordinary human being, clearly attracted to the sensuality of this aggressive young woman. Why did he walk out? The answer came back in a unified voice. David Richards and David Moses were of one mind. "The fool confuses love with lust." He wanted love. Hidden in Hannah's easy affection was bitterness and alienation.

David looked up, and the hospital loomed in front of him. He glanced at his watch and decided to chance Shula was still awake. The light was on in her room.

David cracked the door slightly.

"David!" She beckoned. "Come in. Come in. I've missed you."

He scooted a chair close to her bed. "Shula, do you know Hannah Sarid?"

"I know everyone here." Her matriarchal voice emerged. "Why do you ask?"

"Can you tell me something about her? About her background?"

"Of course, of course." She sounded like Shlomo Cohen. "Hannah was born here. Her parents Roni and Ya'el came here seeking refuge. Roni was killed up on the Golan Heights during the Six Day War. Terrible." Shula looked at David with great lament. "Unfortunately, Hannah didn't finish her schoolwork before she joined the army in 1980. She wanted to study film at Tel Aviv University but lacked the high school diploma. In the meantime Ya'el died of cancer. The girl is quite alone in the world."

"She's still in the army?"

"When the Lebanon war broke out in 1982, Hannah drove an ambulance. As best we can tell, she saw some horrible things. She returned here as a reservist and hasn't left since." Shula shook her head sadly. "So much talent and so much pain. Hannah's life seems to be on perpetual hold."

"Hmmm," David moaned more than answered. "Just wondered." He moved closer. "Shula, in the morning, I must leave. I want to find the place where my father died. Time here has been invaluable, but I have other places I must visit. I want you to know you haven't failed. You have been part of a noble experiment. Some of us are just meant to go."

Shula's face dropped. Disappointment was in her eyes.

"After all," David tried to reassure her, "Abraham and Moses had to go not knowing where. Some of us have to travel longer in the wilderness than others."

"I suppose so," she lamented and turned away. "I'm sorry you're leaving."

"When my mother comes, we will return and visit. I promise."

"Thank you." The old lady squeezed his hand. "Your staying here has meant much to me." She pushed herself up in the bed. "Let me kiss you before you go."

David bent down and once more the bony arms encircled his neck. "May the Holy One of Israel guide your steps, David Moses. May He give to you a vine and fig tree in your own promised place." She kissed his cheek and patted his head. "I anticipated your need." Shula pointed to the drawer in the bedside table. "Yisrael helped me make a map. You should have no trouble finding the place where your father was killed."

David quickly opened the drawer and found the hand-drawn map clipped to a printed road map of Israel. Lines were drawn in red ink clearly marking the route. "Thank you. Thank you." David slipped the map in his vest pocket.

"Be cautious, my son." Shula shook her finger in warning. "Travel is still dangerous."

"I will be careful." David stood up. "Shalom."

"Shalom aleichem," Shula Schransky answered.

David hurried back to his room and began packing his few things in the duffel bag.

He set his alarm clock and turned out the lights. In the darkness he looked at the opaque ceiling until his eyes adjusted. The moon was shining across the far hills over the top of the buildings. He could see the outline of the fences and the entryway running out to the highway. He could not possibly imagine who he might have become if he had grown up in Afikim rather than Oklahoma City. George and Mary Richards came to mind. All David knew for certain was what had been. The world of his past was all he had; the time at hand was all he would receive.

TWENTY-FIVE

David rose early to find Yisrael Dinitz before the pressing demands of the kibbutz avalanched the old man. He caught Dinitz coming out of the cafeteria. Yisrael listened briefly before looking away as if distracted by something happening somewhere else, but his disappointment was obvious. "So?" he grumbled. "You want to get away from us."

"No, no. I simply need a little space." The excuse was a concession. "I'm sure I'll be back to stay." David's explanation was duplicitous. He struggled to find the most soothing words. "I can't go on until I complete an important piece of unfinished business."

"What?" Yisrael frowned.

"I want to find the place where my father was killed. You said I might use one of the old vehicles. I thought I might drive up to Nablus. I'm sure a little time up there would help put things into perspective."

Dinitz rubbed the side of his head and thought about the request. His lip protruded, and he looked down at the sidewalk. "Sure," he finally drawled. "Yes, I understand." He brightened. "You need to find this place. Maybe such a trip would help you see everything more clearly. I will get you the keys to one of the pickups." He smiled broadly. "Exactly what the doctor ordered. You need to touch the past more fully." He walked quickly toward the administration building.

David fell in alongside him. "I have maps you and Shula prepared."

"You must be very careful." Yisrael warned. "Everyone is

— **228** —

a terrorist! Matters are tense around Nablus. All West Bank cities are suspect now."

"Come on," David chided. "You're dealing with an Oklahoma cowboy. Remember? We're well acquainted with fighting off the Indians."

Dinitz didn't laugh at David's joke. "You're not watching a John Wayne movie," he groused. "Palestinians are murderers. Don't forget it!" Yisrael unlocked the back door and went in.

"Why are matters getting worse?" David leaned over the front counter.

"Maybe a million Palestinian refugees live in the West Bank and Gaza. Jordan, Lebanon, Syria have possibly another million and a quarter. Their cities are a blight on the land." The old man pulled a key out of his desk and put it on the counter in front of David. "The Arab population is under our military control so they blame *us* for all of *their* problems."

"Why doesn't the government improve their condition?" David asked.

"Why didn't your American president prevent Selma, Alabama?" Yisrael shot back. "You are embarrassed by George Custer; we must endure Ariel Sharon." He shrugged. "America had Indians, and we have Arabs. The losers always hate the winners." He tossed his head indifferently. "That's life!"

"Of course," David answered dryly. He picked up the key. "I will take good care of the pickup."

"Take as long as necessary." Yisrael shook David's hand. "Go find yourself, so you can come back and settle down."

"I'll try to get everything nailed down," David sounded casual and lighthearted. "Don't worry if I don't return quickly. I want to see as much of the northern area as I can."

"Sure," Yisrael waved him on. "Fill up with gas as you leave." He pointed to reserve tanks near a barn.

"Thank you very much."

Yisrael held up his hand. "A final thought." He shuffled some papers nonchalantly. "Hannah Sarid is trouble." He put the papers down and began fumbling with a pencil on the desk. "Everyone knows about her. If there is a problem, I can help."

David blinked rapidly several times. "Hannah? The kibbutz is a rather small world. Don't worry, Yisrael. I'm a big boy."

The old man pursed his lips for a moment and then winked. "Be careful." He pointed to the north. "Just follow your map. Take the road toward Lod. You'll see signs pointing toward Ram Allah. Remember where you are, big boy."

David was relieved to be on his way. The old green pickup ran well, and the road was easy to follow. Rickety vendor stands offering vegetables and fruits dotted the roadside. Old men in worn dirty business suits and traditional black and white Arab kaffiyehs sat smoking and talking, oblivious to the lack of customers. Their clones led small donkeys down the highway. Even though the air was already quite warm, the country gentlemen wore vest sweaters under their dull brown and black coats. The Palestinian world seemed to spin at a slower speed.

Periodically David passed Jeeps parked by the side of the road; soldiers held M-15 assault rifles casually in hand. The IDF, the army, was always a clear and formidable presence. The troops waved; the Arabs only stared. *Strange*, he thought, the Palestinians almost seem to know me.

Driving through a small Arab village, David was reminded of how different Palestinians were from their Jewish counterparts. *Their pace of life seems unbearably slow*, he thought. *Jews always run scared. We would have turned this local dump into a tourist stop even if it meant building an olivewood factory in the center of town.*

Brothers of the road vendors sat in front of every cafe sipping coffee and talking endlessly as if the paupers owned the world. Their wives in brightly colored embroidered dresses scurried up and down the streets, in charge of nothing but responsible for everything.

Everyone seems to notice me. Why? He slowed to turn a corner. The buildings were remarkably alike with one-story flat roofs and colorless gray concrete-block exteriors. *Life is obviously as plain as the rocks jutting out of the ground everywhere,* David thought, *and probably as hard.*

He stopped at a small stand on the edge of the village and bought a Coke. A toothless old Arab made no attempt at friendliness. When David returned to the truck, he noticed the yellow license tag. *I forgot! Arabs must use distinctive blue plates. That's the reason for the cool reception. The truck could be a liability.*

For the next hour and a half, David drove from the flat coastal plain, up the backroads climbing into the mountainous hill country. He sped through Ram Allah and on to Al Birah, which the map said was the site of ancient Beeroth, the burial place of Nahari, the armor-bearer of Joab. The winding road toward Ofra was lined with never-ending rows of vineyards. Settlers' huts had changed little since the days of Abraham and Abimelech, the Babylonians and Romans. Ofra looked like a friendly village with its open, unfenced fields.

Need a seventh-inning stretch, David thought. He slowed down, and spotted a little cafe not far ahead. *Let's leave the Israeli license plates behind.* He walked the block and a half to the Arab watering hole. *Seems like I remember someone at Afikim saying there was a Jewish underground operating out of Ofra. Strange thought.* He looked around. *Doesn't appear subversive, but I'm sure Ofra was the place. No one looks hostile.*

Inside the cafe, Arab men were talking so loudly David could hear them from outside. He opened the door and walked in. The environment became frigid. *I'm in trouble,* he sensed. Several men looked up as if they might attack. *Keep cool,* David stopped at the first chair next to two men and a woman.

"I'm an American, a tourist," David raised his voice. "Does anyone speak English?" He smiled and tried to radiate southwestern hospitality.

"Sure," an Arab answered. "Can I help you?" Immediately the atmosphere lifted.

"Probably need ya'll to help in ordering," David tried his best Oklahoma drawl. "David Richards is the name." He extended his hand, knowing Moses would not be the best choice of surnames. "Sorry, I don't speak Arabic."

"Taher." The young man extended his hand. "Please meet my friend Jaher and his wife Naimi. We would be pleased to have you join us. Let us order for you. Have you taken your noon meal yet?"

"No. Actually I'm quite hungry." David kept smiling and looking around the room. Even though no one was staring, he was clearly the center of all attention.

"What part of America?" Taher's small mustache reminded David of King Hussein of Jordan. The dark-skinned Arab's eyes were soft brown with bovine gentleness. "My cousin studied at the University of Texas." The man had a small scar above his right eye.

David laughed. "Our archrival! I attended the University of Oklahoma."

"Va-ry interesting!" The old man's words rolled up out of his throat. Jaher's face was pitted as if from a childhood disease. He had a small black and white beard. Jaher's hair was gray, and he looked around sixty. His wife seemed to be about the same age. "You must tell us more of this place called Oklahoma." He offered a cigarette. David accepted out of politeness and an urgent desire to be "one of the boys."

The conversation quickly became animated, with questions, answers, and laughter filling the air. David was toasted like a celebrity making a guest appearance. Falafel and pita bread were set before him. Other men pulled their chairs closer. The woman said virtually nothing but watched intently.

After an hour David decided to press his luck. In a confidential voice, he said, "I picked up a strange tip recently. Is this the town where there is a Jewish underground?"

"Where did you hear this?" Taher's countenance changed, and his eyes became hard. He leaned back and stared.

"I overheard a conversation while visiting a kibbutz." David tried to sound indifferent. "I was looking at olivewood products. I was intrigued."

"Sure." Jaher interjected. "Everyone knows Jewish terrorists live here."

"Tell me more about these people." David tried to sound

like an American journalist. "We don't hear much of this side of the story in America."

"Four mayors of West Bank towns found bombs placed in their cars by these people," Jaher muttered. "This information is public knowledge."

"And the murderers bombed the college in Hebron, killing our students." Naimi virtually spat out the words. Her hair was streaked with gray, and wrinkles crossed her olive skin. "The swine are butchers and murderers." She slapped the table with the side of her hand. Two fingers were missing on her right hand.

"Such stories interest you?" Taher sounded skeptical.

"Absolutely." David kept smiling. "I know about the problems you have in living with this modern Jewish state. After all, people will ask me questions when I return home."

"Some of those people in Ofra even plotted to blow up the Dome of the Rock Mosque," Taher slowly answered. "They are unquestionably terrorist."

"Frightening," David commented. "I assume you are Moslems."

"No." Taher shook his head. "We are Christians."

"Christians? I thought . . ."

"Many Arabs are Christians," Jaher interrupted. "My family has been Christian for at least sixteen centuries. It would not be possible for us to be otherwise."

"I am amazed."

"Americans don't understand us," Taher continued. "You have been so busy studying what the Germans did to the Jews you have completely overlooked what the Jews have done to us." He turned to Naimi. "Tell him your story. Her family survived the Turks, the British, and the Jordanians, but the worst have been the Israelis."

"I was forced to live in Balata Refugee Camp," Naimi growled. "I quickly learned what it is like to have sewage run down between the houses. The IDF broke into our homes at will and often tore our few remaining treasures to shreds." She snarled. "Soldiers beat and humiliated us at will."

Jaher leaned over the table to make his point in David's face. "Should they want to run a pipeline through our orange groves, they just cut the trees down without repaying or replanting!" He seethed with anger.

"These attacks made you followers of Arafat?" David probed.

"Did anyone say that?" Taher looked around the group in mock consternation. "We only want justice."

David scratched his head. "But I thought Arafat was the leader of all Palestinians."

"Arafat and all the Fatah commanders are greasy politicians living in luxury while we exist in squalor," Naimi accused.

"Quiet!" Jaher put his hand over hers. "Political allegiances and opinions are best not discussed in public."

"I don't care," the woman defied her husband. "There is no hope, unless we take matters in our own hands. We must rebel!"

Jaher looked nervously around the room. "My wife is under a great deal of strain. Anger produces statements that are not always representative."

Naimi began softly thumping the table with her tightly closed fist. "One rock killed the giant Goliath; rocks can destroy once more. David can be toppled by a well-placed stone to the head."

"Watch yourself," Jaher warned. "You speak too freely."

"You give the Jews your best American airplanes, and everyone knows they have the atomic bomb hid somewhere." Naimi talked even louder. "Your country pours in money like turning on a water faucet! But I tell you we will not take the injustice much longer!"

"Please," Jaher warned his wife. "You are saying far too much."

"I am going to tell you something to never forget." Naimi punctuated each word by pointing her finger in David's face. "You will see the day—"

Two old men rushed through the cafe door screaming in Arabic. Chairs fell backward as the men nearest the door ran out to the street. The owner jerked off his apron and threw it on the floor. Taher was right behind the first wave pouring out onto the street.

"Stay here," Jaher cautioned David. He pointed his finger in his wife's face. "Don't you dare come outside. I remember last time all too well. You stay *here!* Understand?" Jaher warned and was gone.

"What's going on?" David rushed to the window. "What did the old men say?" He pressed his head against the pane to see as clearly as possible. Men were running between the buildings.

"Trouble has broken out." Naimi pointed out a side window. "At the school." She pointed behind the building. "Our children are confronting the soldiers."

"I must see." David raced after the two men.

"No." Naimi grabbed at him. "Don't leave this building."

David rushed down the narrow passageway between the cafe and the next building. When he reached the alley, he saw Taher and Jaher running toward the next street. "Wait for me," he yelled after them, but the roar of shouting drowned him out.

When David turned the last corner, he saw a large flat field in front of a one-story school building. Children and large boys were gathered on the side near the school. Opposite them, a line of IDF troops slowly and menacingly advanced across the playground. A soldier was sprawled on the ground behind the Israeli line. The Palestinians had stopped on the adjacent side of the playground and stood watching.

Just as David caught up with Taher, the children loosed a barrage of rocks at the soldiers. Instantly the troops charged. Shots exploded; canisters of smoke bombs hurled through the air. The children fell back, but the older boys kept throwing rocks. The troops raced forward, swinging clubs in the air.

"We've got to help the children." David darted out onto the playground. "I must do something!"

Taher grabbed his arm. "No! No!" the Arab screamed. "They'll kill you!"

The first wave of soldiers plowed into the big boys. Most got away, but two boys fell under the blows.

"I can't stand by and let this happen!" David broke loose

and started to run. He froze in place. A troop carrier swung around the corner and screeched to a halt ten feet behind him.

Soldiers leaped out and charged the men. The Arabs froze in place with their arms over their heads, but David turned back toward the children. He started to run. Suddenly, searing pain shot through his head, and his knees became rubber. He stumbled forward before he heard a horrifying thud. The paralyzing blow detached his body from his mind. He tumbled forward gasping for air. The last thing he saw was the ground surging up into his face.

At first there was nothing but pain. Eventually David heard movement. The sounds of large vehicles moving away was more like formless objects floating past in a terrible fog. Shouts punctuated the amorphous flow of sound and noise. He sunk to another depth of oblivion only to find the blackness filled with his terrible repeating nightmare. Once again the dreaded fireball shot straight up in the night like an atomic explosion. Pieces of metal and debris floated by overhead in the slow-motion replay of the recurrent horror. The all-consuming dread of abandonment unto death returned, and perspiration erupted all over his body. He tried vaguely to identify whether sweat or blood was running down his neck. Everything dissolved again.

"My friend!" An unknown voice probed the abyss. "My friend! Can you hear me?" The accent was strange. David tried to nod his head but wasn't sure anything moved.

"Medical Assistance!" the voice pleaded. "Somebody help! Don't let this man die! Get help over here!"

Someone lifted David up and turned his head. Burning sunlight jolted his senses. He tried to shield his eyes but couldn't move his arm. David forced one eye open.

"You should never have run at them." The face was unfamiliar except the man looked like King Hussein with a small scar above his right eye. "You are lucky the IDF didn't shoot you. We must get you out of here . . . back to the cafe."

David felt hands setting him on his feet. He tried to walk but was nauseated with pain. The voices around him faded into a white blur, and once again he slid into unconsciousness.

TWENTY-SIX

Noise . . . pain . . . blurred, merged in a . . . black . . . impenetrable . . . fog. A word broke in . . . from somewhere . . . dissolved. Eventually light . . . maybe overhead. Words attached to voices . . . sentences connected . . . no meaning.

"His ribs could be broken." The man sounded distinctly English.

Every muscle in David's body rebelled at the slightest movement.

A man with Arabic inflection asked, "Doctor, could his kidney be ruptured?"

"I don't think so. Rather badly bruised, I should say."

"*Keef halak!*"

David had no idea where he was or why he hurt so fiercely.

"Then again, the ribs may be only badly injured," the English voice diagnosed. "Shouldn't be moved unless he runs a high fever. Call me if there are any problems." The sounds faded.

David opened his eyes. Far overhead he saw a dirty ceiling splotched with water stains. A ceiling fan whirled but didn't dispel the sweltering heat. Nothing fit.

"How are you feeling?" A man with a salt-and-pepper beard looked down into David's face. "Remember me?"

David blinked uncomprehendingly.

"Remember? I am Jaher."

"Where am I? What happened?"

"Ofra." The deeply suntanned man put a wet cloth on David's forehead. "You are in my house." He pulled a sheet up over David's shoulders. "We carried you here when you passed out on the street."

David tried to touch the side of his head but could only feel a thick bandage.

"I'm afraid the doctor had to sew you up. You took three terrible licks." Jaher shook his head. "One blow can kill a man."

"And you are . . . ?"

"Jaher Kabha. Do not worry. We take good care of our friends. The doctor said you are to take this pill." He offered a glass of water. "A sip will help it go down."

David tried to push himself up but felt the tight bandage around his chest preventing movement. "I don't feel very well."

"Most understandable." Jaher held the glass to David's lips.

The medication quickly dropped David back into a bottomless and forever night. When he awoke, time seemed to have been suspended. The ceiling fan was still on, and everything felt much cooler. The room was dark. Slowly his memory returned.

A riot . . . a demonstration . . . a tumult erupted. Why was I there?

David tried to get up, but the pain was excruciating. He fought through agony until he was able to sit up in bed and put his feet on the floor. The room moved in a slow spin; he was uncontrollably dizzy. David clenched his teeth and clung to the sheets. Eventually the gyrations stopped. He tried to stand but quickly dropped back on the bed. Springs squeaked. One attempt was enough.

The door opened slowly, and a head peered cautiously around the corner. "You are awake? It's Jaher."

David nodded weakly. "Come in."

"I am sorry to bother you, but a few questions must be asked."

"I have a few myself." David's response was labored.

Four men followed behind Jaher.

"What time is it?" David asked. "Must be after eight o'clock."

"Closer to nine," Jaher answered. The men gathered around the bed.

"Heavens." David rubbed his chin. "I've been out for six or seven hours."

"More like twenty-four," Jaher explained soberly.

"You've got to be kidding!" David had to catch his breath to speak. He forced himself back up again. "A whole day passed?"

"Remember me?" The man had a thick bandage covering his head and over one eye. "I'm Taher."

David couldn't remember. "What happened to you?"

"About the same thing that happened to you," Taher answered. "But Arabs are a tough lot, my friend. We shall see if Oklahomans are our equal." He pulled up a chair. "I'm sorry, but we must ask you some questions."

"What?" David breathed carefully and slowly.

"You are either a very brave or foolish man," Taher began.

"Or a deceptive one," another man accused.

"I don't understand," David groaned.

"Why did you run after the soldiers?" Taher smiled, but his question was hard and serious.

"The soldiers?" David tried to remember. Slowly the schoolyard scene returned. "Someone had to help the children," he said thoughtfully. "The children? What became of the children?"

"Why did you run *at* the soldiers?" Taher persisted.

"Why?" David looked incredulously at the men. "Why did you?"

"We didn't." Taher clarified. "We watched. You ran."

David blinked and puzzled at the strange question. He said slowly, "Then why weren't you running to help? The children were in great danger."

"See." Taher looked around the room. "I told you."

"I don't understand," David looked at the man.

"We did not run," Taher continued, "because that was exactly what the IDF wanted. They would only chase the children, but given the chance they would kill us. You were about to be shot dead."

"Nothing makes any sense." David held his throbbing head.

"You have a car?" another man asked.

"No," David answered. "I drove a pickup, a green truck parked somewhere in your town."

"Yes, we know," the man persisted. "The truck has an Israeli tag. Where did you get it?"

"A friend at a kibbutz loaned it to me for the trip," David explained wearily. "Please tell me what is going on."

"That should cover the questions about the truck," Jaher said firmly. "I think he has answered well." Abruptly, Jaher spoke in Arabic. The men nodded and quickly left.

"What's this all about?" David groaned.

"Sorry," Jaher apologized. "Your intentions were not clear. What you did yesterday was quite courageous but a bit on the foolish side. We had to make sure you were not a plant from the Mikhabarat."

"The what?"

"The Mikhabarat is the Israeli intelligence service. You might have been a *jasus*, a spy."

"Oh, come on." David sank back on the bed. "Really now." He suddenly felt nauseated. "I need you to call Professor . . ." His words became thick and garbled. "Please," he begged, "I'm an American. I need . . ." Words would not come anymore. David closed his eyes and drifted away. Susan's face smiled and beckoned. David desperately wanted to touch her, but she was out of reach. Everything slipped away.

The ominous frightening roar of some great machine shook David awake. Bright morning sunlight streamed in. The pain had lessened, but the noise was deafening. The entire bed trembled. Thunderous rumbling increased and the walls vibrated.

David panicked. He swung his feet to the floor and struggled to stand. To his astonishment he was wearing a long nightshirt and his clothes were nowhere in sight. Consternation gave him the momentum to stand. Even the floor trembled. He hobbled to the door, trying to shout. "Help! Help! What's happening?"

The door opened before he reached the latch. "It's me, Naimi!" The small gray-haired woman reached out to support him. "Please be careful. Sit down."

Perspiration popped out on David's forehead. He reached for a chair. "Are we under attack?"

"No, no." Naimi eased him down. "The IDF is bulldozing a house."

"Why?" David gasped.

"Retaliation." Naimi clenched her fist tightly. "One of the boys who started the riot two days ago lives next door. A soldier was struck in the head, so the army will get revenge by tearing the family's house to pieces."

"What about the boy?"

"Tamir was taken into custody. They may kill him, deport him. No one knows."

Cracking sounds of timber breaking apart jolted David. He held his head with his hands, breathing as deeply as he could. His palms were sweaty, and his heart was racing. "Why am I here?" he spoke rapidly.

"We were afraid to take you to the hospital lest you be arrested," the Arab woman explained. "While the soldiers chased the boys, some of the men carried you down the back street. We were afraid you had broken bones or worse."

"One blow did all of this?"

"They hit you several times while you were on the ground."

David could hear walls breaking apart. The bulldozer kept roaring in loud bursts of energy like the jaws of a primordial dinosaur grinding and crunching its prey. "Will they attack us next?"

Naimi shook her head. "No one knows you are here but our men. Once they have made an example of Tamir, the IDF will leave. He threw a rock; they hurled back a boulder. The issue is never justice but always intimidation."

"Where are my clothes?" David blurted out.

"They were ruined." Naimi pointed to a door. "But we

found keys in your pocket and took the bag from the truck. It is in the closet. No one is holding you here."

"Thank you." David sounded apologetic. "I think I'm rather shaken right now."

"Of course." The little woman smiled for the first time. "Something to eat or drink perhaps?"

"I think . . . I suppose . . . I just need to compose myself." David ran his hand nervously through his disheveled hair. "I'll be fine in a few minutes."

"I understand. Call if you need anything." Naimi shut the door behind her.

David looked around at the plain stucco walls and the strange makeshift furniture. Nothing was familiar, normal, except for the crucifix on the wall. He didn't belong. He was displaced, and the feeling was awful. The bulldozer moved away.

A strange inner dread arose from somewhere in the center of his very being. The sensation was worse than death. He wanted to run but couldn't. David tried to close his eyes, but a memory would not be denied.

Large faces were peering down at him. The room was strange, alien, filled with foreboding smells and sounds. A man kept tickling his chin with a huge finger that looked more like a sword. Little David could see the bright red lipstick of a woman coming in and out of focus as she swooped down on him with wet, juicy kisses.

"What an adorable child, George," she cooed. "Just perfect for us."

The man laughed with a roar that shouted like a river rushing out of control down a deep canyon. "We'll take him!"

Little David felt himself being lifted up in the air. His feet dangled helplessly, and he felt suspended dangerously above the floor. Another face pulled alongside. A man with a mustache was holding him at arm's length. Little David heard the woman saying, "Now you're ours! All ours."

"Come on, Mary. We don't have much time to get the

papers in order to get out of the country. And what is the name?"

"David," the other male voice boomed. "He's well trained to the name. Be a bloody shame to confuse him, now wouldn't it?"

"David!" the women shrieked. "You will be ours forever and ever."

Little David had the terrible sensation of being whirled around and around. Total abandonment swept over him, and he thought he would die. He wanted to scream but was too frightened.

"We're taking you with us now, little David." The woman's large mouth whispered in his ear. He felt she had the capacity to bite it from his head.

The bulldozer roared back to life. David forced himself to open his eyes and dispel the long repressed memory, but nothing stifled the emotional backwash. His fingers dug into the edge of the chair until his nails cracked. Tears ran down his cheek, and his body shook uncontrollably.

Nothing stopped an overwhelming avalanche of emotion he had run from all of his life. The anguish of abandonment rolled over him, and David expected to die. Thirty minutes later he was dismayed to find he had survived. Rather than death, he had walked through purgatory.

During the following days, David gradually increased the amount of exercise he could tolerate. His walks took him farther and farther across the village of Ofra. He returned past the pile of rubble that was once the home of a boy named Tamir. No one knew what had become of the youth.

David generally stopped at the little cafe. His bandaged head gave him something of hero status. The Palestinians were naturally friendly and curious about him. He tried to avoid the bitter black coffee and constant cigarette smoke but increasingly looked forward to the afternoon banter. The villagers seemed to want little more from life than the comfortable enjoyment of the moment at hand and to live out the simple ways inherited from their fathers over countless centuries.

Near the end of one afternoon, a tough-looking young man strolled into the cafe. Rope-like black cords held his kaffiyeh in place at a cocky angle; the black and white checkered scarf was pulled over the right side of his head. He was unshaven, and his clothes were particularly dusty as if from travel. He sat down, and talking ceased.

The stranger rattled away in Arabic. He stopped, lit a cigarette, and blew the smoke nonchalantly in the air. Once again he resumed his report as if continuing a casual conversation. Men smiled and looked at each other knowingly. Their chatter resumed.

Jaher leaned close to David. "Seems there's been an unfortunate accident up the road from Ofra. Apparently a bulldozer driver was on his way home when the truck caught on fire." Jaher rolled his eyes innocently. "Our friend reports idle gossip that a molotov cocktail was thrown into the driver's face. Who knows? Nothing was left of the IDF soldier." Jaher sipped his black coffee.

David looked around the room. Each man smiled at him as if he were now part of the inner circle, their eyes sparkling in secret delight. David smiled back nervously and knowingly. A chilling realization settled over him. Each man had in some way been involved in the revenge.

Jaher emptied his cup and set it on the saucer. "I believe the rabbis have a saying. 'An eye for an eye; a tooth for a tooth.' "

TWENTY-SEVEN

After two weeks of recuperation, David knew Ofra quite well. Arabs greeted him as though he were a resident. Jews never spoke; their settlement on the edge of town was clearly off-limits.

"Your hair will soon hide the laceration," Jaher observed as they strolled along a side street. "No one will be able to see the evidence of your considerable adventure."

"How tragic," David joked. "Hard to be a hero these days."

"You have learned much about our ways," Naimi commented thoughtfully. "I hope you will be able to take a good report to your people."

"Certainly." David slowed to watch two Palestinian women drying watermelon seeds on the ground. They smiled shyly and looked away. "Your people are good, great friends."

"And fierce enemies," Jaher added.

David didn't respond. At the corner, they passed the road sign to Nablus. "Been quite a detour," David mused, "but it's time for me to get on my way again. People must wonder what has become of me."

"I'm sure your letter to the friend who loaned the pickup was received days ago," Jaher reassured him. "You must not be in a hurry."

"By my world's standards, I've been here forever."

"That's what's wrong with your country!" Naimi chided. "You even walk too fast."

"Not lately," David protested. "But I'm getting there again.

For several days I've been thinking about returning. Tomorrow would be a good day to start for Nablus."

"We have suspected as much," Naimi answered. "Yes. We will miss your funny talk, but we understand."

Jaher pointed beyond the sign. "If you go farther to the north, you might visit Barta, where I was born."

"Do they sell souvenirs of the event?" David kidded. "Every other place has mementos of famous occasions."

"Touché," the Arab grinned. "Perhaps, you would find other aspects of Barta to be more instructive."

Naimi did not smile. "In 1949 the Israelis and Jordanians cut our village in two pieces. One morning we awoke to find a new border drawn through the center of Barta. No one could cross over."

"We were permanently cut off from our relatives on the other side of the street." Jaher wiped his hand down like a slashing saber. "Israelis and Jordanians maintained the line with machine guns. During our cousin's wedding, we had to sit on our roof with binoculars to watch the festivities."

"Now we have become two very different peoples." Jaher shook his head. "Political boundaries have also separated our souls. The Jews have divided us against ourselves."

"Hussein and the Jordanians took away our identity as a nation," Naimi complained bitterly. "The Jews stripped us of whatever was left. They made us the living dead."

"Please," David stopped her. "People have choices. Politicians have only as much control as we give them. No one can own your soul."

"Americans are very naive." Jaher's voice took on a sharp edge. "When my grandmother died, we knew nothing until we heard wailing across the border. Only when we looked through the binoculars did we understand." He pounded his fist into his hand. "There was no choice to attend the funeral! No choice in standing by the grave. Such things eat away at you for years."

"Brutality flourishes in this land," David answered. "Believe me. I have been touched by injustice more deeply than you know. But we can rise above circumstances."

"Only an American could say such a thing!" Naimi sounded indignant. "We cannot conceive of such a foolish idea."

"I can't stop evil," David insisted, "but I can keep it from engulfing me."

"Really?" Jaher smiled cynically. "Live a little longer with us. A few weeks have not yet taught you what a lifetime of injustice has ground into us. A few more weeks and we shall see *who* is devoured by *what*." Jaher's anger was barely concealed.

"Maybe Jonah will swallow the whale this time." David tried to keep smiling. "You are people of great wisdom. I respect your experience and ponder every word. Unfortunately the winds blow my boat on to other shores before I have learned all you might teach me. How can I thank you for all you have done for me?"

"Spread our story," Jaher answered immediately. "Let your people know of our suffering."

David put his hand on Jaher's shoulder. "I will not forget."

"Once our friend, always our friend." Naimi reached into the pocket of her long flowing dress. "We will remember you risked your life for our children. Take this gift with you." She put a little cross on a chain in David's hand. "Our priest asked a blessing for your safe travel."

David looked at the silver crucifix on the thin linked chain. "A symbol of suffering. How appropriate. I will treasure this gift forever." He closed his fingers over the cross. "I will pray all pain will be transformed."

"Listen carefully," Jaher lowered his voice. "A fire has started, and it will become a raging inferno in the days ahead. What you have seen is a small beginning. A revolt will soon sweep the entire West Bank."

"Nablus is dangerous." Naimi squeezed David's hand. "Don't take any more brave chances. See this place you seek and then move on. We already have too many dead heros."

Jaher shook his finger in David's face. "You may believe they can't steal your soul, but by now you should have no doubt. They can certainly kill your body!"

• • •

The August sun's merciless roast began with sunrise. David left immediately after breakfast. By ten o'clock, the green pickup was bouncing along the backroads going to Nablus. David kept the window rolled down, allowing the breeze to blow through the cab.

Should have started earlier, he thought and took a drink from a thermos of water. *I hope I can find "the place" from Shula's instructions.* He spread the road map on the seat.

David thought about the bitter conflict between the Arabs and Jews. Yisrael Dinitz and Jaher Kabha had identical attitudes about opposite sides of the same problem. Their hates were ancient and intransigent. Reconciliation and resolution seemed impossible. Yet each man could be generous, loving, thoughtful, and at times, quite flexible. Products of war and strife, both had the capacity to be gentle and self-sacrificing.

David envisioned Yisrael leaning over the dining table making his point by jabbing away with a fork inches from David's nose. "I tell you Arafat and the Fatah mafia are more vicious than Hitler and the SS. Incarnations of evil is what they are! Living by drinking our blood!"

Jaher's voice seeped into his reflections. "Hear of Meir Kahane? He's a Jewish countryman of yours. Kahane teaches Jews are commanded to run all Muslims and Christians into the ocean. He only says out loud what Jews believe but don't yet have the courage to admit!"

The two Davids came to mind; David Richards and David Moses marched before him. Products of vastly different worlds, they, too, were linked by strife. He remembered the contempt of his alter ego. One persona was a product of social compromise; the other evolved from political deception. Like Arab and Jew, his inner war had gone on as long as Israel had been a nation. His own emotional barriers were no easier to cross than the border between Jordan and Israel.

What price peace? he anguished. *Reconciliation costs more than any man can pay.*

A stop sign and crossroad loomed ahead. David slowed and

remembered Yisrael's instructions. The road had been unpaved until increased farm traffic north to Tulkarm brought improvements. The *place* would not be far ahead.

David nervously turned onto the main highway and drove for about a kilometer before he saw the cutoff. The Y in the road was just as Shula described. He turned off the highway and coasted up the incline until the truck rolled to a complete halt. David pulled onto the shoulder and got out.

The hills along the side of the road gently sloped up into little mounds covered with sage underbrush. Red lilies of the valley bloomed everywhere. Birds were singing. Summer's heat had burned the grass brown, but the scrubby thick brush was still green. The countryside was serene, but David felt edgy. Beads of perspiration broke out on his forehead, and sweat trickled down his chest.

The road could not have changed since the terrain allowed no other passage between the hills. This section had to be the *place*. Everything fit. He walked slowly up the road looking for some vestige, some remnant, anything that might have survived forty years. At the top of the rise, David saw an open, flat area about twenty feet ahead. The clearing was overgrown with weeds but was obviously man-made. On the opposite side of the road, an incline gradually slid down to a dried-up creek bed.

David immediately plunged into the underbrush on the slope. The spindly pine trees wouldn't have been there four decades earlier. Their regularity in rows indicated intentional planting. Several yards below him, hunks of brown rusting metal stuck out of the ground. He quickly scampered toward the twisted debris. A long metal carcass seemed to have rolled down the hill, lodging against rocks. With time, the vehicle's frame became a makeshift retainer wall, piling up dirt as it washed down the hillside. One axle still stuck out of the ground. The rest of whatever it had been was long since rusted away, but the residue was unmistakably a truck's frame.

David scrambled back up the slope and crossed the road. The clearing still had broken concrete blocks scattered around the edge. The shape of a foundation with an entrance was clear.

He walked in just as someone would have done when the structure was standing and felt the space around him. A large boulder in front of the apparent entrance formed a natural fortress for a child to play behind.

He closed his eyes and tried to imagine how a pickup might have chugged up the hill and pulled over in front of the little hut. The place could have been a vegetable vendor's stand or more likely a roadside rest room. A small child would naturally have been placed at the base of the rock, perhaps, to play in the tall grass. The truck probably turned around to be ready to return to the main highway. A wide swing to the right would have cut across the center of the road. An explosion would have hurled the pickup over the side of the road; the force would have smashed the wooden building to pieces. The child behind the boulder would have only seen fire, debris, pieces scattering in every direction.

Such a sudden and violent explosion might not have registered as sound but shock and horror engraving the child's mind forever with recurrent shapes of disintegration, the cataclysmic movement of fire and fury burning an all-engulfing brand of terror on the soul. A child would have vibrated for hours like a quivering reed before the ravages of a wind-driven forest fire. Stripped of parents and protection, desire to survive would become the paramount emotion.

David could envision the scenario, but his heart would not unlock the door. Reruns of the recurring dream apparently were reserved only for midnight showings. And yet the moment was disorienting; everything was slightly out of focus, like a movie filmed at a warped angle, making him feel unstable.

A nauseous bubble of fear rose from David's stomach. He wanted to swallow the eruption but feared nothing could stop the intrusion. He sat down on the rock and lowered his head between his knees. He felt like he was going to die . . . not the quick death from an instant explosion but the agonizingly slow demise of life sucked away into the blackness of an unending, all-consuming night. His heart pounded ruthlessly.

ALL THAT REMAINS

After a few minutes he sat up. The wind blew lightly through the pines while birds fluttered from one branch to the other. His life-denying chill subsided.

Akiba, that strange Hebrew word, came back to mind with frightening clarity. *As Isaac was bound*, David thought, *this was the place of my binding.* He looked again at the large boulder. *On that dark night, this was my Mount Moriah.* He felt the hard surface worn smooth by the ages. *Why me? Why us? For what obscure reason did God turn His back and look away? We were not patriarch and son living out some great divine scheme shaping eternity and molding time. We were only a family seeking a reprieve from a world run amok.*

No answer came. The breeze gently bent the pines. Birds hopped to the lower branches and sang solitary songs. Clouds floated before the sun. For a moment the heat subsided and a shadow covered the clearing.

I was not bound! Yaacov Moses was the victim! David inhaled deeply. *On this unholy place an akiba, a sacrifice, had been made, but not the same as Abraham's.* The insight rushed at him with demanding intensity. *The ancient story turned upside down, the drama was reversed. The father had given himself for the son.*

A new notion emerged. *God did not look away nor hide His face.* The answer came immediately and intuitively. *No! The Holy One had never closed His eyes.* David felt primordial fear dissolving into something not yet named. *Across their labyrinthine path had been endless minefields, but Ruth and I survived with far more intact than life and limb.* Tears filled his eyes.

I am what remains of the oblation of Yaacov Moses. David wept. *My father's personal holocaust was not without meaning. I am the continuance. I was chosen for life! L' Chaim!*

In still uncharted regions of his psyche, the ground shifted and the earth trembled. The father had died for the son. No further sacrifices were required.

Four hours later, David was back at the kibbutz of Afikim. He tried to tell his story as quickly and sensitively as possible. Simma leaned on the counter in the administration building shaking her head. Yisrael and Rosalie Dinitz listened with rapt attention. Rosalie pushed David's hair aside to look more closely at the scar on the side of his head.

"You are very fortunate the Arabs didn't cut your throat while you slept," Yisrael concluded. "Only the Holy One spared your life."

"They probably hoped to extract information from you." Rosalie patted the hair back in place. "Does the wound still hurt?"

"No, I'm fine." David kept smiling and acting nonchalant. "I've come back to work."

Yisrael wrung his hands. "We were very concerned. Your letter came, and we forwarded it on to Professor Cohen, but everyone worried. We did not send help for fear of upsetting some delicate balance."

"I have other bad news for you," Simma added. "Shortly after you left, Shula Schransky died. Her heart finally stopped. We buried her a week ago on the kibbutz."

David grimaced. "How sad! I'm so sorry I wasn't here. I will put a stone on her grave."

Yisrael tilted his head back and forward. "But what more could anyone ask? Her life was full, and she died as a true daughter of Israel, surrounded by a roomful of friends who mourned her passing."

"I never get accustomed to the loss of my friends." Rosalie sighed. "I miss her." She looked away. "I always will."

"I will write my mother at once. She will regret waiting so long to come."

Yisrael stood up slowly. "We need the pickup. It will be good to have it back."

David laid the keys on the counter. "I need some time to digest my experiences. I'm not up to full strength, but I will be glad to return to the fields and work with the men."

"No, no," Yisrael frowned. "You've proved yourself. Besides I need you to help Simma. We have letters that require accurate translation. The two of you will make an effective team."

Simma smiled pleasantly.

"Give me a few more hours." David reached for his duffel bag. "In the meantime, I'd be glad to be back in the old apartment."

Simma handed him the key. "I'll be here when you are ready to work."

"Let me get a letter off to my mother." David scooped up the truck keys from the counter. "She would want to know about Shula's death immediately. Maybe I can persuade her to come for Yom Kippur and Rosh Hashanah. These holidays are not too far away."

"The Days of Awe," Yisrael acknowledged. "A most appropriate time for families to gather in Jerusalem."

TWENTY-EIGHT

"Can't believe the summer is gone." David looked out over the taxi-filled plaza, watching tourists gather in front of the Jaffa Gate. The street cafe faced David's Tower, which jutted up out of the Citadel, forming the side of the gate and the boundary of the Old City's ancient wall. "Sure hasn't cooled down much. All in all it's good to be back in Jerusalem and gone from the kibbutz." The broad street running through the Armenian quarter of the Old City was lined with little shops, tourist junk, and places to drink coffee while watching sightseers stream past in steady procession.

Shlomo stirred the thick black coffee. "Huh! September's nearly past. Time flies when you're having great adventures and chasing women."

David laughed. "No question. The Dinitzes had very definite plans for me and Simma. Nice person, too."

"But not of your world," the professor concluded for him. "Of course, of course." Shlomo leaned back in the chair, his rotund frame draped over the edge. "I'm sure everyone wanted you to stay on. Who knows? You might have had a career at Afikim!" He laughed.

"The people understood," David stirred his coffee. "Yisrael took it rather personally, but even Simma knew I didn't have a place among them. The time had definitely come for me to go. I think I had learned everything they had to tell me."

"I should say so! Look at you! You are as dark as a kibbutz farmhand, as disheveled as an Arab, as battered as a demonstrator, as wiry as a sabra . . . and as distraught as the Hasidics! You have become a true Israeli."

"I suppose I have been reborn," David observed thoughtfully. "A Richards was sent down the river, and it would appear a Moses came back up the stream."

"You are lucky to be alive." Shlomo shook his finger at David. "You could have been killed on the West Bank," he scolded. "What can I do with the likes of you!" He shook his head before breaking into a smile. "And yet what a student! What you have learned! I suspect much about being a human being!" He grinned broadly. *"Oi vey!"*

David watched an Armenian priest in a black robe walk by. The high-pointed back hood pulled over his head made him look more like a sinister phantom than a Christian clergyman. He seemed oblivious to the stares of the tourist. David watched the priest turn on David Street. "Must be going to the Church of the Holy Sepulchre," David surmised. "How many times has Jerusalem been rebuilt?"

"Countless!" the professor answered. "To be exact, forty times in thirty centuries."

"The cycle never stops," David mused. "The Romans obliterated everything, and yet two millennia later, we are in the same city, at the identical places, watching people still dressed like the ancients. Jerusalem is truly the capital of 'starting over.' "

"Of course, of course." Shlomo rolled his eyes. "Our resurrection rate is the highest in the world!" He laughed and shook all over. "Our fathers first came from the desert and our ancestors returned again from Babylon. My generation immigrated from Europe. Jews always come to this holy city to begin again."

"How does one start over?" David asked. "How did *you*, Shlomo?"

"My wife and son . . . died . . . were murdered." He spoke with a finality that forbade further questions. "I tried to hide in the world of ideas. I started again by going to the university. I journeyed into the Enlightenment and came out into the world of politics. Spinoza, Kant, Hegel, Maimonides, and the rabbis— even the likes of Shabbetai Zevi and Nathan of Gaza, the Baal

Shem Tov, Jesus, and Paul too—as well as Marx became my boon companions. Unfortunately, my new hopes dwindled and melted into disillusionment. Even in this quest I was forced to commence again. But in the end I returned to the faith of Abraham, Isaac, and Jacob to find peace. I went forward by going back. David, I believe in the future of our people. We are masters of starting over because we believe in destiny."

"But is this *my* world?" David reached in his pocket. "The Palestinians gave me a gift for trying to help a child." He took the cross from his pocket and laid it on the table. "I cannot renounce what I believe is true."

Shlomo picked up the silver crucifix and bounced it in his hand. "The image of a Jew dying because of religious prejudice and the cynical politics of power. A fitting symbol to represent all of us and yet so divisive." He put the cross in David's palm but held to his hand. "I agree with Yosef Blum. Anyone qualifying for Auschwitz is surely a Jew! The Arabs would have slit your throat without caring a whit for some subtlety of theological difference over inclusion or exclusion. But unfortunately, my son, history doesn't afford you the luxury of straddling the great dividing wall between the world of Christian and Jew. One has to decide."

"I can't accept the alternative of having to choose," David argued.

"The Wall and the crusader's sword forever divide Judaism and Christianity," Shlomo concluded. "Our friend Ilan Sharon and his Messianic followers notwithstanding, I see no genuine possibility of synthesis ... except one chooses to rise above all strife ... as a true human being. When I look at that cross, I don't see Israel's Messiah, but I am reminded of what it is to be a genuine human person. And I know Jesus would have gladly died again to keep His followers from doing what they have done century after century to His kinsmen."

"I can't let it rest on that note." David looked at the high stone wall running around the Old City. "There must be a more complete integration." Everywhere he saw massive rock partitions and barriers.

The professor gently pressed the tips of his fingers together and then pressed his hands against his face. "I think there probably is a better answer, but history isn't ready to receive the larger truth yet. Such a solution is too radical now."

"Try me," David persisted.

"The great Maimonides wrote a very instructive insight in his *Mishneh Torah*. He considered Jesus of Nazareth as preparing the way for the whole world to worship God with a unified heart." Shlomo smiled slyly. "Maybe the only important thing is to recognize that Jesus the Jew has done more than any Jew in history to spread faith in the God of Israel."

"But Christians believe in Jesus' resurrection. What will you do with the miraculous dimension?"

"Perhaps . . ." Shlomo clicked his tongue and pursed his lips. "Perhaps I expect the miraculous to come packed in more ordinary wrappings. I do not need the rock rolled away on Easter morning to believe the power and justice of God can still break into history." He cocked his head sideways and said pensively. "Let me tell you two stories."

David leaned back in his chair and crossed his arms over his chest.

"Before World War II Schechter was a renowned Jewish conductor. The Nazis arrested him and transported him to Terezin. Because of his reputation, the camp commandant assigned Schechter the job of directing an orchestra composed of other prisoners. Many were also outstanding musicians. This select ensemble of the incarcerated were to play for the entertainment of the SS officers." Shlomo shook his head vigorously. "This assignment was no honor! As soon as their concert was over everyone would be sent to the gas chambers at Auschwitz."

David uncrossed his arms and scooted his chair closer to the table.

"But Schechter knew how to use even culture as a means of resistance and confrontation. The conductor selected Verdi's 'Requiem Mass' for his symphony because of the meaning of the words and the power of the music to touch the emotions of the Germans." Schlomo leaned forward and grinned. "Verdi was not even a religious man, but Schechter well understood the lyrics of this outstanding work! Schechter even requested prisoners to sing to the masses. He rehearsed the musicians so fiercely they nearly dropped. Each person knew they would be dead the day after the concert and yet their work was so outstanding that even Adolph Eichmann was specially invited for the concert."

Shlomo stopped and cleared his throat. He feigned a cough but could not cover how close he was to being overcome with emotion. "After the performance, the Nazis stood and cheered the orchestra and the choir. The fools! Not one of the Gestapo understood what had really happened. The musicians had just sung in their faces, 'you will be judged for every evil deed. You will come before the bar of divine judgment to answer for every crime.' The SS butchers had not the slightest notion they were applauding their own final sentence of eternal damnation rendered on them by a Jewish jury composed of their victims!" Schlomo suddenly smashed his fist into the table. Tears trickled down his face. He stopped to breathe deeply.

David could not respond.

"A stagehand named Yitzhak working behind the scenes later escaped." Shlomo sniffed several times. "He was young, fast, and fortunate. Yitzhak told me this story. Yitzhak said, 'The devil is clever, but stupid. He always underestimates our tenacity. Even culture can be a weapon for people of discernment.' " Shlomo cleared his throat again. "When you speak of miracles I think on this story. I believe the performance of Verdi's 'Requiem' in that concentration camp was a miracle. The Holy One of Israel gave the victims of Terezin the final victory, the eternal triumph over their captors. The choir and orchestra of Terezin still play from heaven, and the Nazis continue to listen in hell."

"This is a true story?" David asked more in astonishment than disbelief.

"My wife played in the orchestra." Shlomo could barely speak. "My son lived in one of the barracks." He immediately looked away. David slowly covered the old man's clenched fist with his palm and squeezed gently.

"I understand." David could say no more.

The two men silently watched people pass. Three young soldiers clomped up the street; their heavy boots clicked against the cobblestones. Uzi machine guns swung casually from their shoulders. With military berets tilted leisurely on their black hair, the boy soldiers talked and laughed as if they had not a care in the world. Casually dressed tourists gawked in curiosity at a bent old woman hobbling on a sticklike cane and shuffling down the ancient sidewalk. A brown hood of coarse cloth covered her head, draped over her shoulders, and hung down her back. Shriveled lips no longer buttressed by long since departed teeth sunk back into the lined, creased face. Sad, cloudy eyes peered out from beneath folds of hanging skin. Suffering and wisdom met in her countenance.

"But I promised you two stories." Shlomo began again. "Two examples of the miraculous. Perhaps even of resurrection. Let me explain why the Six Day War was so short and decisive." His voice ceased to tremble, and Shlomo sounded more detached. "It was June 1967. Syria was ready to sweep on to the Golan, and Jordan had reinforced their troop positions on the West Bank. Suddenly Gamal Abdel Nassar sent his troops roaring out of Cairo toward the Sinai Desert. Obviously, Israel's enemies were about to strangle the nation. We too were about to face crucifixion. Few people know the complete story of what followed."

"Don't stop now," David urged. "Everyone remembers Israel's decisive victory."

"For a decade the Israeli air force had been working on an incredible idea called *Moked*, Hebrew for 'focus.' General Ezer Weizman first developed the concept. Later, General Mordecai Hod perfected the plan. This strategy would attempt to obliterate the enemy's air force in one blow! The entire Israeli air force would have to strike in a moment by flying so low all radar would be avoided. There would be no radio contact whatsoever. No nation in history had ever attempted such a thing!"

David smiled. "I have a hunch I'm about to hear the modern version of Joshua marching around the walls of Jericho."

"Nearly two hundred jets would fly at treetop levels over hundreds of miles attempting to strike targets scattered across thousands of square miles." The professor waved his finger as if lecturing a class. "One *single* random sighting from some isolated solider with a radio could ruin everything! To add to the difficulty, every military target had to be hit at exactly the same precise minute to guarantee protection to other planes flying over their targets.

"On Sunday night, June 4, General Hod summoned the base commanders to his headquarters to tell them Operation Moked would be executed the following morning. Once the attack was launched only twelve planes in all Israel would remain on the ground. The rest of the forces would hit in waves five to seven minutes apart, making three passes each time. When the pilots entered the briefing room at 5 A.M. the next day, one number was written on the blackboard, 0745. Zero hour!"

David studied his friend's face. Shlomo's eyes flashed, and his words spewed out like the rapid fire of a machine gun. He talked with a zest David had not seen before.

"When the first attack jets flew toward the sea, they were so low it felt more like riding in a high-speed boat. Even one slight split-second miscalculation could send a pilot and his plane into oblivion! Yes, many miracles would be needed on this day."

"This time I'm not going to wait for the end of the story," David interrupted him. "I think you are also far more a part of this episode than you have admitted. Tell me, Shlomo, what was your part in this adventure?"

"You get ahead of me." The professor frowned.

"With good reason," David shot back. "One must get ahead to end up even! Level with me."

"Of course, of course." Shlomo shrugged and gnarled his forehead in mock consternation. "I had a certain role in those events."

"Be specific." David pushed.

"Well . . ." Shlomo's voice rose in pitch, "everyone had to serve in the military. Shortly after I arrived in Israel, I enlisted. Someone discovered I had an unusual sense of space and depth perception, so the air force made me a pilot even though I was really too old for such things. In time, I became a commander."

"Ah! You were leading the attack!" David asserted.

"Let's say I was just one of several leaders." Shlomo nodded his head. "Yes, my unit led the attack on Egypt. We flew French Mirage jets and Ouragans which could match the Soviet MiGs and Egypt's Sukhois jets."

David laughed. "My friend, you are one of the most amazing persons I have ever known! Teacher, survivor, philosopher, pilot!"

Ignoring David's commentary, Shlomo continued. "At exactly 7:30 A.M. we took off from a landing strip at Lod. I was so close to the ground when I crossed the Sinai border that I terrified the Bedouins. When I soared over the Nile delta, I even had farmers raise up from their irrigation ditches and wave. Precisely at 7:45 I saw the El-Arish airfield. On the first strafe we took out their battery of radar-controlled 57mm guns. By the time we came back around, two MiGs were on the runway with their canopies closed. Unfortunately for them, it took one minute to warm up the engines. We were only supposed to make three passes, but we were so successful we made five passes, leaving at least fifteen planes burning on the ground. By the time we were through, every single plane was destroyed. Our little squadron turned homeward a total success."

"And what happened to the rest of Israel's air force?"

"Our combined first strikes destroyed two hundred and four Egyptian airplanes. About half of their total number and twice what any of us might have thought possible. We lost only eight planes." Shlomo thumped on the table with his finger and puckered his lips. "In the next wave that followed minutes later, one hundred Egyptian planes were burned, and we lost only one. Our first strike strategy traumatized the Arab's psychologically as well as physically. But this great victory was no accident nor only the product of our cleverness. The hand of

God had smote Pharaoh once again. Yes, my son, I saw a miracle on June 5, 1967."

David looked back toward the apartments where Shlomo lived. "Several times I have thought that no one could have a home in your location unless they were a very important person." David studied Shlomo's eyes. Profoundly intelligent and equally sad, they were also the eyes of a humble self-effacing man of courage. "The other day I was looking at a book in your office and noticed pictures underneath a pile of books. I wasn't sure, but the first picture looked like you and Ezer Weizman eating in a restaurant. The other two were unmistakable. Anyone would recognize Moshe Dayan and Menachem Begin. Obviously you were good friends with all of these historic figures."

"I get around." Shlomo pushed aside the compliment. "We each tried to do our part. Some of these men were very religious; others not at all. We were all just little Jewish boys who grew up and went off to war. But I say to you as I would to them this very moment: the existence of this nation is itself a miracle of resurrection. Jews and Christians stand on the same foundation. We share a common faith of sorts in resurrection. The remnant of Israel has been raised from the dead more than once." Shlomo pursed his lips, measuring his response carefully. "As the Christians trust in Easter, so Jews believe in the nation of Israel rising from the graves of the Holocaust." The professor smiled as he talked. "You see, Jesus' cause is really the same hope undergirding our nation. Maybe we can someday gather around a common faith in the one God who raises His faithful righteous ones to life again."

"Extraordinary idea." David shook his head. "I must keep chasing such a possibility."

"You are looking for a burning bush, David Moses." Shlomo's voice was guttural and probing. "Only a divine revelation can satisfy your quest."

"Have you seen such a fiery sight lately?"

"Maybe yes, maybe no." The professor pulled at his beard. "Love is a fire which burns and a bush which is not consumed.

Can you accept such a possibility? True descendants of our father Moshe have not so much been devoured by such flames as transformed through them."

"What are you suggesting?" David leaned forward.

"Perhaps that there is no answer to your question except to learn to love *regardless*. Maybe we have to be the fuel for the fire to kindle upon."

David searched Shlomo's round face. This nearly bald old man with heavy jowls and large sad eyes had surely walked through his own fiery furnace. At such moments David could almost smell the smoke. Shlomo Cohen was a magnificent human being.

"While you ponder such weighty issues, I have several less demanding matters for you." Shlomo reached in his pocket and pulled out a crumpled letter. "Got here just before you returned. I could not but notice the postmark was from California."

"It's about time I heard from my little mother." David tore open the letter and quickly scanned the page. "She's coming after all! Says she's bringing Edward. Ruth will be here for the high holidays. Terrific." He laid the letter down. "She'll be here in a couple of days!"

"Marvelous. Delighted to hear it." Shlomo waved at a passing taxi driver. "We shall have quite a Rosh Hashanah for your starting over this year. Most appropriate."

"I'm sorry Shula died before Ruth's return." David folded the letter and put it in his pocket. "I know she'll want to visit the kibbutz and Shula's grave."

"And I have one other message for you," the professor took a small piece of paper from his shirt pocket. "Perhaps this man may help you with these troubling questions." He handed David the paper.

"Father Panos." David read aloud. "Jebel Qarantal? What's that?"

"Jebel Qarantal is Arabic for Mountain of the Forty Days. The place is high above Jericho where the wilderness begins,"

Shlomo explained. "A Greek Orthodox monastery sits on the edge near the top. You will find Father Panos living up there."

"A monastery?"

"The hills are also filled with caves." The professor switched to his factual tone. "Men fleeing this evil world live there, keeping vigils of holiness. Sometimes the idea doesn't sound half bad."

"You know this Father Panos?"

"No. A friend from the States called while you were gone. The suggestion was his."

"Father Kendall!" David snapped his fingers.

"A slight joke," Shlomo smiled. "Yes. Your spiritual shepherd called to check on your progress while you were up in the north fighting the IDF. He wanted an accounting of what I had been teaching you. I had to confess you were educating yourself."

"I'm sorry I missed his call, but who is Father Panos?"

"Oh, a very holy man, I am sure," Shlomo answered. "Such a man spends all his days in prayer. From what I gathered, he was a teacher to Paul Kendall some years ago. Paul wrote this monk about you and said one of these days you'd be showing up. Apparently all you have to do is walk up a mountain and the good priest awaits your arrival."

"We don't have much time before Ruth comes," David thought out loud. "Perhaps, I should go tomorrow."

"You could catch a bus down to Jericho. You'll probably have to stay overnight. The climb up to the monastery should be no problem for such a soldier of fortune as yourself." He eyed David mischievously. "Of course, we are faced with the problem of your walking through Jericho, as you might want to stop and supervise another riot."

"Okay." David threw up his hands. "I promise to walk the straight and narrow."

The professor sounded stern. "You are going back into hostile country. Just don't talk to people on the bus and act American."

"Believe me!" David rubbed the scar on the side of his head. "I've learned my lesson."

Public transportation had none of the luxuries Yosef Blum offered his Fellowship Tours customers, but the sights, sounds, and smells were far more authentically biblical. David glanced up and down the aisles at the strange mixture of race, dress, and class. IDF soldiers mingled with the Arab travelers. There was little conversation, and tension filled the air.

As soon as the bus pulled out of Jerusalem, turned the corner around the mountaintop, and passed Bethany, the quick steep descent to the Dead Sea began. David's attention riveted on the rugged terrain of eroded valleys and flood-washed gullies, streaked with a pastel of color. He thought of how far he'd come since the first time he took this route with Yosef Blum's tour group. At every turn of the road, the land offered inexhaustible variations of contour and form. Endless canyons beckoned like forgotten mysterious avenues into the ancient past.

Occasionally the bus passed a Bedouin family plying their ancient trade of goat herding. Dirty-faced little children waved, and David waved back.

In a little over an hour the bus came to the bottom of the descent at the Dead Sea. After letting a few people off, the vehicle swung straight west toward Jericho. Trees reappeared and green patches replaced the parched soil. Soon the timeless oasis town came into view.

David piled out of the bus, trying to maintain a neutral tourist look. "Looking for Jebel Qarantal," he told a soldier. "Christian pilgrim," he nearly shouted.

The young man pointed to the high mountains towering above the city. "Good luck." He grinned. "Hope your shoes are in good shape." David waved and started walking through the town.

Jericho was much like Ofra. Life moved leisurely with the same toothless old men peddling fruit and soft drinks to the tourists. A few of the patriarchs wore faded brown robes. Their heavy, black, plastic-rimmed glasses strangely and incongruously imposed on the rest of their ancient dress.

David followed the main highway until he found the excavations of ancient Jericho. He listened to a tour guide lecture his group of Americans about the excavations of Kathlyn Kenyon. They wandered back to the bus and he cut across the open field toward the long climb up the mountain.

The monastery was not difficult to see. The stone buildings seemed to be cut into the side of sheer cliffs, rising almost straight up out of the flat plain. The high bluffs towered over the valley like eternal sentinels over the Jordan and the Holy Land.

By the time David reached the base of the mountain, he needed to rest. A simple parking lot was provided for visitors to the monastery, but from that point on everyone was equal. The journey was steep, winding, and by foot.

Halfway to the top, David stopped to absorb the intoxicatingly beautiful view. *You can almost see all the kingdoms of the world from here*, he thought. He looked toward the east and thought he might see the outline of Amman, Jordan. *Before Canaan even existed, caravans and armies passed this strategic entry. Joshua marched up this valley, and Jesus might have stood on this very spot.* He shook his head in amazement.

The higher he climbed, the more numerous the small caves became. The hermitages of thousands of long-dead ascetics dotted the sides of the cliffs. David stared.

What sort of man would go to such extreme measures to find peace? Someone like me, David concluded. He started walking again.

Beyond the final bend, a large entryway loomed up, built out of the rock. The huge, gnarled wooden door was secured from within. A chain hung down like a primordial doorbell. David heard nothing, except the wind. No one passed him on the trail, neither were there cars in the dilapidated parking lot. Feeling foolish and gullible, he yanked on the chain. Somewhere far off inside the religious fortress, he heard a bell faintly ring, but there was no response.

ALL THAT REMAINS

Must be the maid's day off, David thought cynically. Taking a longer look, he realized the monastery was much larger than it appeared from Jericho. *Maybe no one even lives here anymore.* He looked at the empty caves below him and yanked on the chain again.

David paced up and down the cobblestone landing. Periodically he stopped and stared at the awesome panorama beneath him and then began his nervous walk once more. Somewhere far inside he thought he heard footsteps. The faint padding of sandals. Someone was walking down stone stairs!

The enormous door creaked, groaned, and slowly swung open. A young man in a black cassock peered out. He said something that sounded faintly like Greek.

"Please," David pleaded, "I am here to speak with Father Panos."

"Father Panos know you?" the man answered in English.

"We've not met, but Father Panos is expecting me."

"Come in, come in," he beckoned quickly. "We will see." Once David stepped inside, the man pointed to a small, stark sitting room and bolted the outside door shut. Without another word, he bounded up a seemingly endless flight of stone stairs and disappeared at the top.

At least I'm inside . . . as usual someone from somewhere who knows nothing must sort out what they don't understand before anything can happen. He sat down on a rough bench and tapped his foot impatiently. *Just wait and learn "to be." To be ... the hardest task in creation.* David turned uncomfortably, trying to find a more comfortable posture. *I wonder if it took Jesus this long to get in here.*

The sound of clopping sandals again finally broke the imposing silence. The steps seemed heavier than the young man's. A shorter gray-haired monk wearing an identical black cassock descended the stone flight of stairs. He wore a tall black hat shaped like a baker's bonnet. The man's black eyes, olive skin, long, shaggy, graying beard, and proud nose marked him as a Greek Orthodox priest. A large gold pectoral cross swung from a chain around his neck. David immediately stood up.

"Can I help you, my son?" the monk spoke softly in a bass voice with the touch of an accent. Thick, bushy eyebrows hung down into his eyes.

"My name is David Richards." He extended his hand. "I am here because I was sent by Paul Kendall. Father Ken..."

"Of course!" The priest exploded with enthusiasm, opening his arms and hugging David, kissing him on both cheeks. "You are the one! Welcome to our humble house."

"Thank you," David mumbled.

"Yes!" The Greek boomed. "I am Father Panos. We have been expecting your visit. Come with me."

Father Panos bounded up the stairs, giving a running description of the ancient monastery as he walked. His gold cross swung back and forth in steady rhythm with his continuous gestures. Along the way he pointed out large jagged cracks in the cliffs left by terrible earthquakes from past centuries. At the top of the stairs a large plaza opened underneath the overhanging cliff. Walls built from chunks of stone concealed rooms and chambers hidden away behind ancient doors.

"Where do you stay?" David looked over the courtyard and up at the massive rock overhang. "Do you have bedrooms?" The pungent fragrance of incense drifted out of the cave.

"We live in the outside rooms." Father Panos pointed down the corridor of rock walls. "See the cave?" He pointed to a large opening in the middle of the walkway. "In that exact place our Lord confronted and confounded evil. Very holy to us."

"Incredible. Can I go in?"

"We worship there." The priest's words took on solemnity. "You must enter with great respect."

"Sure." David smiled. "Are there many of you here?"

"Time has taken its toll." The monk shook his head. "Once we were a legion. Today not many seek a holy life. Only five of us are left."

"You have a church here?"

"We *are* the church!" Father Panos held up his index finger in an instructive, monastic gesture. His second finger bent to touch his thumb as the last two fingers curled into his palm. He looked like a saint in an icon raising his hand in a gesture of blessing. "We, not bricks, are the living stone."

"Very interesting." The dryness of the air made David cough.

"My son, you must be very thirsty after your climb. Come back to my study and let us take a little refreshment." The monk led him across the courtyard and down another dark passageway tunneled into the mountain. At the end he opened a large, cracked door. "Come into my personal study."

The cave was lined with bookshelves. The stone walls and floor were stark and austere, but the room was invigoratingly cool. Hanging in the center of one plain wall was a large icon of Christ. A long table and two heavy chairs nearly blocked the other end of the room.

The monk rubbed his hands together quickly and smiled knowingly. "Now we can talk about David Richards."

TWENTY-NINE

We are simple men." Father Panos offered David a chair. "We live very basic lives. Our strength comes from simplicity." He picked up a brown clay jug of water from a shelf. "Quench your thirst." The monk filled a cup and handed it to David. "A hot day outside."

"Thank you, Father." David sat down. "Your English is . . . well . . . almost American."

"I did graduate work at the University of Chicago and taught there for a time. Paul Kendall was one of my students."

"But you are a Greek?"

"Native-born, but I've traveled farther and more widely than Ulysses could ever have imagined. Now I pray and wait here for the world to come to me."

"And so I have arrived." David pulled his chair closer to the table. "Father Kendall felt you could help me put my experiences in better perspective. I'm not sure where to begin or why I am here at this place of the temptation of Christ. Actually my life has been far more confused than evil."

"We do not think of evil in terms of deeds." The priest smiled. "Rather in this holy place the issue is *perspective*. The greatest temptations are ones of misinterpretation. Our most difficult task is to learn to see correctly. We must reconsider circumstances, relationships, needs, and most importantly ourselves in the clearest light." The monk took off his tall, black hat and set it on the table.

"So?" David thought for a moment. "Why are you up here in this completely remote mountain?"

"Because our monastery allows us the opportunity to stand closer to ultimate truth." Father Panos's words sounded certain and final. "Your noise-filled world of fighting, manipulation, confrontations, money-grabbing, business is reality? Surely not! From morning to night you live with distraction. Madness masquerades as expediency; delusion presents itself as trend and fashion." The priest's eyes became like two black lasers. "In the absolute solitude and quiet of this place, we listen *only* to God."

David shook his head. "I hear your words but . . ."

"You are like the goldfish in a bowl." Father Panos pulled at the gold chain around his neck. "If someone tried to explain water, the fish would ask, 'What water? I see no water.' Only one who stands outside the fish tank can correctly understand."

David looked around the room. "From the top of this silent mountain you look down on the confusion in my world of pandemonium and are able to sort the illusion from the real?"

"From this place of *temptation*," the monk corrected David. "Remember the ultimate lure of evil is the enticement to listen to the world rather than to God. In this place we try to listen only to the voice of God."

"And your perspective is changed?"

"Purified!" He thumped the table.

"I see," David spoke slowly. "I would never have concluded . . . but yes . . . I understand. So I need to tell you what has happened to me and—"

Father Panos held up his hand in the same beatific gesture that ended all discussion. The index finger pointed up, the second finger touched the thumb like pinchers and the last two fingers curled underneath. "Perhaps you need not say anything." He smiled. "Here we are not psychologists but simple people, sinners who work very hard to be men of God. Possibly we both only need to listen to what the Father is saying."

"I don't understand." David blinked.

"When Father Kendall wrote of your coming, I began to pray at once. For days I included you in my daily prayers. After contemplation, I wrote down what I felt in my heart. I think it is more important for me to share those promptings than to listen to you talk."

"I'm a goldfish," David confessed. "I am humbly grateful for your words and hopefully will be transparent to your observations. Please continue."

"As I prayed, I saw shapes of someone making pictures. Are you an artist?"

David stared dumbfounded. "Amazing! Yes, I paint, draw. I particularly sketch people's faces."

"Yes," the priest drawled slowly. "Maybe you draw others in an attempt to see yourself?"

"What an amazing suggestion!"

"You have been trying to discover yourself for a long time," the old man's bass voice rumbled, arising from the deep. "You have sought to find yourself as one seeks a lost object or a misplaced treasure." The monk's eyes burned intensely beneath his bushy eyebrows. "Your quest has not been wrong, only misguided."

David frowned. "What would have been the correct way, Father?"

"People in your world think they are autonomous. You assume you are little gods with total freedom to do as you choose, to be whatever and whoever you wish. Of course such ideas are illusion."

David ran his hands nervously through his hair and rubbed the back of his neck. "I'm sorry." He pursed his lips and blinked again. "I'm afraid I'm a little slow today."

"In the beginning is always the Word." Father Panos drummed on the thick wooden table. "We come into being because God speaks the Word. He calls our name. Our name summons us into existence. Our only true identity is in the name by which He addresses us. Understand?"

David shook his head.

"You exist only because every morning God the Father calls out through all eternity, David. David? Are you there? Do you see?" The priest smiled compassionately. "When you are able to hear and answer, then you have found yourself." He waited for his observations to sink in. After several moments of silence, the monk continued. "It makes no difference what name you have on your driver's license, what you call yourself, unless that earthly name reflects the heavenly name."

"But you see," David protested, "I am caught between the worlds of Judaism and Christianity. I don't know which way is correct. I am confused . . ."

Father Panos held his hand up in the priestly gesture once again. "Do we not all come from Father Abraham, the first man to understand that the Creator is our common source of life and existence?"

David fought to frame his question correctly. "But the problem is the cross, the death of Jesus. For the Jew this is a painful issue that—"

"A stumbling block, yes!" The priest clutched the cross at his neck. "But even in the beginning, Abraham knew a sacrifice was necessary. He discovered at the place of the binding that God had already made a provision." The priest held up his gold cross. "Abraham came even then in the beginning by the way of the cross. None of us can save ourselves."

"A provision was made . . ." David suddenly felt a surge of emotion. "When death seemed unavoidable . . ." A knot formed in his throat. "God provided a way."

"And He always does," the priest assured. "The answer begins when He calls our name. Through the centuries, monks were martyred in these caves by barbaric invasions. These monstrous barbarians and terrorists are our true adversaries. We must never forget Jews are not the enemies of Christians; Christians are not the enemies of Jews. Our common adversary seeks to destroy both of us, snuffing out forever all eternal perspective."

David swallowed hard. "I see," he said slowly. "My quest has been to find the *eternal perspective* on who I am?"

"Yes," the priestly voice rumbled, "and all such struggles for integrity require significant suffering."

"But John's Gospel says no one comes to the Father except

through the Son," David argued. "I have met Jews who tell me that belief in Jesus ends the possibility of being Jewish."

"Perhaps the more urgent question is not one of theology or doctrine." The priest pulled at his long beard as he talked. "Possibly the deeper issue is the division within David. Huh?"

David stared again.

"I do not believe the *Pantokator*, God the Almighty, lied to either Abraham or Moses about their destiny and redemption, my son. Of course, we are looking into a great mystery of grace. We are trying to understand if God continues to maintain a way for the Jew while opening the door for the gentile. But is this any different from trying to understand how David Richards's past can make peace with the present?"

The old man stood up and walked to the icon of Christ on the wall. "We call this picture *The General*, the one who directs." The priest leaned over and kissed the picture. "He is the one who orders all things. We do not always understand how the Christ comes to us. Often we are not even aware of His coming. Our Lord is the master of many disguises. Many times we look back over our lives and discover He was with us and we didn't know. Confounding, isn't it?"

David immediately thought of Susan. Paul Kendall came to mind. David felt undone and profoundly touched without being able to grasp what was happening. To his amazement, he also thought of Uncle Edward; profane, impure old Edward Crownover who loved him so deeply. Tears filled David's eyes. "I think I understand." He reached for a handkerchief.

"You and I cannot solve one of the greatest mysteries of the ages even from the top of this lofty mountain," the priest continued. "The best we can do is solve the mystery of the man named David. His brokenness can be healed by this cross of which we speak. One word will heal the division within you. Are you ready for the Word?"

David nodded and gestured with his fingers. "Don't stop."

"You are the son of the Eternal Father. You are His *son*. Every morning before He calls for the sun to rise, the Divine

Abba cries out, 'Son, my son! Where are you?' Be a son, David. And the rest will fall into place."

"And what does a son do?" David's voice was barely audible.

"He is simply like his Father." The priest smiled kindly. "Like his Father whose very nature is love."

"A son?" David whispered.

"Can you hear Him calling?" The priest took hold of David's hand. "Son, where are you?" Father Panos cooed like a turtle dove. "Son? You are My son." He squeezed and released David's hand. "My son? Are you there?"

David gently reeled back and forth, silently absorbing the words. He closed his eyes, trying to etch the moment on his soul. "Son," he said. "That's the name. Son."

The priest said nothing. David sat with his eyes closed for well over five minutes. He finally looked up. Father Panos was sitting with his hands folded before his face in devout prayer. David watched the old man's lips silently move, intoning the prayer of his heart. David remembered Father Kendall praying for him. He thought again of praying before the great Western Wall. Like inhaling the offering of sacred incense, David tried to breathe in the holy aroma. He closed his eyes again and sat in silence, losing all sense of time.

When David opened his eyes, the priest was sitting back in his chair stroking the beard around his chin. There was no discernible expression on his face except for the laser stare that seemed to read David's thoughts.

"Did the Holy One call your name?" the priest asked.

David sighed. "Yes, I heard my name."

The priest nodded his head as if he were only affirming the obvious. "Your life will be different now. You will be a whole person," he said matter-of-factly.

"Thank you," David choked.

The priest stood up. "We have lost track of time, and you have missed the bus back to Jerusalem. We can only offer you a very uncomfortable monk's bed and simple supper tonight. I'm afraid you don't have many choices."

Robert L. Wise

"I would be very honored to stay with you, Father Panos."

"Shortly we must light the candles and say the evening prayers. I am the only one who speaks English so you will be spared the imposition of idle talk. Solitude will be an aid to you." He walked to the door. "Please follow me."

David was surprised at the depth of the shadows falling everywhere. The priest led him back down the corridor to the plaza and on to the cave.

"Let us say a few words about the temptations that confront anyone who has discovered who they are. Men and women who become sons often assume the work is done. We must remind them Jesus' temptations came immediately after the Father's declaration and disclosure of the identity of the Son."

David looked over the rock ledge down on the desert plain beneath him. "What did the temptations mean?"

"The first was the lure of trying to control the world. The issue was indulgence and tangible security." The priest leaned over the wall. "You would probably call this form of enticement materialism."

"I know something about trying to turn stone into bread," David answered.

"No one escapes," the priest replied dryly. "The second provocation was the lust for importance. In America you refer to this desire as 'the applause of the crowd,' being number one. Would you also know something of the inordinate need for admiration?"

"Selling my soul for the sake of appearances?" David asked. "Oh, yes, an addiction as powerful as any narcotic. I'm no stranger to the problem."

"In the final temptation," the monk explained, "the Christ was offered all of the kingdoms of the world to which, of course, He already had claim. The devil offered to strike a deal for the sake of absolute authority and ascendancy. It is the final temptation because it is the most alluring. Nothing is as seductive as the drive for power, the politics of conquest. Omnipotence is the ultimate obsession, an appetite never satisfied."

David turned his back to the panorama hundreds of feet beneath him and asked, "Is there an answer? I can tell you unequivocally I understand the problem. I've already failed the test."

Father Panos held up the gold cross around his neck. "Our Lord knew there was no solution unless one is willing to lay his life down. Jesus, the Jew, understood the answer is not some simple religious solution we put on like a new coat, a new facade we wear. We must be willing to sign a death warrant against our own egos."

"Like becoming a monk?" David asked.

"No, no," the priest shook his head vigorously. "Such a vocation is a unique calling. It's not helpful either to immerse oneself in religion as an escape. Such delusion only corrupts the religion and produces fanaticism. Nothing is more frightening than power-hungry clergy!"

"So what must I do?" David implored.

The monk frowned and puckered his lips, obviously pondering his response carefully. "Don't go seeking some noble cause, a dramatic act of contrition. Don't try to make yourself into a religious sacrifice." Father Panos began nodding his head. "I would suggest you seek out one or two persons who need your love. Decide to do whatever is necessary to allow them to know they are truly loved. After you have laid down your life for that person you will know what to do next."

The evening breeze picked up from the plain and swept up the side of the mountain in a cool gust. The shadow from the high bluffs extended nearly to the city limits of Jericho. Far off to his left the Dead Sea had taken on a golden sunkissed glow. The world looked peaceful and serene.

"Do you understand, my son?"

"Perhaps, I do," David concluded.

"Then let us go into the cave," Father Panos pointed inside. Other monks were lighting candles and kneeling for prayer. "You will need the help of the One who pioneered and perfected this path."

• • •

David finished his sketch of Father Panos. Most of the outline was made with quick, vague flourishes of his dark pencil. The long beard came with broad strokes of the side of the lead, but he labored over the eyes. The ominous eyebrows took shape from many quick, precise thrusts of the point of the pencil. He bore down to capture the black penetrating eyes. Satisfied, he blew out the candle. The walls of the monastery's guest room disappeared into the night.

David looked out of the tiny cell into the opaque darkness lying across the valley. The street lamps of Jericho broke the overlay with pinpoints of light. Toward the distant horizon were other isolated specks and somewhere beyond the line between sky and land was far-off America.

The thought gripping his mind was unthinkable. Never could David have imagined such a conclusion to his journey. And yet the notion made perfect sense. He had made a business out of creating appearance. Now the challenge was to do something authentic. The aroma of incense floated through the window and smelled holy.

"I must return from the far country," he spoke into the darkness. "The time has come to go home."

Sleep came quickly, and serene peacefulness followed. There were no violent dreams of explosions. Somewhere near dawn a very unexpected vision slipped into David's slumber.

A large house with a split down the middle appeared. From a side road Abraham Lincoln walked in. He laid down his tall stovepipe hat and picked up a hammer. As he banged away on the side of the house, the division began to disappear. In a short time, the house was unified. The president laid down the hammer and turned toward an invisible audience. "With malice toward none and charity toward all, let us be about the business of binding up the nation's wounds." As he finished the address, the dream slowly faded.

David awoke with an astonishing sense of well-being.

THIRTY

An endless flow of humanity poured from the exits of the Ben Gurion Airport. Tourists and immigrants, Arabs and Jews marched forth in waves. David hopped up and down trying to see every person coming out of the customs door. Multitudes of the observant flocking in for the high holidays made it hard to see a small woman.

"Shouldn't be difficult to spot Uncle Edward," David told Shlomo Cohen. "His height and mustache stick out in any crowd."

"I'll stand on the far end with the taxi drivers." The professor pointed to the opposite side of the sidewalk. "I remember the picture of your mother well. Don't worry, they won't get past us."

"There she is!" David pointed at a gray-haired woman carrying only one suitcase. "Ruth! We're here. Over here!" He darted into the crowd with the professor at his heels.

Ruth Moses dropped the bag and opened her arms. She was wearing brown slacks with a sweater tied across her shoulders. "Look at you! Dark as an Arab." She laughed and hugged David. "I would have mistaken you for a tour guide."

"Meet my friend, Professor Shlomo Cohen."

Shlomo made a sweeping bow and kissed Ruth's hand. "My greatest honor."

"Most gracious," Ruth beamed. "Thank you for all you have done for my boy. I feel like we are practically related. I'm sure he's told you my life history."

"We have a great deal in common," the professor answered.

"Yes, I must confess I feel like I've known you all of my life. Wonderful that you are now here."

"Edward is still clearing customs?" David asked.

"Unfortunately no." Ruth shook her head. "At the last minute he was . . . ah . . . well, unable to come with me."

"What?" David gasped. "Not coming?"

"I will tell you all the details in the car." Ruth kissed him on the cheek and pulled him along. "Let's get away from this mob. Don't worry. I'll explain everything."

"Let's hurry." The professor pointed toward the car lot. "I would suggest we get the car out of here before the rest of New York City descends on us."

David tossed Ruth's single bag into the trunk. She got in the backseat, and they quickly pulled out of the parking lot. "About Edward?" David asked. "I am shocked he is not here."

"Let me just look at the city for a few minutes." Ruth had the distant, vague sound David knew was impenetrable. "I must absorb the atmosphere of it all again. Then we shall talk." Ruth stared out the window. "Everything has changed! All the buildings were the boxy, white, international style the British favored. Now there are so many different shapes. So modern!"

Shlomo maneuvered through the tangled mess of Tel Aviv traffic. Taxis honked and drivers shook their fists at each other, but eventually he got through the airport traffic and into the city. Shlomo told Ruth, "I want to drive through the area bordered by Bograshov and Yehuda Halevy Streets. The old look is being restored." Shlomo turned from Hashalom Road on to Giborei Yisrael Street until he eventually passed the Great Synagogue on Allenby Road. Ruth oohed and ahhed at every corner, consumed in fascination.

"Look at how the date palms, the orange, and jacaranda trees have grown! I've not been here for thirty-five years," she sighed. "Simply unbelievable what has happened!"

"Eighty-five years ago the town was nothing but a pile of sand a mile north of the ancient seaport of Jaffa," Shlomo told David. "In 1909, our European ancestors wanted to build a completely secular city. Today it is a great metropolis of the world. We have a university, a Philharmonic, and even six ballet companies! Not bad, huh?"

Ruth kept pointing out places. Her running dialogue was punctuated with exclamations of surprise and delight. "There's quirky, old Sheinkin Street!" She pointed out the window. "Best shopping area in town."

"Over there is Carmel Market," Shlomo pointed out. "The Nahlot Binyamin Mall is close. Good place for Turkish coffee."

"And of *afarsimonim!*" Ruth added. "Love apples. Wonderful treat."

"I think we should quickly make our way to Jerusalem," Shlomo concluded sorrowfully. "I know you'd like to stop, but we can come back. You must see the restoration of old Jaffa, but the jet lag will catch up with you if we don't go on."

"A wise man," Ruth agreed. "My tired old body could use a long soak in a tub of hot water. Yes, I think we should go up the mountain to the queen of all cities."

"I've made reservations at the King David," Shlomo added. "Nothing but the best for you."

"About Edward?" David talked over his shoulder.

"Yes," Ruth said slowly, but with resolution. "I must tell you about Edward." She cleared her throat. "Actually the problem began with high blood pressure."

David turned nearly completely around in the front seat. "What has happened to Edward?"

"I'm sorry to tell you, but Eddie had a stroke. Things aren't good. We had planned to make connections in Rome and take an El Al flight into Tel Aviv. Three days ago I got the phone call from England." She looked down at her hands. "He never did take care of himself. Drinking, running all over the globe, eating the richest gourmet food in the world!" She shook her head in disgust. "The old fool never paid attention to anyone's advice." Ruth stopped abruptly and began to weep. "He can't talk and is in a hospital ... in London ... the University College Hospital ... on Gower Street." Her words were barely audible. "So very sad." She pulled a handkerchief from her pocket. "A nurse called me."

"How bad is it?" David grimaced. "Will he live?"

Ruth nodded her head. "They know he's going to have some paralysis but are sure he'll live . . . at least for the time being. No one knows if he'll ever be able to talk or walk again." She covered her eyes with her hand. "So very, very sad."

"Who'll take care of him?" David gestured frantically.

"For the moment Edward has good medical attention and a private nurse," Ruth reassured him. "But there isn't anyone left to look after him . . . except me."

"And me!" David protested.

"Of course." Ruth smiled and patted his shoulder. "But you have the rest of your life to live. We've lived ours. I've closed up my house in California. I'm only going to remain a few days before I go to London. Edward stayed with me through the years. Whatever mistakes he made, Edward was the one who nursed me back to health when I was a nameless face in a hospital bed. Heaven knows how much money he sent me over the years." She looked at David with great pain in her eyes. "In the end he was my link to you, Son. I owe him a debt that only I can pay. Now my turn has come. I am all that remains."

David slowly turned back in his seat and looked out the window, rubbing his temple. "What an unexpected turn of events!"

"We will have ample time to talk, but I must not delay too long." Ruth seemed to be thinking out loud. "I'm sure Edward must be terrified. Being alone and helpless . . . is . . . almost . . . unspeakable."

"Yes." David looked straight ahead at the road winding steadily upward. "No one should ever be left in such a condition."

"We will have plenty of occasion to return to Israel, David. One day we will go to Leipzig together. But now Edward must be looked after."

"Of course," David quickly agreed. Silence fell between them. The professor drove but offered no comments.

Ruth finally spoke. "I did not tell you that I returned to Europe once after I left Israel. I had to see if any of the pieces were left. Because of the iron curtain, I couldn't go back to Leipzig, so I went to Auschwitz and then to Terezin and on to Buchenwald. I became obsessed with the death camps. I tramped through each one like an archeologist looking for any remnant of humanity. Maybe some shred of evidence was left of my family. I needed to see what remained." Her voice sounded far away. "I suppose I was going mad."

"No," David answered, "you didn't tell me about this trip."

"My soul was gripped by a terrible fear the entire Jewish race was going to be consumed by death itself. I started to believe somewhere beyond the edge of reality, an invisible creature existed by devouring our flesh. The taste of innocent Jewish blood alone soothed the beast. Since the thing had devoured everyone and everything I loved, I believed the day would come when the wicked creature would catch me. Although I didn't know when, I was sure my own demise could happen at any moment."

David turned back over the seat to his mother and offered her his hand. She pressed his fingers against her cheek.

"Yes, I think I became quite mad." Ruth kissed his palm. "Too much loneliness can twist the mind."

"And . . . ?" David probed gently.

"It wasn't until several years passed I fully realized millions of Jews had survived. The state of Israel was not obliterated. The demons had not annihilated our race. Only then was I able to go back to a synagogue and once more get in touch with my past. No matter how great the loss, this faith of ours always seems to remain."

David looked at this small woman who hardly appeared sixty-seven and at the same time paradoxically seemed to have the wisdom of the ages etched in her ancient face. Wrinkles ran together like lines in the portrait of an aged soothsayer. With her grayish-white hair pulled back tightly at the back of her head, Ruth's face looked more severe than usual. Profound sadness lined her black eyes, which had momentarily faded into a lighter brown, increasing her melancholy appearance.

"The night at your house," Ruth continued, "was the first

time since your father's death I observed a Seder with a member of my own family. I didn't think I could go through with it." A slight smile broke through the heaviness. "You helped me, David. We got through it arm-in-arm. And we will get through Edward's problem together."

"Together," David affirmed. "Tomorrow is the twenty-second of *Ellul*, 5748, September 22, 1987. A new year for both of us. A new year, indeed."

"And so we start again," Ruth answered.

"Professor Cohen has invited us to join him for the Rosh Hashanah services at his synagogue."

Shlomo slowed down for a checkpoint, but the solider waved him on quickly. "If you wish," he spoke over his shoulder, "we can all go together."

"Certainly." Ruth released David's hand and settled back in the seat. "We would be honored, Professor. As always, we need each other to do these things right."

The car sped on into the outskirts of Jerusalem.

"We really don't have much time." Ruth tugged at David's sleeve. "We must get to Yad Vashem Memorial and back before the start of the service. I will have to change clothes at the hotel. We don't want to inconvenience Professor Cohen in any way."

David put his drawing pencil down and closed the sketch pad. "I'd almost forgotten what it was to worry about time. Are you trying to push me back onto the fast track?"

"Come on." Ruth nudged him toward the door. "Catching a taxi in Jerusalem can hardly be compared to fighting a Los Angeles freeway. Besides, I don't want to be hurried at the Memorial."

Ruth needed no instruction in how to find her way from the professor's house out of the Old City and to a taxi stand. David was pushed to keep up with her.

"Some things just need to be done *before* Rosh Hashanah," she explained as he led the way. "I've had this task on my mind for a long time. I'm not going to let another year slip by."

"Of course, of course," David answered, nearly trotting alongside Ruth. "I'm even starting to sound like Shlomo."

The cab only took ten minutes to reach the Holocaust memorial. The parking lot was sparsely filled with tour buses. David paid the driver, and they hurried up the tree-lined path of tribute to righteous gentiles who had saved Jewish lives. David held the glass door open at the entry hall, and they walked through to the display rooms.

"I've been here before." David fastened his yarmulke in place. "Rather grim for starting a new year."

"For finishing an *old* year," Ruth corrected him. She slowed before the pictures and posters lining the exhibits. "Oh, yes. I remember all of this. Seems like yesterday."

"Must be painful."

"At one time," Ruth said thoughtfully. "Not today." She stopped in front of a picture of a German storefront with *Juden Verboten* scrawled across the windows. "More like visiting old friends and just remembering the way it was." She pointed at the cloth star of David pinned on a child's shirt. "I had to wear such an insignia."

David stopped in front of a large poster of Jews being herded out of the Warsaw Ghetto. A forlorn little boy had his hands in the air; a Nazi solider kept a rifle trained on the child.

Ruth smiled. "What a striking resemblance, David. The little fellow looks so much like your baby pictures. Certainly a remarkable likeness."

David looked at his mother. "How can you look at a picture like that and take it so . . . so . . . almost . . . lighthearted?"

"One must find a balance in these things or go crazy," Ruth said sternly. "I know. Yes, I've seen that famous picture many times, and I thought it looked like you the very first time I saw it decades ago. I cried then. Today I am looking at it with my son. Now it is appropriate to be amused at how much my son looks like one of our people."

They passed a dark screening room with benches. A handful of people watched a black-and-white film showing a boat sailing into view. Powerful background music swelled as people surged out on the deck. The boat's flag dropped, and the flag of Israel went up.

"Refugees!" Ruth clapped. "I came on exactly such a boat. Look at the people! We all looked exactly the same."

The film depicted and described the British attempt to embargo all refugee boats. With resonant voice, the narrator told the story of the clandestine landings of the DPs and their successful evasion of the soldiers.

"Look at their faces!" Ruth spoke so loudly several people turned around and looked. "Hope and despair all mingled together. One moment optimism, the next terror. That's exactly the way it was."

"We're going to run out of time," David whispered. "The children's memorial section is next."

"No." Ruth took the lead again. "I know where I'm going. I've come for a particular purpose, and I know exactly where the area is."

"Far be it from me to get in your path." David threw up his hands and followed.

"We must go to the top floor," Ruth explained as she trudged up the stairs. "The Hall of Remembrance is where the records are kept of those who perished."

On the top floor signs directed them to a dimly lit room filled with endless rows of books. Ruth walked the length of the corridor slowly, looking up and down the shelves.

"So many," she said more to herself, "so many . . . but each one remembered."

David walked silently behind her.

Ruth stopped at the registration desk. A young man wearing a yarmulke and thin wire-rimmed glasses worked with a microfilm magnifier. "*Bevakasha*," Ruth said. "May I have four pages of testimony?"

The young man immediately handed her the forms and pointed to a desk. "Please use that place to complete the applications. I will take them when you are done."

Ruth hurried to the desk. She opened her purse and found two pieces of cardboard held together by rubber bands. She peeled the bindings away and carefully took out three yellowed photographs.

"What on earth are you doing?" David peered over her shoulder.

"I thought the pictures had been lost long ago." Ruth held one in a clearer light. "Seemed like a miracle when they fell out of an old diary I kept years ago. I made copies for you, David, but I felt the originals should be placed in the archives. These photographs are of my parents and my sister Margit."

David picked up each picture and Ruth filled in the blanks on the pages of testimony slowly and carefully. She completed the form for her father, printing in bold letters, "David Israel Eidinger." Next Ruth filled in the sheet for her mother, printing "Rebbeka Rive Eidinger" on the line. Finally she made a page for Margit. In the selections marked, "circumstances of death," she wrote in small print, crowding in as much as possible.

Ruth took the pictures from David and affixed them to the documents. "They will not be forgotten," she said resolutely. "They will always be remembered here." Ruth signed her name at the bottom and returned the forms to the man at the desk. "We can go now." Ruth took David's arm and turned toward the door. "I am ready to go on."

They walked slowly toward the steps. David stopped at the banister and took Ruth's hand. "I must tell you of a decision I've made. I, too, must put my house in order. I must go back to America and fulfill the obligations that I have as a son of the Richardses. Only then will I discover what I am to do next."

"I . . . I . . . I don't understand." Ruth blinked several times, and her face fell.

"You must take care of Edward. A debt must be paid." David looked his mother full in the face. "Perhaps the obligation can be fulfilled with greater love than you ever thought possible. Maybe the old hostilities will dissolve because you act from the heart, but you will be released from the past by what you do. Yes, you are about to fulfill a very important task."

Ruth's eyes moved rapidly back and forth across David's face. She nodded her head slowly.

Robert L. Wise

"And so I must return to Oklahoma City and be a good son. I must take care of George and Mary Richards. I will try to help fill their emptiness, and as I do so, I believe the rest of what I am to be about will fall into place. I will return to America shortly after you leave for England."

Ruth looked down at the marble floor and started to reach for the railing on the stairs. She clutched at his arm.

"You will not lose me," David said resolutely. "A good son never forgets where he came from. I will not forget that I am all that remains for you."

For a moment, Ruth paused at the step and then reached up to touch David's face. She gently felt the contour of his cheek and ear. "What we are is more important than what we do." Ruth kissed him. "I have no fear of ever losing you again."

"We don't have a great deal of time left. Taxis may not be quite as easy to find out front as in the city."

"Each one does still live on in you, David." Ruth's voice was kind and thoughtful as they walked down the steps. "Yaacov, Rebbeka, my father David . . . a part of me . . . yes, we are there in different ways. Today, I particularly see my father in you. He was a gentle, kind man. No one taught him to be so sensitive. It was simply his nature, as it is yours." She stopped on the landing. "I look at your face, and I see little reflections, an eyebrow, the turn of your nose, the cleft in your chin, something of all of us is there, but your heart is most like my father's." Ruth stopped and squeezed his hand. "Please don't feel you have to live up to some description or grand design I've given you of our family. Just be yourself. It's all there and it's more than enough."

ABOUT THE AUTHOR

Author of twelve books, including *When the Night Is Too Long*, *Where There Is No Miracle*, and the "People of the Covenant" series, including *The Dawning*, *The Exiles*, and *The Fall of Jerusalem*, Robert L. Wise, Ph.D., is also a well-known teacher, lecturer, and student of Jewish culture. He has traveled extensively in the Holy Land and across the world.

Robert lives in Oklahoma City with his wife, Margueritte.